Surviving The After

Emilee King

ISBN-10: 1966173038
ISBN-13: 978-1966173038

1

I didn't know how long I'd been staring at the wall. At least a few hours, probably, without stopping. I'd gotten really really good at it.

A slight shiver went through my body, making me tighten the blanket around me and huddle closer to the generator. The air was hot and sticky. It was hard to breathe. It made my lungs a little sore. Or maybe I was just imagining it.

Does it really matter? Probably not.

I still had a few hours, I guessed, until it was dark and the Compound went to sleep. The late-night hours were the only times I left the second floor of the maintenance building—even then, it was only by necessity. The newly sanctioned night guards were ordered to not play nice if they caught anyone wandering around past curfew, but I didn't want to leave anyway.

I hadn't decided yet if I was going to take a stroll tonight. I was out of food, which didn't seem like a big deal now because I wasn't very hungry, but my water was gone. Water was important, right? How long could a human survive without water? Two days? Maybe three?

I tried to remember the longest I'd ever gone without water. I couldn't think of a time. It probably didn't matter.

No, I decided, I wouldn't leave tonight, especially after my extra trip last night. Two guards noticed me stealing through the dark and chased me down. To avoid getting caught, I ended up in the elevator to Cyrus' office, surprised the screen would still take my fingerprint, and hid out up there until I thought it might be safe.

His office had been empty. I poked around a little, finding all the drawers and cabinets locked, then wandered over to the bookshelves. Most of what he had was in different languages—German, mostly, I thought, along with French and Italian and others—and what I actually could read looked boring. I was prepared to leave when a name caught my attention: Philo Castor.

Despite everything that he'd indirectly caused in my life, I found myself curious about the formula's creator, Philo Castor. Where had he come from? What was he like? What drove him to discover and create something that ended up being so unnatural, cruel, and—in some ways—demonic? What was his story?

I started reading about him and was sucked in, and before I knew it, the sun's rays were threatening to come over the horizon. Throwing the books and files and maps back in their place, I sprinted to my room as fast as I could. Nobody caught me, but I was sure Cyrus knew I did it. I never got in trouble for it though: we both knew there was nothing I could discover in the shelves that would be of real aid to me or threat to him.

No, I wouldn't leave tonight. I wasn't hungry anyway.

The seconds ticked by and I counted each one. Two. Three. Twenty. Four hundred and ninety-seven. Nothing to do, nothing to say, nothing to think. Just me and my blanket and the wall. And the generator. Couldn't forget the generator. I had to think of a name for that thing. It was big and powerful. Maybe Caesar? No, that just made me think of pizza. Alexander? Ivan? Was I looking for a good connotation or a bad one? Probably a good one. True, the generator had burned me on multiple occasions, but that had been my fault. It kept me warm. I could always count on it being there. Maybe Steve. Roger? They sounded like nice guys.

Then I realized I was trying to name a generator.

Should I be concerned about that? Probably not. There was nobody here to judge me besides Steve and he seemed like the forgiving type. It was good to have a friend like Steve.

Steve was good for a lot of things, but keeping track of time wasn't one of them. How many days had I been in here? He didn't know. Neither did I, though I guessed about two or three weeks. All I knew was that Cyrus had let me live on the condition that I wasn't seen by anyone else. I accepted the terms at the time. Now I often wondered what would happen if I wandered out into the open during the day and let the world see me. How fast would he kill me? Did speed really matter as long as the result was the same?

I never did though. Part of me knew Cyrus was bluffing. I'd survived his little key extraction process despite his prediction I wouldn't. He was still baffled by that. So was I. I was the farthest he'd ever gotten with a key, but he didn't know what that meant or where it left me. He'd taken the key essence—whatever that meant—out of me. Was I still infected? Was I still the key somehow? What if he needed me at some point in the future? I didn't know what for and I didn't think he did either. Regardless, I was his insurance policy. He was too careful to let me go too soon, just in case.

Cyrus was the only one I'd seen since I woke up. I didn't know where anyone else was or what they were doing or what they thought of me. All I knew of Vanessa is what Cyrus told me: she was a success. She was stable in her new body. She was up and at 'em and training and taking over all of my responsibilities. Everyone had met her. Everyone knew who she was. She fit the niche we were designed for much better than I did. She was an even match for Micah, executed all assignments on time, patrolled like a perfect policeman. I wasn't needed anymore. I'd been relieved of my duties and told to make my own quiet existence away so I wouldn't bother anyone.

"And I would stay away from your family, Arie," Cyrus had told me before our lovely conversation was over. "She's informed them what's happened. They know who she is. You don't want to face that, do you?"

No, I didn't. I didn't want to look into the faces of those I loved—those who had put so much work and energy and faith in me to beat the very key that had stood in front of them—and hang my head in shame. I couldn't do it. It was over. I lost.

Cyrus was using the guilt against me, a way to keep me silent. I knew that. I continually proved him right, choosing to stay away from everyone and everything. It was just too hard. I didn't have the motivation or guts to face anything. I barely had the will to eat and sleep and keep myself alive. I'd probably be better use to the world if I were dead: then I could keep a watchful eye on the good guys and haunt the bad.

Useless was an understatement to describe my current state to all parties involved. I was sure Cyrus—not to mention Roland—were both giddy beyond belief to have their key, their captain and commander. I'd heard the stories of what I was supposed to be, the war general, the stoic soldier that follows orders just as well as it gives them. Like Micah but with no rage. No emotions. No personality. I wondered how Micah was faring with a new teacher's pet that didn't even understand when he teased her. He was probably just happy to have a partner that would actually do the job and do it well.

Congrats, Micah. Hope you love your new best friend.

I hated to admit it, but it was weird without her. My head wasn't empty, exactly, but it was weird to have a thought she would normally tell me, only to realize I was alone.

Now that she was out of me, though, I wanted to meet her. I didn't know much about the transfer process or how it had affected her. Maybe she didn't even remember me or who I was or anything before she awoke in her own body. Maybe she did. I didn't know. Part of me wanted to see how she walked, how she spoke, how she moved. I wanted to see how she compared to the monster in my head with ripped out hair, exposed flesh, a half smile and a solid blue eye. I wanted to punch the guts out of her. I wanted to beat her to her knees just like she had done to me. I hated her.

But the other part of me was terrified of her. I tried to never admit that when she was in my head, though that didn't really help. She knew I was scared of her. And who wouldn't be? Anyone would be horrified to wake up one day and discover a blue monster was talking back. At least, that's what I told myself: anyone would be terrified. Nobody would have the courage to confront her. After all, she pretty much ruined me when she was safely locked in my head—I couldn't imagine trying to face her when she had her own arms and legs she could move freely.

I was a coward. I knew it. I lived it, inside a giant cavern of generators I was too afraid and apathetic to leave. It was my jail, and I was both prisoner and guard, letting myself drown in self-pity. Even I was repulsed with how pathetic I was.

Today I was sitting next to Steve with my blanket around me, my usual stance, as I stared at the wall and played with the edges of my long sleeves. I still kept my arms covered despite the fact I was always alone. They weren't blue anymore, much to my astonishment and relief—Cyrus couldn't give me an explanation besides that my potential had been used up at the right time.

I didn't care why, really. You could still see where it used to be though, faint greyish pink raises in the skin where the symbol and its vines had scalded themselves onto my body. The scars ran from head to toe but you could only really see them on my arms, like monuments made to the beginning of what would be my failure. I hated them. I kept them hidden from my eyes.

There wasn't much else to look at. I felt like I had the wall opposite from me completely memorized, every line, chink and crevice. I decided to mix it up a bit, turning to look at Steve the generator head on to get a different view.

A bubble of voices echoed below me. I tensed but didn't panic. The maintenance building was still used by cleaning crews and such to store supplies, which meant that I was often visited by a blab of indiscernible conversation as they retrieved what they needed. Nobody ever knew I was up here. I often wondered if anyone I knew was down there, if my mom ever came by to grab her cleaner brush and thought about our conversation that day outside—if she ever thought about me.

Suddenly, something crashed through the window that I used as a door. I jumped as a can clanked on the ground before sliding to a stop several yards in front of me.

What the heck?

I leaned forward cautiously, as if to inspect in from afar, when it started spluttering out sparks. Fire. Everywhere.

I couldn't understand how it happened—the building was made of metal, at least on the inside, and there was nothing for the fire to catch onto and burn. But flames were everywhere, suspended throughout the whole space, as if the air itself was on fire. The temperature instantly ballooned hundreds of degrees and clouds of smoke obstructed my vision.

Pulling the collar of my hoodie over my nose, I made sure to grab my blanket before fighting through the smoke and airborne flames, flinching when I felt a piece of skin on my forehead singe. I forced the broken window up and started climbing down the fire escape, getting halfway to the ground before realizing that's as far as it went. Someone had taken out half of the ladder.

I looked back up at the window, seeing the gobs of smoke coming out and floating up toward the sky. It wasn't too high but I didn't really have much of a choice anyway. I jumped. The shock of the landing vibrated up my legs, and I leaned over, breathing in gusts of clean air.

And there it goes. Take note, everyone. I'm destroying the pathetic monument to her name…

Wait a minute. With a start, I realized I was hearing thoughts that weren't mine. No, they weren't thoughts. I was hearing my voice—my voice *out loud.*

Slowly, I walked down the side of the building, my voice getting louder, and peeked around the corner. A gathered group of eighty or so employees were standing a few feet from the maintenance building, watching the billowing smoke with melancholy or otherwise blank expressions in a rigid stance. And standing in front of them with a smirk on her face was me.

I gasped and dropped my blanket on the ground, which was when she saw me. It was like looking into a mirror. Her eyebrows shot up and she gasped, the same short sound.

A grumble went through the incredulous crowd, but everyone's feet stayed glued to where they were. I only had eyes for me. At least, she looked just like me, but at the same time she didn't. She held herself with poise and power, wearing a bright pink dress that had a much lower neck and much higher skirt than anything I would've ever dreamed of wearing, exposing perfect skin. Perfect arms. Perfect legs. No freak symbols or blue vines or nasty scars. Though I knew she had to be wearing gobs of makeup, her face was beautiful, her hair full and luscious, nothing out of place. Her blue eyes were deep but narrowed, pointed, as if looking for a fault to expose or a weakness to exploit. She was me but she wasn't me.

"They told me you were dead," she whispered, disbelief written all over her flawless face. "They told me you didn't survive the transfer."

It took me a moment to realize I didn't say the words even though they were in my whisper. A transfer, she called it. They had transferred her. A transfer to another me.

"Vanessa?" I asked, my brain hurting as it tried to wrap itself around what was going on.

Her expression completely shifted, shutting out all disbelief and putting arrogance on full display, though she couldn't hide the boiling anger she kept underneath the smooth surface. She couldn't hide from me.

"The princess is alive!" she shouted then laughed gleefully. Those around her flinched and stared at the ground, though she barely noticed. "Wow, you really are a hard person to kill, aren't you?" She struck a pose, highlighting her exposed leg and putting a hand on her hip. "What do you think of the new suit?"

I just stared at her, trying to make the connection. It was me. But I wasn't in a mirror. This wasn't some home video I had a recollection of. This wasn't even a nightmare where I was more or less in control of my own actions. This was insane.

"At first I thought it was yours that I'd overtaken," she went on, "but then I realized it couldn't be. It's too perfect and new." She waved her hand at me like I was old news. "Not like your scarred, shabby old thing. Then Cyrus told me I was right—they took me straight out and put me in a brand new one. Yours would've worked, I guess, but this is just so much better."

Then I understood: Cyrus and Micah had put in so much painful energy into giving me—my face—the reputation it had. So rather than explain all the science transfer stuff and still be scary, they just kept the same advertising. The monumental project in the research lab had been creating my clone. But at least part of it had gone wrong; I could tell that much.

"What's wrong with you?" I asked, taking a step toward her in an attempt to play offense. She wasn't going to win this opening confrontation. "Have they figured that out yet?"

She laughed once but it was off. Fake. "Excuse me?"

A corner of my mouth pulled up. "They're disappointed, aren't they?" She glared and opened her mouth, but I beat her. "Where's their commander in chief, huh? They asked for a perfect soldier and instead they got a skanky showgirl that parades herself around and won't shut up."

Vanessa glared fire darts at me before smiling sweetly. "I'm unprecedented. Being special isn't a bad thing. Plus, I'm better than you ever were. It wasn't too hard to fill your shoes."

I shrugged. "Still. That's got to be a tough blow for you. I guess being a disappointment runs through both of our veins, you know, since you took mine."

Her head tilted slightly, her eyes narrowing as she analyzed me, and I knew we were headed into battle.

She stretched her arms out, taking two steps toward me. "Your veins or not, it's great to be free. I can't even tell you—I thought being cramped up in your head was bad, but it wasn't until I got out that I realized how truly deprived I was." She slid her hands down her fitted form. "You were only into long black stuff that belonged in a convent, which, let's be honest, was your relationship status."

She winked at me and I willed any implied images away. "I've fixed that. Now I can wear whatever I want, get whoever I want, and say exactly what's on my mind. All the time. It's great." Her hand spread out in presentation over the still and silent crowd behind her. "And I used my talents to build up the reputation you never had nor deserved, so now I can get any idiot here to do whatever I want. Who's the princess now?"

I took a step toward her, counting on my fingers. "Right. Everyone here is scared of you because of the strength *I* gave you and the skills *I* learned in training that *I* passed on. You dress *my* body to attract the attention you crave, but every worker is too afraid of you to lay a finger on you, so you either have to scare them or go pick up a stupid guest, which gets you in trouble." I gestured to her mockingly. "Look at you—you're a cheap copy of me. You need me. You would be nowhere without me."

"Oh, princess." She stuck her bottom lip out and took a step closer. "You are in so much denial, aren't you? That's not healthy, darling, you should really get that checked out."

I laughed once. "See? That's how I know when I'm right: you rail on me instead of coming back with a legitimate response. You've got nothing."

She gave a tight grin. "Clever."

We had walked toward each other so now we were toe to toe, staring each other down only to see ourselves reflected back, ensnared in a chess game. One move. Then another. A war of words in which my enemy knew me as well as I knew myself.

I hated her even more, if that were possible. I hated the way she smirked, flaunted, paraded, the way she stole my very body and nearly my identity, how she almost made a better me than I did. I hated that. And I hated it even more because the face I was looking at with so much disgust was my own.

"Yeah," I muttered. "Clever." I cleared my still smoky throat. "Regardless, it's nice to have a clear head again. I was getting sick of hearing you yap on all day."

She just looked into my eyes knowingly, as if she still had access to my every thought. "Oh please, princess. I'm sure it's like I never left."

That statement left an acid pit in my stomach. I tried to ignore it.

Vanessa stiffened and her head tilted ever so slightly. I knew what that meant, probably because that's how I imagined I would look when a transmission came through the earpiece.

"Duty calls, huh?" I asked smugly. "How's that going, by the way? I wouldn't peg you as the loyal dog type, but I guess they lied to you about me, so there must not be a lot of trust to begin with."

She tried to smile, but it was too much of a scowl. "I've got a job to do, unlike some people who sit around all day wrapped up in a blanket crying over themselves."

The edge to her voice—to my voice—just added to the confirmation I knew was true. The disappointment in Vanessa was a two-way street.

"You aren't free," I told her with a small grin. "They just tricked you into a longer leash. And now you get ticked off every time you want to run but realize you're still chained up."

That hit an exposed nerve. Acting on raging impulse, she lifted her hand to hit me and I caught her wrist reflexively. Both of us stared at our interlocking arms for a moment before dropping them, realizing the magnitude of what it meant—if this blew up into an actual fight, nobody would win. We had literally trained in the same head with the same mind and body. Every attack would be anticipated, every decision predicted, every action contested. We'd kill ourselves out of exhaustion before one actually could take out the other.

"It doesn't matter what you say to me," I told her, meeting my eyes evenly, "or how you think you can make my life miserable. I'm glad you defied orders and smoked me out because you should know that I'm still here. I'm still breathing. And as long as I'm standing, in whatever bad shape that may be, I'm still winning."

Vanessa clenched her teeth, glaring at me as she backed away. "Fine. I don't know what you did during the transfer to screw this up, but I know you, princess—you're at a breaking point, and I'll barely have to blow to topple you right over." Almost too fast for me to follow, she jerked her hand out to her left and snatched an unsuspecting employee. Three snaps—leg, arm, shoulder—and then the girl was on the ground crying in agony. Vanessa never took her eyes off me. "And I'll do it with your face."

Ignoring her victim, Vanessa turned toward the crowd. "Everyone back to work," she barked, annoyed her display of victory had gone all wrong. Then she smiled at someone I couldn't see behind a group of scurrying people and bopped her head forward and backward. "You too, sweetheart." She walked away as the crowd turned to dust. The place was cleared in twenty seconds.

I didn't allow myself to fully take in everything that just happened, worried that I'd fall into an abyss of nervous breakdown and never be able to climb out. Instead, I picked up my blanket and dusted it off, then went over to the girl crying on the ground.

"Come on," I said, gently helping her up and supporting her side with the broken leg. "Let's get you fixed up."

We hobbled together down the side of the Compound—away from everyone—to the research building where I handed her off to a surprised doctor. I didn't wait for questions. I apologized to the girl again before heading to the bathroom to splash water on my face and decide what to do.

Horrible gagging sounds greeted me as I went through the bathroom door. I walked forward to see a girl crumpled on the floor of an open stall, her face sunken and sickly, and I stopped, blinking in surprise. It was Zoe.

Her deadened eyes widened in terror when she saw me, a squeaky gasp escaping her mouth as desperate tears welled up.

I shook my head before she could get too upset. "It's not me," I said, though it died into a whisper. My voice had been stolen.

Two perfect eyebrows creased. "There are two of you?" she asked, her usually smooth and powerful voice small and cracked.

I nodded. She thought for a moment then nodded back at me, the fear gone from eyes, just accepting it—accepting me—without question. I felt a pang of guilt at the fact that all these months I'd thought of her only as a two-dimensional doll who only loved to be looked at.

Way to be a hypocrite.

She dropped her eyes and watched her manicured fingers tap against her leg. I stood there, wondering what I should do. It was stupid, but even in her state of fragility she still intimidated me.

"Are you okay?" I finally asked. "Do you want me to get a doctor or something?"

"No," she answered, a little too quickly, confirming what I'd guessed. "I'm just feeling sick. It's nothing major."

I knew she wasn't sick. Miss Welch used the f-word often in rehearsals, and even ordered costumes in impossibly small sizes on purpose so we'd have to lose weight to fit. All of us—boys and girls alike—had starved ourselves on multiple occasions to accommodate, but several team members developed nasty disorders. It was our giant elephant in the room. We all knew it happened, but we'd never ever talk about it.

Weakness is death.

"Well, um…" I cleared my throat. "Is there anything I can do for you?"

Zoe glanced up at me, brushing her blonde hair behind her ear. "Like what?"

The question wasn't mean or sarcastic. It was honest, almost childlike. She was really asking if I could help, if there was some way I could pull her out of her hopeless situation, some magic dust I could sprinkle over her to heal the hurt. And suddenly, I felt like this girl understood me better than anyone I'd ever met.

We just looked at each other, marking the realest moment I'd had in a long time, every part of us vulnerable and out on display. Both of us devoid of our makeup and sparkles and fancy shoes, revealing pale and lifeless faces, tired eyes, and feet that threatened to collapse underneath us, her leaning over a toilet and me clutching a dirty blanket to my chest. People without the production. Just humans.

"I don't know," I admitted. "If you…just, if you do think of something, let me know."

I internally winced. *That sounded so stupid.*

"Thanks," she responded, her tone slightly warmer. "I will."

Once I got outside, I remembered my situation: my 'Vanessa on the loose and being temporarily homeless' situation.

What do I do?

I stood in place for a few minutes, my body rigid and still, as I tried to keep myself from breaking down. Deep breaths. In and out.

I knew it was probably a bad idea, but it was all I had. I wrapped my blanket around my shoulders and trudged down the length of the Compound, past the training building, almost to the giant wall that kept out the rest of the world. My foot kicked against a circular metal lid locked into the ground. I sat in the dirt next to it and waited.

It had probably been an hour or so when I saw him walking to me. He looked angry at first until he got closer and really saw his visitor. His eyes widened as he ran the rest of the way to me, stopping, out of breath though he couldn't have actually exerted himself.

Micah looked at me, then behind his shoulder, then at me again. "Whoa. You're…" He blinked a few times, taking it in. "Wow."

I sighed. "I need a place to stay."

"As long as you don't invite your evil twin," he told me with a laugh of disbelief, "you can stay as long as you want."

2

One week. That's how long it took for everything to get much worse than the absolute disaster it already was.

Vanessa knew I'd go to Micah first—within two hours of me hiding out, she brought two strike teams down on me. I went willingly of course, mostly because I really had no other choice, keeping my head down as twenty-four armed guards escorted me across the Compound. It was like a parade. Vanessa gave a smug smile when I clenched my fists as the crowds of infecteds watched us go by.

We went right to the administration building, up the elevator, to the right where all of administration was sitting at the conference table. I was led to the seat at the other head—directly across from a closed off Cyrus—Vanessa sat to my left, and the tribunal began.

I stayed silent throughout the whole thing. Apparently, Cyrus didn't tell anyone, not even Roland, about me still being alive, which I could tell caused a stir. They debated forever. After Cyrus beating around the bush for ten years, he finally admitted he didn't know why I was still alive or how I survived. That caused another stir.

I just wanted to get on with it. After Vanessa's speech expressing that I should be publicly executed, it was put to a vote. Out of the eleven votes (since when was Vanessa considered an administrator?) seven of them were in favor of execution, while four were against. I was surprised that Miss Welch wanted me spared, though Dr. Bragenhurst and his two cohorts—the people over the research building—didn't surprise me at all, as they'd made a case for the unknown scientific aspects of everything. Scottsman was about to vote for sparing, but then Roland growled something under his breath, effectively changing his mind.

The rest of them wanted me dead, or at least seemed indifferent one way or the other. I tried not to be offended when Miss Zebedee raised her hand for death—I'd worked under her in the kitchen even when I didn't have to, and she'd once told me she was grateful for my help.

You think you have friends one day, and the next they're pitting you against a firing squad. And people wondered why I had trust issues.

I don't know why they even voted, because in the end it didn't matter: Cyrus' vote counted for ten thousand.

He'd been oddly quiet throughout the entire meeting, his usually jumpy eyes still and focused. When the voting was done—Vanessa practically bouncing in her seat next to me—he sat still for what seemed like forever, staring at a spot right above my head. Then in a quiet, drawn-out voice he said, "Overruled. Arie lives."

I'd been imagining how my blood would spurt after being shot eighteen thousand times, so I was just as shocked as anyone at the verdict.

"What?" Vanessa's voice was like the fire of a sniper rifle. "Are you kidding me?"

Cyrus let out a small sigh. "Vanessa, we—"

"You're going to leave her alive?" she practically shouted. "After all that, you're just going to let her *walk away*?"

"Remember your place, dear!" Cyrus snapped sharply, silencing the already quiet room. "Arie will be spared. She will be reduced to the bottom rank of laborers, be given her own working assignment that shall be hers alone and done in seclusion excluding when her supervisor checks in. She will live, eat, and work away from everyone else here. No one is to address her. No one is to kill her—and that includes you. You have direct orders to not harm her in any way." He took a breath, as though tired. "Do you understand?"

Vanessa gave a muttered, "Yes, sir," then stalked out of the room.

So, Cyrus saved my life. Whether he liked gambling or wanted to test loyalties or really did have some sick and twisted paternal feelings for me like he claimed, I was to live.

The order went out to all supervisors before I even left the building: ignore the person who looked suspiciously like the Arie that was supposed to be dead. Do not talk to her. Do not interact with her. Don't even look at her. Any questions, concerns or challenging behavior would be taken up with Cyrus himself. End of discussion.

And that was that. A guard from the strike team took me to my own personal worksite near the edge of the Compound. I didn't ask questions—like who my supervisor would be or how in the world I was supposed to build a whole building by myself—but the answers came soon enough. Lennon was doubly assigned, charged with overseeing my work. Vanessa came to check up on us too. As for the second question, they simply didn't care. It was my work. My problem.

So I worked. Most nights I didn't even leave the work site, taking a nap against some propped up wood or just working through the night. It wasn't like I had anywhere to go anyway. The night Lennon decided to stay, though, I went to Micah's, who was nice enough to house me in his underground hole.

My progress was laughable, since there was hardly any of it. I fell ten thousand miles behind just on the first day of work despite going as long and hard as I could. Vanessa wasn't allowed to hurt me, of course, but she looked the other way when Lennon wanted to hit me, and I couldn't even find it in me to care.

The third night of the new arrangements, I had visitors. I didn't see them coming, mostly because I wasn't given even one industrial light, so I had to work off of the distant light of the maintenance building, but I still wasn't expecting anyone.

"Arie?"

I jumped at my whispered name, turning around and blinking in shock. There was Ellen, Sark and Peter, breaking at least forty-six rules to be standing there in front of me in the night.

Ellen darted forward and gave me giant hug. I froze over, still choking on surprise, until she took a step away from me.

"I had to see for sure," she told me in a quiet voice. "See for myself. After...after..." She took a steadying breath. "What the heck is going on? There's...there's a girl who looks—" She pointed behind her, then shook her head. "Arie, she looks just like you. We thought she *was* you. And then you're here. Why...why would..."

I just stared at her, finally able to force mumbled words. "Why did you come?"

Peter took a step toward me, leaving an expressionless Sark a step behind. "Why didn't *you*? Did you even know what was going on?"

I think I nodded but I wasn't sure.

Ellen's eyes filled with tears. "Why didn't you tell me? You knew this was going to happen and you...Arie, I...I knew it was bad, but *nothing* like this. Why didn't...and after..." She sniffed and wiped her eyes. "Why wouldn't you tell us you were still here?"

"Or at least warn us about her," Peter cut in. "It's been insane. They're having to go kidnap more infecteds because she's killed so many workers."

That made me wince. "I, uh…I…" I cleared my throat, gesturing to the pathetic scene behind me and saying the first thing that came to mind. "I have to keep working."

Ellen's eyes widened. "You have to keep *working*?" she repeated in disbelief.

*Say something. Something better. Say…*I didn't know. I didn't know what to say. I didn't want to lose another great friend out of ignorant action— lose another great friend to Vanessa—but I didn't know what on earth I could possibly say, how I could even begin to explain.

I'm so so sorry.

"Come on," Sark muttered, motioning for Peter and Ellen but watching me. "She's working. Let's get back before the night guards round up."

Tears started streaming down Ellen's face as she turned and walked away, Peter following close behind. Sark gave me a small nod—not necessarily angry or mean, but not really nice or happy. Kind of acceptance. Maybe some understanding. He wasn't surprised I reacted the way I did. He didn't like it, but he wasn't going to condemn me for it. And he would take me if I decided to come back.

He let me know all of that with one look and nod, then he turned and disappeared into the dark. Once they were really gone, I sat down on the foundation and cried for fifteen minutes, then got up and kept working.

A week of the new arrangements passed by. I ran out of nails, which meant I had to make a dreaded trip to the administration building. I had to clear anything and everything with Cyrus—even a stupid box of nails—even though it would be a trillion times easier to just get it from the supply closet.

With a sigh, I started off, watching as my feet took stiff and quick steps toward my destination, only glancing up from time to time to make sure I was still heading in the right direction. That's when I caught a glimpse of Vanessa walking into the Dome.

I knew she wouldn't care about the kids unless she was aiming to hurt them, but Cyrus would never allow that. He viewed them as investments, not pets. However, I couldn't shake the feeling something bad was going on. I stopped walking and waited.

After a few minutes, Vanessa exited carrying Bea, who was glancing around the outside world in fearful curiosity, thumb stuck in her mouth. Then I heard Hadley shout from the door, "Arie, don't take her! Don't do that to her! You really wouldn't want that!"

And it clicked. Bea's eyes locked on me from a distance and her eyebrows furrowed as she looked back and forth from me to her captor. Then she let out a shattering scream that shook the entire Compound.

I broke out into a run. Vanessa caught sight of me right before I reached them, and she jerked Bea away from me at the last second.

"Leave her alone," I demanded, clenching my fists. "You don't have anything to do with her."

"Wow, princess," Vanessa said with a mocking laugh. She swayed, making her yellow skirt flow with her. "I think that's the most I've heard you speak all week."

Bea whined, the sound disfigured by her thumb in her mouth, and reached her other hand toward me. I stepped toward her, but Vanessa pulled her away and Bea cried out again.

"You don't have the rank to decide what happens to her," I said, my tone hard. "Get out."

Vanessa held on tighter to the wiggling Bea. "Actually, I put in an order at the lab for this little girl. She isn't infected yet."

"They know that, idiot. She's too young. They said they'd wait at least another year." I gritted my teeth in frustration because I knew Vanessa knew that.

She shrugged with a smile. "Not after I talked to them. Funny how rank doesn't seem to matter when I look like you."

"You're a fake!" I glanced behind me to see Hadley at the door of the Dome shouting with a red face and balled fists, Jacklynn and Ranger hanging behind him. "You're just a stupid fake copy and you'll never be as good as the real Arie!"

Vanessa glared at him, shifting from ostentatious to predatory. She took a step toward him the same time I stepped in front of her to block her path. I heard Jacklynn mumble something and the Dome door shut behind me.

Good girl.

Bea started hitting Vanessa with slobbered fists, wailing and reaching for me. I realized I would have to do something unexpected—I would have to be on offense instead of defense. Vanessa expected me to defend, per usual, rather than start the fight myself.

"Shut up," Vanessa snarled. She went to hit the poor girl, and I threw myself at them, tackling us all to the ground. Using the surprise to my advantage, I punched Vanessa in the face twice, stood and smashed my foot in her face too, then scooped up the crying Bea and made a run for the one person I could trust to take care of her.

I found the labor group easily, and my heart thumped wildly in my chest when my scanning eyes couldn't find the worker I was looking for. Then I caught sight of him several yards away from the work site, kneeling on the ground in front of Hadley, whose mouth seemed to be talking a million miles an hour.

Hadley saw me first. With wide eyes but straight and brave shoulders, he pointed at me, and Sark turned around right as I dashed to him. His eyebrows shot up in surprise as he got to his feet just as I shoved a terrified little girl in his arms.

"Take her," I said, breathless, glancing behind my shoulder and ignoring the stares from the workers. "Keep her safe until I—"

A scream cut me off. I turned to see a vengeful Vanessa tearing through the labor camp, leaving destructive chaos in her wake. Workers scattered while I pushed Sark and Hadley forward. An object thrown at my head sent me to the ground momentarily; I pulled myself up to see Vanessa chasing Bea, Sark, and Hadley down. I ran after them, noticing too late the way she was cornering them. Having nowhere else to go, they ran into the half finished building on another work site, empty because of workers on lunch. I couldn't push my legs fast enough, my heart lurching in my throat as they disappeared behind a wall one by one, Vanessa following right behind them.

The place was a danger zone, the floor littered in sawdust and boards and nails and tarps. Vanessa's steps were predatory, nearly feline, as she backed the three of them up against a half finished wall. Sark stood with a square jaw, one hand steadying Bea as she clung to his back, and the other on Hadley's head, who was hiding behind Sark's legs.

I ran to intercept her, then slowed to a stop three feet away. She was holding a hammer, a hammer that looked lethal in her hands as she twisted it threateningly toward Sark. We all knew she could throw it at his skull faster than I could stop her or he could find room to get out of the way. The smug smile she gave was aimed at me, but her eyes danced with wild anticipation as she watched him.

"You won't touch him," I muttered through clenched teeth, my fists beginning to shake with murderous fury. The raging emotion felt white hot compared to the numb empty tomb I'd been the last few weeks. I didn't know how to handle it.

She laughed, waving a hand like I was absurd. "Oh please, princess. Torturing Sark is too easy. I don't have to touch him to hurt him."

Before I could ask what that was even supposed to mean, she shifted, so suddenly and completely that I staggered back a step in surprise. Her face contorted and twisted itself into a mangled expression, her shoulders tightening and crunching in on herself as she let out a string of awful, bloodcurdling screams.

My body tensed and recoiled at the sound, the familiar sound, expecting the kind of pain that caused that sound to come from my mouth. I tried to quickly block the suppressed memories as they surfaced—memories of death and torture and pain I once didn't believe could exist.

"Make it stop!" she shrieked over and over again. "Please!" The sounds were savage. Horrible. They paralyzed me as I fought an internal eternal war to keep myself here.

It's not real it's not real it's not real.

Bea started crying, scared and confused, and Hadley scrunched his nose and pressed his hands against his ears. The effect on Sark was slower.

"Please! Please, Sark, please!" Another shockingly loud screech of agony in between my—her—begging. "Sark, make it stop!"

He closed his eyes, trying to take a deep breath but nearly started hyperventilating instead. He shook his head, his body trembling visibly from where I stood, and his forehead creased.

"Sark, it hurts! Don't, please, Sark, please stop! *Sark!*"

The creased lines in his forehead seemed to deepen, to spread, like fault lines running through him, and within fifteen seconds of tortured screams he went from fierce protector to broken victim. He rocked on his heels like he would crumble; Hadley pushed against his legs as though trying to keep him up.

The pain was written all over him. Vanessa was too loud for me to hear him, but I watched his mouth form the words: "Stop. Please."

Vanessa flipped the switch as suddenly as she did the first time. The screaming ceased, her face evened out, and she beamed with arrogance. "Told ya. I can send him down without lifting a finger." She turned to me, still swinging the hammer. "Where'd *you* go, princess? Huh? Back to the box? The ring with Micah? Ooh or when Cyrus strapped you to that chair for days and *broke* you." I shuddered, trying to stay in control, as she took a step toward me. "Or did we reach farther—Dalton? You know which day at Dalton's place was my favorite." She cocked her head, running her tongue along her teeth. "Or did you go all the way back to the beginning—to when a devil named Mr. Sark would beat you like an animal just to do it all again the next day."

The flashes of memories tore into me like bullets. My breathing went ragged. My lips quivered.

"I'm here," I whispered to myself, even though I felt myself bending, breaking, shattering under the voice that had been pounding me for months. "I'm here, not there."

"No," Vanessa said, closing the last of the distance between us and taking my chin in her cool hand. "No, princess, you're there. You're screaming and you're begging and you know there isn't a way out. And the teeny tiny rational part left intact doesn't want a way out, because you know you'll never ever be the same. Those scars, those screams, still haven't left you, and they *never* will."

My knees buckled. She hit the hammer into my gut, knocking the wind out of me and sending me to the ground. Gasping, I didn't realize why she'd leaned down next to me until my arms were secured behind me. Vanessa straightened and I pulled against the restraints; she'd zip tied me to a support beam.

Still choking on nothing, I caught a glimpse of Sark behind Vanessa. He was leaning down, talking to the kids, oh so quietly reasoning with them. Hadley puffed out his chest and nodded, taking Bea's reluctant hand. I understood: he was getting them to run.

"Vanessa," I snapped as she was about to turn around. I needed to keep her attention. Sark wouldn't run but the kids had to get out.

"Hmm?" she drawled, a slow smile spreading on her lips as she took me in: beaten, tied up, and kneeling before her, and she'd barely put a finger on me.

"Let me go. Fight me one on one."

She rolled her eyes halfway through my demand, already turning with boredom. Hadley was starting to drag Bea across the space towards the opening. She wasn't thrilled, pulling and quietly whining for Sark.

I continued hastily, begging for Vanessa's attention, and struck a nerve I just realized existed.

"He'll never pick you," I found myself saying, unsure of where exactly it was coming from. Her body went rigid, the smug smile frozen on her face. "You know that, though. You can trick or force him into anything, but you know he'll always *always* pick me over you. And you can't stand that."

Vanessa snarled and moved so fast, I didn't catch what she did until my face was already bleeding. Then she was kneeling over me, one hand pinning my head back against the beam and another holding a red-stained nail.

"I'll make you look like I did," she seethed in my ear, "when I was locked up in your head. That hideous blue monster you imagined—I'll tear you up, just like her." I winced at my stinging cheek, trying to pull away, but she held fast. "Then we'll see if Sark can stand to be near you." Her thumb pulled on my temple and she positioned the nail above my eye. "Let's start here, shall we?"

My mouth went dry. I squirmed, trying to get my legs out from under me, hearing Hadley gasp in horror somewhere. Somewhere in here, somewhere he shouldn't be. Because under no circumstances would Vanessa stop, and under no circumstances could Hadley witness what she was about to do.

"Vanessa."

She paused. And I knew she only paused because it was his voice, and because he said her name—not mine—and while it was strained and still tinted with hurt, he said her name softly, keeping all distaste out of his tone.

I hated it.

I wanted him to tear her apart. But when Vanessa lowered her hand and turned to look at him, I saw him standing loosely with his hands half raised in surrender. His eyes were deep and imploring and so lost, and something dawned on me, something that had probably been determined weeks ago—something I'd completely missed.

It was clear now though: Sark would always pick me, but he would never hurt her. If he could've once before, her screaming episode had taken that right out of him.

Sark would be no help. If we had to fight out of this one, I was going to have to fight alone.

"Put that down," Sark went on, looking at the nail still clutched in Vanessa's manicured hand and trying not to seem panicked. "We can go somewhere—anywhere. We can…" He almost dropped the word but managed to keep his voice even. "Talk. We can go talk. Just put it down."

I heard her teeth slam together when she snapped her jaw shut. One deep breath. Then two. Three. Time seemed to slow down as Vanessa reigned in her fury. Some of the tension left Sark's face, but I still felt it, still knew it. She wasn't calming down. She was reigning in her fury to sharpen it and control it and strike with it.

"You're right," she said. The nail clattered to the floor, and she put on a sweet smile. "I'm acting rashly. I'll cut her up another time. We should *talk*." She gave me a knowing glance. "Although I don't think Arie will like our talking sessions much, Sark. Maybe we should try something new."

I scowled. "You're not taking him anywhere."

She ignored me. Instead, she stood and started for the two children that were frozen in terror against the wall across the room. She was freaking fast. Bea barely had time to scream before they both started running, and a choking sound came from me when Hadley pushed her so she wouldn't get caught. That made it too easy for Vanessa to snatch Hadley's arm and yank him back. Bea ran outside—hopefully to safety—in terror.

"That's okay," Vanessa crooned, not even struggling with Hadley's attempts to get away from her. "I'll get the little girl later—I already have a plan for her anyways. Right now, I just need you."

A horrible stab of ice-cold terror went into my chest, stabbing over and over again, stab stab stab.

"Vanessa," I breathed. "Vanessa, please."

Her grin only grew at that word. *Please*. She wanted me to beg. And she wanted me to know it wouldn't matter.

Once she got close enough, Sark grabbed Hadley away from her, and she let them go only to push them to their knees on the ground.

"Okay, Arie," she said, standing over both of them. Neither could run without the other getting caught. "We're going to play a game."

Sark hovered over Hadley protectively, and I strained against my restraints, feeling the plastic break skin around my wrists. My blood went cold when Vanessa slid a little silver gun out from under her skirt. The thing didn't seem like it could cause much damage—it looked like it could be a futuristic water gun—but I shuddered at the knowledge of what it could do. What I'd seen it do to others. What it had done to me.

When Cyrus strapped you to that chair and broke you.

"Vanessa!" I squeaked. "Vanessa, please, please don't. Me. Me, I'm here, I'm tied up. Do it to me. Carve me up. You hate *me*."

"Oh, I will, believe me." She stroked the side of Sark's face with the gun. "But, let's be honest, you don't care what happens to you anymore. It's not nearly as fun as it used to be. But these two— I'd say you care a lot about what happens to them. That's always been your downfall point, really." She smirked. "Well, one of them."

"Vanes—"

"Here's the game," she cut in, beginning to lose patience. "I take this fancy nerve juice and you pick who I use it on."

"Me."

"Uh, yeah, no. That's the game: you aren't an option." Vanessa gestured to Sark and Hadley, then pretended to check an invisible watch. "You have ten seconds to decide or I will."

I was shaking my head viciously before she was through. But it didn't matter. Nothing I did would matter. I was tied to a beam and not able to *do* anything.

"Ten."

"Vanessa, please, just think. I'm right here."

"Nine."

"Vanessa."

"Eight."

"Don't, please."

"Seven."

In one slick move, she reached underneath Sark and pried Hadley from his grasp. Hadley yelped; Sark growled, but Vanessa held him down with her foot.

"Six."

"Arie," Sark breathed.

"Five."

I started hyperventilating. "Vanessa!"

"Four."

Sark was lax on the floor. Acceptance. Preparation. He could prepare all he wanted, but nothing would help him stand against the excruciating pain of that stupid gun. "Arie, it's okay."

"I'm here!" My wrists ached from yanking them. "I'm right here! I swear, I'll do anything. You can do *anything* to me. You—or me, I'll do anything to myself, anything you say. But please. Please not them. Me."

"Three. Better pick one, Arie."

"Arie—"

"Vanessa." Tears started crawling down my stinging cheek. "Please please please."

Huffing with impatience, Vanessa nicked Hadley's neck with the tip of the gun. Even that short little contact sent him into hysterical screaming.

"Arie!" Sark shouted at me, struggling to reach Hadley's flailing form. "Arie, now!"

She went to dig into Hadley for real this time, and I choked on the name, feeling it tear into what was left of my soul. "Sark."

Instantly, Vanessa released Hadley, who stumbled over his growing legs as he ran to me, ducking behind me and crying into my back. Grinning, she pushed Sark flat on his back and climbed on top of him, like a cat finally able to pounce on her mouse.

I didn't watch—I probably owed him at least that much—but I closed my eyes and doubled over and sobbed along with Sark's screams. He tried to muffle it at first, tried to be brave, but I knew she would push until she found his limits, then push even harder, because I knew—I *knew*—exactly how that gun had found and pushed mine. Even Micah did what was necessary to evade that gun, to escape the liquid inside.

Because that liquid would make you think you were dead—no, make you *wish* you were dead. It was pushed into your system little bits at a time, targeting your nerves, squeezing them and burning them and yanking them. It literally turned your body against you, made you feel excruciating things that weren't actually even there. It was just the liquid tricking your body into believing it was being picked apart piece by piece.

That's why Cyrus loved it: the whole thing was a mind game. Sure, the agony would completely tire a person out in every way, make them beg and compromise and do just about anything, but unless it was used in huge amounts, there was no sustainable damage. If the victim was pushed too far or passed out or something, Cyrus would just give them a fifteen-minute break before they would go again. And again. And again. Until they gave up.

I would know.

Please make it stop.

It seemed it would never end. Sark's screams seemed to break open, shattering into pieces, the shrapnel lodging itself into me. I shrieked and sobbed and cried so hard, choking on tears and snot and saliva, trying to find the numbers to count but they were failing me. Four was too long. I needed five. I needed five *now*.

But five wasn't coming. We'd be in four forever.

I didn't know how long I cried there, useless, before Hadley finally gave me a shove. I'd nearly forgotten he was still there. When he shoved me, I fell forward, automatically catching myself on my hands before realizing that my hands were free. Hadley's splotchy tear-soaked face held a grim yet triumphant grin as he held up the nail Vanessa had wanted to cut me up with.

Hadley had cut me free.

Lurching to my feet, I tackled an unsuspecting Vanessa off Sark, beating my fists against any and every part of her. She'd been so wrapped up in her torture that I caught her completely off guard, making her unable to defend herself. I punched her with ferocity until her face turned red and her body went limp and her hateful eyes closed.

Hadley was already at Sark's side, rogue tears still falling from his eyes as he fluttered around Sark's crumpled form. I crawled to them. Sark was shaking and moaning and spasming, slick with sweat and blood.

Trying in vain to breathe normally and stay calm, I first checked to see where the blood was coming from: deep scratches all over him. Had she used her nails?

"Oh Sark," I whimpered, not sure if I should touch him. He choked on some blood from his face, and I gingerly put my hand underneath his neck to help him breathe better.

He flinched. I didn't know if it was from my hand or from my voice, but it was clearly in response to me.

"You," he whispered heavily.

I tensed, waiting for him to shrink away from my touch since it probably felt exactly like hers. Heart breaking, I started to lean away, but his hand nudged mine, and he tried to move his head. It took me a few moments to understand what he wanted. My breath caught the mangled sob before it left my throat as I picked him up as best I could and just held him, cradling his head against my chest and burying my face in his hair.

Somehow, he relaxed into me, crumpling in, letting me hold him up. "It's you. Really you."

"Yes," I whispered back. I was crying again. "Oh, Sark, I'm so sorry."

"No, it's okay. I told you. You did the right thing."

I shook my head. "It doesn't feel like it."

"You did. Hadley..." I felt Sark shudder slightly beneath me, and he groaned in pain. "That can't happen to him."

I closed my eyes as the tears kept falling, nodding.

"It happened to you," Sark stated. "They did that to you."

My sore throat closed up. I tried to clear it. "Yes."

His breath stuttered for a second. "It hurts," was all he commented.

His words broke something in me. "Oh, I know." I kissed his head softly. "I know, I know, it…it's awful. I'm so *sorry*." My voice cracked.

Sark spasmed again, groaning through his teeth as his body twisted violently. Hadley, still frozen in terrified shock, hiccupped, whimpering. I held Sark tight and stroked his face softly, knowing the liquid would have to work its way through completely. Eventually, he got in control enough to open his eyes. The first thing he looked for was Hadley.

Hadley's hair was a rumpled mess, half sticking out in all directions and half stuck to his tearstained face, making him look years younger. His mouth opened like he was going to say something. He just sobbed instead.

"Hey," Sark said softly, his voice still strained tight. He tried to stretch his arm toward him. "It's okay. Come here."

Hadley's eyes widened with fear, glancing at me as if for permission.

I nodded and said, "Just be careful," the same time Sark said, "It's okay."

Sobbing again, Hadley burrowed himself forward into Sark's chest, clenching Sark's shirt in his little fists and shaking. Sark held him tight, and I held them both, as though I could somehow spread all my broken pieces over them and protect them from getting hurt ever again.

"You did that," Hadley cried into Sark's shirt, muffled. "You did that for me."

Sark half held back his next groan, further relaxing into me. "Of course I did."

"Thank you."

"Of course," Sark said again. He held Hadley's head against him. "I told you—you always have me. Okay?"

Hadley nodded, face still buried. "I know."

My breaths hitched with the overwhelming emotion I felt for these two, and I felt a pang of hurt at the fact that I'd missed when Sark had promised him that. I hadn't been there when Hadley needed someone.

Because I'd left them. I'd *left* them.

How could I leave them?

Something snaked around my throat and yanked up, choking me and nearly jerking me to my feet. Hadley yelped when I dropped him and Sark. I put my hands up just in time to catch the industrial wire before it completely dug into my neck.

Vanessa hissed in my ear and pulled harder, forcing me against her body, as my hands went slick with blood. I jerked and twisted and finally jammed my elbow into her face. She lost her grip momentarily—enough for me to throw the wire—but all too soon she had her hands on me again, jerking me around and pressing me against the floor. The smug grin was gone from her face; her eyes glowed with manic hatred as she climbed on top of me, holding my arms down with her knees, then dug the nerve gun into my shoulder and squeezed the trigger.

My shoulder contorted in on itself, twisting my muscles and tendons and bones with it. I screamed and kicked my legs wildly in the air. Then Vanessa's hair was a mess of hands. It took a moment to realize it was Hadley trying to tackle her. Vanessa snarled and slapped him viciously, giving me just the right angle to push her off. Then the real brawl began.

We rolled around in the sawdust, punching and hitting and kicking and yanking and clawing and biting. Our movements were in sync without us trying, and often we'd accidentally block the other's attack just because we were doing the same thing. Then we'd both growl in heated resentment and hit twice as hard.

I managed to nail Vanessa in the head with a board. She sprawled onto the floor, and something small fell out of her ear, rolling halfway to where Sark was hiding Hadley in an alcove. I saw Sark reach for the object just as I noticed a hammer on the floor. Vanessa and I lunged for it at the same time.

My fingers curled around the hammer first. I turned to use it right when Vanessa's knees slammed into me. My breath left me in a quick whoosh and she seized my wrist when I went to hit her off me.

"Nice try, princess," she smirked, face bruised and cut and bloody, beating my hand against the ground until I released my weapon, tossing it a few inches away. She leaned forward to get it and I used my other hand to grab a fistful of her free-flowing hair and yank on it, keeping the hammer out of her reach. Then I slammed my knee into her gut and kicked her away. A cry pierced the air as I felt the chunk of hair still in my hand.

Vanessa held her palm against her now bald spot, scowling at me and preparing to charge again. I staggered to my feet and threw her hair on the ground, bracing myself. Attack and dodge, again and again, like clockwork, until we both died. And we would. We'd both die to tear the other apart.

We went for each other right as Roland grabbed her wrist and Micah barreled in front of me, grabbing my shoulders to keep me in place.

"Vanessa!" Roland sputtered in between curse words, completely enraged. *What do you think you're doing?"*

She barely acknowledged Roland, snarling and breaking out of his grasp. We both lunged at each other but were both held back. Then the strike team surrounded us, guns aimed and ready.

"Back off, Arie," Micah muttered as Roland let out another stream of colorful curses on Vanessa.

"She started it," I muttered back in breathless frustration, jerking myself out of his hold. Then I realized I sounded like I was ten again, complaining to my mom that my brother Kieran had stolen my toy. "I hate her."

"I can see that." He gave a quick glance to Vanessa before focusing on my puffy face. "I don't think I've ever had to pull *you* out of a fight before."

Vanessa shrieked, aiming words at me now. "I'll kill you, Arie! I swear, I will *murder* you!"

I sidestepped so I could give her a wry grin from behind Micah, raising my hands in mocking presentation. "You're doing a great job so far, aren't you?"

She snarled again, moving toward me, but a guard let off a warning shot next to her head and she stopped.

"Get off me," she shouted, yanking her arm away from Roland again, then glowered at me. "This isn't over. Not by a long shot." Then she turned and stalked away with Roland, the strike team slowly following after a gesture from Micah. We both surveyed the war zone as the adrenaline started to leave my system.

"She almost killed you," Micah said under his breath, noting the red spotted sawdust everywhere.

"She did worse."

He pointed to the awful gun on the floor, voice thicker. "She used that."

Then the adrenaline was gone and hurt—so much *hurt*—took its place, with so much exhaustion, and I collapsed. Micah caught me on the way down, effortlessly holding me up against him.

"Where's Bea?" I asked, whimpering as my shoulder strained with my gasping.

"What?"

"Bea," I insisted. "Where…is she okay?"

"I don't know who you're talking about."

"The little girl. She…she's so small."

Micah let out a frustrated breath through his teeth. "You mean you started this whole thing because of that freaky kid that won't talk?"

I shook my head, heart still hammering, and groaned. "Don't tell me…that if I could go back to the moment when they dragged you from the

Dome to infect you…you wouldn't want me to stop them."

Micah stiffened in stunned silence. I waited a few seconds, trying and failing to get my bearings, before I didn't want to wait anymore. I made it a few steps before my legs gave out again. Micah caught me again, silently helping me to where I wanted to go.

A big board had been placed in front of the alcove. I pushed it softly aside to find a trembling Hadley hiding behind a pale and bloody Sark.

I collapsed again, on purpose, and this time Micah let me go. A mangled choke of pain escaped me when I sat back against the wall next to Sark. I felt Hadley reach his hand out to touch my shoulder, and we both whimpered. I knew his wasn't for me though.

"It's okay," I told Hadley, my voice raspy and spent. "He won't hurt you."

Micah huffed under his breath and crouched down, taking in our pathetic group with hard eyes before he held out his hand expectantly. I didn't know what he wanted, but apparently it wasn't for me. Sark was rigid and stoic as he placed a little round object in Micah's palm. Vanessa's earpiece.

The peaceful, if not tense, exchange gave Hadley the courage to believe me. Wide eyes on Micah the entire time, he extracted himself from behind Sark and burrowed himself in my lap, trembling. I winced, and Sark wrapped his arm around my leg. I gently leaned against him and sighed.

Hadley's here. Sark's here. Micah's here. We're safe. I'm safe. She's gone.

I couldn't stop trembling. I wanted to believe it was from the pain my body was in, but I knew I was terrified. Because I would never be safe. She would never stop. She would never go away.

"I'm supposed to take you in," Micah said in a low voice, playing with the earpiece in his hand. "Keep you out of sight until they can get Vanessa under control."

I shook my head and winced again. Sark's hand tightened on the back of my knee.

"You need medical?" Micah asked me. He was still all business, in mission mode, but never once had he ever asked me that. If I'd ever been critical, Roland had brought in a doctor.

"No," I rasped, stroking Hadley's hair. "I'll be fine."

I expected Micah to shrug it off, to let me just deal with it like we often had to, but instead he squared his jaw. I was shocked when he reached his hand forward and brushed his fingers against the wound on my neck where the wire had pierced me. Hadley hissed and recoiled away, closer to me, and I felt Sark stiffen beside me.

"She beat the tar out of you," Micah commented, probing my neck with fingers softer than I thought he was capable of. "This will need stitches."

I shrugged noncommittally. "Somehow I thought you two would get along."

He laughed once and dropped his hand, and I saw a small hint of my Micah there in his eyes. "Yeah, no. I never thought I'd actually miss you until she came around."

My mouth twitched into a brief smile, then a grimace when the movement pulled at a wound on my face. That snapped Micah back into mission mode. He straightened up and started walking around the room purposefully, inspecting what was broken, and probably going to grab the gun before Vanessa could find it again.

The second Micah was out of our line of vision, Sark gently took my chin in his hand and kissed me, soft and hard at the same time. Despite my surprise, it sparked something in me; I hadn't felt it in a long time. The warmth that his presence gave me, talking with him, touching him—all the contact I'd avoided since Vanessa had crashed my party—rose up inside me again, the flood of emotion shocking my numb system. It hurt to raise my arm and hold his face, to lean closer, to move my mouth with his, but I didn't care. I just wanted him here, wanted him with me, wanted him okay. I thought I would explode with how much I cared about just one person.

Maybe I'm still human after all.

Sark sighed into my mouth, almost in relief. "Oh, I missed *you*."

I couldn't help but grin slightly at his distinction.

Something shifted in my lap. Remembering, I turned my head to see Hadley still sitting there, and despite the traumatic situation, I found him looking between Sark and me and beaming slyly from ear to ear. "I knew it."

A painful laugh burst out of me, and I rolled my eyes. "No you didn't."

"Yes I did," Hadley insisted. "You're Sark's favorite person. All he does is talk about you, and when he's not talking about you then he's watching you with big fat googly eyes."

Now Sark laughed with me, pecking the corners of my mouth. "No I don't."

"Yes you do. You did it at our performance. Your eyes were, like, glued to her. I'm old enough to notice these things."

Sark wasn't paying attention anymore, twisting his fingers in my hair as I twisted mine in his. "Mm, you are, huh?" And then we were lost again, lost in each other, so relieved to have each other on our fingertips again.

"Okay guys," Hadley said after another moment of third wheeling. "I guessed now. You guys can stop."

Sark grumbled something unintelligible in response.

"Seriously." I knew how he would look with that voice, his nose all wrinkled up. He tried to get in between us and push Sark away from me. "I'm glad she kisses you back and all, but it's gross."

Sark just pushed him back and wedged himself in between me and Hadley, wrapping his arm around my waist and bracing his other hand against the wall so he was leaning over me and boxing Hadley out. "Then leave," he told him, only half teasing, before kissing me again like we'd been separated for years.

Hadley wrapped his arms around Sark's neck and pulled him backward, a half whine escaping both of us when we were parted.

"She was my girl first, you know," Hadley told Sark, really annoyed now. "You didn't even like her back then. You can't just take her because now you want to slobber all over her."

Sark grabbed Hadley from off his back and swung him around so he was in my lap again. Then, completely deadpan, he said, "I'll fight you for her."

I had to hold my hand against my mouth to stifle a laugh.

Hadley pursed his lips, considering, as he looked over Sark, noting his build and the thick muscles on his tanned arms, only made more defined from the last months of heavy labor.

"How about we share her?" Hadley finally suggested.

Sark pretended to think it over. I didn't think I could love him more than I already did, but there it was. "Yeah, okay. I guess that'll work." He held out his hand to shake, then pulled back. "I can still kiss her though, right?"

Hadley wrinkled his nose in disgust. "Fine. But not when I'm around."

"Deal." And they shook on it. "But just one more." Then Sark ducked and crushed his lips against mine.

"No!" Hadley gasped, but he was laughing now, a deep belly laugh that shook his whole body, as he fought to get Sark away from me.

And for that moment, I was okay, because we were *here*. Despite the pain and the blood and the fear, we were *here*, and we were together, and we were *laughing*, and I would've done anything to make that moment our permanent future.

Then heavy footsteps sounded, slaughtering the beautiful moment. Micah appeared out of nowhere, jade eyes cold, as he leaned down, gripped my arm, and yanked me to my feet. I cried out in pain and stumbled, trying to find my footing. I slumped into Micah only to be jerked back by Sark. They each kept a hold on one of my arms, standing toe-to-toe and ready to rip the other apart.

"Get your hand off of her," Sark growled murderously through his teeth. For someone who just got tortured, he seemed pretty deadly.

"We have orders," Micah spat back. "I'm taking her in *now*."

I raised an eyebrow, then quickly dropped it because it hurt. "You're not taking me anywhere."

He turned his radioactive eyes on me. "Vanessa—"

"Vanessa is alive, and she *will* come back for them." I took a breath, trying to keep myself calm at the horrifying thought. I almost lost this time. I wouldn't win a second. "I have to find Bea, and then I'm getting them somewhere safe."

Where can you possibly take them that she won't find?

"We're following orders," Micah repeated, pulling on me. Sark advanced on him and I put myself in between them.

"Not now," I hissed at both of them.

Micah grinned at Sark. "Why? Because you know he'll lose?"

Sark bristled. I put my hand on his chest, restraining, without looking away from Micah. "He's hurt." I nearly heard Sark's ego whine that I was making excuses for him, but, despite his urge to prove himself, he wisely stayed put.

Micah scoffed. "So? I could take him out ten times regardless of what shape I was in."

"Now you're being stupid."

"No, I'm serious." He let go of me, only to pull out Vanessa's nerve gun. "In fact, I bet there's still a little juice left in here. Could be fun."

My hand on Sark's chest curled into a fist, feeling when his breath caught. I glared Micah down, my blood going cold as I considered the odds I had of keeping him off Sark. Even if I were whole and prime, peaked and strong, I'd fail. Miserably.

I forced the words through my teeth. "You wouldn't dare."

Micah just smirked, knowing exactly the fruitless defense plans I was running through in my head. "Oh, we both know I would."

Giving him one last dagger glare, I turned to face Sark, stepping close so I could whisper under my breath. "Take Hadley, and please find Bea if you can, and then stay with them. Please. I'll come as soon as I can get out."

I was too close to see his eyes, but I saw the veins in his neck pop. "You're not going anywhere with him."

I ignored him, glancing down at Hadley who was hiding behind Sark and glaring at Micah. "Help Sark, okay? I'll come find you."

Hadley nodded solemnly, and I was struck by just how much he'd grown.

"I'll see you soon," I said to both of them, taking a step away and talking normally. "Please be safe."

Sark was too ticked to talk, but he spoke with his eyes: *please be safe too.*

I nodded, then turned and half limped, half stalked out of the place, feeling Micah fall into step behind me.

"Good choice," he said.

"I hate you."

"No you don't," I heard him mutter under his breath, though it almost sounded hurt, and for a second I wondered if he actually cared.

"It's difficult to say," I muttered back as we exited the half finished building. "When you pull stunts like that, I just want to throttle you."

Suddenly Micah stopped in his tracks, and I tensed, glancing around for the threat before realizing maybe I'd stepped too far and *he* was the threat. I looked at him. He watched me for a second with a look I couldn't decipher.

"Where do you want to go?" he finally asked me.

"Where do I…" I trailed off in disbelief.

"Where would you feel safe?" he clarified, as though I didn't understand the words he was saying rather than couldn't believe he was saying them.

I opened my mouth and it hung there for a minute, empty. Then I got an idea. "Follow me. I guess I need your help with something."

I led him to the maintenance building. I hadn't been there since Vanessa had thrown fire into it. The building itself wasn't really damaged, but the top floor had been filled with so much smoke that nobody had been able to go in yet. Or maybe just nobody cared.

We went around to the back of the building and I pointed to the half ladder. "I need to get up there."

"I didn't think you'd want to go back," Micah said. "Wasn't that like your jail cell for two weeks?"

I shrugged. "Home is home."

Micah cupped his hands and I secured my foot in them, then he helped push me up to the ladder. I grabbed hold of the metal and pulled myself onto the fire escape, ignoring the whine of my beat-up body.

"I'll wait down here," he said. I nodded before shoving open the window and ducking inside.

The place still smelled like smoke, making me hold my breath in between inhales of the tainted air. Besides the smell, though, and the occasional black mark on the wall, the place was pretty much the same.

"Hey, Steve," I greeted my generator friend, just for old time's sake. Then I sat on the floor and sifted through what was left of my pile of belongings.

I'd managed to get my blanket out—that was still tucked safely at Micah's place. It was a good thing too because everything I left behind was now ash. The remains of what I guessed had been my pillow covered up the glint of the kitchen knife I'd kept here. I picked up the weapon to take with me for good measure, but that's all I could salvage of my old home. It made me sad for reasons I couldn't understand. Micah was right. I shouldn't like it. This place held so many bad memories and yet I still felt so emotionally attached to it.

I sat on the floor for a few more minutes, running my fingers over the tally marks on the wall, before grabbing my knife and heading for the window, giving a last glance to Steve the generator.

Thanks Steve. I know you're not real, but you pretty much saved me.

Poking my head out the window, I expected to see an impatient Micah standing there. He was gone.

"Micah?" I called, craning my head in both directions to try and find him. "Micah?"

Nothing.

He probably got bored and left. Micah was possibly the last person on the planet who would understand emotional attachments to metal boxes. It still irritated me, though, that he would leave after being so infuriating about following orders.

I climbed down the half ladder and jumped to the ground. Still no sign of Micah.

Where did he go?

A rustling sounded from around the corner of the building, and I rolled my eyes as I walked toward it.

"Micah, you're so stu—"

I froze, my heart leaping in my throat, when I saw the monster in front of me. A mutt. Out here. In broad daylight. No restraints or Roland in sight.

How did that happen?

It snarled when it saw me and charged. Still stunned, I relied on the instinct that overtook me after months of practicing in the ring. The mutt bounded toward me, and I waited until the last possible second before sidestepping, digging my knife into its gut as it went by me. It howled and crumpled to the ground, writhing as bluish red liquid seeped from the wound, hateful eyes on me. The knife wasn't enough to kill it but enough to let me get away.

I ran toward the center of the Compound only to see my attacker wasn't the only one: mutts were everywhere, running rampant, chasing terrified employees and guests alike.

What is going on?

Instinctually, I made my way through the chaos to the Dome, hoping someone had taken my advice: if there was ever a crisis, go to the Dome. I'd said that because the Dome had extra security measures, a fortified wall that could be raised to defend from enemies while a series of tunnels led you to back exits in case you needed to escape. It was arguably the safest place to be, especially with unsupervised mutts running around.

The past few weeks I'd been the worst friend, acquaintance and family member ever, so I really hoped that those I loved would've listened to me anyway.

I burst through the front door of the Dome to see a mess—cots turned over, toys dumped everywhere, books littering the floor. The back half of the building was obstructed by a white wall. The security wall.

Someone already put it up.

"You came!" someone shouted. I looked to my left to see Hadley run up to me and give me a giant hug. "We didn't know if you would come or not."

"Of course I did," I said as I glanced around at Ranger, Sharna, and two other kids who were making a purposeful mess of the place. Then I understood: it was their version of a blockade. "Do you guys know what's going on?"

"No." Hadley shook his head, his shaggy hair swaying along with it. "The monsters started attacking people out of nowhere, so everyone came here to be safe. They said that's what you told them to do."

I felt a bit of hope. "They're here?"

"Yep." He pointed to the wall. "We tried to figure out how to put the wall up and it finally worked, but we couldn't get behind it in time since we didn't know where it would be. I told everyone that you would come and fix it."

My shoulders slumped slightly at his resolve, his belief that I was a hero that could do or be or fix anything.

"Yeah," I said, heading for the wall. "Let's see if we can figure this out."

It took a few minutes of exploring, but I finally managed to stack two cots to stand on and find a loose panel in the wall above my head. Gritting my teeth, I pushed on it. Eventually it gave way, and I was able to pull it out and hand it to Ranger to set on the floor. The hole was big enough for someone to climb through, the wall thick enough that there was a ledge to sit on too, should anyone be able to get up there.

"Hadley?" I heard Sark's voice call from the other side.

"He's okay," I called back. "Is everyone there with you?"

"Everyone but you."

I breathed a sigh of relief. "Okay, brace yourself. I'm sending you some packages."

One by one the kids climbed up on the precariously balanced cots with me, grabbed onto my arm, and scrambled to the opening as I pushed them with all my might. The first kid climbed up, paused for a second to wait for confirmation from Sark, then pushed off. Then the second. Then Sharna. Then Ranger.

Almost there.

Hadley hopped up next to me, ready to take his turn, when I heard the front door slide open and close again.

"And sadly," someone said, as though finishing a monologue, "no matter how grand the empire, it will always meet its complete and utter collapse."

I froze at the voice, recognizing it. Where had I heard it before?

Hadley's eyes widened in fear when he saw our visitors. I turned my head, and a silent scream escaped my open mouth.

Twelve people, two women and ten men, ranging in ages but all scraggly. Thin. Pale. Dirty. Wearing orange jumpsuits.

The young man who stood at the head of the group smiled at me, highlighting the bird tattoo on his jaw.

I've been waiting a very very long time to meet you, he'd told me one day, long ago, as he tried to drag me into his cell and rip me to pieces. *I've been waiting a very long time to kill you.*

The prisoners had escaped.

3

"Brothers and sisters," Bird Man said in a booming voice, spreading his arms out in presentation. "After our years of devotion, we will finally see the end of Cyrus' reign of tyranny, the end of another one of Castor's keys, and the end of the monster that is Arie Nolan." His dark eyes searched mine. "Though I wonder if you've come to your senses, accepting the fate that's best for all. Letting us out was a sign of faith. I'm sure you'll be rewarded for that wherever you end up."

They're crazy. Why do they always have to be crazy?

Initial confusion mixed with my terror until I understood. I took my finger off the screen and turned to face them, stepping to the left so I was partly shielding Hadley.

"You've got the wrong one," I said, my voice high but not shaking. "I didn't let you out. There are two of us."

Bird Man laughed once. "Cunning." He snapped his fingers and a woman behind him walked forward carrying a machine gun the guards carried. "We borrowed this. I don't think its owner minded."

"Arie?" someone called from the other side of the wall. I willed them to shut up.

Bird Man beckoned to me, the woman aiming the gun at us threateningly. "Come join us for the ceremony." Six of the other prisoners took out boxes from underneath their clothes, wires connected in ways I didn't understand, then they went around to different areas of the Dome to set their treasures up. My stomach dropped when I realized what they were. Bombs. Disarming the lady with the gun would get me nowhere but buried along with everyone else.

Without much of a choice, Hadley and I stepped off the cot and took slow steps to the center of the Dome. I tried to keep my mouth from moving too much as I whispered to him.

"When you get the chance, run."

"No," he whispered back. "I'm staying with you."

I didn't get the chance to chew him out. Bird Man and his guard closed the gap between us, two men following suit. Each of their necks held the same tattoo as their leader: the symbol that used to be on my wrists.

The two men each grabbed one of my arms and forced me to my knees.

"You've got the wrong Arie," Hadley told them, puffing out his chest. "Leave her alone."

"Hadley," I warned through my teeth before looking up to Bird Man. "Let him go. He's just a kid. He doesn't know anything."

Bird Man raised an eyebrow in surprise but kept up a mocking tone. "I didn't realize you cared so much about your pets."

A gun barrel pushed against the back of my head, forcing me to look at the floor.

"Brothers and sisters," Bird Man announced. "Today marks the end of an era, the end of an anarchy, the end of an evil that's plagued this fallen world. We've dedicated our lives to eradicating the evil that Castor unleashed. We've been faithful. We've been successful. And now we seal that success with a sacrifice."

"Hadley, run," I said, my hands starting to shake. "Run now."

The confidence was gone from his voice, replaced with fear. "No. I don't want to leave you."

"Hadley." My tone was harsh with desperation. "You get out right now. *Now*. Run."

I heard the sloshing of liquid around the Dome, purposeful splattering onto the floor, and the distinctive smell hit my nose right as a bucket of it was thrown over me. My hands shook harder as I started coughing in response to the fumes of the gasoline.

Pushing against the gun at my head, I glanced up at Bird Man. "You're going to burn me alive?" I asked in between coughs.

The bird on his jaw flew as he grinned. "Like the witches of old."

My blood went icy in my veins, my body going numb.

"No!" Hadley shouted in panic, kicking at one of the men that held me down. "No! Stop! Let her go!"

I jerked against those restraining me. "Hadley, run!" I screamed over and over, able to kick down one of the men holding me. "Get out now!"

Bird Man kneeled down in front of me, and I froze over, holding myself perfectly still, trying to keep from breathing as my eyes locked on the small flame from the lighter he was holding inches from my face.

"Fire is powerful," he told me, as enchanted with the flame as I was petrified. "It symbolizes destruction and rebirth, punishment and passion, warmth and blister. The phoenix and the apocalypse. It cleanses. It melts even the strongest metals and shapes them into something new."

"Please don't," I breathed, the small burst of air bending the flame away from me. "Please."

Bird Man ignored me, raising his voice so it echoed. "We come to bring an end to—"

Hadley tackled him to the ground, surprise on the kid's side, and he threw the lighter across the room. Following his brave lead, I ducked my head and forced my body backward, ramming into the gun lady. The weapon went off and shot one of my captors in the foot. He shouted and let me go, and I used the new free hand to punch my way through the other guy and the lady with the gun. Then Hadley and I made a break for the security wall.

We hopped up on the cot and I grabbed Hadley roughly by his shoulder. "Get up there!"

His eyes were wide with whispers of tears. "But what about you?"

"Now, Hadley!" I shouted. He obeyed, climbing up my body and standing on my shoulders before peeking his head through the opening.

I felt the rumble before the blast, the floor beneath me vibrating angrily until the first bomb— the farthest away from us—went off. Hadley slipped off my shoulders and I lost my footing, nearly falling to the floor.

"Arie!" he howled, his legs flailing in the air before I put a hand under each of his feet and heaved him up.

Bullets shot as us haphazardly from behind, and I jumped up into the hole with Hadley, straining my arms to keep half my body inside as there was only room for half of me. Now I saw what had made the kids hesitate: the ledge peered over complete and total darkness. Someone must've cut the power in the emergency tunnels. I couldn't see much of Hadley's face in the dim light, but what I could told me enough about his thoughts of jumping into the blackness.

"You have to go, Hadley," I said, harsher than I meant to, as the commotion behind me grew louder and more chaotic. My shoulders burned with the effort of keeping my form up, and the edge of the hole was digging into my stomach and taking most of my air. "Go now."

His hands clawed on my slippery arm, grip like a vise. "I can't. It's too dark. I can't fall."

"You won't fall. Sark?"

"I'm down here, Hadley," Sark called up from the black nothingness. "I'll catch you. It's okay."

I felt something explode by my dangling leg and wondered what was keeping the prisoners so busy. Then a deep rumble from the earth told me the walls wouldn't stay up for much longer.

"Arie," Hadley cried, his nails still digging into my arms as he tried to shuffle backward, away from the ledge. "Please don't make me. Please. I want to stay with you."

"I'm right behind you, Hadley, I promise." The desperation in my voice probably wasn't comforting. "Sark will catch you, I swear, and you'll be okay. You have to trust me."

"Hadley, it's okay," Sark called again. The echo from his voice put a pit in my own stomach. He sounded so far away.

"No!" He turned and barreled into me, nearly knocking me off the wall. "I can't! I can't be brave anymore. Please, Arie, please, I'm just too scared."

Tears sprang in my eyes at the betrayal in his when I started to push him to the edge. "Hadley, we have to. We have to. Be brave just for a minute more, okay? Please."

"No, Arie!" he shrieked, and suddenly he looked so small and little and so terribly afraid.

"Don't let me go! I don't want to anymore. Please!"

"It'll be okay," I chanted to him as tears fell down my face and I pried his hands off my arm. "Sark will catch you, he will, I swear, and it'll be okay. I promise." It took nearly everything I had left, but I pushed Hadley over the edge.

"Arie!" he screamed on the way down, and the blow was enough to make me lose my grip. I hit my head on the corner on my way, crashing down into the cots. Chaos ran rampant in the Dome, full of people and mutts and orange jumpsuits that all seemed to be fighting each other, and I couldn't tell who was who or who was on what side, or what sides even existed. Where had everyone come from?

I caught sight of Bird Man just as his glare found me, and I quickly scrambled back on top of the cots when I heard him shout my name.

Steeling myself, I jumped again for the hole, screaming through my teeth as I hoisted myself up and through our escape.

"Arie!" Sark was yelling emphatically from the darkness. "Arie are you there?"

"I'm here," I squeaked out, peering at how my legs dangled into nothing. Suddenly I felt a whole lot worse about forcing Hadley to jump.

You have to, I told myself. *Be brave, just for a minute longer.*

"I'll catch you," Sark told me.

I heard Bird Man's voice from right below me, and another rumble went through the foundation of the building. I didn't let myself think before pushing off the ledge and letting the blackness swallow me whole.

A yelp came through my teeth when I landed hard in Sark's arms, the middle of my spine nearly breaking against his broad forearm. My neck snapped back painfully; Sark swore under his breath and staggered. Before he could right us, I jumped out of his hold and pushed him toward the group of bodies I could sense in the dark.

"Run for the exits!" I yelled at them, hearing the scuffling of bodies as they obeyed, though in the dark it was impossible to tell which direction was the right one. We flung ourselves into the blackness and hoped luck would strike us.

I pushed myself forward, blind, using one hand to feel along the wall next to me as I ran for some sort of guide. I didn't know where I was going. I didn't even know if I was in the right tunnel, or a tunnel at all. I didn't know where anyone else had gone, though I heard and felt bodies in front of me. But not enough of them. Had we been separated?

Bird Man must've finally regained control of his weapons. Bombs shook the ground beneath me. The ceiling began to crack, bits of dust and debris falling on my head. My lungs burned from the exertion or the gas or both. We had to be close. The tunnels weren't very long, if I remembered right. Where was the exit? Did I choose the wrong tunnel? Shouldn't they all lead outside eventually?

Someone screamed in the distance, far from me, walls in between us. Then the last blast went off, the biggest one, the one that knocked me to the ground, pulled the ceiling down, and buried me.

~~~

I ached. That's the first thing I realized as I came to myself. My body hurt.

My eyes finally opened to spotted darkness. Darkness spotted with light. Light coming from the space above me, poking through the holes in the mass on top of me.

Taking enormous amounts of effort, I dug myself out of the pile of rubble and staggered to my feet. A gasp that stung my insides escaped my cracked lips as I saw the world around me.

Half of a frame stood above me, the ghost of the Dome that no longer existed, giving me enough reference to realize I'd almost made it out of the tunnel. As far as I could see, there were piles of rubble and desolate frames from what used to be buildings—the ones that were still standing were on fire. The sky was grey and cloudy with billowing smoke, blocking out the sun. People ran around in a panicked frenzy. Injured or dead bodies littered the ground every few feet. It was if the apocalypse had descended on the Compound.

What is she doing?

The rubble shifted next to me. I knelt down and started digging, finding a battered Sark underneath. Nearly choking on relief, I pulled him to his feet, checked over him for any major injuries, then threw my arms around his neck. He hugged me back tightly, both of us at a loss for words.

The rubble shifted again as Peter dug his way out, then helped Alaina. Sark and I went around
~~~

digging and helping when needed. One by one, we were unearthed. Daxton. Kayla. Lucy. Brennan. Ellen. I pulled my mom out, Sark grabbing my dad next to her. Besides a giant gash across Alaina's neck and Lucy's arms wrapped tight across her stomach as though she were feeling sick, there were no noticeable injuries except cuts and bruises and sore limbs that didn't work quite right.

A horrified gasp sounded behind me. I turned to see Sark several yards away straining underneath a giant slab of ceiling he held up with one shoulder, reaching under it with the other, the ground angled downward as though it opened up into the Earth. I walked toward him to see what was wrong, but he lowered the slab and stood, mouth open in shock, his broken eyes finding mine.

He stopped me when I reached for the slab. "Don't look under there," he told me, his voice airy and cracked, as though whatever he'd seen had stolen his ability to talk.

My voice cracked too. "Why?"

"Just don't." He shook his head and hugged me again, this time as a restraint. "Just don't."

Before I could break away and look anyway, someone else rose from the rubble, generating a few half screams, one of them probably mine. A massacred body with a bloody stump at its shoulder, crawled toward us, its face burnt to a crisp, but I could still make out the bird tattoo, loathing eyes locked on me.

Three shots sounded and Bird Man went down as quickly as he came up. I turned to see Micah standing with a gun, wild eyes glancing everywhere as if anticipating forty different attacks from hundreds of different angles.

"What's happening?" I asked. I tried to take a step toward him, but Sark flexed his arm around me, keeping me in place.

"The Compound is falling apart." He spoke too fast, his eyes stopping their search around the world to search mine. "What do we do?"

I realized that, at least for Micah, this *was* the apocalypse. The Compound was his whole world, all hc knew of life. He was really asking me.

What do we do?

"We're supposed to find Cyrus," I answered automatically, remembering our training for a time of crisis. Then I remembered that might not be my job anymore. "We're supposed to find Cyrus and Roland and protect them."

Or Vanessa is supposed to. I didn't know where I fit into the scheme of things anymore.

"Roland's dead." Micah nodded when I shook my head in disbelief. "In pieces. Evil Twin didn't like him either."

What? I glanced around the burning Compound again. *What is she doing?*

A bloodcurdling scream tore through the smoldering atmosphere. "Arie! Arie! Arie!"

Then I remembered: we were still missing people. My heart pounded as I followed the sound, stumbling over the uneven surface under me. "Jacklynn? Jacklynn, where are you?"

I found the crying girl, tears stained red because of a long cut on her cheek, kneeling in a pile of rubble, leaning over a crumpled body. Hadley.

"No," I gasped, collapsing to my knees next to Jacklynn. "No, no, no."

Kayla and Daxton sprang into action, getting on the ground and checking different parts of Hadley, their work concise and complimentary of the other's. The checkup took about ninety seconds.

"He's alive," Daxton told me, his voice grim. "But…"

"He's critical," Kayla finished for him. "I know the research labs were attacked—I'm not sure if any supplies made it through."

"The kid needs a hospital," Peter said from behind me. "A real one."

At that, everyone looked to me. I looked at Micah.

Micah sighed in resignation, as though giving away government secrets. "The nearest town is about thirty miles from here. You can make it, if you hurry."

Leave? My breathing sped up at the prospect, my insides knotting together. *Leave the Compound?*

"Where's Ranger?" Jacklynn asked, her words blubbering. "Where's Sharna and Lotti and everyone else?"

Then I remembered: we were still missing people. Kids.

I looked at Sark, understanding slowly passing over me, but he just closed his eyes, as though that would make everything go away. I glanced back at the maneuvered slab of ceiling, which I now realized resembled a tomb.

Don't look under there.

Ellen half screamed and Alaina gagged and Lucy burst into tears and my body went completely numb. Jacklynn just cried louder that no one would answer her, though she'd probably figured it out. I wrapped my arms around my shuddering form, closed my eyes, and tried to keep the panic attack away.

What do we do?

"You have to leave," Micah said, the words wounded. "You never belonged here anyway."

I can't. He of all people should've been able to understand that.

"You know the codes to get out," he went on, almost hesitantly. "The Compound is compromised—nobody will be able to come after you for a while, at least."

I shook my head.

"You have your family with you so they can't be used against you. Load everyone in a supply truck and get out of here."

"I can't," I whispered. "I can't."

"If you don't then your kid will die here." He took a deep breath. "And I know you don't want that."

No. I didn't want that.

"She couldn't have planned that better," Micah added in a lower voice. "The irony. The full circle. She'll come after you when she finds out you survived."

He was right again. And again. Vanessa was exploiting every weakness of mine she could remember. And she wouldn't stop until we were all rubble. Wouldn't stop even then.

You have to do this, I told myself. *You have to. Put your thousands of issues aside. This is Hadley.*

That struck a chord. This was Hadley. I would do just about anything for him. I had to redeem myself, be the hero he believed me to be. I had to save him.

This is Hadley.

"All right." I opened my eyes and jerked myself to my feet before I could change my mind. "Let's go."

Peter supported a pale Alaina, and Brenna put a protective arm around Lucy. Ellen and I each grabbed a side of Jacklynn and pulled her up, letting her lean on us, as Sark gently scooped up Hadley in his arms. I started leading the way, my parents following close behind, when I realized who wasn't following.

I turned around to see Micah, conflict pinching up his face. "You're going to find Cyrus?"

He didn't answer. He just looked at me with helpless eyes, the most vulnerable I'd ever seen him, mouth halfway open like there were words caught in his throat.

"Catch up when you're done," I told him. It hurt to leave him behind.

He nodded. "I will." Then he turned to go.

"Micah?" I called. He stopped and looked at me again. "You don't owe him a thing."

He nodded again and then started running for the administration building. I readjusted my hold on Jacklynn, who was still sobbing, and glanced at Ellen. Her blonde hair stuck to the blood smeared on her forehead as she gave me an encouraging nod. I felt a little lighter. Somehow, she was still my friend.

I led the way to the hangar, going to the left side of the building, as the right side—the one that housed the planes—had caved in. My hand shook violently, and it took me a few tries to get the scanner to read my fingerprint. Then the door slid open to reveal a garage full of ten white supply vans.

While everyone loaded each other into the first van, I went to the cabinet on the closest wall and unlocked it, grabbing the corresponding vehicle keys and one of the plastic white boxes before running over to the van.

"Here," I said, handing off the box to Daxton. He was sitting at the head of a loose circle, Kayla opposite of him, with Hadley stretched out in the center. It was a tight fit, but it would work. "It's a first aid kit. I don't know if it'll help, but…"

He nodded and took it from me, both he and Kayla in work mode. Another bomb could go off right underneath us and it wouldn't break their focus.

I shut the back door and tossed the keys to Sark as he slid into the front seat. Then I dashed past all the other vans to the control panel on the opposite wall, reaching my hand to scan my fingerprint and open the garage door.

Someone stepped in my path, and I skidded to a stop, just feet from the wall, and blinked in surprise.

"Koa?" I asked, taking a step away from his tense body. Blood smeared the left side of his face—it seemed to be coming from his mangled eye socket. "What are you doing?"

He took a few deep breaths through clenched teeth. "I can't let you leave. Nobody leaves."

"Come with us." I bounced on the balls of my feet in edgy anticipation. "We have to leave now but you can come. You can get out."

Koa spat at my feet and shook his head. "I knew you were a fake from day one." Then he tackled me to the ground.

I didn't realize how much my body had suffered from the collapsed building until I tried to use it. Landing a good elbow to his face, I wrapped my legs around him and twisted us around so I could get a punch in before springing up and slamming my finger on the scanner. The garage hummed to life as the door rose up.

Get them out, Sark.

Koa grabbed me from behind, holding a knife to my neck, and we struggled as I tried to shake him off without decapitating myself. He kicked my leg out from under me, forcing me halfway to the ground and slashing his knife across my collarbone. It grew brighter around us. I threw my head back and smashed it into his nose before pushing him off me. He staggered a few feet away, glared at me, and started at me again.

He didn't get the chance. The van ran right into him, sending him flying, as a skinny arm from the passenger seat reached out. I took the hand and it yanked me inside the vehicle as we drove out of the garage and onto the narrow road.

It was my dad. He and my mom sat in the front bench next to Sark, who was gripping the wheel and staring straight ahead while flooring the gas. My dad gave me half of a sad grin. I let go of his hand before scooting down and squishing in between my mom and Sark.

"You okay?" Sark asked quietly through his teeth.

"Yeah," I answered, catching my breath. "Thank you."

I glanced over my shoulder to survey our sad group scrunched in a van. Jacklynn sobbed in the arms of Ellen, who was crying silently as she stared at the wall. Alaina had her eyes closed, wincing, as Peter went over her bleeding wound with gauze, slowly turning the white cloth red. Lucy and Brennan were an intertwined statue, Lucy in his lap, with both of their arms wrapped around her frail body, staring into space with wide eyes like they were seeing a ghost. Kayla and Daxton were leaning over Hadley, blocking my view of him, as they mumbled things to him and each other. It didn't look like they were getting much of a response.

Panic rose up in me again and I tried to force it back down, turning my head to stare out the front window. Hadley wasn't out of the game yet. We'd make it.

Out of the corner of my eye, I saw my mom grab my dad's hand, intertwining her fingers with his and clinging to him. Both of them were pale. Too pale. His hand tightened on hers when he raised his other elbow to his face and coughed into it. My mom's shoulders tensed until a few seconds after he stopped coughing. Then she surprised me by grabbing onto my hand and holding it tight. I didn't look at her, but I didn't pull away either.

I watched the clock, five minutes turning to ten turning to twenty. We sped along the empty road forever in silence besides the faint mumbles of Kayla and Daxton or occasional cough from my dad or heavy breath from Jacklynn. Time ticked by slowly and painfully, yet all too quickly. The sun began to set, abandoning us, leaving us to our doomed fate. I was beginning to get worried we'd never find civilization when we pulled into a town.

Sark barely let up on the gas pedal despite the traffic, weaving in and out of cars and receiving several complaining honks—it was a miracle we didn't get pulled over. Not having any clue where to go, he followed the blue signs that pointed to a big 'H' and hoped for the best.

We finally found the hospital. Sark screeched into the parking lot and Peter had the van door open before we stopped, everyone jumping out of the vehicle. Ellen, Jacklynn and my parents ran ahead to warn the doctors we were coming, Brennan and Lucy following behind them. Alaina was unsteady on her feet, so Peter scooped her up and carried her. I stayed with Sark as he practically shoved Kayla and Daxton out of the way, picked up Hadley, and made a run for the emergency room entrance.

The nurses had a bed waiting. Sark had barely set Hadley's form on it when they whisked him away, through glass doors and into a room, out of sight. I was left in the otherwise empty waiting room with ugly maroon chairs to await the verdict on my self-adopted little brother's life.

The waiting room was hell. I couldn't sit on the stupid maroon chairs, so I paced back and forth in front of Sark's. Three steps one way, about face, three steps the other. Three steps. Three words.

Hadley will live. About face. *Hadley will live.*

I didn't know how long we waited. Maybe thirty seconds. Maybe thirty years. I'd lost all concept of time when the nurse in happy yellow scrubs came through the glass doors and walked toward us.

Those sitting stood up at her arrival and I stopped pacing. My heart seemed to halt beating for a moment when I saw her face did not match her happy scrubs.

"I'm so sorry," she said, her soft voice like a blanket. "I'm afraid he didn't make it through."

What? My body stiffened and every thought train in my head derailed. It was blank.

"What do you mean?" Alaina demanded, her anger rising with each breath.

The nurse gave a sad sigh. "He's gone. I'm sorry, we tried everything."

"Did you?" Alaina shouted, stepping forward as Peter grabbed her arm. "How could you have tried everything if he's gone?"

"Too many vital organs were crushed." The nurse wasn't put off at all by the emotion, her voice still gentle. "I don't know how he lasted as long as he did."

Peter pulled on her arm. "Alaina—"

She tried to yank away. "But you're a doctor! Do something! Help him!"

Peter pulled her harder and she obeyed, collapsing into him and bursting into tears before he carried her backward and out of my line of sight.

I didn't understand. Hadley couldn't be gone. He had just been in my arms, safe and sound, seconds ago. He was going to make it. He was fine.

The nurse turned her chocolate eyes to my frozen form. I looked past her, through the glass doors, and saw someone wheel out a bed with a sheet over a lanky form. A choked gasp escaped me as they took him away.

"Is there someone we should call for you?" the nurse asked me, her words encasing a blanket around me. A shock blanket. I was in shock. "Who takes care of him?"

I couldn't tear my eyes away from where the bed had been. "Um, me." It took a moment to realize I was speaking. "I told…I told his parents I'd watch out for him. I said I'd keep him safe."

She placed a comforting hand on my shoulder. "I'm so sorry for your loss." Then she backed away to the glass doors. "I'll give you guys a minute."

She's sorry for my loss. I lost him.

I watched the nurse leave before slowly turning around. Sark was behind me, his ocean eyes welled up, but his jaw clenched, fighting the emotion, the reality, of what just happened.

"He's gone," I whispered to him in case he didn't already know.

Sark nodded once. "I'm so sorry."

I stepped forward and fell into his chest, afraid I couldn't keep myself up anymore, and threw my arms around him. He wrapped both his arms tightly around my waist and rested his head on my shoulder, burying his face in my neck. Our bodies shook together, and I felt his tears on my skin. Water stung my eyes, but nothing would come out, as though floodgates had been placed over them.

Eventually the same nurse came back and Sark untangled himself from me. I didn't understand her purpose until I realized what I looked like: gravel and debris stuck into my skin, colored red from a paste mixed of blood, dirt, and sawdust; a bloody gash on my face; cut on my shoulder; and several burn marks on my hands. I hadn't noticed anything until she pointed it out.

"I'll help you take care of that," she told me, reaching out to touch me.

I recoiled and stepped away from her, wrapping my arms around myself as I stared guardedly at her. If it weren't for Sark's restraining hand on me, I would've made a run for it, out of the building and far away.

"Give us a minute," Sark muttered and the nurse went on to the next person. Then he turned to me. "You have to let her help you."

"No." I started to pull myself away from him.

Sark just stepped closer, not about to let me get away. "She won't hurt you. She's here to help you."

My breathing became panicked at the thought he was going to make me see a doctor. "I don't want her to help me. Don't let her. Please, Sark, I'll do anything. Anything but that. Please don't let her come close to me. Please."

"Okay, okay." He let my arm go and hugged me again, pulling me against him, and I closed my eyes. "I won't let her touch you."

"Promise?"

"I promise. She won't touch you."

"Okay." I needed to believe him. "Okay. Thank you."

"Can you calm down now?"

I tried to nod but it didn't work. I was still suffocating. "I need to go walk. I need a moment."

Sark hesitated, debating for a second, and I could imagine the billion things he wanted to tell me, like stay in the hospital or don't go far or come right back. So I added, "I'll be careful. I just need to breathe."

Feeling him nod, he answered, "Okay."

I turned and took stiff, jerky steps away from him, through the double doors that led to the main part of the hospital. I didn't know where I was going. I just needed to leave the waiting room.

The place was busy. The smell of disinfectant filled the air as doctors and nurses bustled about, a sort of stressed calmness on their faces as they focused on their work, moving from room to room. Patient to patient. Problem to problem.

I wandered down the hallways looking for nothing but seeing way too much. A wrinkly man being wheeled urgently down the hallway. A father kneeling at his unconscious daughter's bedside. A little boy in superhero pajamas screaming for his mom to make it stop hurting.

So much suffering. So much pain. Everywhere. The darkness, the loss, the agony, loomed over everything, threatening to suck the entire hospital in a black hole and never spit it back out.

Nothing warranted stopping my pathetic parade until I passed by a janitor standing in the door of a supply closet, talking to nobody with a reasoning tone. I stopped when I recognized the muffled voice that responded from inside.

"Excuse me," I muttered, holding myself tighter.

The janitor turned to look at me with raised eyebrows. "Uh, can I help you?"

I looked past him to see Jacklynn scrunched into the corner of the closet, curled into a ball on the floor and crying into her sleeves.

"You know her?" he asked me.

I just nodded.

His eyes filled with understanding. "I'll give you some privacy."

"Thank you."

The janitor left and I shut myself in the small closet, sitting in between Jacklynn and a mop. I didn't even have to say anything before words spilled out of her.

"He came back for me," she blurted in between sobs. "He came back for me and now he's gone."

My eyebrows furrowed. "What are you talking about?"

"In the Dome. Sark told us to take the kids and run. We were running in the dark tunnels and something fell. I got stuck and screamed and Hadley came back for me." The sobbing got louder. "He came back to help me and then he got crushed and now he's dead and it's all my fault!"

Her cried words were like stabs to my chest. "Oh, no, sweetie." I wrapped my arms around her and she crawled into my lap, soaking my shirt in two seconds. "It wasn't your fault."

"But it was!" She was edging toward hysterics. "And nothing even matters because he's dead! And the doctors couldn't even help him! He's dead!"

I strengthened my hold on her while she thrashed wildly, as though she literally could not stand the pain inside her and needed to flail it out.

"Shh, Jacklynn." I patted the back of her head. "Calm down. It's okay."

"No it's not! It's not okay! He was my best friend! He was my best friend and now he's gone and I'll have to find a new one and that will be impossible!"

I didn't even know what to say, tears stinging my eyes again without falling out as I took a shaky breath.

Jacklynn's sobbing paused for a moment, her body still trembling, before she asked timidly, "Arie? Will you be my new best friend?"

"Of course I will. I'd be honored." I tried to facilitate calming down by distraction. "What do I do for that position?"

"Well…" She straightened up and cleared her throat, her tears momentarily stopping as she considered the serious matter. "There are lots of clubs. And meetings. And you have to come to all of them and be a full participant."

"That sounds like fun. What kinds of clubs are there?"

She counted on her fingers. "Paper airplane club, pet rock club, best jokes club, peanut butter and jelly club…" But all too soon, the tears came again. "Hadley was president of all the clubs. I was vice president. But now I'll have to be president 'cause you…you don't know how." She burst into sobs again on the last word, burying her face in my shoulder.

I just hugged her, no good words, no worthy condolences, coming to my head to say. I just hugged her and let her cry and felt all my insides ache.

She's too young for this. It's not fair.

But then I thought of my poor fifteen-year-old self, infected and lost, thrown mercilessly into a broken world.

Is there an appropriate age for your life to fall apart?

I leaned against the wall of the supply closet with a crying girl in my lap, wondering how the human heart had the capacity to feel so much yet nothing at all.

4

I didn't realize I'd dozed off until I felt a tapping on my arm. My eyes cracked open and I found myself still in the supply closet, Jacklynn asleep in my lap, the door open and Sark leaning down in front of me. The janitor from earlier stood behind him, giving me a nod before leaving us alone.

I straightened up, then grimaced when my back screamed at me. The movement jostled Jacklynn, who stirred, leftover tears coming out of her eyes again before she was even all the way awake.

"Hadley," she mumbled, her eyelids fluttering. "Arie. Arie, where are we?"

"It's okay," I whispered as I rubbed her arm. "You're okay. Can you stand up for me?"

She nodded sleepily and staggered to her feet, Sark and I both keeping a hold on her as she swayed. Sark held out his arm and I took it, painfully pulling myself up, then we all stumbled out of the closet together.

"Can you walk?" Sark asked me quietly, his eyes looking over me with concern. He slid out of his jacket—where had he gotten that from?—and helped me into it, hiding at least some of my injuries.

I ignored my protesting legs and nodded. "Yeah."

He leaned down and picked up Jacklynn. Her eyelids fluttered again, but she didn't open them all the way as she wrapped her arms around his neck and rested against his shoulder. I held onto his arm and let him lead me wherever he had in mind.

I kept my head down, watching my feet instead of those we passed by. Sark took us through the hospital and out the front doors. The last of the sun had died under the horizon, the streetlights switching on in a futile attempt to protect us from the night. As if knowing what the day had brought, the night sent a chilly wind through the sky, blowing frosty air right at me. I huddled closer to Sark and concentrated on matching his brisk pace.

We ended up at a motel a few blocks down from the hospital. Sark balanced Jacklynn in one arm as he used to the other to dig a key out of his pocket and unlock the door to a room. I held the door open for him as he took Jacklynn inside.

The sense of loss hit me like a brick in the face. Impossible sadness hung as thick and suffocating drapes around the room, blocking out any light the awful day might have scraped up from somewhere. There were two small beds—Peter was next to Alaina on one, playing with her hair as she slept, a thick bandage wrapped around her neck; Brennan and Lucy were curled together on the other, engaged in a strained and whispered conversation. Ellen was asleep on a pillow on the floor in the corner and Daxton had crashed a few feet away from her. Kayla sat at the small wooden desk against the far wall, her chin in her hands as she stared out the square window, lost in a different world. She didn't even glance at us when we came in.

Sark bent down and whispered something to Lucy. She nodded and turned herself around, somehow making room on the tiny bed for Sark to set Jacklynn down. Lucy pulled the blankets over the sleeping girl and Jacklynn snuggled into her without waking up. Sark surveyed the room once before ducking out and pulling me with him, shutting the door behind us. Then he went to the next room over, unlocked it with a different key, held open the door and gestured for me to enter.

It was empty. Sark shut the door and had me sit down on one of the beds.

"Your parents should be back anytime," he told me. He didn't offer where they went and I didn't ask. Getting the chair from the wooden desk, he sat in front of me and leaned forward, pulling his jacket off me, then gently touched his fingers to the embedded rubble on my neck.

I flinched and leaned away. "Just leave it."

"There's rock in your skin. If you won't let the nurse take care of it then you have to let me." He reached for me again and I leaned away.

"I don't want it—"

"Arie," he cut in harshly, not with impatience but near desperation, as he met my eyes. "Please. Let me help."

I understood then that he wanted something to do. Something to fix. Something to keep himself distracted rather than think about today. I nodded and he let out a breath before beginning to dig the rubble out of my skin.

It hurt. I clenched my teeth and tried to make no sound as each piece was removed one at a time. At one point Sark had to use the motel key—not the most sanitary thing, but we didn't have anything else—to chip the rock away, leaving torn and sensitive skin in its wake.

"Okay," Sark said, dropping his hands. "We have to figure something else out. This is killing you."

I realized I'd been holding my breath and let it out in a gush. "No, it's fine. Keep going. I can take it."

His eyes narrowed in disapproval. "You don't have to *take* anything. You don't deserve—"

"If you don't do it then I will."

The image of me going at myself with a rusty old key was enough motivation. He sighed and kept working.

"Is that what she would tell you?" he asked me quietly after a moment.

That caught me off guard; I blinked in surprise. "What?"

He glanced at me, eyes uncertain. "You could hear her, couldn't you? Vanessa. In your head. And she'd tell you things like you deserve this pain right now."

I opened my mouth but didn't have a good enough response, caught up in the implications of what he'd said. Vanessa *would* be telling me that if she were still with me and, instead, I was telling myself unconsciously.

Her smug words repeated in my head: *Oh please, princess. I'm sure it's like I never left.*

"How long?" Sark asked when I didn't answer, trying to keep a smooth tone but it slipped.

I cleared my throat even though I didn't need to. "Awhile."

"How long?"

"Um…" I took a deep breath, dragging us both down memory lane. "Remember that night in Denver when we went for a drive and I had such a bad nightmare that you had to pull over?"

Of course he did. I could see the memory replay in his eyes, understanding passing over his face, as he made the connection.

It's not me, I had cried in desperation on the side of the road. *It's not me.*

I know it's not you, Sark had told me, not having any clue of the scope of the situation.

And now, here I was, months and lifetimes later, the full embodiment of everything I swore I'd never become.

"You wouldn't have believed me," I murmured. I knew what he was thinking. "You would've thought I was insane."

Sark kept working on the debris. I'd almost counted to sixty when he spoke again.

"Why didn't you tell me you were still here?" There was a new strain to his low voice and he wouldn't meet my eyes.

My breath caught, but not because of the pain. Tears stung my eyes as the answers flipped through my head.

Guilt. Shame. Embarrassment. Fear. I could not stand the sight of myself and figured you couldn't either.

I hung my head, unable to look at him, as I uttered, "I'm so sorry. I tried to keep her…but…I couldn't do it." The words came spilling out faster than I could realize what I was saying. "You did so much for me and had so much faith in me and I lost. I tried, I swear, I tried. I tried as hard as I possibly could and it wasn't enough and I keep asking myself what I could've done. I don't know. I should've been stronger, but I didn't know how. And then I didn't come back because—"

A knock on the door interrupted my stream of confessions, and I was grateful and annoyed at the same time. We both glanced at it, then Sark squeezed my hand.

"We aren't done with this conversation, okay?"

I just nodded. It was probably a good thing our visitor had shut me up.

Sark got up and opened the door. My parents came in, each carrying a few grocery store bags that they set on the ground by the door.

"You made it," my mom said, pulling off an old purple jacket that was new to her. They must've hit a thrift shop or something.

Sark took her coat and laid it behind me on the bed. "Yeah, everyone's here."

"Good work, son," my dad said as my mom gave Sark a hug and said thanks.

The whole interaction left me completely flabbergasted. They were behaving like they were all old friends.

When did that happen?

It made me feel a tiny bit jealous, though I didn't know of who: my parents for suddenly being so close to Sark, or Sark for being claimed by them.

Suddenly I wanted to know everything about what they knew. Did they know who Sark was? What had they been doing since I left? And what did they think of Alexis and Cyrus and me sprouting a twin out of nowhere?

I planned to ask, but once their eyes turned to me, I couldn't find any words to speak.

My mom's eyes narrowed, and she came closer to look at me. "Why didn't you get the doctor to help you?" she demanded, her motherly tone coming out. I felt like I was twelve again and had raided the candy box before dinner.

For some reason, the question overwhelmed me. Because if I were to really explain the answer, I'd have to go through everything, detailing how big of a screw up her daughter had turned out to be. For the first time since I left home, instead of pretending like I didn't care, I really felt like I had disappointed my mom. And I couldn't live with that.

My expression must've been something because after a few moments of me just staring at her with my mouth open, her stance relaxed and she dropped her head, as if remembering I wasn't twelve anymore and this was our second conversation in three years.

She backed away from me, turning to the grocery bags. "Sark, will you help me pass this out?"

Sark didn't miss a beat. "Sure." He grabbed all of the bags in both his hands and still managed to open the door for my mom. They left, leaving me alone with my dad.

He stared at the closed door for a moment, churning brown eyes wide with hidden panic, before he glanced at me. We both looked at the ground.

I didn't know what to say or how long I would be in here alone with him. Most likely, my mom had maneuvered this whole thing, knowing neither of us would take the step ourselves.

The silence broke when he coughed, hard, and I winced because it sounded like he'd ripped his throat open.

"Never taken a sick day in my life," he muttered.

That was true. My dad never got sick. Actually, his body malfunctioned often enough but he was always too busy with life to take care of himself.

He sighed. "Do you want me to just leave? I'll tell your mother we had a deep conversation, and you can tell her your life was changed forever."

I actually laughed once, lifting my eyes to look at him again.

"Yeah." He took a meandering step toward me, watching his shoe brush against the carpet. "I'm not the best at conversations. You know that."

I did know that. I knew a lot of things about him, this man who reminded me more of the dad who annoyed me but I put up with because I loved him, and less of the evil deranged man who I blamed for every problem in my life.

"Can I just ask you one question?" he asked. "Just one. I probably don't deserve it, but I've been imagining an answer for a long time now."

I shrugged. "If I can ask you one."

"A hundred percent honesty?"

I nodded and waited for him to go first. He shoved his hands in his pockets, his expression hesitant but troubled. "How's my baby girl doing?"

Something got caught in my throat. He hadn't called me that in a long time. Part of me was infuriated by that—how dare he barge in here and assume I would still answer as his daughter. But most of me was drooping in soft compliance and waiting for peace, trying hard to let go. I was so sick of hating people. There was too much darkness in my life.

I found myself answering honestly, my voice quiet. "She's tired. She's so tired and wants this all to be over."

My dad dropped his eyes and nodded, his shoulders hunching, an invisible weight pulling down on him.

I shifted so I was sitting cross-legged on the bed, ready to take my turn. "Cyrus told me you knew I would be the key and you knew about breaching. And that's why you infected me." I took a breath, bracing myself, still unsure how much trust I was placing in this conversation. "Is that true?"

"Well…now that's a loaded question." He hesitated before gesturing to the chair in front of me. I nodded and he sat down, coughing again, then rubbed his forehead with one hand. "Yes, I knew you'd be the key. Yes, I infected you with the hope of protecting you, but…I wish I could say that was the only reason."

"I thought you were crazy." I said the statement as my own kind of experiment.

"You should have. I don't blame you." He raised his head to meet my eyes with his tortured ones. "I wanted to be the superhero dad and save my baby girl. Instead, I got sucked in. I did. I messed up. And…I know this is the last thing you want to hear from me, but Arie, I have regretted it every second of every day since you left."

Even in the best dreams I'd ever had, never had I ever imagined my dad saying those words to me. Ever. I stared blankly at him as I took this new information in, stunned that it actually went out into the universe. My dad had developed a lot of talents in his years but admitting he was wrong wasn't one of them.

"It wasn't even my idea, originally," he went on, looking at a spot on the wall right next to me rather than at me. "I didn't know anything about Castor or his formula. Not a snitch. But one day someone approached me and asked if I knew anything about it. I said no. The guy said that I should because my daughter had a part to play.”

“Who approached you?” I asked, leaning forward slightly. “Did you know them?”

He shook his head. “No. I wish I did. It was over the phone. Don’t know who it was and told them to buzz off. Never heard from them again.”

That would make sense. My dad, being the curious man he was, would’ve then researched Castor on his own. And thus, the game began.

“At first I really believed I was saving you,” he said. “Really. Then I thought I was saving mankind. There was no distinction, no realization of what I was actually doing until you ran away.” He shook his head mournfully. “It destroyed what was left of your mother and I was certain Alexis had found you and killed you. Nothing wakes you up like a good spoonful of regret. By then, though, it was too late. And it always will be.” He scowled at the wall. “Mankind’s not worth saving anyway.”

A coughing fit overtook him out of nowhere. He covered his mouth with his hand and hunched over, the few muscles in his back tensing.

“Are you okay?” Concern colored my tone as I raised my arms as if to do something and then dropped them when I didn’t know what.

My dad nodded mid-cough, cleared his throat and straightened up. “It’s getting pretty annoying but that’s it.” He put his hand on his lap, but I still saw the slight stain of red.

“Dad, you just coughed up blood.” My forehead creased with worry. “What’s wrong?”

"Nah, it's just a nasty virus. Well, it's cancer, actually. Esophageal kind." He gave a small grin. "That's what I get for shouting so much, huh? Karma came back to bite."

My mouth fell open. "Whoa, what? Cancer?"

He held his clean hand up. "Now, don't freak out on me. It's not nearly that bad, as far as cancers go. I'll be just fine."

"Since when?" All this time I'd imagined him building himself a Frankenstein in an evil lab while I starved on the street. "What about treatment?"

"We aren't sure when it set in, actually. I tend to not notice when my body is signaling something's wrong. I'd guess probably two years. And I've seen all the doctors I need to so don't lecture me on medication. I'm doing what's recommended."

I raised an eyebrow. "That's your code for 'I'm doing whatever I want.'"

His grin grew and he nodded. "You got it."

The door opened again, my mom and Sark coming in, now with only one grocery bag. My mom suppressed a smile when she saw my dad sitting in the chair by me, and I had to keep myself from rolling my eyes. Subtlety had never been her strong point.

It wasn't my dad's either. "Well, see Candace, I guess your scheme worked out after all."

She shot him a disapproving look. It took me back in time again, to when I was thirteen and wanted to go skydiving and my dad said he'd take me.

I shook my head, trying to clear it, or at least somewhat organize it. Instead, I was left with a headache.

Slowly to avoid hurting my sore body, I stood up from the bed and attempted to look nonchalant. "Well, I still smell like gas so I'm going to take a shower." I started to head for the bathroom, but Sark stopped me, his expression concentrative, as though he'd just realized something.

"Why *do* you smell like gas?" he asked me.

Again, I opened my mouth, but no words came out, the raging memory stealing my voice.

The liquid dumped over me. *You're going to burn me alive?*

The flame dancing in front of me. *Like the witches of old.*

I shuddered and wrapped my arms around myself. Sark's eyes widened with alarmed understanding right as I heard my mom gasp from behind me. My eyes stung with tears again, distorting my vision slightly, but it didn't matter because I could only see Hadley's smashed body.

Motions stiff, I turned, stepped around Sark and shut myself in the bathroom. Turning on the shower as hot as possible, I stripped off my disgusting clothes and grabbed the small soaps on the counter before stepping under the stream of roasting water.

I scrubbed myself clean. The water hurt my skin, but I guess I didn't care because I never turned it down. After washing my hair twice, I just sat in the yellowish tub and let the water rinse over me.

The bathroom door opened, making me jump, and a shadow went across the shower curtain.

It was my mom. "Arie, I'm leaving some clean clothes in here for you, okay?"

I felt like I was ten again, going through a stage where I wore the same outfit every day until my mom intervened.

A few seconds passed before I could answer. "Okay. Thanks." Then the shadow disappeared and the door shut again.

I stayed in the shower until the water got icy cold. Shaking slightly, I got out, dried myself off with a stiff white towel, and got dressed with the clothes folded neatly on the counter: a pair of dark jeans, mismatched socks, white tennis shoes, a bright purple sports bra, a slightly discolored white tank top, and a navy sweatshirt with a hole in the hood. The fabrics were worn and smelled musty, but I was happy to have them.

My eyes accidentally caught a glimpse of what I had been avoiding. Once I looked in the mirror, though, I couldn't look away. It wasn't the pinkish wound on my jawline or the skin on my neck rubbed raw that warranted my stare—it was the whole package. It was me. It was her. That was the real problem. I looked into the mirror and didn't see myself but my worst enemy. She even stole my reflection.

Suddenly the bathroom felt way too small, like the walls were coming in closer and closer, threatening to crush me. I threw open the door and stepped into the room. The lights were off. Sark was gone but my parents were asleep in a bed, holding hands, the slight snore of my dad wafting through the still air.

The room didn't feel much bigger than the bathroom. Afraid of a nervous breakdown, I did what I did best: I pulled my hood over my head and left.

It was freezing outside and my wet hair did not help the situation. Still, I walked on, out of the motel and down the sidewalk, getting further and further into a sleeping town. There were only a handful of people out —mostly wanderers, it seemed, like me. None of them appeared to be threatening to me, or really even seemed to notice me, but I kept my senses sharp just in case. A couple passed by me across the street. They only caught my attention because his leather jacket and her gray trench coat were much newer and nicer than anyone else's clothes I'd passed. I gave a slight glance to them as they went by me. My body jolted when I thought I saw a flash of bright blue.

Heart pounding, I jerked my head around to watch them go, waiting for a mutt. A stone settled in my gut when nothing happened. The couple continued to hold hands and make their way down the empty sidewalk.

You're going crazy, you're going crazy, you're going crazy.

I took a deep breath and kept going, pushing myself faster. I didn't stop until I came upon a small twenty-four-hour convenience store, not realizing I made the decision until I found myself inside.

The blasting heater was worth it. I basked in the hot air for a moment before walking deeper inside.

There was one cashier working and two other customers. I kept a mental tab on each of them as I made my way to the beauty supply aisle, pleased that I was the only one in it. There wasn't much to pick from but that was fine. I didn't need anything fancy anyway, just something that would get the job done well enough.

The decision was easy: I didn't want to be blonde, red was Alaina's thing, and any shade of brown wouldn't change much. Black. That was my best option. I picked up a box of black hair color and inspected it.

So what do we do now?

It was a stupid question to ask myself because I already knew the answer. I felt slightly sick as I slid the box in the sleeve of my hoodie, safely hiding it, and made my way to the exit.

I considered writing a twelve-page letter to the cashier about why this box was essential to my partial sanity and ask to please make an exception but decided against it. Still, though, it was ridiculous I had just escaped hell with an evil twin and deadened soul and still felt so incredibly guilty about stealing twelve dollars' worth of cheap hair color.

The cashier was busy helping a customer when I left, and I had to keep myself from walking up to the checkout and turning myself in.

We can now add 'thief' to my list of colorful descriptions.

When I got back to the motel room, I found it unlocked, the lights still off but my parents gone. The place was empty. Just how I liked it.

Part of me wondered where they went but I decided not to care. They were adults. If I wanted to take a half hour trip to the store and turn to a life of crime whenever I wanted, then they could come and go when they wanted too.

I went back into the bathroom and took off my hoodie, not wanting to get color on it. The white tank top did nothing to hide the scars lining my arms. I decided that was the right way to do this. I hated the scars, but I wanted to see them. The imperfections set me apart, making me who I was, separating me from Vanessa. I hated them but I needed them.

The next chunk of time I spent working on my hair. I followed the directions on the box as best as I could, only making a minimal mess. The cream sink turned grey when I washed out my hair and I had to scrub for a second to clean it all off. It was slow work, but it kept me busy and somewhat fascinated as I tried to paint myself differently.

Once I was done, I looked at my reflection again, my hair successfully darker than it had been. The change was subtle, but it was enough for me to differentiate and that's all that really mattered to me.

I was attempting to wash the spots of color from my fingers when I heard the front door open. Turning off the sink, I stepped out of the bathroom, trying to decide how I was going to explain my homemade makeover to my mom. Instead of her, though, I saw Sark.

His shoulders were heavy, his eyes tired and lifeless, so pale and still that he could've been a part of the cracked wall behind him, as he looked over me in silence. I felt like an idiot at the thought of explaining my actions to him, actions that probably seemed stupid and trivial when I should've been planning what our next step was.

He didn't ask. He closed the distance between us with slow steps and dropped his eyes to my wrist. My heart sank and my veins burned in humiliation when I realized what he was staring at. Slowly, he raised his hand to my shoulder, barely touching me with the tip of his finger, and traced down one line of the raised scar on my arm, all the way to the deformed circular shape on my wrist.

I braced myself, wishing I could shrink or melt or disappear, waiting for the apprehension or revulsion or pity my repulsive deformities would bring. Apologies bubbled on my lips, my shame keeping me quiet.

What does he think of me now? Something terrible, I was sure.

But Sark completely shocked me. Pulling on my arm, he cupped his other hand behind my neck, brought me closer to him and kissed me.

Stunned he would even want to look at me when I was so grossly exposed, I hesitated at the contact, waiting for him to change his mind. He didn't. His touch was gentle but still firm, holding me to him as I felt him unravel, dropping all pretenses. He was hurting. He was hurting so badly and he still trusted me enough to come for help.

I caved. It was easy to fall into it, even after I avoided it for so long, and I found myself gripping him as tight as he was me, both of us desperately trying to fill the crushing void in our souls with something besides more darkness.

Sark kissed my scarred fingers, palm, wrist, shoulder, and back to my mouth, leaving a trail of fire on my skin in his wake. Not the scalding fire I was used to always burning me, but the warm kind that seemed to somehow thaw out the vast coldness inside of me.

He made me feel loved. Human. Not quite so alone, even in both of our impossibly oppressing grief.

How could I have left something like this behind?

"I'm sorry," I breathed, drowning in my own complex emotions I didn't understand, my eyes watering in response. "I left. I left and I'm so sorry." I didn't have a good explanation, at least not one that made sense. Taking his face in my hands now, I kissed him everywhere, mumbling apologies in between as if sealing them. "I'm sorry."

He stayed quiet, letting me apologize as I kissed his face over and over, until my breath went ragged and I ran out of steam. Then I slumped against him, afraid my knees were going to buckle under the weight of my own body.

"I missed you," I told him. "I missed you so much and I should never take you for granted. I won't. I won't ever again." My voice faltered. "I'm so—"

Sark put his finger over my lips, smashing my words together. "It's okay."

My insides swelled at the amount of acceptance and forgiveness in his tone, but the choice of words shattered me—I had hurt him. I had hurt him really bad.

"You're here now," he said as he gathered me up in a hug. A slight sigh escaped him when I leaned my head against his shoulder, and I felt his mouth in my damp hair. "You're here."

I'm here.

Blinding pain flashed under my neck when Sark accidently touched the sore spot on my back. I flinched and a mangled whimper went through my teeth. My hammer wound from Vanessa must've bruised into something awful.

His hands fell to my hips and he turned me around. I tried to stop him halfway, but he was having none of that.

"Let me look at it," he asked me. "Please."

I consented, only because I knew he wouldn't let it go. I braced myself as I felt him move my hair around my shoulder and pull down the top fabric of my tank top, waiting for the flash of pain again, hoping I'd be able to rein it in. A short, disapproving breath came from Sark.

"It looks bad," he admitted.

I tried to shrug. "Can't be *that* bad."

His fingers felt around the edges—it was tender, but he was soft enough that it was manageable.

"It's swollen," he said. "I can't tell if it's filled with blood or not. It's all flesh though—we're lucky she didn't hit your spine."

The touching paused for a second, then the pain shot across me again. I half moaned and clenched my fists, swaying on my feet.

"It's fine," I managed to get out.

Sark wasn't buying it. "Come on, Arie. It's me."

I had to take a few deep breaths to stabilize myself. "It hurts. But it'll get better. I'll just have to be careful."

The fabric was carefully put back in place, then his hands were on my shoulders, lightly massaging me. His quiet voice had a hint of its old teasing tone, trying desperately to come back to life, when he talked in my ear.

"Your back is a wasteland of nasty knots." I could almost hear his smile nearly forming. "You don't have anything to be stressed about, do you?"

The corners of my mouth twitched. "Nothing comes to mind."

I leaned my head against his shoulder, wincing at the sting of my back. That got me thinking about Vanessa, hopelessness threatening to pull me under again, but then another thought occurred to me.

"How did you know...?" I replayed the conversation Sark and I had earlier, in this room. He knew I could hear Vanessa. That didn't make sense. Nobody knew. They may have been able to guess, but he had seemed too certain about it. Who could have told him? Cyrus wasn't even aware, unless Vanessa had filled him in after I was out of the picture...

Sark leaned his head closer to me. "What?"

My mind started racing with horrible possibilities, the pieces coming together in my mind. I'd been gone for weeks after the transfer. How stupid was I to assume Vanessa and Sark had no contact during that time? Why hadn't that occurred to me?

What did she tell you?

"Can I ask you something?" I asked, my voice still quiet, part because of embarrassment and part in fear I'd wake up the next disaster that would strike us.

He rested his head against mine. "Anything."

What else did she say that would turn you against me? What could she...

And suddenly I knew. I knew exactly what had happened.

Sark felt the change in my posture. He stopped working on my shoulders and turned me back around to look at my face. "What's wrong?"

My heart sped up at the thought, my breaths becoming shallow. "Will you be honest?"

"Of course." His forehead creased. "What's going on?"

"Did she kiss you?"

The question froze him, showcasing his guilt so he couldn't lie to me even if he wanted to. He seemed to shrink back under my searching gaze for a moment before he sighed. "Yeah."

Instantly my insides burst into heated flames of pain and jealousy and hatred. My gaze turned to a glare, the question slipping from my mouth before I could stop it. "How was that?"

Now he was scrambling. I watched his eyes flip through a bunch of different things, fear and shame tainting each one because he understood how deep he'd just fallen. It was nearly physically painful to watch, to wait, because each passing second I got more and more terrified he'd say she was amazing or wonderful or much better than me.

But Sark didn't say any of those things. He thought for a few more moments before he answered, hesitating, like he was balancing on the edge of a cliff. "Confusing."

Confusing? I wrapped my arms around myself and took a small step away. *He just said confusing.* His expression remained somber, but his eyes were frantic, waiting for my reaction. I didn't know whether to cry or yell or rip my hair out or all three.

I tried really hard to keep my voice even. "*Confusing?*" I didn't even know where to aim my rage: Sark for doing it, Vanessa for stealing someone so important, or me, for sitting idly by, wasting my life away while he was with someone else.

But it wasn't just *someone*.

"I know, I…" He ran a nervous hand through his hair, readying himself to defend a side he knew had no case. "She looked just like you. She sounded like you, felt like you—as far as I knew, she *was* you, just a…a different version. I wanted you. I wanted you back so badly, and she knew that." He dropped his eyes. "So when she cornered me after work one night, I…I didn't hold up very well."

My teeth made an audible sound when they snapped together. Of course she did. *Of course* she did. I felt I would explode at the image I couldn't rid myself of—because she would've been all over him. Everywhere, in her stupid little dress, ready to say anything, or do anything, to get him to seal a betrayal.

Sark went on hastily before I could go on a rampage of hot tears, glancing up to meet my eyes. "But it didn't last. Nothing…after, um, a minute, I decided I didn't like it and pushed her away. She got mad and tried to talk through me, but I left. I swear, that was it."

"You didn't *like* it?" I repeated, my words harsher than I meant them. "What, she wasn't good at it?"

He winced. "No, she…that wasn't it. She just wasn't you."

That calmed me a degree. I knew he was doing his best to be honest, even if he didn't want to be, and I had to give him points for that. Really, it wasn't fair that he was the one left to deal with the repercussions. He'd been a victim as much as me—I couldn't imagine what the rest of that night must've been like for him.

"So," I said slowly, trying to choose my words right. "You're saying she kissed you differently than I do? Because I thought she…I mean, she only knows what I know."

Or at least she did. She probably knows a whole lot of new things now.

Sark nodded, almost too quickly. "Yeah."

"How?"

"It's hard to explain, but she…it's bizarre. It's like how technically she *looks* just like you, but when her face would twist up in bloodlust…I mean, then she wasn't you. She was Vanessa. Because you could never make your face look like that. It's the same thing: at first she felt just like you, and I would be lying if I said I didn't encourage it, but then…" He shook his head, and I thought I saw him shudder slightly. "You're different than she is. You're…"

I felt my chest swell. *Wonderful? Magnificent? The best in the known universe?*

"Soft."

I could almost hear Vanessa cackling in my head. My forehead creased and my voice went flat. "I'm *soft*?"

"No, it's a good thing," he reassured me. "Like…" He brought his hand to my face, gently caressing my cheek—a move that usually burst butterflies in my stomach, but the magic just wasn't as powerful right now. "When you kiss me, I can feel you care about me. You're doing it because you care about me, not to prove you can or play mind games with me or try to hurt me. I didn't realize there was a difference until I was with her. I hated it. It was such a…disgusting way for her to try and disfigure your memory."

My arms tightened around me, his words extinguishing some of the fiery rage inside because I knew he meant them. I could only imagine the frenzy Vanessa would sink into when Sark— probably the only guy she actually wanted—ended up refusing her for me.

And she'd probably known exactly what to say. She knew him as well as I did. Somewhere amid my violent emotional tsunami, I felt my heart ache at the awful things she must've crooned in his ear, in my voice, just to break him in every way only I could.

My voice went delicate as my shoulders relaxed. "It was bad, wasn't it?"

He shook his head as he flinched, the expression in his eyes letting me know the severity. "Yeah," he said, his voice nearly cracking. "It was bad. I don't know how you survived this long with that level of cruelty in your head."

That's the thing: I didn't.

I couldn't help it. I lurched forward and wrapped him in the biggest hug I could manage, holding his head against my shoulder and burying my face in his hair.

"I didn't mean it," I whispered in his ear. "I didn't mean any of it. Everything she said, I didn't mean it. It was all a lie. I promise you. It wasn't real." I kept whispering the words over and over to him. He clutched me like his life depended on me, and I went on forever, not stopping the repeated words until he loosened up. Then when I felt he was somewhat okay again, I turned his face to me and kissed him gently.

"It's okay," I told him, and I meant it.

"Arie..." His voice was strained with hurt. "I know that's literally the worst thing I could've done—"

I shook my head. "I don't blame you. I really don't."

"I don't know how you can't. That, uh...that doesn't really inspire good faith in me, but I..."

"It's not you." As stupid as this would sound, he deserved honesty from me. I dropped my gaze to the crusty crushed motel carpet. "It's me. And her. I..." I sighed. "I just can't stand the thought of her taking someone else away from me. You more than anyone."

He put his fingers under my chin and lifted my head until I looked at him again. "You aren't her. And she could never be you. Not by a long shot." The corners of his mouth pulled up ever so slightly. "Besides, I'm only interested in the real thing."

That made me smile, the first bit of happiness I'd felt in what seemed like years.

"You're mine," I told him, leaning into his shoulder. "Not hers."

He smiled. "That's all I want."

A knock on the door interrupted us. Sark let out an annoyed breath before heading to open it. I scrambled into the bathroom and yanked on my hoodie to hide my scars from whoever it was.

Daxton was slumped in the doorway, sent as the honorary messenger. Sark and I went back with him to the other room where we held a meeting with everyone. Unfortunately, like me, nobody really knew what to do. In the end we agreed on one thing: we couldn't stay in one place for too long. Just because the Compound had gone under didn't mean someone wasn't tracking us now.

Nobody said the name we were all thinking as we filed back into the van. We drove for hours, the sun going from barely showing to high in the sky, not knowing where to go. We just kept driving.

The mix of emotional trauma and no sleep started to catch up with me, leaving me exhausted. I settled against the wall of the van as we bumped along.

Ellen surprised me by resting her head on my shoulder. "I like your hair," she mumbled. "It's a good look for you."

It took me a few seconds to relax from her contact. "Thanks." Then I remembered that my scars were covered, which was probably why she didn't have any qualms being so close to me. Still, though, with the whole Vanessa situation, I was surprised Ellen would touch me at all.

We're friends, I reminded myself. *That must be what friends do.* I hung to that warm thought, the only positive thing in my head, promising myself I'd thank Ellen later when we were alone. It was truly amazing to have a friend like her. I couldn't let myself forget that.

Despite the shuddering of the vehicle as it went along, everyone in the back dozed off at some point, including me. Ellen's blonde hair tangled with my now black as we slept against each other. Every once in a while my head would hit against the wall or a monster would appear behind my eyelids and I'd jolt awake. Not wanting to wake up Ellen, I wouldn't move except my eyes, looking around at our party. Alaina was awake the first time and our eyes met—I instantly felt weird and we both looked away, but I didn't know why. Every other time I woke up she was asleep. Lucy stayed glued to Brennan, Jacklynn moving from Lucy to the floor and back again as she slept. Kayla actually fell asleep against the wall, but Daxton didn't—an uncharacteristic swap for those two—and Daxton watched over her with a longing gaze I'd never noticed before.

Sometimes I'd glance up at the front seat. My mom's head was often resting on my dad's shoulder, blocking my view, so I didn't know if she got to sleep. Sark's eyes never closed, at least when mine were open, but that wasn't surprising. I tried to get his attention a few times to ask how he was doing but he never looked at me.

We didn't stop until the gas tank was empty. My dad pulled into the gas station, and we all stumbled out to stretch our legs, leaving the still sleeping Jacklynn inside. The more the poor girl stayed out of reality, the better.

My ankles cracked when I stood. Ellen popped her neck as she got out and we joined our small circle next to the car.

My dad sighed. "I love driving nonstop in a van as much as the next guy, but where are we going?"

That was an excellent question. We stood in uneasy silence. I watched my feet as I shifted on them, not able to come up with a good answer.

"Do you want to go to the police?" my mom asked when nobody responded.

My dad scoffed. "What, see if the blasted government can do anything for us?"

I snapped my head up and said, "No," the same time Peter snorted, "And say what?"

Kayla shook her head. "We don't know what Cyrus has infiltrated." She glanced at me. "Unless you do."

I gritted my teeth. "He's everywhere. We can't."

"Okay, so no government." He coughed twice and my mom grabbed onto his arm instinctually before he straightened up. "Any other ideas?"

I glanced at Sark but everyone besides him and Alaina—who were both interested in the sidewalk—glanced at me. My stomach flipped but, thankfully, my mom spoke up.

"Let's just keep going," she suggested, patting my dad's shoulder. "We'll keep driving and find a place to stop tonight. Then we'll make plans."

Nobody had any objections, so we all agreed on that. My dad used some of the cash he had withdrawn from one of their last functioning accounts to pay for gas while my mom went into the store to buy water and food.

Lucy had to go to the bathroom *really* bad, apparently, and said she couldn't wait in the line at the gas station. There was a twenty-four-hour breakfast place across the street, but for some reason Brennan was nervous about her going so Ellen and I volunteered to go with her. We stuck by her side as we jaywalked the street and went into the quaint place.

The smell of bacon and coffee hit my nose as Ellen explained the situation to the hostess in an ugly green uniform. The hostess was nice enough and pointed us to our destination.

After using the bathroom myself, I washed my hands with the pink soap and studied myself in the mirror. My hair had mostly dried and wasn't as black as it was when wet, but I could still tell it was different. It was my reflection.

Your name is Arie Nolan and you are nineteen years old. You have blue eyes and dark hair and scarred arms. You're infected and a person and you're trying to figure out what that means.

I sighed and dried my hands on a paper towel. *My name is Arie Nolan and I have no idea what to do.*

Once we were ready, I followed Lucy and Ellen out of the bathroom and headed for the glass front doors. I watched the people we passed out of the corner of my eyes, people drinking coffee or eating eggs, people laughing with their families or talking business with their coworkers. In my distraction, I didn't notice someone had stopped Lucy and Ellen until I bumped into them. Recognition melted into terror when I saw who it was: a woman in a dark gray trench coat, blonde curls spilling out from under a beanie—the same woman I'd passed the other night on my way out.

I hadn't been crazy. One of her eyes was sea green, the other bright blue, and the brilliant smile she gave me was much too animalistic to be human.

A mutt? She had to be one, but she was a far cry from the ferocious mutts at the Compound. *What is she?*

Before I pull Ellen and Lucy out of her grasp, a thick hand wrapped around my neck from behind and my body froze over. I didn't move as the male mutt in the black baseball cap and leather jacket entered my peripheral vision, bracing myself, waiting in anticipation for him to snap my neck or sink his teeth into me.

"Just do it," I said through my teeth, staring straight out the front doors to see Brennan running across the street.

The mutt's hot breath plastered my face, his head moving up and down against my skin, as though he wanted nothing more than to dig into me, but something was physically holding him back. "Arie," he whispered, his voice a silk growl like the woman's. "Arie. Arie. Arie." My name dumped out of his mouth over and over, as if it was the only word he knew. I stayed perfectly still and trapped the scream behind my teeth.

Brennan had reached the doors now, but couldn't get in. The doors were locked. His eyes widened in horror as he pounded on the glass and shouted Lucy's name.

The smell found me the same time it happened. An artificial smell, something metallic and created, hit my nose, leaving a sterile taste in my mouth. As soon as I registered it, every patron in the restaurant started dropping, one by one. I could only see a few in my limited line of sight but I heard the others—people choked, convulsed, screamed, or just passed out, a few falling dead. They thrashed and shrieked as blue vines began searing onto skin, marking them up, changing their demeanor. Some people went still during the process but those who survived it morphed from human to creature, baring their teeth and snapping at nothing while they burned.

I nearly screamed again when I realized what was happening. They were becoming mutts.

Sark, Peter and Daxton had caught up to Brennan, and all were berating against the glass as they watched the horrific scene unfold. Lucy half screamed and Ellen struggled against the mutt's hold, but they weren't affected by the mysterious gas.

It's because we're already infected. It can't hurt us.

The mutt holding me brought his face even closer to mine, brushing his nose against my cheek, and I flinched. "Hey, sweetheart. Hey, hey, sweetheart."

A choked shriek escaped me and I tried to jerk out of his grip, but he just held me tighter.

"Arie. Arie. Arie." I heard his teeth snap together over and over again in my ear. He was trying so hard not to attack me. "Arie. She wants to talk to you, Arie. Arie. She wants to talk to you, Arie."

Then the mutt shoved me forward just as the other shoved Ellen and Lucy, and all three of us crashed into each other. Among the chaotic screeching and snarling, I heard glass shatter, and I straightened up just in time to see Brennan grab Lucy.

I barely processed the fact that the two mutts were gone. My eyes searched for a half second, then I lunged forward, tackling Sark to the ground and slapping my hands over his mouth and nose.

"Don't breathe!" I shouted at him. "It's in the air!"

Sark's eyes narrowed, then he nodded once. I yanked us up and shoved him out the door, snatching Ellen's hand before running with everyone else across the street, narrowly missing getting hit by oncoming traffic.

My mom's bewildered expression matched my dad's, and Alaina said something to Kayla when they saw us dashing for the car.

Peter jerked open the van door and shoved Alaina inside. "Get in now!"

We all followed the order, Sark at the wheel now. He was speeding out of the gas station lot when a pack of twenty or so mutts burst through the door of the restaurant, roaring at the sky. Then they descended on the road, and everything fell into madness.

Cars were ripped apart, people thrown and chewed on and slaughtered, bodies both red and blue everywhere. Sark weaved in and out of disasters, and we tumbled around in the back of the van like clothes in a dryer.

My head slammed against someone else's, and something scraped against the side of the car, making Jacklynn shriek. I sat up just in time to see a mutt running up next to us get smeared by an oncoming car. Then an explosion sounded and the ground shook underneath us. I turned my head to see the gas station we'd just been at in the distance, up in flames.

The carnage ended after that. No more mutts followed our speeding van as we fled the gruesome scene.

Nobody spoke the entire drive. We all sat in stunned silence, staring at the ground, terror taking our words and voices. The attack played over and over again in my mind: the blue, the screams, the bodies. I shivered. It was just like one of my nightmares, but this time I would never wake up.

When the sun had set and darkness settled, Sark pulled into another motel. My parents went to get a room while Sark got out and opened the door for us. Our shoulders were heavy as we slowly filed out.

I was last. Sark shut the van door behind me, and I leaned into him, needing a hug. Instead, he started walking after the others and I almost fell over.

What was that? I knew he had seen me—he was right next to me. Confused, I followed him to our room.

We all stayed in one room this time. It was a tight fit but we'd rather all be together in case we got attacked again. Water bottles, granola bars and fruit snacks were passed around for dinner, though nobody ate much.

The attack was on the news that night. We were a captive audience, unable to look away from the train wreck even though the retelling was almost as disturbing as being there had been. After the gas station exploded, the mutts had taken off and nobody knew where. The reporter informed us the body count was close to fifty, but that wasn't conclusive and didn't account for those who were injured or missing. Nobody had any sort of explanation for what had happened.

What is she doing? There was no way this recklessness was all from Cyrus: he wasn't wasteful. I racked my brain, but I couldn't understand what the point was, not to mention the questions of where she got mutts like that or where she was operating from or how much Cyrus was involved.

"Our hearts and prayers are with those affected by this monstrous and devastating attack," the reporter closed. "The government has put several task forces on the case of this disaster, and if you have any information, they urge the public to make contact. In the meantime, they ask you to please stay inside as much as possible. As always, we'll keep you updated on the situation as we get more information. Stay safe." Then it went to the weather.

A collective silent sigh went through all of us, as though we'd all been unconsciously holding our breaths through the newscast. My parents settled into their bed—I insisted they take one—Brennan, Lucy and Jacklynn in the other, while the rest of us stayed on the floor. It wasn't the most comfortable, but nobody expected to get much sleep anyway.

I glanced at Sark from my spot across the room, who, I could've sworn, was purposely avoiding my gaze. Was I just being paranoid? Or was there really something going on? I thought back to our last conversation early this morning, which seemed forever ago now. *He* had kissed *me*, first of all, and didn't seem angry that I was hurt about the Vanessa situation. Did I say something that had upset him? Maybe he was shaken over the mutts. Maybe he was just stressed, as all of us were, over what on earth we were supposed to do. Or maybe I had done something wrong. I couldn't think of anything, but I continued to analyze every word I'd said, every look I'd given him since he last had his arms around me, the anxiety making my stomach feel sick.

Ellen and I took the first watch—she sat by the door and I by the window, waiting for something, anything, to find us. Not that we could do much if we were attacked again, but a few seconds warning to the others was better than nothing. I watched the dots of snow slowly start to fall onto the sleeping town as I heard the mutt's voice over and over.

She wants to talk to you, Arie.

5

There were six more attacks over the next week. Only two of them were near us—the others were spread across the country, including New York, Chicago, and Denver. I pretended to not understand the significance of those places, purposefully forgetting that at different points in my life I'd called all of those places home.

A military force was actually assembled as the attack on Denver commenced, but that just made the slaughter worse. Only three men out of the entire group weren't killed or turned into a monster. Their bullets and tanks and fighting style were no match for the ruthless mutations, and panic spread like wildfire at their uncontrollable nature as the body count continued to rise.

We'd already talked through our own strategies—in short, we didn't have any. Emotions ran high, and eventually our strategy sessions would fall into heated arguments within minutes. We kept relocating, kept running from the nightmares we knew had been caused by us. By me. We watched so many people on TV lose their lives to the formula that had stolen ours years ago.

The stress was causing a major strain on our group. Peter and Alaina got into an explosive fight (and, honestly, I wasn't even sure what it was about) and barely talked to each other for two days, making it awkward for the rest of us. Jacklynn sobbed loudly for hours every night and no amount of calming from Lucy or me would help. She just cried herself to sleep, keeping everyone else up until she was out.

Besides to soothe Jacklynn, Lucy didn't speak a word unless it was whispered to Brennan, and even he was unusually unhelpful, closed off except to Lucy. Sark and I didn't interact except once when I was obliviously standing in his way and he asked me to move—I still hadn't figured out what our problem was and was too afraid to ask. Kayla remained her diplomatic self, Daxton stayed out of everyone's way, and Ellen stuck to my side whenever possible.

My parents helplessly watched us fall apart, my dad's coughing fits causing both my mom and I to wince and hold our breath until they were over.

We were all just a messy disaster. We even had to go back to getting two motel rooms just because people needed space.

It was awful. I hated feeling so powerless, so vulnerable, unable to help those closest to me when our suffering was all so obvious. But the situation was just too huge. Too hard. Too much was out of my control. There was so much pressure to find a solution to an impossible problem and it was nearly suffocating me.

I couldn't take it. I couldn't handle everything. I struggled to find menial distractions to keep me from acknowledging the cloud of hopelessness that filled my every breath, but nothing helped much. I stopped eating. I picked all my nails off until they bled, and when I ran out of those I started picking skin off my fingers instead, afraid of the sense of familiarity I felt when I glimpsed a dot of blood. And when Peter and Alaina started going at it *again*, I made myself stand and told Peter to come with me on a trip to a store for more food, if only to separate the match from the gunpowder and keep Jacklynn asleep.

We only ending up getting more water—neither of us cared enough to put actual thought into what we needed. As we trudged back through the motel parking lot, I lifted my eyes from my feet to see one of our room doors ajar, several people moving around inside. People I didn't know.

A pit formed in my stomach and my feet turned to lead. I stopped in my tracks. Peter did the opposite, surging forward to see what was going on. Once he got to the door though, he stopped too, and my breath caught when I saw his shoulders sag in defeat. Something caught his attention, dragging his gaze to the right, but a parked car blocked me from seeing what he was looking at.

I found control of my feet again. I forced myself to take steps forward, forced myself to not think through the hundreds of things that could've happened, the people I could've lost. I was almost to Peter when he turned and faced me. I stumbled when I saw the fierce heartbreak in his eyes, as though he would've given anything to protect me from what I was about to see.

He took me by my shoulders, voice thick and uncertain. "Arie…maybe you—"

I pushed past him. He kept an arm on my shoulder as I staggered toward the doorframe, staring at the strangers bustling around the bed. I was about to enter when a quiet voice stopped me.

"Arie."

I ripped my eyes away from the room to the sound. Sark was sitting on the ground against a post a few feet away from me, his arm around my mom who was sobbing into his shoulder.

He shook his head once, his eyes mournful, telling me without speaking. *Don't go in there.*

A choked gasp escaped me and I felt like I couldn't breathe, my eyes darting back and forth between my mom and the undefined lump on the bed. Peter's grip tightened on my shoulder, as if afraid I would fall.

"No," I whispered inaudibly to the universe, wrapping my arms around myself. "Not yet. Not yet."

I gaped at the doorway for a few minutes, my mom's muffled cries the background music, and I started to feel lightheaded.

I have to leave. I needed to run. I needed to run away, run far away, and leave everything behind, curl in a corner and convince myself I hated my dad anyway and it didn't matter that he was gone because I was too afraid to admit that it did.

Sark said something to Peter—I wasn't focusing hard enough to hear—and Peter nodded once before squeezing my shoulder again and slipping into our other motel room. With his exit and the tears pounding against my head, desperate to leak out, I decided I was running too.

Turning to take my first step out of there, I saw Sark and my mom again. He was watching me with an expression mixed with grief, shock, and concern, while I wasn't even sure my mom had noticed I was there yet. My soul felt heavier as I watched her sob for a moment, this woman who'd now lost every member of her family at least once. She needed me to stay. She needed me to cry with her like we used to years ago.

But I didn't want to. I didn't want to be her daughter again. I didn't want her to be my mom again because inevitably she would be taken away from me. I was so sick of losing people.

I could feel it: I was at a crossroads again. The way I reacted now would dictate our relationship for the rest of forever.

Swallowing the storm inside me, I stumbled over and collapsed on the other side of my mom, gently pulling on her arm. She glanced over at me with puffy eyes, giant tears rolling down her face and staining her cheeks.

"Arie," she whispered in between sobs. "He's…he's gone."

I nodded. "I know."

She buried her face in my shoulder and I hugged her, resting my cheek against her hair as tears stung my eyes and I patted her head. Words escaped her lips, words I knew she would've never said to me if she weren't disillusioned by her anguish.

"We were getting better. It was…it was so hard, but we were fixing us. We were going to do it. We were going to fix us. We were."

My breath caught and I hugged her tighter. "I know, Mom. I know. Me too."

She cried on me for what seemed like forever. I just held her and stroked her hair and let her cry it out. There was nothing else to do.

I glanced at the silent Sark, seeing him staring at the ground, almost tears in his eyes.

"How long?" I whispered to him.

He looked up at me a few moments before whispering back. "I found her about twenty minutes ago. I don't know how long she was alone."

I nodded and bit my tongue so I didn't cry at the image of my mom alone in a random motel room with my dad's corpse.

I should've been there.

Eventually, the strangers took my dad away. Paramedics wheeled him out on a stretcher, and I was grateful they'd covered his body with a sheet. I didn't want to see it.

Sark lied when they asked for personal information—he said the loss was too much now, that we would follow the ambulance and work out details later, even though we had no intention of doing so. Just like how we'd snuck out of the hospital before giving any identifying details. Couldn't have anyone logging our names in a database only to have Cyrus or Vanessa flag us down in a few hours.

My mom scrambled to her feet and lurched after them, begging them not to take him away yet. I held her back, knowing it was useless to reason with her, until she finally stopped fighting my hold and collapsed into me. Supporting most of her weight, I half dragged her back into the empty motel room and put her down on the bed my dad hadn't been on. She fell asleep almost instantly. Tears still ran down her face as I pulled the blankets over her thin form.

Straightening up, I twisted my hair in my hand and took a deep breath before walking stiff steps to Sark. He was standing in the doorway, one foot in the room and the other out, unsure where he wanted to be.

I stopped in front of him and wrapped my arms around myself. "I'm going to stay here with her," I said, keeping my voice quiet. "Does anyone else know?"

He shook his head. "No. I was alone when I found her. I just told Peter to keep them inside the other room."

"Okay." Another deep breath. "That's good. Can you just stall them until…" *Until what?* "Until I figure something out?"

I became panicked at the thought of our situation. Not that my dad had been in charge of anything, but I suddenly felt a giant weight of responsibility on my shoulders, matching the one that was already there.

What are we going to do?

"Yeah. Sure." His face was expressionless, but the emotion still bled through his eyes. "Take as long as you need."

The response wasn't anything grand, but it almost pushed my tears over the edge. Really, what would I do without him?

"I can trust you with anything," I told him, my voice nearly breaking. "Don't let me forget that, okay?"

I wanted one of his hugs, but then I suddenly remembered our blatant lack of communication in the last few days. Nearly swaying on my feet, I started turning to go. Sark grabbed my arm softly and pulled me closer, wrapping me in a tight hug, and kissed my temple lightly. "I won't."

"Thank you," I breathed. "I can't even say how much."

He left and I staggered over and sat on the foot of my mom's bed, watching over her. The grief, the age, shone through when she was asleep. You could see every slight wrinkle marking every heartache. It made her seem years older. How many of those wrinkles, those grief marks, those heartaches, had come from me?

Too many.

I thought back to the last grief mark I'd etched onto her skin, days ago when I'd finally found some courage and asked to speak to my parents alone. Through thick tears I told them about the last time I'd tried to escape the Compound. I got caught, obviously, and was sentenced to the Box as punishment. Before he put me in though, Cyrus showed me video, claiming it would give me some perspective.

It was of my older brother Kieran, on the military base he'd shipped himself off to—the base I'd hated for years because it was the place he had chosen over me when I'd needed him most. And it was the place that had killed him.

I'd watched with absolute horror as the security footage showed Kieran meeting with one of Cyrus' inside guys. I'd heard them discuss things, threats that hadn't made sense to me until later, when the guy had left and Kieran had taken a small photo out of his pocket. A photo of me.

"I'm coming for you, Arie," he'd told the photo. "I'm coming."

I'd choked on my own grief as I told my parents in the shortest terms I could that Kieran hadn't left us at all. Kieran had been planning on running away with me, a place Alexis would never find, and Cyrus hadn't wanted that. He struck a deal with Kieran—Kieran disappears and I stay alive. He steps foot in my life again and I'm dead.

I told them how I watched the video in which Kieran got fed up, the video in which he decided to come get me anyway. I told them that the explosion that killed him wasn't on a routine ride, like we'd been told, but on his way to come save me.

I told them Cyrus blew up my brother to keep him from getting to me. I didn't tell them how

Micah had to hold me down to keep my flailing limbs from hurting themselves. I didn't tell them how loud I had screamed when I watched the awful scene unfold that I was powerless to stop. I didn't tell them how I'd thrown up upon seeing a photo of the bloody stump that had once been my best friend in the world.

Both my parents cried. That was the first time I'd ever seen my dad cry, further softening me toward him, but when he leaned to give me a hug, I'd sidestepped out of his way. I told myself I wasn't ready for that yet. He had just cried harder.

And now he's gone.

I wasn't sure how many grief marks that conversation had added to my mom's face, but I tried to count them as she slept.

She didn't sleep for very long. I was staring at the wall questioning my existence when all of a sudden she started talking.

"He usually wakes me up." Her voice was cracked but void of tears as she stared at the ceiling. She must've cried herself dry. "Every day of my life for over twenty years, he wakes me up at five thirty. Claims we have to get a good start on the day, that sleeping wastes our time." She laughed once. "Practically an insomniac, that man, for most of our marriage. It used to drive me crazy."

I wanted to agree, comment, add my own story of being victimized by my dad's owlish habits. Say something, at least. But my tongue stuck to the roof of my mouth, so I just nodded.

"This morning, I woke up. On my own. I thought maybe it was the middle of the night until

I saw the sun shining through the curtains. I turned around to check but I already knew." She sighed. "Every day for twenty years."

I swallowed before finally managing to get out, "I'm sorry."

She acted like she didn't hear me. "You know, we almost got divorced. Four times, actually. Four times in twenty-one years I was prepared to walk away from him forever. It would be hard with you kids, for sure, but I couldn't take his antics. The first time was when he lost his job for…what, the sixth time? We almost had to declare bankruptcy and he didn't even care. Didn't even…the last time was when he infected you. He tried to explain it to me, but I didn't understand. I didn't think he'd actually do it, either. And then you were gone anyway." She shook her head. "I hated him for taking you away from me. So many times I questioned my own sanity, questioned if I'd been blinded by something I thought was love but was actually poison. I wouldn't believe that could happen, but I remember you with Connor, and if you could fall for it then so could I. Right?"

I just pursed my lips and tried to keep my expression neutral. This wasn't exactly what every kid hoped to hear about their parents, but my attention was hers. Whatever she needed to say, I would listen, no matter what.

"But every time I'd get up in arms and prepare to leave, he'd do something. Unconsciously. And I'd remember why I toughed it out all those years in the first place." She shrugged. "I really did love him. So much. Fatally so."

Her eyes shifted to me. "He was diagnosed right after you left. The combination was a bombshell. I'd lost my parents, my kids, my marriage, and now I would lose my husband too. He didn't move off the couch for a week—can you even imagine that?—but when he got back up, he was a different person. Kinder. Slower. Loving. He'd already told me he wouldn't be treated for his illness, and I took it personally, like I wasn't worth living for. But that wasn't it."

The corners of her mouth pulled up slightly. "He treated me like I was the single most important thing in the world, even when Alexis took us hostage and forced him to work. It was like he was making up for twenty years of affection he'd been too busy to give. We worked hard on our relationship, and it paid off. Finally, I figured it out: the cancer was karma. He thought dying was punishment for what he did to his family and he took it without complaint." She laughed once but it was a lifeless sound. "No complaining. That was a new one for him too."

Her eyes closed and she sighed. "I guess I just never thought the day would come, you know?"

"Yeah." I cleared my throat. "It usually sneaks up on you."

She was still for a long time, but I wasn't sure she was asleep. I waited until she cracked her eyes open and asked if I'd get her some water.

My joints were stiff as I pushed myself off the bed and headed outside, knocking softly on the other door. Ellen answered.

"Do you have any more water bottles in there?" I asked.

She shook her head. "We drank what Peter brought, but I think there's more in the van. I'll grab the keys." She left for a moment before following me out into the parking lot with keys in hand.

"Is everything okay?" she asked me as I pulled out two bottles from the back of the vehicle. "I don't know Sark very well, but it seems like something's wrong with him. Besides the obvious, of course."

I didn't want to say the words out loud, afraid the universe would think I was accepting them, but something about Ellen made me feel I could tell her.

"Yeah, um…" I slid the van door closed and turned to look at her. "My dad just died."

Her mouth fell open and her eyebrows shot up. "Whoa, what? Are you serious?"

I nodded, brushing my hair behind my ear. "He was sick, so…yeah. My mom's pretty upset."

"Oh, Arie." Tears welled up in her eyes and that made them well up in mine. She surged forward and hugged me. "I'm so sorry."

"I am too, I think." It was confusing, trying to piece the emotions together. My dad had been a stranger to me for years. Why should I care? Just because I understood an inkling more about his actions didn't mean I forgave them.

I guess that was the problem: half of me didn't. Half of me was still hurt and angry, with no intentions of being called his daughter again, the half that was spiteful and hardened and knew how the world treated her. But the other half of me had gone and gotten used to him a little, the half of me that was alone and scared and cautiously hopeful and wanted her daddy again. I should know by now that I shouldn't let people into my life. It's just painful.

Ellen kept her arm around me as we walked back to the motel. She waited outside as I took my mom the water. I stood there for a moment, my eyes darting back to the other bed, the bed where my dad had taken his last breath, and suddenly the walls started closing in, the pink patterned curtains threatening to suffocate me against the matching comforter.

Pulling my mom up, I went past Ellen to the next room and knocked on the door. Alaina answered this time.

"I was hoping you were room service," she muttered, moving to let me come in.

"Gather everyone up," I said. "We're leaving." Then I turned to get my mom and head for the van.

The news must've dripped down the grapevine quietly as we assembled in the vehicle because everyone was quiet and avoided looking at me, and nobody asked why we were a person short.

I sat in the front with my mom and told Sark to drive wherever he wanted—I didn't care how far we went as long as we slept in a different place than last night, which was safer anyway, in case the paramedics came back looking for us. He just nodded and drove.

An hour later we arrived at another motel. We just got one room this time, as the cash from my parents' last account weren't going to last forever, and I planted myself in the far corner on the floor.

Except for the occasional bathroom need, I didn't leave that corner for two days. I couldn't make myself stand underneath the weight of life.

Our motel room was a sad place to be. People rarely spoke. Jacklynn's random cries were the only sounds besides the card games that would get going every once in a while. Food lasted longer because nobody had the stomach to eat. The darkness was like cigarette smoke to an addict—no matter how much we hated choking on it, we wouldn't stop smoking. We inhaled the miserable atmosphere, absorbed it into our being, then exhaled the darkness for the next person to breathe.

The only one who had a speck of enthusiasm was my mom, and not in a good way. She became everyone's mom on steroids, fluttering around wiping clean things with a discolored towel and asking if she could refill the water bottle she had placed in your hand thirty seconds before. If you asked her if she was okay, she'd blink in surprise and say, "Yeah, why?" then launch into a speech on how you were looking rather skinny and could probably use a granola bar, backing it up with the nutritional value of each flavor. It was scary.

I was going on day three of devastating immobility when someone pounded on our door. Everyone stiffened at the sound because everyone was already in the room. We had an unexpected visitor.

Sark stood and looked through the peephole, then let out an annoyed breath. For a second I thought he wouldn't answer it but eventually he cracked the door open and said, "Get lost."

Micah pushed past him and came inside, carrying a big black duffel bag. His eyes were narrowed and focused, his face and clothes dirty and worn and wet from the rainy night, as he stalked into the room, picked up the remote from off the bed and turned on the TV. The newscast came on, detailing yet another awful attack. They were becoming more frequent and deadly; I'd stopped watching them.

I kept my eyes on Micah rather than the screaming people. He gestured to the screen with the remote. "You know, this seems like something you would care about."

I just glared at him. *Nice to see you too.*

He tossed the remote back on the bed. "I learned a bit about your whole cloning process—you were supposed to die on the table. Instead, you used your talents yet again to defy the odds and come back."

I scoffed and shook my head derisively.

He ignored me. "I want to know why. If you're just going to sit here and watch her burn the world, why would you choose to come back?"

"Okay, you know what?" I dragged myself to my feet, my legs sore from being cramped so long, and started for the door. "I'm not having this conversation."

Truthfully—though I would never say out loud—that question scared me to no end. Because the only answer I could come up with was "I don't know."

Micah blocked my path. "Well, too bad. We're having it."

Apparently, everyone decided we needed some space because they cleared out. Sark lingered for a few seconds before shutting the door behind him.

Frustrated, I folded my arms across my chest and scowled at Micah.

"This is it?" he asked. "This is when you decide to give up? You're going to throw everything away?"

I wasn't in the mood for a lecture and his words infuriated me. What right did he have to judge me? It wasn't like he was all that saintly himself.

Again, I gave him no answer. I just tried to melt him with my eyes.

He shook his head. "You know what you said to me once when we were trapped at Dalton's place?"

I automatically winced at the name, surprised Micah had brought it up.

"You said just because we lose a battle doesn't mean we lose the war." He gestured to me. "Where's that girl, huh? Where's the girl who was trapped in a hellhole waiting to die and still said stuff like that?"

My hands balled into fists. "She *broke*!" I shouted. "*You* helped break her. Congrats, it worked, I'm done! I'm out. Do you not understand that? It's over. The war's over. I lost." I jerked my chin at the door. "Now get out and let me live the rest of my miserable life in self-loathing."

Micah raised an eyebrow. "It's over? Really? For you, Arie, it's never over."

"Well, it is now. There's nothing I can do."

"I doubt that." His tone got edgier. "She came from you, right? Just—"

The rage boiled in my veins. I stepped forward to shout in his face. "Just what? She is *not* me! I can't control her." I thought of the past few days on the run, the stolen glances at me, the unrest, people waiting for something. Waiting for me. "Is that was this is about? You really think that just because she came from my head I can make her do whatever I want? That I have some special secret weapon I'm sitting on? What power do you think I have? She's not me and I have nothing to do with her!"

The slight alarm started showing through in his eyes. "I don't buy it. You can—"

"How many times did I say I can't get caught? Huh? And how many times did you really take me seriously? 'Arie, would being the key really be the worst thing?'" I spat his own words back at him. "Oh sure, it's all fun and games, the key is so mysterious and exciting, until it actually happens. And now you're freaking out because you realize *you were wrong*!"

I took a few deep breaths to calm myself down. "Besides," I continued, stepping away from him but still glaring, "you don't actually care about all the people she's killing. You don't. You're just a stupid little puppy dog who lost its master and is scrambling to find a new one because you don't know how to live with your dripping ledger without puppet strings for excuses. Don't pretend you're so much nobler than me."

He didn't flinch but his eyes seemed to, and I knew I'd hit a nerve. Still breathless from my rampage, I took several deep breaths to try and calm myself, and guilt for what I'd said to him started to creep its way into me.

"I guess you can't find Cyrus?" I finally asked, the rage gone from my voice.

Micah dropped his gaze to the floor. "No. I'm assuming he's with Evil Twin."

Which is why you came here. "I don't know where she is. Really. I'm sorry."

He nodded. "I believe you."

"Do you think he's working with her?"

"No," he answered promptly, but it wasn't quite right. "If so, he would've taken me with them."

Yeah, keep telling yourself that. Vanessa was ousting everyone, wasn't she?

"I've just been doing some groundwork. Tracking." He patted his duffel bag. "I was able to snag a little bit of weaponry before I left the Compound. Been taking out the mutts I run across." He shook his head. "The new ones are freaky."

I perked up at that. "You have the bullets?"

"A few. Not much but it's kept me alive this far." He unzipped his duffel bag and dug through it, handing me a handgun and a magazine of blue bullets—the special bullets Cyrus engineered, the only ones that could take a mutt out. "You should take one. It doesn't seem like she's got them attacking you yet, but just to be safe." He glanced at me, something new in his eyes I didn't recognize and got the feeling he didn't want me to see. "She'll do anything to get the chance to tear you apart."

I took the weapon, about to say thanks, when a scream echoed from outside, followed by the sound of shredding metal. Lurching forward, I jerked open the door and ran outside.

Rain was coming down in torrents, obscuring my sight in the darkness, but I finally caught sight of my family running from our van. About five mutts were climbing all over it, literally ripping apart our vehicle, while five others were chasing the runaways down, the two mutts from the restaurant at the helm.

Slapping the magazine in my gun, I sprinted after them, sensing Micah right behind me. He started shooting at those on the car while I went for the running group. I gunned down two of them before they realized what was going on.

The mutts had caught up to the group—Lucy was trailing behind. The blonde mutt in the trench coat nabbed her by the hair and yanked her to the ground. Lucy screamed and Brennan turned and shouted. Water sloshed in my shoes as I ran toward them, shooting the mutt in the shoulder. It shrieked, and I tackled it off Lucy and fell onto the asphalt.

The mutt's shoulder bled red then blue, but she still managed to roll us over, so she was on top of me, forcing the gun out of my hand and tossing it away, then snarling over my struggling form.

"She wants to talk to you, Arie," the mutt told me, rain rolling into her smile. "She wants to talk to you."

"Tell her I have nothing to say." I elbowed her in the jaw, and she raked her nails across my neck. Four gunshots sounded, sending her tanking, and I rolled out of the way. Convulsing, she roared at the sky as the blue lines on her body grew thicker and brighter, her face puffing and swelling, both eyes going glassy blue. Then she stopped moving.

Panting, I jumped to my feet to find both Sark and Micah armed and aiming at the dead mutt. I snatched up my gun on the ground a few feet away, but I didn't need it. All the mutts were either gone or dead.

Sirens wailed in the distance, along with strangers' alarmed screams. Sark, Micah and I walked over to our group huddled in the rain.

"Is everyone okay?" I asked over the storm.

There were several nods and mumbled assurances, then Lucy said, "Thank you."

Sark glanced around at the forming crowd in the street. "We need to get out of here."

I nodded, taking in our surroundings. We were about four blocks down from the motel, which we couldn't go back to, since that's where the police would go first. We couldn't be around for questioning; we had to find a new place. I glanced around to see the businesses around us closing for the evening. A few cars went by, but it was pretty vacant.

Sark led the way, Micah and me bringing up the rear, as we went down the street, looking for a place that might take us in. My clothes were soaking wet, my bones shivering inside me. It was cold. Wherever we ended up, it would be a long night.

What am I going to do?

Sark finally ducked into the only open building, everyone following suit. I hung back when I saw what it was: a church. The look was of a European cathedral, beautiful stain glass windows glinting in the rain, giant spires reaching up to the clouds.

My eyes followed the spires all the way up and I started to feel sick. *I can't go in there.*

It was stupid that it was such a big deal—religion had never really been my thing—but now would be a really bad time to be wrong.

I didn't realize anyone had noticed me until Ellen nudged my shoulder. "What's wrong?"

I planned on saying 'nothing' but something else slipped, as it usually did with Ellen. "Are you religious, Elle?"

She turned her eyes to admire the building. "Not really, but my best friend growing up was. I'd go to church with her sometimes. It was nice." She glanced sideways at me. "You don't want to go in?"

Her tone was genuine—nothing about her was ever judgmental. It was that tone that cultivated honesty from me.

"Not really."

"Can I ask why?"

I twisted my arms slightly to hide my covered wrists, a habit now. "I'm a device in a borderline demonic cult. That's not exactly church friendly."

She was quiet for a few moments. "If it makes you feel any better, you can't tell. It's not like they'll card you. What's the worst that could happen?"

I didn't know, but I couldn't get the image of lightning out of my head. What were the chances of getting struck by lightning? It wasn't *that* common, right?

Ellen took my arm in hers. "Come on. It'll be okay." I held my breath and let her lead me inside.

It was quiet. That was the first thing I noticed. The rain pounded on the roof, soft voices sounded, and I could barely hear organ music in the background. But it was quiet. Still. Rows of pews took up the middle of the space facing a risen stage with an organ and podium, lit candles lining the front adding to the stillness.

Ellen waited with me for a moment before sitting down on the last row. Our group had slid into the left side of the pew, each bent with exhaustion and shivering from the rain. A priest was putting his few blankets around whoever would take one. The only other person inside was a man in what looked like an old police uniform—he was sitting on the second to last row, shaking hands with Sark and my mom like he was introducing himself.

Too restless to sit, I wandered off to the right, pretending to admire the art on the walls but not really paying attention.

Why did I come back? I really didn't know. Why had I survived up to this point if I was just going to sit around and waste my life away? That's what I wanted to do, though so far it hadn't been very fulfilling.

I didn't realize I'd been unconsciously listening to the older man's story from across the room until something caught my attention.

"Of course, this was back before they kicked me off the force," he was saying, his voice gruff but nice at the same time—like what you'd expect Santa's to be. "My sobriety wasn't all there to begin with but when we found her body…" He let out a quiet whistle. "I couldn't see a young girl take her life and not be affected. I hit the bottle hard that night, a rainy night like tonight, and sat on the curb, drinking it all away. Then this other girl stumbles up to me from no man's land. She was wobbly on her feet. Emaciated. Almost deranged. Kept whispering to herself. She was in bad shape."

I tilted my head to hear better. "After getting some water in her system, I finally got her to talk. She said she just escaped her abusive uncle and needed to get to Denver, Colorado as soon as possible. I told her not to worry, young lady, I was a police officer, and I'd take care of her. But that only made her go into a panic frenzy. She said her uncle *was* the police and she couldn't trust me, but I told her I wouldn't tell anyone and would take her where she needed to go. Poor kid didn't have a choice."

I turned all the way around now, getting a closer look at this man, but the captive audience didn't notice me.

"So," he went on, "I stowed her in the backseat and drove straight to Denver. Shouldn't have been driving either, with the amount of alcohol in my system, but I needed to help her, ya know? Especially after the call that night. Anyways, once we made it to Denver, I stopped to fill up the gas tank. When I came back, she was gone." He shook his head wistfully, his tone taking a slightly dramatic turn. "I never saw her again."

My hand covered my mouth, muffling my gasp of surprise. Slowly, I walked to the middle aisle, each step bringing back another piece of a suppressed memory.

The man turned his attention to me, his brown eyes soft, his small smile highlighting the short white beard on his face. I knew him.

"Officer Moss," I remembered.

His smile grew slightly, and he nodded politely at me. "Erin." My face must've given me away because one thick white-brown eyebrow arched. "Your name isn't Erin, is it?"

I shook my head, sitting down on the opposite end of his pew, watching him closely as though he'd disappear when I blinked. "No. It's Arie."

He cleared his throat. "Well, Arie, you look a lot better now and it's not just 'cause you cleaned up—you've grown quite well."

My response was a little late, my voice still airy with disbelief. "Thank you."

"You still on the run from your uncle?"

I shook my head again. "He, uh, he wasn't my uncle. His name was Dalton."

Another eyebrow arch. "Was?"

"Yep."

Moss nodded, almost in approval, then glanced at Lucy and Brennan. "So who ya running from now?"

"Um…" I twisted some of my wet hair around my finger. "Myself, I guess."

Moss whistled again and nodded. "Aren't we all."

Peter snorted and a few people laughed once, including me, confusing Moss, but he didn't ask.

Moss leaned back against the pew behind him, rubbing his beard. "Well, Arie, I was just telling your friends here that when I found you on the curb a few blocks down, I wasn't—"

"Wait, what?" I interrupted, my eyes widening. "It was here?"

"Well, yeah, it was. Don't you recognize it?"

My eyes didn't but my soul had. Immediately, I started running through calculations in my head, trying to gauge how far we'd driven, walked, travelled, if it could really be possible that I was here, again, just miles from the place Dalton had held me captive and stole eight months of my life. I looked at Micah for confirmation. He gave me a small, apologetic smile. "I didn't want to tell you, in case you freaked out."

My mouth hung open and I glanced at the front door, my insides tingling and prickling at my new revelation. I slapped my hands over my eyes. Of course. It was so obvious now.

"Arie?" Micah asked. "Are you okay?"

I hesitated, knowing that once I acknowledged the revelation, I'd be forced to act. "That's her kingdom," I whispered to myself.

"What?"

Straightening up, I took my hands off my face to look at him, speaking louder. "That's where she is: the one place she knows I would never go again."

Micah's eyes widened with the realization and I knew I was right. How did I not guess that from the beginning?

The information settled on all of us, changing the atmosphere from damp to electric. Instantly, people started running through scenarios.

"So, she's building an army," Brennan started. "Then she can do whatever she wants."

"Yeah, but it's not very organized," Peter said. "She's just unleashed her monsters to wreak havoc. Where's the strategy in that?"

"Maybe that's not the strategy," Ellen chimed in. "Maybe she wants to infect everyone, so they'll all be like her."

Kayla spoke up then. "But that still doesn't make sense—the mutations that she's produced are more advanced than anything we've seen but they're still just mutts. That's worlds different from the perfect soldier the formula is supposed to create. Why would she waste life on a formula she knows doesn't work?"

"And that doesn't explain her," Daxton added. "Why she is the way she is. Not exactly the key everyone was expecting, including Cyrus."

My mom cleared her fragile throat, grabbing everyone's attention because she sounded like she was breaking, then leaned forward to look at me. "Maybe it doesn't work."

"What doesn't work?" Peter asked.

"The whole thing." My mom shook her head. "I know it's all become life to you by now, but this whole infection thing has been crazy from the start." She shrugged. "I don't think it works. Not the way it was meant to, anyway."

Daxton's mouth hung open slightly. "Vanessa isn't a perfect key because…"

"The perfect key doesn't exist," Kayla finished. "Infection is just a means to an end that doesn't exist."

The more I thought about it, the more it made sense, despite it going against years of reinforced belief. "All she knows is the stories that we knew—that I believed. The key is supposed to be this great commander to the perfect army. That's her goal. Now she has the 'improved' formula and keeps dumping it into tons of people but only getting more mutations, if the subjects survive at all." I glanced at my mom. "I think you're right. It doesn't work. It probably was never supposed to."

Brennan nodded slowly, trying to grasp this new train of thought. "So she's panicking."

"Without a successful formula, she has no purpose. What else was she created for? What else can she do? She doesn't want my life; she wants to be more than me. That's why she'll never stop, even if she could kill me. She wants to fulfill what she was created to do, but she can't because it doesn't work. It has never worked. They've tried dozens of times and I'm the farthest they ever got with a key and I still don't work."

Sark raised an eyebrow. "Dozens of times? There's more than one key?"

I nodded. "I didn't know either until Cyrus told me. That's why he waited so long to bring me to the Compound—he didn't know if I was worth it. Dozens of keys have failed throughout the years, since Castor first created the formula. Nobody can get it right."

"You mean Castor was a failure from the start?" Kayla asked.

"Come on: creating the perfect human?" I shook my head. "I don't think that's possible. We're meant to have flaws."

Peter rubbed the side of his head. "So philosophy aside, Vanessa is bent on finishing something that doesn't work which is why she's scary angry."

I nodded again. "Exactly. If it had worked, she wouldn't be able to *be* angry." My hands fidgeted in my lap. "That makes it more dangerous though. She knows in the back of her mind that she's already lost, which is why she wants to take down as many people as possible—she knows she's on a crash course that can't end the way she always hoped."

Peter pursed his lips. "Yeah, I can see that. She just wants to set everyone and everything on fire and watch it burn."

"But where does Cyrus fit into this?" Ellen asked. "This still doesn't sound like his plan. Do you think he died when the Compound fell?" There was too much cautious hope in her voice to miss.

That part, I couldn't explain. Where was that strange man? And what could he hope to gain?

"Wait, hold up." Peter scrunched his eyebrows like he had a headache. "You're basically saying we are the failed experiments of a larger experiment that also failed?"

I thought for a moment. "Pretty much."

He rolled his eyes. "Well, there's a confidence booster for you."

"So what are we going to do?" Brennan asked. "We can't let her keep going. And we have to destroy the ones she's already created."

"We can't storm the place—we don't have numbers and she's got a billion mutts." Peter looked down the row to Micah. "How much firepower you got?"

Micah seemed surprised to be addressed by someone other than me. "Not enough. Four handguns and ten mags. That won't even get us through the front doors." He started digging through his duffel bag. "I can probably get more though." Then he straightened up and tossed something at me. A Compound radio. "The Compound's pretty desolate as far as supplies but I don't think she touched the offsite labor camps. I don't think she even knows where they are."

I glanced at the box in my hand and could've sworn it got heavier as I realized what he meant. I shook my head. "Oh no, Micah, they don't want to hear from me."

"I can't do it. You're the only other one with the clearance to get them to listen. We don't know how much they know about what's happened."

"They'll know the Compound's been compromised. They'll think I'm just weeding out rebels. They're not going to believe me."

"Then make them believe you. That's our only shot."

I stared at him for another moment, then stole a glance at Moss. I'd forgotten he was there for that absurd conversation. His eyes were huge like quarters, and he leaned forward slightly, as if taking in our every word like it was the best film he'd ever seen. When I still didn't move, he gestured at the radio. "Well go on, now."

With a sigh, I brought my legs up and wrapped one arm around them, twirling the radio in my hand. Staring at the bench so I didn't have to look at anyone else, I counted in my head.

One. Two. Three. Then my finger pressed the call button.

A crackling sounded as contact was made, then a strained male's voice came over the speaker.

"Labor camp, what's your clearance?"

Don't screw this up.

I kept my voice from shaking as I answered. "One, one, nine, alpha, six, thirteen."

"Okay, go."

"This is Arie Nolan from base to labor camp. How are we doing over there?"

The strain in his voice just got worse. "Everyone is accounted for, and we are in crisis management level three. Is it true that the Compound has been compromised?" He had that same horrorstruck awe that Micah had, unbelieving of the idea that the Compound could really fall.

Don't screw this up, Arie. Don't screw this up.

"Yes. Yes, it's true. The Compound is down, and I need some help while the operation is weak."

There were a few beats of silence that nearly killed me. "Aren't you supposed to be with Cyrus?"

"Yeah," was all I said, letting that sink in. I could almost hear the gears turning in the kid's head as he tried to figure out what game I was playing.

"Is this a drill?" he finally asked, suspicious fear coloring his tone.

"No, I'm afraid it's not."

"Look, we're loyal to Cyrus one hundred percent. I'll send someone to shoot anyone that wavers, but you can count us good."

"I'm not doing a count and I'm not with Cyrus." I sighed, moving to the next level. "Put me on with one of your workers."

His voice was still distrustful, but he didn't think he had a choice. "Who?"

"Liam Harrison."

In my peripheral vision, I saw the slouching Alaina perk up at the use of her brother's name. I'd told her a long time ago that he was relatively safe but that's all the information I had to offer.

"Hello?" a voice asked uncertainly, and I felt myself relax slightly at the familiarity.

"Liam, oh, it's so good to hear from you again. It's me, Arie. Are you okay?"

There were several moments of empty static. "Uh, yeah. I'm all right."

For some reason, his reaction caught me off guard—was it dumb to assume he'd be jumping in joy to hear from me too? "I need you to trust me, okay?"

His tone was layered with discomfort and cautious fear. "Arie, I...I don't know. I think...look, I'm just going to get off now."

"No, wait! Why?"

"There's been a lot of stories going around about you. I think it's best if I...look, I've got stuff to do, you know?"

I doubled over and bit my finger to keep from crying in pain at the words. Peter groaned and a few people sighed in exasperation. I fought to keep the welled-up tears inside, my insides aching as I remembered how I used to play guitar with this guy lifetimes ago, when he was my best friend's brother.

I tried to keep the hurt out of my voice, resting my forehead in my hand. "I know. I know. I just—"

Another crackling sounded, quieter than the first, as though there was some scuffle on the other side. Then a different voice came over the radio.

"What's up, Arie?"

I blinked in surprise. "Mark?" Last I'd seen Alaina's cousin and his twin, Mara, they were in the hospital in critical condition. "You're alive?"

"You better believe it, baby. I must apologize for my friend Liam, here, he seems to have a headache this evening and doesn't have his priorities straight. We trust you one hundred percent."

My voice nearly broke with relief. "Really?"

"Arie, there are only three people in the known universe I'd follow blindly to the end of the Earth: U.S. soccer player Landon Donovan, Captain Kirk, and you. What do you need?"

I smiled the biggest, stupidest smile. "I need you to convince as many infecteds as possible to be on our side, break into the hangar at the camp, load all of the weapons and storage onto a plane, and fly to Washington state so we can run headfirst into a suicide mission. You still in?"

Mark didn't miss a beat. "Absolutely. I like the odds stacked against me. Keeps it entertaining."

"You're literally the best person ever, Mark."

"I know. I haven't heard it in a while, but I never stopped believing. Journey is my inner muse."

"You sure this kid can pull it off?" Micah asked me. "Sounds like an idiot to me."

I opened my mouth to defend but Mark beat me to it. "Okay, I heard that, and whoever you are, you obviously have no idea who you're dealing with. We got this."

"I have no doubts, Mark." I gave him instructions on how to break into the hangar and what codes to use where. "Let me know when you've made it that far. Keep the radio on you and please be safe. A lot of the infecteds there are going to try to take you down because of Cyrus. Just let them know whoever isn't with you is free to go."

"Don't worry, I'll use my incessant charm to commit them to the cause. Works every time."

"Good luck. I'll talk to you soon."

"Roger that." Then the radio went silent.

I cleared my throat, watching the black box as I tossed it around in my hands. "Well guys, we've got a war to end." I glanced up at them. "Anyone interested in coming with me?"

Peter grinned, leaning forward to give me a high five. "Always."

6

Preparations started immediately, and the next day and a half was absolutely insane.

I borrowed Moss' cell phone and called Lindsey Carter, my contact in the Office of Cultist Intelligence. My heart swelled when I heard her voice, reminding me how much she had pulled me through, and she was ecstatic to find I was alive. I told her I knew where the mutts on the news were coming from and I was going to put a stop to them—I just needed some help. She told me she'd send the few agents in my area straightaway, adding promises she'd get on the next plane out here.

Four agents met us at the church. The one in charge introduced himself as Agent LeBlanc and I explained where I was going and what I needed. The OCI didn't have the power it used to, but LeBlanc was still able to provide us with three tactical military units, a warehouse to gather and work, and the blueprints of the building Vanessa was hiding in, since it was the agency's building in the first place.

The first floor seemed innocent enough: offices, cubicles lined up outside of conference rooms, kitchens and break areas. The secret basement level, though, was used as confinement, the prison Micah and I had been illegally sentenced to. It seemed strange to me that it was a year ago that I'd escaped.

Micah, Peter and Alaina made a trip back to what was left of the Compound, rounding up any extra supplies they could find and bringing back the infecteds who had miraculously survived the downfall. I was happy to find Elijah, Zoe and Cameron among the battered faces.

The real triumph came when Mark showed up. Not only was he towing over a dozen crates full of weapons and gear, but he also came with almost a hundred infecteds, familiar faces in the pack: Carlton, Tristan, Sasha, Dustin, Elizabeth, and so many others from the club in Denver. The reunion was wonderful, but I had to pretend I'd been called and ducked away when I heard someone ask where Hadley was.

The prep work was massive, and I threw myself into it, not allowing my mind the time to wander and really consider what was going to happen. Because if I really thought about it, I would lock myself in a closet and cry until I drowned.

It was going to be rough—we all knew that. There were no guarantees, but it was a battle we had to fight. A battle *I* had to fight, despite being petrified to the point of physical illness. I hated the lack of consistency my enemies had provided me over the years: first it was my dad. Then Sark and Felix. Lennon and Jefferson. Alexis. Then Dalton. Cyrus. Now Vanessa. I'd learned to live in fear of the next thing that would pop out and surprise me. Today, I would end that.

I was in the back room of the warehouse with my team—Sark, Micah, Peter, Brennan, Ellen and Alaina—sorting through the weapons for the last time and dividing them up between those who said they'd fight. It was getting down to the wire and we all tried to ignore the future that hung over our heads.

Micah was standing next to me as we worked. "You're oddly chipper for someone about to walk back into hell," he stated.

I shrugged, watching my hands as they placed guns in different piles. "And you're pretty smiley for the guy who volunteered to go with me."

He sighed, his tone getting serious. "Have you actually thought about it?"

"Nope." I popped the 'p' with my lips. "That's not really my style. I'm more of the 'avoid it until you face it' type."

"Right." He seemed annoyed with my answer but didn't get the chance to press it.

"What are we going to do when this is over?" Peter asked, and I was grateful for the change of subject. "Assuming we survive, of course."

"I don't know," Alaina responded. "It'll be weird. No Alexis. No Cyrus. No running. What's a freak to do?" She paused for a moment. "I think I'm going to go ice skating."

Peter laughed once. "Where did that come from?"

"I don't know," she admitted. "I always thought it was tacky but now I just want to."

"Okay." His tone clearly made fun of her. "While you're ice skating, I'm going to a football game."

"Which one?" Brennan asked.

Peter shrugged. "I don't even care. Any of them. All of them. What about you?"

"I want to watch a movie. Just sit on the couch, make some popcorn and chill. I don't even care what movie." Brennan glanced at Ellen. "All right, Ellen, your turn."

"On what I would do?" she asked before thinking for a moment. "Um…I don't know. I've been at the Compound since I was eleven, so I don't remember a ton. Probably…work on a campaign."

I lifted my head to look at her. "A campaign?"

"Yeah, you know, like a political campaign. When I was a kid I wanted to be the first woman President of the United States. That's the next best thing."

I nodded with a smile. "All right, that's cool."

Only Brennan would be considerate enough to include everyone. "Okay, Micah, what are you doing when we get out?"

I saw Micah stiffen slightly, but I chose not to help him out, just to see where it would go.

"Uh…" He shifted on his feet. "I guess I'd actually see the world through my eyes instead of a sniper scope. Apparently, I've been missing out—I heard something once about Galaxy Wars. I guess it's the thing to watch."

Brennan's eyebrows furrowed. "Watch Galaxy Wars?"

"Yeah, you know, 'in a galaxy far away' and the guy is his father or something."

We all laughed, and Micah glanced around self-consciously. "What?"

"Oh, brother, you need help." Brennan slapped Micah on the back and looked to me. "Should we survive, do I have permission to educate him on the finer things in life?"

I smiled. "Absolutely." And for a half second, I thought maybe this could all work out after all.

Of course, the moment was slaughtered. Kayla came walking in, her eyes on me.

"We're done," Peter said before she asked. "Time to get this murder show on the road."

"Everyone knows what's going on, more or less," Kayla said, "but it might be good to talk to them all at once before we go. Rally the troops to unification. We're all marching to death, after all."

At that, every eye shifted to me, and I almost threw up. "What, me? You've got to be kidding."

Kayla shook her head. "You're up, Arie."

"Whoa, why me? I'm the reason everyone's here."

"Exactly."

"No…" I sighed in frustration. "That's not what I meant."

Peter smirked at me. "Too bad. You're our great leader."

"Leader of what? Sucking at everything?"

Nobody was on my side. "I know you may not realize it, Arie," Kayla told me, "but you are quite influential, especially with the different representations we've got here. If anyone should do it, it's you. We'll wait out here until you're ready." She turned and left, taking almost everyone with her. Sark and Brennan lingered behind.

"Break a leg!" I heard Peter call at me from outside the door.

I gritted my teeth and shook my head. The stupid speech would kill me before Vanessa's mutts could get the chance. Equal parts annoyed and terrified, I turned to needlessly pick up guns and put them back in their same piles, so it looked like I was doing something.

Stalling. You're stalling.

Brennan walked hesitant steps until he was standing next to me. "Hey, uh, Arie? Can I…clear something with you?"

"Yeah." I abandoned my pointless work to turn and look at him. "What's up?"

His hands fidgeted and he kept glancing away, avoiding my eyes. "I'm having Lucy sit out. Of the fight, I mean. I just…want her to be safe." His tone tried to close it, but I sensed there was more to the story.

"Okay, that's fine." I wasn't one to pry, but I knew Brennan wouldn't take a person from us when we were already outnumbered unless he really needed to. "No problem."

He nodded, short and stiff. "Okay. Thanks." He turned to go but I spoke before he could.

"I'm not going to ask, Brennan, and you don't need to tell me. I trust you. Just know that you could if you needed to."

"No, I know. I know. It's just…" He finally met my gaze and a wall came down in his eyes, showing his anxiety. "Lucy's pregnant."

I blinked in surprise, somehow managing to curb my expression of shock. "Oh. Oh, okay. Um…how long?"

"About five months now. Almost six."

Now that I thought about it, Lucy had been wearing looser clothing and her frail form had seemed pudgier, but those weren't exactly things I would comment on. The stress Brennan must've been under the past few months had probably been massive, trying to protect three people instead of one, dealing with the thought of being a dad before he turned twenty. And I couldn't imagine how poor Lucy must've been handling all of it.

I didn't ask any questions or give any advice—it wasn't like I would know what to do either. "Of course, Brennan. Don't worry about it. I'll have her stay with my mom and Jacklynn and make sure they take good care of her. She'll be safe." I hesitated before adding, "If you want to stay too, that's totally fine."

He shook his head. "No, I have to go. There's no way I could sit out of this one." He sighed. "It's just that she wants to keep it, which—and I do too. I do. It's just…the timing…and we didn't want to tell anyone yet and with this…"

"You need to make it out alive," I finished for him. "And you will."

Brennan took a shaky breath. "I hope so."

"You will." I gave him a quick hug. "I won't tell anyone, I swear."

"I know you won't."

I grinned. "And just so you know, Arie makes a great baby name. Middle names too. Works all around."

Brennan cracked a smile. "I'll keep that in mind." Then he turned serious, his eyes genuine. "Thank you."

"No problem. Thanks for telling me."

He nodded at me and left the room. I let out a long breath, shaking out my hands, then glanced at Sark, who didn't seem surprised.

"You knew?" I asked, my tone almost accusing.

Sark took a meandering step closer to me. "Yeah. Poor guy had to tell someone. You should've seen him the day they found out."

Of course he told Sark. It was funny how Sark had gone from one of our worst enemies to the one we all trusted with everything.

Suddenly I was hit with the freight train of reality, the knowledge that this was it for us. Granted, this was the most positive interaction we'd had all week, but I realized I didn't know if it would happen again. I just looked at this guy who had come into my life and stolen what was left of my heart, something stirring in my deadened soul that left my skin all tingly.

I cleared my throat, trying to shake myself out of it. "Yeah, well, I'm glad he's keeping her out. And it's sweet he wants to protect her."

Sark looked me over for so long, I thought he might not have heard me, then he blew out a long breath. "I know the feeling."

Glancing down again, I puttered around with our supplies, but my attempt at stalling was pitiful. After a few seconds, Sark stepped next to me and started fake rearranging too.

"What about you?" he asked, trying for a conversational tone. It didn't quite work. "Is there any way I could get you to sit out too?"

I snorted, though I wasn't sure why. "No. Why, you don't want me there?"

"I'm conflicted: there is nobody else on Earth I want fighting by my side more than you. I trust you with my life. But…" His hand touched mine, then he just grabbed it. "Please don't go."

I turned my head to look at him. "I have to. You really think I'd stay?"

"Not a chance." The corners of his mouth turned up, and he used my hand to pull me closer to him. "I just thought I'd try."

My feet closed the rest of the space just as Sark wound his arm around me and kissed me hard, like he never had before. It was scared. Desperate. Flowing with the knowledge that this might be the last time he'd ever kiss me again.

I broke away first, mostly because the tear in my soul was killing me. This wasn't the clean break I was hoping for. Of course, I was kidding myself at the thought of a clean break with Sark.

"Come with me," he whispered, touching his forehead against mine. "We'll get out of here, somewhere nobody will ever find us. We can leave all this behind."

I couldn't help thinking about that, just for a second, and the irresistible draw I felt toward the image made me kiss him again. Then I shook my head. "You don't mean that."

"No," he admitted. "Unless you said yes."

"I wouldn't. And you couldn't leave either." I put my hand over his heart and grinned. "I'm sorry to tell you, Sark, but you've learned to actually care about us."

He smiled and held my cheek in his hand. "That's your fault. Caring about you..." He laughed once. "That wasn't part of my plan."

"Mine either."

Sark glanced over me again, a storm in his eyes, like he was trying to memorize every square inch of my face. "Arie, I—"

"Whoa, whoa, whoa," I interrupted, trying to step away from him but he wouldn't let me go all the way. "That sounds like you're going to say serious things and this is not the time to say serious things."

"I don't care. Arie, I love you. I'm so crazy in love with you."

And those words brought everything to a screeching stop.

I shook my head, not able to keep all the panic out of my voice, trying again to back away from him. "No. No, you don't. You think you do, but you don't. You're just in the moment and I'm the only one—"

"No, you're downplaying this because you're afraid to fight for it. You don't want to feel any responsibility to walk away from this." He took a deep breath. "I love you. And I want to be able to say that for a lot longer than two more hours."

He's telling me this now? Now, when I was about to walk into my sure destruction, as there was no way Vanessa would let me live, one way or another.

I couldn't respond because I didn't want to feel the hope that would inevitably destroy me later, but I couldn't get myself to lie. Instead, I kissed him again. Then I nuzzled my face against his, my favorite feeling in the world, and the words spilled out of my mouth with only half permission. "I don't know what's going to happen. I don't. But if we do make it through this then I want to have a very serious talk with you about us."

Sark kissed my forehead, my nose, then my cheek before whispering in my ear, the desperation creeping into his voice. "Promise me we'll get that talk. Please. Give me something to fight for, Arie, because I'm grasping at straws."

"Okay," I found myself saying. "I promise." But when I gave him a last hug before we walked out of the room, I wondered if that would be the first promise I'd ever knowingly break.

I'd forgotten about the whole 'Arie gives the last speech thing' until I got into the main part of the warehouse and saw everyone gathered. The energy in the room was electric, people pumped up on adrenaline and fear.

I grabbed Sark's arm and jerked him back to whisper to him. "What if I'm leading over a hundred people to be slaughtered? What if we all die and it doesn't make any bit of difference?"

Sark looked at me for a moment, his face grim, before sighing. "Then I would remember that everyone volunteered. They've already given themselves over to the cause. You're not making them do anything."

I was grateful he didn't sugarcoat it, but I didn't like that answer. I didn't like the idea of assembling an army for any kind of 'cause' no matter how noble. This wasn't about nobility. This was about humans.

"Just remember," Sark continued, "they don't need a superior and they don't need a key. They need Arie." Then he backed away to stand next to Peter in the front row.

There was a crate at the front of the assembly—I assumed it had been left there for me. My heart pounded harder in my chest at the thought of standing in front of so many, of being so vulnerable and exposed.

I can't do this.

But they were waiting for me. And if I didn't do it then I'd look like a coward, and then everyone's confidence would be at an all-time low. Taking a deep breath, I pulled myself on the crate and straightened up. The first few rows of people noticed and stopped talking, turning to face me, and slowly it travelled back like a wave until the warehouse was silent and I had everyone's undivided attention.

I had wanted to sound professional, like I knew what I was doing, like I was capable of leading them this way, but then I decided to bag it. This situation called for authenticity more than anything. After all the shows, the lies, the facades and reputations, it was time we were real with each other. I owed them, and myself, that much.

They need Arie. They need a person.

"I find it stupidly ironic that I'm up here," I started, making my voice loud and clear, "in front of all of you, after years of avoiding being the key that leads an infected army. I guess sometimes, despite our best efforts, life forces us in a direction and there's no way around it. We end up in places we never wanted to be." I paused for a moment, my eyes searching over every face. "But you should know that when I look at all of you, I don't just see a number. I see a person. I see hopes and dreams and fears and heartaches. I see so much pain and triumph. Each of you matter to me."

Well, that was corny.

I took a deep breath, trying to keep my fingers from fidgeting. "That being said, I know some of you will die. I know we might all die. This isn't going to be easy, and I can't tell you it will be worth it because I don't even know and I'm not going to lie to you. We've all been fighting these battles for years now and this is where the war has brought us."

I felt I was rambling now and hadn't made my point. Why did they ask me to do this?

"The point is, we aren't soldiers. You weren't drafted and I'm not going to make any of you go. But if you're going in for the honor and glory and credit then I don't want you here. Go look somewhere else because that's not what this is about. If anything, you should be going in for yourself."

I stole a quick glance at the expressionless Micah. "You all should know that Vanessa is probably with Cyrus, which means she has his data and research. If we can win this fight, we'll get his completed reversal files."

A rumble went through the crowd and I waited to let it fully sink in, the information raising the stakes on its own.

"We aren't soldiers or crusaders or rebels. We aren't heroes. We aren't victims. We are survivors. Surviving to the end takes strength. It takes guts. And you should all be proud that you've made it this far. Don't let your endurance, all your experiences and heartaches and triumphs be in vain. Let's make them mean something."

Someone shouted, "Yeah!" from the back and everyone burst into cheers and applause, several whistles echoing throughout the space.

I jumped off the crate. That was it. The only thing left was to get going.

Everyone split into their groups, weapons were passed around, last instructions given. I said my goodbyes to my mom, Jacklynn, Lucy and Kayla—I was making Kayla stay to receive and interpret reversal files, to oversee the project and make sure these kids got their lives back. She had accepted the job without question and volunteered to help out with the paramedics who would be waiting at a safe distance for anyone who made it out.

Carlton was another person I needed to stay back. He was notorious for his hacking skills and I would need his help to get into Cyrus' system once I found it.

He handed me a small circular device with a USB drive on the end of it. "Get to the computer and plug this in. I'll do the rest from here." Then he tapped his left ear. "I've got a com too, so I'll be listening. Let me know when you need me."

That was it. All too soon we were leaving the warehouse and walking down the deserted streets, puffy clouds in the sky making the sunshine spotty. The military units had evacuated every building within a three-mile radius of Vanessa's fort, though the work hadn't been hard since most people had left a long time ago. The place was torn up, buildings in shambles, bloodstains on the sidewalks. You could tell the mutts used the area as a playground.

Though I'd made it so I didn't really belong in any group, I walked with a few of the entry teams so I could stay with Sark, Micah, and the rest of our crew until the last moment. I was trying to talk myself up in my head, but all efforts stopped when the building came into view.

My feet halted movement and I almost tripped over them, as a sharp gasp went through my teeth and my hands started shaking.

Everyone else stopped with me, thinking it was part of the strategy, but I barely remembered anyone else was there. I couldn't feel the ground underneath me—I felt the car. The car that had bumped along the road as it sped, the car I was shoved into the backseat of, my hands and feet bound, after watching Erika die. The car that had ripped me from my life and brought me here, to the place that would truly break me.

Then I felt my feet again. My feet slapping against this road as I ran, not daring to look behind me, my heart threatening to explode out of my chest because it was pounding so hard. The fear, the all-consuming terror, of both being captured and being free, knowing the monsters were right behind me.

Micah's shaky breath brought me back to reality. "I hate her," he muttered.

I tried to agree but I'd lost my voice. Instead, I stared at the place as though it were the deadliest train wreck in history: disturbing and scarring but you still couldn't look away.

Finally, Peter broke the silence. "We're still going in, right?"

No, we're not. And here I was again, at another crossroads, this one infinitely more impossible than any of the others.

Because what do you do? When the epitome of every fear, every inadequacy, every dark nasty thing that found its way into your head, every hellish experience that made you question life itself, is up against you? When you realize just how much the darkness has controlled your life and turned you into a shell? Do you keep running and hiding? Do you succumb to the urge that tells you to quit because there is nothing on the planet as addictive as self-destruction and you've given up so many times before? How can you possibly rise when your legs are broken, your soul is crushed, and your heart only pumps blood through a body now rather than life into a human? When it seems all hope is lost, how do you find the power, the courage, the strength, the audacity, to take that first step forward?

I didn't know. I didn't. Because, just as I'd told the infecteds in my lame speech, I wasn't a hero. I wasn't the heroine I read about in so many books when I was in high school. I was just a damaged girl who'd been beat up too many times in her life.

But then I remembered those next to me. I remembered Kieran, my dad, Erika, Hadley and Bea. I remembered every day someone had made me laugh and every night I'd cried myself to sleep. I remembered the times gathered with those I called my family and the times loneliness numbed me to a corpse. Every moment that took me from being a fifteen-year-old girl who didn't know a thing about the world to a near adult who'd seen too much of it. I remembered everything I'd lost and everything I'd gained, everything I was proud of and everything that killed me.

I cleared my throat and raised my gun. "Yeah. Let's go."

7

She knew we were coming.

I could tell that much from the welcome banner she'd left on the front door. Really, though, I wasn't surprised. This was her big moment and I was sure there were no limits to how much she'd orchestrated this whole thing.

A pile of bodies nearly blocked the front door and our point of entry, each of them pale and lifeless, swollen blue veins contorting their ashen skin. One of the bodies had been half strung up on the door and I tried not to gag. It was Lennon.

Peter spat on him as Alaina's face went white, but she glared and nodded as if almost in approval. Sark was the one who stepped forward and cut down Lennon, softly kicking the body to the side, then waited. I took a deep breath, stepped over the dead and led the way inside.

It was dark. The rows of rectangular lights had been shot out, broken shards hanging by electric wires from the ceiling. The open space spread out forever before us, cubicles torn to bits and desks ripped in half, an eerie stillness ringing through the emptiness.

I took a step inside. Then another. A piece of something cracked underneath my foot and I tightened my hold on the powerful gun hanging around my neck. Nothing else sounded, nothing else moved, as I made my way through the disaster zone. When I was about a quarter of the way through, I stopped and pressed the button on my earpiece, my eyes fixed on the far wall of the building somewhere in front of me, clouded by darkness.

"We're inside," I said, keeping my voice low. "No sign of anything yet. All entry teams proceed with caution. They're around here somewhere."

I didn't know a thing about tactical team entries, which is why I wasn't in charge of any of them. Each group had its own leader with its own purpose—most of them were mutt control, as we couldn't leave any of them alive. I had a different mission to lead on my own.

"Copy that," a dozen people replied in my ear. And that was it. Now everyone's life was on the line.

You can't think about that now. Just focus.

I gave a nod to Micah and Brennan—leaders of other groups—before turning to head down the third hallway, my skin prickling as I ran through the blueprints in my head to make sure I didn't get lost. I would spend no time poking around upstairs where it was arguably safe. I'd never been upstairs until now. I'd only been down in the basement, which is where I knew she'd be.

Sark followed me despite my thousands of previous protests. True, I probably needed backup, as downloading the files off the computer was a main priority and Vanessa wasn't just going to hand that to me. At the same time, having Sark around Vanessa was a bad idea, and not just because of my infuriated reservations: he couldn't defend himself. Though he swore to me he'd do whatever he had to, we both knew there was about a two percent chance of him doing anything that would hurt her, just because of me. And there was about a ten thousand percent chance she would take any opportunity to rip him to shreds, just because of me.

Still, he followed. We left the other teams to do their checks of the vast building while we crept down the hallway, he on the right side and me on the left, hugging the wall with guns at the ready, slowly getting farther and farther away from the exit.

We passed by doors, a few closed but most of them broken in some way, hanging at an odd angle in the doorframe. Offices. Conference rooms. Interrogation rooms. At least, they used to be. What I guessed was once a break room contained a bloodstained fridge with what looked like half a body in the sink. I moved on before I got a good look.

Sark glanced at me in question and I shrugged. Vanessa must've hoarded her army in the fortified basement for added protection. Maybe the whole upstairs was clear and all the teams would blaze through the place in no time, corner the mutts and get them all in one swoop. Maybe this whole thing would be a cakewalk and we'd all walk out without a scratch.

Right, 'cause that's not overshooting anything.

My heart sped up with each step until it was practically jumping out of my chest. I stared at the locked double door at the end of the hallway. The padlock was broken. My hand shook violently as I reached to push the door open, but I couldn't get myself to touch the metal.

What am I doing? I can't do this. I can't. How did I ever think I'd be capable of handling this? *You're a complete idiot.*

Sark took my hand in his and squeezed it. I glanced at him, but his presence only heightened my alarm.

He misread my distress completely. His sincere eyes met mine and he said, "I'm not leaving your side."

That statement tore me right in half. Because two of the worst things that could happen to me were being here alone and being here accompanied by those I loved most. My breaths were shaky and uneven as I shook my head. "I never wanted anyone to come here. Especially you."

Sark opened his mouth but then he was gone, me right after him. A force shoved us through the metal doors and sent us tumbling down concrete stairs. Somehow Sark stopped himself halfway down and grabbed me before I could keep going. I jumped to my feet and dashed back up to the doors, pulling on the handles with everything I had. They didn't even budge. We were stuck down here.

My words were rushed and breathless as I pressed my earpiece. "All teams check in. Is everyone okay?"

Brennan was the first to respond. "We're in the basement now. Seen a few mutts but it hasn't been bad so far." Everyone else had the same answer.

Nobody's dead yet. For some reason, that was difficult for me to believe. Nothing good could dwell or happen here. It had to be a lie.

"I'm okay too," Sark said from behind me. I turned to see him cast in shadows, half of his mouth pulled up. "Just in case you were wondering."

It worked. I tried to hide the smile that spread across my face as we walked the rest of the way down the stairs. "Don't do that."

"Do what?" he asked, feigning innocence.

"Make me smile. This is a serious situation."

"Serious, huh?" He thought for a second. "I don't know, I'm getting sick of our lives being in danger all the time."

I was going to agree but my foot took the last step and I stopped, my eyes searching for anything in the dark cavern set out in front of us. The musty air smelled like wet dog and dried blood, the faint dripping of a pipe the only sound in the still silence.

Sark waited for me to take the lead since I was the one who knew where to go. As quiet as possible, I filled my lungs with the stinky air and began to take cautious steps forward, hands clenching the weapon I jerked around in every direction, my eyes squinting to make something out in the near black.

Where are you? I thought with each step. *I know you're here.*

I'd gone about fifty yards when a body came out of nowhere, hurling itself onto me. Sark gunned it down before I registered what it was, and the gunshot was like the trumpet of war. Mutts descended on us from every direction, their snarls echoing through the darkness, the blue lines and eyes becoming visible seconds before they attacked.

I let instinct take over, as any form of rational thought would've gotten me killed. Mutts yanked and hit and bit and snarled. The first thirty seconds were dicey until Sark and I found each other in the madness. Standing back-to-back, both for comfort and strategy, we started shooting wildly into the space in front of us, blasting down mutts as they jumped to assault.

Our plan was working until one got past the blockade of bullets and Sark went down. I was able to kick the mutt off of him while still shooting, but then a monster caught me from behind. I fell onto Sark, part of his gun plowing into my back, then a mutt grabbed me by my neck and dragged me a few feet away. I kicked its head and used the distraction to aim my gun, but it was too late. The mutt grabbed my weapon just as I fired, redirecting the bullet into the darkness. We fought like that, the monstrous remains of a middle-aged lady growling on top of me, pushing the length of the gun against my throat, choking me off.

Finally, I landed a knee to her gut and used the momentum to push me over, rolling myself on top of her. Throwing my elbow in her face, I jerked the gun and pulled the trigger. The mutt screamed, convulsed, then went still underneath me, its blue eyes glassing over.

Panting, I jumped up to find myself surrounded by a pile of dead mutts. The wave was over. I was alone.

"Sark?" I called quietly, poking my gun through the mass of bodies, both afraid of finding him and hoping he was there. "Sark, please tell me you're there."

No sound greeted me besides the dripping of the pipe and my own near hyperventilation.

I pressed the button on my earpiece. "Sark, where are you?"

No response from anyone.

My voice started to shake along with my hands. "All teams check in now."

Drip.

Drip.

Drip.

Nothing.

Please answer me. Please. Don't leave me here by myself.

But nobody answered. I was alone.

"Your name is Arie Nolan," I whispered to myself in a panic. "Your name is Arie Nolan. Your name is Arie Nolan." For some reason, I couldn't think of anything past that. "Your name is Arie Nolan. Your name is Arie Nolan."

What else? I forgot everything. I forgot everything but my name and that I was going to die here. *What else?*

I glanced around at the mutts. *You're looking for someone.*

"Sark isn't here," I told myself. "Sark isn't here. You've looked for him here. The doors are locked and you can't go back upstairs. You have to keep going." I closed my hands around my gun and looked at the darkness looming in front of me. "Your name is Arie Nolan and you have to keep going."

And I did. My feet carried me forward, my arms jerking my gun at every made-up sound. Farther and farther I went. Deeper and deeper I sank into the blackness.

Your name is Arie Nolan and you have to keep going. Your name is Arie Nolan and you have to keep going.

I walked for years without seeing or hearing from anyone. No mutts. No Sark. No Vanessa. No Micah. No Peter. No Brennan. The darkness played tricks on me—I'd surge forward to attack a body only to find nothing there. This happened too many times, and a new kind of panic set in.

Maybe I'm insane. Maybe I'm imagining this whole thing. I'm dreaming or in the Box or... My stomach lumped into a sharp rock. *Maybe I'm still in this place. Maybe I never broke out and I've made up everything that happened in the past year.*

The scary thought took hold for a second, but I shook it out of my head. It was those ideas that gave Vanessa home court advantage. She was real. She hurt me. But she didn't define me. As long as I concentrated on the fight between her and me, I could focus. I could keep taking one step after another.

My paranoia overdrive came in handy—I came across a mutt but spotted it way before it saw me. My breath caught, grabbing its attention, and I shot it to the ground right as its blue eyes met mine.

I braced myself for another onslaught, but nobody else came. This mutt had been acting on its own. I walked closer to its crumpled body and found it had been standing in front of a steel door, one of the cells, as though guarding it. There was something in there.

The only way I could get myself to open the door was to remind myself that this wasn't my cell. It looked just like it, but mine was farther down the hallway: number nineteen. This was number two. Completely different.

I didn't allow myself much time to think about it; I just forced open the door.

The small amount of dim light from the hallway spread out in a triangle among the pitch-blackness of the room, barely illuminating the scrunched form shackled to the wall. He flinched when he saw me, but his agitated green eyes lit up after a moment of studying me.

"Arie, dear," Cyrus said, his dignified voice cracked and raspy. "You found your way after all."

I instantly straightened up and held my breath to stop my gasping, a desperate attempt to cover up my weakness.

She locked him up. She's not working with him at all. She's on her own.

"I was so hoping you'd survived," he added, blood from his scars dried on his cracked lips. It looked like his scars had been cut open again, crudely, and his jaw was swollen so he could barely move it. "It'd be a shame to lose you after all this time."

That sent fire through my veins and I felt I'd nearly explode with hateful rage. This man had done so much to me. To my family. To so many others. He deserved to rot in this cell and have his flesh eaten away by maggots. That's what I wanted for him.

I unsheathed the handgun from the holster around my waist, not wanting to waste my bigger gun's precious few mutt bullets. Cyrus' eyes widened, focused on the weapon, and I thought I could see fear in them. I wondered when the last time was that he'd been afraid.

Raising the weapon, I aimed the barrel right at him, glaring him down, catching a hint of a smile on his face—a smile that did not match the fear in his eyes. A smile of triumph. A smile that knew despite his greatest achievement backfiring and leading to his ultimate demise, at least he had managed to turn me into the cruel killer who got her revenge.

I pulled the trigger. And again. Again. I blasted the handgun with ferocity until it clicked empty.

Breathing hard, I tossed the useless gun on the ground.

After a moment, Cyrus cracked his eyes open, his tiny body shaking furiously, as he tilted his head up to see the massacred wall three inches above him. With his mouth hanging open in horrified shock, he glanced back to meet my glare.

I cleared my throat to make sure my voice rang out. "I win."

Then I turned, walked out and shut the door, leaving Cyrus shackled to the torturing darkness.

After that I started checking every cell, even though none of them had mutt guards, holding on to the hope that I'd find Sark in one of them. I didn't. My hands got shakier, my heartbeat got faster, and my mouth got drier with every cell I opened, each door getting me closer and closer to my own.

That's probably where she's hiding out. She knows I couldn't set foot in there again.

Cell number seventeen was empty. The lower half of my body went numb as I approached number eighteen, where my prison mate had spent his time. I was surprised to find the door ajar, a faint gasping coming from the open crack.

Slowly, I pushed the door open and it creaked, making the hair on the back of my neck stand up on end. My eyes adjusted to the new level of light, and I saw someone curled up on the ground, clutching their stomach and nearly convulsing, the veins in their arms and face getting bigger and brighter, as though they would pop any moment.

I gasped and yanked the strap of my gun over my head, tossing it to the side, then lurched forward and dropped to my knees next to Micah.

He cast his eyes on me and they boiled with hatred. "Monster," he spat through his clamped teeth. Then he really saw me, my face screwed up in panic, and his eyes softened. "Arie."

"Micah, no." I pressed my hands on top his, desperately trying to stop the blood that was seeping from him.

He tried to push my hands away but couldn't move that much. "Doesn't matter," he said in between labored gasping. "It's a mutt bullet. It'll kill me. There's nothing…nothing to do."

My eyes filled with tears, and I shook my head fiercely. "There has to be something. You can't go." I thought back to the moment in the warehouse before we left, everyone talking about what we were going to do. "It was going to work. You were going to have a life."

Even on the brink of death, Micah still found the energy to scoff at me. "Who are you kidding? I wouldn't…have made it anywhere. You know that."

"No I don't," I insisted. "I don't. The world would've accepted you, Micah. You just had to try."

He shook his head once, a tremor rolling through him. "I think…I think work as an assassin would've popped a red flag on…on most background checks."

I laughed once and it edged a tear over the rim of my eye.

"Besides," he said, wincing, "you were the only one who would've...accepted. I couldn't make it. I wouldn't have. It's probably...probably best."

My voice shook without resolve. "Don't talk like that. You're going to be fine. Just fine." I gave him a half grin. "Sunshine and roses, Micah. That's where you're headed."

The corner of his mouth turned up. "Come on...Arie. We both know there's...there's no sunshine where I'm going." Then the faint smile was gone. "But you...you and I...you..."

A giant convulsion went down him, and a half scream went through his teeth. His body shook and his veins got bigger, making his face get swollen and puffy. He gave me one last glance before his green eyes went glassy blue and he stopped moving.

"Micah?" I whispered, grabbing onto his limp hand. "Micah, please don't go. Please get up."

But he didn't. The glassy blue eyes stared at the ceiling, empty.

My tears began flowing down my face. "Come back, Micah. Come back. Don't leave me here again. Please."

But he didn't answer.

"Don't leave me here!" I shouted, pounding my fist on his chest. "You can't leave me here again! You can't!" I wrapped my arms around myself as the sobbing started to take over. "You can't leave me here again!"

A crackling sounded in my ear, interrupting my mourning and making me jump. I heard muffled voices set at a weird pitch, as though a signal were trying to get through to me. Then Brennan's voice rang out.

"All right, Arie, we're in position. All groups ready to go in ten. Nine. Eight."

In position for what? I hadn't given any instructions for any team. That wasn't my job.

"Seven. Six. Five."

A dagger of ice went into my chest, and I lurched forward to check on either side of Micah's head but found nothing.

"Four. Three. Two."

I nearly bashed my ear in when I slammed my finger on the button. "Stand down!" I screamed into my earpiece. "It wasn't me! Stand—"

Then a giant explosion tore through the building. The ground shuddered underneath me, making the door slam shut, enclosing me in complete darkness. The blast lasted about fifteen seconds, though it seemed to be more of repercussive vibration: I was on the outskirts of the destruction zone.

I heard parts of the ceiling fall outside the cell, but I didn't care. I just held the button on my earpiece like it was my lifeline. "All teams check in. Check in now!"

There was no answer. Not even silence like before. Just static.

The tears were back, if they had ever stopped. I clutched my fist to my chest as though I could hold myself together. "Is anyone there? Is anyone okay?"

The static greeted me, its sharp edges cutting me deep. There was nobody there.

Another explosion shook the foundation, the ceiling raining gravel, and the force of it knocked a dead weight into my lap. I glanced down and froze, though it wasn't the old puffy blue veins that still glowed dimly that caught my attention—it was the thin wispy black hair that met my fingers when I accidentally touched the infection victim's head. I'd know the feeling anywhere, after countless days of the little girl in my lap, glancing with wonder at the world around her. Bea. A corpse.

My scream was so loud I thought I might have ripped my throat open. I jumped to my feet and scrambled through the black to the direction of the door, pounding my fists on the wall. "Let me out! Let me out now!" Finally, my hand found the handle and I jerked the door open, staggering out into the hallway. I turned to run out the way I came, ready to leave these horrors far behind, when I heard a voice in my ear.

"Having fun yet, princess?"

I stopped at my voice—at *her* voice. She was here. Part of me had begun to wonder if I'd made her up.

Her tone was smug and I could imagine the smirk on my face that matched. "I told you: this is my kingdom. This is where I reign. Pretty great, huh?"

I glanced back down the hallway to where she was keeping Cyrus. His situation was the biggest indicator of her plan, confirming what I'd guessed: there was no plan.

What's she even going to do with herself when I'm dead?

"You've got it wrong," I told her, my voice still thick with dried tears. "You've got this whole thing wrong."

"Really? You want to explain that one to me, princess?"

I took a stiff step to my left, closer to my cell and farther from my exit. Then another. One more so I could peek around the corner. A dim light shone through from a room halfway down that hallway.

The control room. Of course that's where she'd be—the room with the systems, the cameras. The room where I had contrived my last escape.

"Philo Castor created the formula," I said. "You think he wanted you to do this. You think he wanted you to be a monster."

She wasn't amused. "Uh huh. Are you trying to talk through to me like one of your stupid mutts?"

I ignored her, slowly making my way down the hallway. "Everyone knows Castor as the man who created the formula, but nobody ever asked why. Nobody ever talks about his life before the formula. Do you know why?"

"When did you do your homework?" she asked, trying to hide her curiosity. How dare I know something she didn't.

"When I was on house arrest. Did you know that he lived in Europe in the late thirteen hundreds? Do you know what was going on then?"

"Of course I do." I could almost see her rolling my eyes. "The Black Plague. Quite a big deal, according to your history teacher."

"Yeah." I was halfway to the control room now. "Castor had three girls and the oldest caught

190

it. He couldn't stand the thought of his daughter dying, so he went up north to Scandinavia with the hope that he could find a cure. He stayed away for months, giving his life trying to create something that could help, despite his wife's letters begging him to come home and be with his family."

She didn't interrupt so I guess she was just as captivated with the story as I had been.

"By the time he had come up with the formula—the supposed solution to the 'perfect' human—all three of his daughters had been killed by the disease. His wife was so devastated by the losses that she hung herself. Castor lost everyone."

I stopped right outside the doorframe of the control room, knowing she could hear me without the earpiece now. "The world remembers him as this crazy guy who only wanted to take over the world. But that's wrong. This whole thing started because a dad wanted to save his daughter."

Steeling myself, I took the last step and turned into the control room. She stood on the right side by the motherboard of controls, dressed in all black—same as me—watching the twenty giant screens on the wall. I stifled a gasp when I saw the video feeds of every area of the building, infecteds battling waves of mutts, surrounded by piles of bodies. The broken walls that had been taken down with her explosion only amplified the chaos. The last screen showed the hallway I had just come from, now empty. She'd been watching us this whole time.

Two of the mutt guns were on the ground in front of the control panel, which was when I realized I'd lost both of mine.

Vanessa turned around to face me, an arrogant smile on her face. With her hair in a ponytail and her face devoid of makeup, she looked just like me. "Cute story. How about I tell you one now?"

She took meandering steps around her side of the room. "Once upon a time there was a princess named Arie. Beloved by her kingdom, the princess ruled her dutiful subjects with light and compassion, and they fell all over their princess, their inspiration and hero."

Then she stopped and faced me. "And while a lucky few got close enough to see through her cracks, nobody truly saw how messed up their princess was. That the princess wasn't a princess after all—she was a fraud." Her eyes narrowed and her tone got darker. "And even when they were given the perfect replacement for the throne, the stupid subjects rejected her and still trailed after their fake princess. Despite everything I could've done for them—everything you weren't—the kingdom still chose their beloved damaged princess. But even with a kingdom behind her to back her up, the princess still fell. She still failed every one of her subjects, including herself." She matched my glare. "Once upon a time there was a princess who turned into a monster once it got dark. And she lost everything."

I lurched forward to hit her smile off my face, but she caught my wrist and spun me around so she was behind me, then wrapped her other hand around my neck, pinning my arm behind my back. It was then I saw the unconscious body in the far corner: Sark. A giant bloody gash took up the side of his head, but his chest still went up and down. He was alive.

"You know," Vanessa said in my ear, "I still haven't decided how this story ends. Initially I was going to lock you back in your cell and bury the place, trapping you in forever." I struggled against her, but she held fast. "But that just wouldn't give me enough closure. So then I thought, 'why not bring the nightmares to life?' I'll just turn Sark into a mutt and let him rip you apart. That'd be fun."

I threw my head back to hit hers, but she ducked just in time. "But I still can't shake the idea of killing you myself. I waited forever for my mutts to herd you here. And now that you're here I don't know what to do. Do I have you watch me kill Sark first? Or should I let you watch the screens for a while so you can see how you brought everyone to die?" Her voice turned to steel. "We both know I should just kill you first, though, before you ruin something else."

"Good luck," I muttered, kicking back my left leg. She moved her left leg instinctually, but I angled at the last second, nailing her right knee, and the contact threw her off balance, bringing both of us to the ground. We rolled around for a minute, me on top of her punching the life out of her face until she turned it around on me, grabbing my hands and using them to choke me.

"I'll admit," she said, her heavy breaths on my face, "there is one thing I've always admired about you: your survivability. The way you adapted after being thrown into the dark and kept going. But your strongest asset is now your greatest weakness." She pushed harder on me. "Your eyes adjusted. And now poor Princess Arie is scared of the light."

Something like a snarl escaped my gasping mouth and I kicked her off of me, both of us jumping back up in the same moment.

She shook her head derisively. "I know you plan on killing me, but you plan on dying here too. You have to because you're afraid if you kill me then things will get better. And you don't know how to live without something hideously wrong." She spread her arms out in mock presentation. "Welcome to the dark side, princess."

I glowered at her, spitting blood from my mouth. "You are nothing without me."

She met my eyes evenly and stepped right in my face. "You are nothing because of me."

I went to slap her, but she ducked and kneed me in the stomach right as I brought my fist down on the back of her neck. Snatching her ponytail, I snapped her head back and punched her square in the jaw. She grabbed my fist and twisted my arm the wrong way until something popped in my elbow. I landed a kick to her chest that sent her sprawling.

"You don't have anything," I scowled at her. "You don't even have your own face. Everything you have came from me!" I dropped to my knees on top of her and hit her until her nose broke. "And now you don't even have a purpose. You can't handle the fact that *you are a failure*! You're a useless monster who's already been damned." Her face was turning red underneath me. "*You are nothing*!"

Vanessa growled and lashed her fist out, connecting with my temple and I went down, my vision going blurry for a second. She punched me in my side, bruising a rib for sure, then rolled me on my stomach and bent my arm back until my shoulder dislocated, a cry of pain escaping my rattled mouth. Staggering to her feet, she stomped on my kneecap and something snapped. Then she picked me up by my shirt and slammed me over and over against the wall, my brain rattling in my head. She released me and I crumpled to the ground but only got a second's rest. Vanessa grabbed my ponytail and smashed my face against the control panel, knocking out one of my back teeth.

A mix of a whimpering and wounded gasping came out of me as blood dripped from my mouth and into my throat, my body succumbing to the pain.

Vanessa's jaw was broken. She stood over me with a crooked scowl. "It's only fitting that you'll die here. After all, this place stands as the epitome of your failure." She gestured to the still unconscious Sark. "Did you tell Sark yet about how you basically chose to stay here? How it was easier to lose your life here than put in the effort to get it back?" She stomped on me with every word and mangled shrieks escaped me. "You are weak and you lost!"

I couldn't move, crumpled in my own blood and waiting to die, horse-like sounds coming from my mouth. And here I was, yet again, lying on this floor, hopeless. I could feel myself giving up, a natural thing now. It was too much. She was too much.

I can't do this, I realized, the weight of it pulling me into the ground. *I'm going to lose.*

"Once upon a time," Vanessa spat, limping toward Sark, "there was a princess named Arie. History will only remember her because she let her entire kingdom fall. She did not get her happily ever after because the perfect Princess Arie wasn't a princess after all."

Taking every ounce of energy I had left, I tilted my head up to see the guns on the floor about two feet away from me. I tried to reach for it, but my shoulder screamed at me, making me stop after two inches. My arms were noodles. Dead noodles, slabs of flesh that wouldn't work. Groaning, I reached again, the pain nearly making me black out, but I resurfaced once my fingers clenched around the cold metal.

Vanessa was about a foot away from Sark. She stopped and turned when she heard the metal scraping against the ground, distorted laughing coming from her uneven mouth when she saw me trying to pick up the gun.

"Oh, please, princess," she scoffed. "You're gonna do the honors for me? Or do you really think you can use it on me? We're the same, Arie. You don't have the guts to shoot yourself. Just like how Sark can't lay a hand on me and Micah's finally dead."

Clenching my swollen jaw, I used everything I had left to prop myself up on my uninjured elbow, my hand shaking so hard I could barely get my finger on the trigger.

"You. Aren't. Me." Then I unleashed a stream of mutt bullets on her. She dodged the first two, but the third caught her shoulder, the fourth her stomach, fifth her head. A ripple went through her body, her knees going out one by one, then she dropped to the floor. First blood, then brilliant purple liquid gushed from her wounds, then her ears, then her mouth. She shook violently, snapping her head back and forth as a high-pitched shriek echoed past the choking on the liquid. A loud cracking sounded and the body still shook, but in a lifeless way, without the head. The thrashing had snapped her neck.

All at once the sounds stopped. Her body went still, her skin already graying and growing thin, like paper, as though it would wither away. Just like the mutts, her eyes glassed over blue, though hers were so bright that you couldn't see her irises anymore, exemplifying the empty tomb of her body. Vanessa was dead.

Tossing the empty gun to the side, I moaned as I spat out more blood and dragged myself across the room to Sark, then gently shook his shoulder.

"Sark?" I whispered, the words burning my lips and throat. "Are you okay?"

It took a few moments, but eventually he stirred. He sucked in a sharp breath of pain and cupped his hand over his bloody head, slowly sitting up. Then he opened his eyes and choked on air, his body rigid and his eyes widening in horror, his skin going paler than it already was. His gaze looked right past me to her.

"It's not me," I whispered to him. He didn't even hear me. He just stared in frozen shock, unable to catch some air, wheezing on nothing.

Finally, I grabbed his chin and turned his head so he could only see me, the blood on my hands smudging onto his cheeks. I didn't even know whose it was: mine or his or Micah's or Vanessa's. Maybe a mix of all.

"It's not me," I told him, staring into his panicked hurricane eyes. "It's not me."

Sark looked over me a few times, his body relaxing ever so slightly, then he gave me the faintest nod. His face was still too pale though and I worried about the damage from his injury. Could he even understand me?

"Get yourself out," I said, trying to make my voice stern. "Now."

As if caught in a different world, Sark gradually picked himself up and staggered out the door, giving a last unfocused glance to my defaced corpse on the ground.

Once he was gone, I turned my attention to the screens. The images were once full of life, but now they were only full of bodies. The fighting was over. Either everyone was dead or everyone was out.

I nearly screamed again as I dragged myself past Vanessa and over to the control panel. My voice broke when I pressed the button on my earpiece.

"Is anyone there?" The words were frail and broken. "Please. Please someone answer. Please."

Only silence greeted me, and my eyes filled up with the tears I didn't have the energy to cry.

"Please," I tried for the last time, my voice trembling. "Please someone answer."

A burst of static sounded and then Carl's voice came through. "Arie, are you there?"

Something like a cry escaped me. "Yes! Yes, I am."

"All right, then, can you send me the files?"

I blubbered like an idiot. "Yes, yes I can. I can do that."

Bless you, Carlton Kenton. I love you so much.

It was painful work to roll myself over to retrieve the USB device from my pocket, but I got it. My hands shook so hard that I had to try about six times to get the drive into the slot on the control panel.

"It's in," I said breathlessly, my voice pretty much gone.

"Give me a minute."

My arms gave up and collapsed underneath me, my face nose-diving into the floor. I spat out more blood and closed my eyes in a desperate attempt to ward off the agony my broken body was in.

Carl was back in a few minutes. "Okay, I got the goods. Their system's wiped. Do you still want me to blow the place?"

I used my last bit of life to press the button on my earpiece and utter the word, "Yes."

"I'll give everyone the warning. Most everyone is out anyway. They're pretty sure they got all the mutts."

Oh good. Most everyone is out anyway.

I was almost unconscious when Carl's voice jolted me back. "Uh, Arie? You know you just set the place to blow up, right? You need to get out of there."

If I'd had the energy, I would've huffed in annoyance. How many white flags would I have to wave before the universe understood that I was finished? How many times would I have to give up before the world realized that I was really tapping out? Arie Nolan was done.

Poor Carl didn't know what to do, his awkward nerves seeping into his voice as he tried to talk to me. "Um, Arie, I already sent the coding over. You have less than ten minutes. You know that, right? You probably do because you're smart. I don't need to…" He stopped for a second. "Are you actually getting out and you're just not telling me? 'Cause that's not cool."

I've done my part. I can't do anymore. I just can't.

I'd thought my eyes were closed but I could've sworn I saw my dad sitting on the ground by me. "How's my baby girl doing?"

"She's tired," I whispered, a tear falling down my cheek. "She's so tired and just wants this to be over." I had to spit out more blood. "I can't do anymore. I just can't."

It was Carl's voice that I heard next. "Arie, I've got your mom here. And Jacklynn. They keep asking when you're coming. Oh, and Sark just came in. He's going to realize you aren't here. Don't make me tell them, Arie. Please. They need you."

They need me.

I opened my eyes, but my dad wasn't there. Just a decaying Vanessa who already looked like she'd been dead for days. The part of me I'd never wanted to admit existed.

She was right: I'd become a creature of darkness.

"Arie?" Carl asked again. "Can you even hear me? You need to get out, like, now."

They need me.

I reached my hand out and began dragging myself toward the door, crying out in pain with each movement. Once I got to the doorframe, I used it to pull myself somewhat up, having to bend slightly at the waist to keep my ribs from completely burning me up from the inside. Then I staggered down the dark hallway, doing my best to ignore my protesting body that barely worked. Somewhere along the way I lost my earpiece—it must've fallen out somewhere—but I repeated the words to myself on my own.

They need me. They need me.

The farther I got, the harder it got to maneuver myself. Dead mutts were everywhere and I tried not to look too closely at the bodies in case the mutts weren't the only ones there. Debris from the earlier explosion created blockades I had to climb over or under, and I sliced my arm at least twice on broken shards of glass.

I reached the stairs and had to climb over a beam that had fallen down. It wasn't until I got closer that I saw movement underneath, pained groaning coming from a pinned figure.

I didn't think I had the energy to get us both out—or myself, really—and was about to lie down and bag the whole 'leaving for safety' operation when I saw who it was underneath the beam. Brennan.

"Arie?" he muttered in pain when he saw me. "Is that you?"

I didn't waste my energy answering. Instead, I kneeled down and began digging him out.

Brennan snatched my wrist and looked under my sleeve—checking for the scars, I realized, to confirm it was me. Then he shook his head, his expression contorted with pain and resolution. "No, Arie, just leave. They've given the bomb warning. Get yourself out."

"You have a baby," I said, letting my words be the fuel for my actions. "It needs you." I dug faster. "They need us. They need us."

Finally, it got to the point where he could wriggle himself out. We supported each other, tripping over our own feet, as we dragged the other up the stairs.

They need us.

The upstairs was in even worse shape, as it didn't have the fortifications that the basement did. Sunlight poked in from breaks in the roof, guiding our footsteps back out to the world, away from the black hole we were in.

Then we were outside. The sun stung my eyes as we went as fast as we could away from the building that would blow any second. Faster. Farther. I could see the warehouse, the wall facing us rolled open to show the collection of bruised and bloody kids tending to each other inside. There were way more of them than Vanessa had made me guess.

They need us.

The first bomb went off the second our feet hit the warehouse flooring. The earth shook slightly underneath us, and it was enough to knock both Brennan and I off our fragile balances to the ground. A collective stillness went through the warehouse as we all watched six other bombs bring the dark building down on top of itself, burying Vanessa and Micah and countless others inside.

Lucy found us first. With tears flowing down her flushed cheeks, she collapsed into Brennan's lap and planted a giant kiss on his lips before hugging his head tight to her chest, mumbling something to him as she cried.

Ellen bombarded me, dropping to her knees next to me and wrapping her arms around my neck, crying into my shoulder without words. Peter pulled us up, a huge bandage on his head, and both he and Alaina surprised me by giving me giant hugs, Alaina's only half because of the sling that held her right arm.

I hung onto Ellen as we searched the crowd. It was only a few moments before I heard my name being shouted in the distance. Jacklynn ran up and threw her arms around my waist, then Ellen's, as my mom pulled me to her chest.

"Oh, baby," she whispered, dampening my face with her tears. Then she stepped back to look over me, her expression confirming my thought that I looked absolutely awful. She just cried harder and hugged me tighter. "I'm so glad you're alive. It's over now. It's all over."

It's all over. That thought brought a hint of feeling back to my numb fingertips. *It's all over.*

The crowd moved slightly, exposing a desperate Carl talking to a heavily bandaged and agitated Sark. Carl and I locked eyes, and he sighed in relief, then pointed to me. Sark turned, his eyes taking a moment to find me, then he started running as fast as the crowd would let him. I took a few shaky steps forward, giving a nod of appreciation to Carl as he saluted me, before Sark practically bulldozed over me. He picked me up in a crushing hug that made it difficult to breathe, but even with the pain I couldn't get myself to stop him.

It's all over now.

I clutched the collar of his shirt in my fists, afraid if he let me go then my bones would turn to dust and I'd crumble into nothing. He held my trembling body as though the wind would blow me away forever. My mom spread her arms around both of us, Jacklynn hanging on to both Ellen and me as Ellen took my arm and rested her head on my shoulder. And for those few seconds we were all attached to each other, I felt as whole as I ever could be again.

We didn't separate until Agent LeBlanc came up to talk to me. His eyes were filled with compassion as he extended a sheet of paper to me.

"Arie Nolan?" he asked, his voice sincere.

My mom, Ellen and Jacklynn backed off of me, but Sark barely gave me enough slack to face the man. I looked him up and down but saw no immediate threats from him. I nodded.

"Sorry to do this to you," he said, "but this is the list of everyone who didn't check back in. You were the last one out—is there anyone we missed?"

A lump formed in my throat as I glanced down through the list of about thirty names, not sure whether to be happy there were so few or devastated there were so many. My heart sank when I saw Cameron's name on the list.

I had to spit out more blood onto the floor before I could talk again, though my voice was barely audible. "There's someone else." Tears stung my eyes again and I looked at the ceiling until they went away. "You probably don't have any record of him. His name was Micah. And he was a person."

A soft gasp came from Brennan, who was standing about a foot away with his arm around Lucy, sad eyes on me. "No. Really?"

I nodded and had to look at the ceiling again.

"Thank you," I heard Agent LeBlanc say. "We'll make sure he's recognized."

"Thank you," I said as he walked away.

My bad knee finally gave out, but Sark caught me before I fell. I rested my head against him and closed my eyes, every part of me aching in some form.

Your name is Arie Nolan and it's all over. Your name is Arie Nolan and it's all over.

A grumble was going through the crowd, though I didn't feel the need to pay attention to it until it reached us. I cracked my eyes open to see several cars driving up. I shuddered in spite of myself when I saw a glimpse of Cyrus being put in the backseat of one—someone must've found him and dragged him out—and Sark tightened his already tight grip on me.

I heard shouting, but it took a moment for me to make out the words.

"Where is she?"

Sark heard it in the same moment, both of us knowing who the random stranger was asking for. Really, who else would it be?

"Where is she?" The angry voice was getting louder and the crowd parted as they were shoved aside. Sark jerked me behind him, hanging onto my wrist, while my mom, Ellen, Peter, Brennan, Lucy and Alaina stood with Sark, in front of me. I peeked over Sark's shoulder to see a tall man with dark hair come through the crowd, wearing a navy blue suit that looked like it could pay for the college tuition I never needed.

"Where is she?" Tall Stranger shouted again, his dark blue eyes going down the line of my self-imposed protectors.

Because of everyone's attention being on Tall Stranger, I was the only one who noticed the tactical team surround us from behind, each armed with a nice big gun. Hands shaking, I raised them in the air, breaking out of Sark's hold, and stepped in between Sark and my mom, ignoring their quiet protests, placing myself in front of Tall Stranger.

"Arie Nolan," Tall Stranger announced with professional authority. "You're under arrest."

8

Both Sark and Peter stepped forward with menace, as if to beat the tar out of Tall Stranger, but then they noticed the tactical team closing in on us—on me—and stopped. My head felt light and airy and buzzy as one of the tactical team members walked slowly forward and handcuffed me.

"You can't just take her," Sark growled.

Tall Stranger glared at him. "I've got an old, crippled scientist, a mixed-up poison among the public, and a body count rising above five hundred—all of which are linked to this face." He pointed a long finger at me. "Until we come to a true understanding of what has happened, she's in my custody."

My stomach threatened to throw up everywhere and I had to will it to stay down. The guard moved to take me away when three wonderfully familiar faces stopped him in his tracks.

"She's in our custody," Keaton said, his long trench coat blowing slightly behind him.

"And who are you?" Tall Stranger asked in annoyance.

Keaton met his stare evenly. "Terrance Keaton, Director of OCI." He gestured to the two standing behind him. "These are my associates Lindsey Carter and Brody Jaynes. Nolan has been our case for years now. You have no jurisdiction."

Tall Stranger shook his head. "Tell that to the Senator. This is borderline terrorism and no longer concerns you or your little team." His threatening eyes glanced around the crowd, as if in warning. "I should have all of these infected monstrosities locked up, and I will, once I can get it cleared." He glared at Keaton again. "I'm here to protect lives, Director Keaton. I suggest you do the same."

The guard proceeded to pretty much drag me— my legs weren't working well—through the group of infecteds and agents and military personnel, the fury rolling off of them in waves, to one of the cars. Lindsey tried to stop him, but he pushed her out of the way and shoved me in the backseat. I stared at the seat in front of me and heard muffled arguing through the car door as Lindsey and Keaton fought over me with Tall Stranger.

After a few minutes, Brody walked around to the other side of the car and slid in the backseat with me. Tall Stranger's voice got louder but he didn't do anything, so I guess that was part of the deal.

"Don't worry, kid," Brody muttered to me. "We'll get you out. Somethin's not right here."

I had to look at the ceiling of the car to keep the film of tears inside my eyes. Tall Stranger would not get my tears.

"They think I did it," I stated, my voice soft and cracked.

Brody sighed. "Yeah. Yeah, they do."

But I didn't.

I could've sworn I heard Vanessa's voice echoing in my head. *Sure, princess. Keep telling yourself that.*

Tall Stranger got in the passenger seat, a guard sat behind the wheel, and I purposely avoided looking out the window as we drove away.

I was blindfolded, driven and dragged in darkness until I was handcuffed to a chair in a small square room. Brody insisted I see a doctor before questioning and his request was finally answered: a woman in scrubs came to patch me up. I didn't speak or move—I barely blinked—until another woman in a black pantsuit came in and sat on a chair in front of me. She told Brody, who was leaning against the wall on my right, to leave, but he refused, and finally she just started the show with him there.

"My name is Agent Grant," she told me, her tone sharp and clipped. "Answer my questions honestly and this will go much smoother. Is your name Arie Nolan?"

I nodded but she cut me off mid-head movement.

"Answer me," she barked, making me jump.

"Yes," I said quietly.

"You are the daughter of Kurt and Candace Nolan?"

"Yes."

"You are, as I understand, the coined phrase of 'infected'?"

"Yes."

Her questions got progressively harder, and I had to branch out from one-word answers. Within the first five minutes, I understood that she was not someone on my team.

"So why did you do it?" she asked, her penetrating hazel eyes glaring into my soul.

I braced myself, knowing I'd pretty much already lost. "There were two of us. It was her, not me."

Grant laughed once. "If I had a dime for every time I heard that one. You realize that your defense is utterly laughable, if not completely unbelievable?"

"I know what it sounds like, but that's what happened. She wanted it this way."

"Uh huh." Grant tapped her pen against her chin. "*She* wanted it this way or *you* did?"

I shook my head. "Why would I want to risk my friends' lives like that?"

"I don't know." She leaned forward slightly. "The monsters like you have to explain that part to me."

She stayed for eons, and her presence drained me and agitated me at the same time, and though she was frustrating and downright mean, I couldn't bring myself to hate her. She was just doing her job, just trying to do what was right. I guess prosecuting me until I went insane was her version of what was 'right.'

I didn't do it. I didn't make an army of monsters and murder hundreds of people. Vanessa did. But the more I talked to Agent Grant, the more I wondered if I had actually made Vanessa up.

Maybe I am crazy. And with that, the urge to throw up my guts until I died came back.

Eventually—mercifully—Grant left. I stared at the floor for a very long time, questioning everything I'd ever known about myself, my life and the way the world worked.

"I didn't do it," I blurted, desperation leaking into my voice. "I didn't."

Brody, now sitting on the floor, blinked in surprise at my break of silence, leaning forward to rest his elbows on his knees. "They're trying to get you to admit you did. Nail a confession. Interrogation one-oh-one."

I glanced at him. "But I didn't."

He looked at me a moment before nodding. "Yeah. You didn't."

"You know that, right? I'm not making this up."

He nodded. "Yeah, I know."

But Brody's reassurances weren't quite enough.

Your name is Arie Nolan and you didn't do it. Your name is Arie Nolan and you didn't do it.

We waited for another eternity in silence before Agent Grant came back with three armed escorts. More handcuffs, more blindfolds, more driving. I was given my sight again once we were in a new room. This was one was white with just one chair. Brody leaned against the wall next to me as we waited some more.

"It's gonna be a hearing," he told me. "Just try to hold your ground, okay?"

I nodded and stared at my white sneakers that were stained with dirt and blood.

"What's going to happen to me?" I asked my gross shoes.

Brody sighed. "I don't know, kid."

Without warning, the door burst open and one of the escorts came in, grabbing me roughly by the shoulder and pulling me down the hallway.

"Hey!" Brody shouted from behind me. "She's not supposed to go in yet."

The escort ignored him, herding Brody and me through thick wood double doors and into chaos.

It was bright. It took me a few moments to get my bearings. The room was huge. A large circular table stood elevated on one side, official looking people sitting around it, including Tall Stranger. The other side had rows of benches that were all full as well. All the attention in the room was focused on a sobbing woman standing in front of the circular table and talking to those sitting there. I stopped when I saw her.

The double doors shut loudly behind me and everyone glanced over to see who the addition was, including the sobbing woman. Instantly, her face contorted with hatred and she pointed at me.

"That's her!" she screamed. "She did it!" The woman tried to charge at me, but two security guards grabbed her and dragged her out of the room. "You killed my husband! You killed him!" she shrieked right before the doors closed on her.

I was frozen in horrified shock, my mouth hanging open and eyes stinging. The escort had to push me, forcing me forward, then sat me down in an empty chair at the circle table and attached my handcuffs to it. Despite the protests of the escort, Brody stood right behind me.

My head was spinning as I watched my hands shake in their shackles. The woman's shrieks played over and over in my ears, nearly drowning out Tall Stranger's voice.

"If that isn't enough evidence, I don't know what is," he said. "I suggest we skip the lies she has to say and move right on to a vote for the death penalty."

I snapped my head up and a commotion of shouting erupted from the benches. I glanced over to find the crowd mostly consisted of people I knew: a bunch of people who stormed the fortress with Sark, Mom, Ellen, Lindsey, Peter, Alaina, Brennan and Lucy on the front row.

Tall Stranger ignored them. "The rest of her infected cohorts should be put in prison at the very least, until we can find out what threat they pose."

A woman at the circle table said, "You don't have the power to do that, Dr. Hammond."

Another man, who seemed to be at the head of the circle somehow, nodded. "Slow down there, Ben. There's more evidence to look at. We need to understand what's happened."

"You think she'll tell that to you?" Hammond asked. He went on to describe essentially how everything was my fault and I deserved the judgment he was trying to get. But I wasn't listening. I was focused on his name.

Benjamin Hammond. Dr. Hammond. Maybe I was just crazy and desperate, but I could've sworn that sounded familiar.

I glanced up at Brody until he met my gaze.

"Do you know him?" he asked under his breath.

I gave the smallest nod. Brody snuck his phone out of his pocket and used one hand to text 'Dr. Ben Hammond?' to Lindsey.

I looked to my crowd of support, mouthing the name with creased eyebrows. Peter shrugged and Lindsey shook her head. Sark thought for a moment but couldn't come up with anything. But Ellen and Mom both had a pinched up look on their faces, like they were concentrating. They recognized it too.

Why would Ellen and Mom recognize the same name?

Someone leaned forward from the bench behind and tapped Ellen on the shoulder—I got a brief glimpse of Zoe—and they had a small exchange that made Ellen's greyish blue eyes go wide. That's when I remembered a night in the Compound when I'd fallen asleep on the kitchen floor after a long evening of working a fundraiser that Ellen was in charge of. A fundraiser for a Dr. Hammond.

There's no way I could've heard Mom's gasp through the chaos but somehow I did. We locked eyes in the same moment I realized how I really knew this man. Memories of scales and popsicle sticks and character stickers from my past life, pre-infection days, came surging up as the last real question I had was answered.

"It was you," I whispered, the rage in my voice slowly raising my volume and cutting Hammond's speech off. "It was you. You told him."

Hammond met my eyes and I could see the truth in them. I was right. Cyrus would only throw a fundraiser for someone important, like Dr. Hammond, who ran one of the most successful national medical offices in the country—who had a branch not far from my home in Saratoga Springs, New York. The office that I went to for regular checkups since we moved there when I was twelve.

I imagined my dad home one day, getting a call from my doctor's office, maybe even from head Hammond himself, informing him that something was very wrong with his daughter. My dad would be self-righteous on the phone, but would secretly be stricken with worry and curiosity, sitting down to the computer to research, eyes wide, slowly getting sucked into the world that would overtake his life.

"You told him!" I shouted, standing up from my chair and Brody held me back despite the handcuffs. "Did you know he's dead now? His guilt killed him!"

"Please calm down, Miss Nolan," the man at the head of the circle said, and I finally saw a nameplate that told me he was Senator Whyme. Brody pushed on me until I sat back down in my chair, fuming. "Now will you explain this to me?"

I was too furious to find words for a moment, trying to melt Hammond with the laser vision I now wished I had.

Finally, I forced an explanation through my teeth. "Dr. Hammond is a doctor."

Senator Whyme waited for a moment, unsure of what I meant. "Yes, that's correct. One of the most successful in the nation. Not to mention an attorney. Isn't that right, Ben?"

For once, Ben Hammond didn't agree with his success. He just glared daggers at me as I continued.

"He's my doctor. He's thousands of people's doctor. So successful but he didn't earn that success. He bought it. From Cyrus."

"Cyrus being the crippled man in our custody now?" a woman at the table asked.

I nodded. "Cyrus struck a deal with Hammond—he would fund whatever Hammond wanted so long as Hammond provided Cyrus with the information he needed: medical records." My voice got louder again. "That's how he finds kids all over the country with the biology needed to create his infected slaves. That's how Cyrus knew I was the key. How he knew where I was and how to contact me, how to control my life. Hammond approached my dad, which is how he got involved in the first place, and—"

"Stop this absurdity now!" Hammond shouted. "Sir, I will tolerate an honest questioning of a monster like her, but I will not stand here and listen to her lie about my personal integrity." He pointed to me. "Can't you see what she's doing? She's manipulating the situation to save her own skin. She *murdered* over five hundred—"

"Will you just shut up?" I yelled, Brody's hand on my shoulder the only thing keeping me in my seat. "Stop turning this on me! I didn't do it. You're the only monster here." I looked at the senator. "He's trying to hurry and get me killed before I can expose him."

Hammond stood and leaned forward from his spot at the table across from me. "It's your word against mine, Nolan, and I think you of all people know our organization isn't something you can go up against."

I decided to call his bluff—all the practice Cyrus gave me pretending to be fearless was actually paying off. "No, I think Cyrus must be in a world of hurt if his last line of defense is someone I might recognize. I'll take my chances."

The circle table was shocked into silence, all except the senator, who was rubbing the side of his head. "Are you accusing a government officer of treason, Miss Nolan?"

I actually laughed once. "It wouldn't be the first time. Take a closer look at his businesses and banking. You'll find it."

"You aren't really going to believe her, are you sir?" Hammond asked in disbelief. "This is the prime example of how dangerous she is—she's just going to cause more destruction the longer we let her breathe.”

I ignored Hammond, trying to strike a chord of humanity in the senator, who seemed genuinely concerned about finding the truth. “Sir, I don’t know how far Hammond’s reach goes or what damage he’s done. All I can tell you is that if it weren’t for him and Cyrus, I’d be home in New York right now, uninfected, going to college, living with my not dead dad and not dead brother.” I gestured to the rows of benches to my right. “And I can direct you to ninety other kids who have the same story. It’s not us, sir. I don’t know what you’ve heard about infecteds, but I think you know I’m telling the truth.”

The senator sighed and looked at Hammond. “Ben, you wouldn’t mind an investigation of your financials, would you? Surely you have nothing to hide.”

Hammond clenched his square jaw so hard I thought the vein in his forehead would pop. “Of course, sir.”

“Good. While the investigation is under way, you will stay in our custody. Understood?”

Hammond’s eyes widened. “But sir—”

He was cut off by the security that surrounded him and marched him out of the room. The senator met my eyes and he let out a long breath.

“As I was planning on bringing up before he interrupted, I believe you, Miss Nolan. Unlike some associates of mine, I did my homework before showing up today. I’ve read through research, spoken to a few other infecteds and your friend gave me a look at Cyrus’ notes. I believe there were two of you, however we need proof that I will work to get. Don't make me regret that belief."

I breathed a silent sigh of relief, but it was halfhearted. I knew where we were headed. I knew since the moment Hammond put me in handcuffs.

"That being said," the senator went on, "your life isn't in the clear just yet. If the destruction and death caused was largely out of your control, how can we be sure that doesn't happen again?"

A moment of understanding passed between us. The senator had done his homework.

"You know about reversal?" I asked him.

He nodded. "Does it work?"

"Cyrus once told me it did, but I don't know for sure."

"I don't understand," a man in military uniform said. "Reverse the so-called infection? How is that different from execution?"

"You can't kill me before reversal," I explained. "I don't know what part of me allowed for the key to become real, I don't know if it's still active in me or if it will die with me, but I really can't take that chance. If someone can just dig up my corpse and still get the power of the key…"

Military Man nodded. "I see your point."

"So you can be the test," the woman added. "Attempt the reversal process on you—the most severe infection case, as I understand it—then make any needed adjustments to reverse the rest of them, eradicating the infection problem for good."

Another man with eyes only half open nodded, juggling his four chins. "That makes sense, as it's a fifty-fifty shot: either the process kills her or she wakes up with no power to harm anyone. The trial can continue then if it needs to."

The senator debated for a moment and the whole room was reduced to complete silence. Anticipation. I waited, sweat beading on the back of my neck, absolutely terrified of both answers.

"All right," he finally said. "Keep the press out of this. Miss Nolan will undergo the reversal process as we continue to review the case, including Dr. Ben Hammond and his associates. Should she return, the investigation of her supposed actions will resume with her full cooperation. Effective immediately."

Immediately? I didn't know what I expected, but nothing that fast. I was yanked out of that room faster than I could blink, put in a car, then on a plane, flying to an uncertain future.

9

I ended up in yet another room, this one white with two chairs and absolutely no clues as to where I was. They didn't keep the handcuffs on me, but they made sure I knew there were six armed guards standing outside the room, waiting for me to do something wrong.

Brody stayed with me through everything and sat in the other chair for a while. Several times I almost told him to just go but couldn't bring myself to say the words. Part of me wanted him to leave so I could have my last mental breakdown,

The more rational part of me kept him there so I would force myself to keep it together.

We sat in silence for hours before the door opened. Keaton walked in, carrying a duffle bag on his shoulder, and shut the door behind him. We stared at each other for a moment, then he reached into his pocket and handed me a flash drive.

"I read it," he told me. I realized it was the story of my life I'd given him before I fled the hospital to go after Alexis. "It's good. You should finish it."

I looked at the flash drive before taking it from him. He put the bag down on the floor next to my chair, then gave me a nod.

Brody stood up. "Good luck, kid. I hope it goes okay." And with that, they both walked out the door.

After a few seconds of looking at nothing, I picked up the bag Keaton left and opened it to find a silver laptop. Of course, I didn't have internet—can't have the monster Arie leading a cyber-attack—but I didn't need it. I just needed to type.

I spent the next chunk of eternity writing down the rest of my story, from leaving the hospital, going to the Compound with Cyrus and everything that happened there, Hadley, my dad, finally ending Vanessa, to Hammond and the people who tried to make me doubt my own sanity. Writing it all down gave me some peace, solidified it somehow. Because if I could read it back to myself, it came to life, and maybe I wasn't crazy after all. I had it in writing. This really happened to me. This was my story.

My name is Arie Nolan and I am not crazy. My name is Arie Nolan and this is my story.

By the end, I was crying, though I'd probably been crying the whole time. I forgot how much had happened, and how much I would miss, until I read back through it all.

And now they're going to reverse me, I typed through blurry eyes. *And it might kill me. For real this time. I don't know what's going to happen to me.* I couldn't think of a good ending for that, so I just left it.

A lady with shocking white-blonde hair came in and finally gave me some answers: I was in a medical research facility. I'd been here for three days while the brightest minds available had gone over Cyrus' reversal notes with the government's big guys breathing down their necks. The process was scheduled for tomorrow.

She made me shower for sanitation reasons, which only reminded me of how much pain my body was in, then she brought me back to my room and told me I'd been cleared to have one person wait with me until reversal. Who did I want?

The answer slipped through my mouth before I really thought about it, which only somewhat surprised me. Sometimes a girl just needed her mom.

I was sick of the chair, so we sat on the floor, me practically in her lap, and I closed my eyes while she brushed my wet hair with her fingers. Sometimes we talked. Sometimes we didn't. I tried to focus on her presence rather than the destructive butterflies in my stomach or my overactive imagination, part of me stewing. This was cruel.

Fine, perform a crazy medical experiment on me, whatever. But make me sit and wait forever as I imagine just how awful it will be? That was just cruel.

"What was it like?" she asked after a while, swatting my hand away from my mouth so I'd stop biting on my nails. "When you went into that building to stop Vanessa?"

I shrugged, not wanting to think about it. "It wasn't the best time of my life."

A stroke of fingers through my hair. Then another. Again. "They all love you, you know."

"I got pretty lucky that way." I thought for a moment. "If Jacklynn doesn't end up having parents, will you take her?"

"Of course I will. I'll need…" she trailed off, her voice getting quiet, and I knew what she almost said.

I'll need a daughter after you're gone.

"You can help me with her," she finally said. "She loves you."

"She used to be scared of me."

"Clearly not anymore." Some more hair brushing. "You know, I never heard your side of the story. With Sark. He told me you weren't always besties."

I laughed once but it was empty. "No, we hated each other."

"What changed?"

Everything changed.

"I guess…I see him as two different people. Mr. Sark was an awful monster of a human being. But Sark is…one of the best people I've ever known. I just had to find him."

"So?" Her voice turned slightly teasing. "Do you like him?"

I rolled my eyes. "Oh, Mom."

"You're right, you don't have to answer. It's obvious you two are crazy about each other."

Obvious, huh? I thought back over the months of our short and senseless relationship, a lot of words coming to mind but 'obvious' wasn't one of them.

I decided I only had a little bit to live and knew Mom would absolutely love a boy talk session—something small that could make us feel more like a regular mother and daughter.

"He told me he loved me," I said. "Right before we went in to stop Vanessa."

She started braiding my hair. "Well, now, you don't sound very excited about it."

"No, it's just…" I thought for a moment. "I'm not sure what he means."

She stifled a laugh. "Um, sweetheart, it probably means he loves you."

"Well, he didn't…act like it. Not that it's his fault or anything, it's just…" I counted on my fingers. "The first night, he kisses me. I'm eventually ecstatic and things are great for a few weeks. Then Vanessa comes and I fall off the face of the Earth. He makes out with her because he thinks I'm gone. I come back but I'm dysfunctional and avoid human life, but when I need him later, he comes right back to me. And then all of a sudden he's ignoring me and won't talk to me up until we go on a death mission, then he tells me he loves me." I sighed. "Can you see why I'm confused?"

She was thoughtful. "Yes. Yes, I can. But I don't think you're looking at the whole situation."

"The whole situation is that I don't think he really loves me."

"Why would you say that?" she asked in surprise.

"Because it just…" I went back to biting my nails. "It just doesn't make sense."

Mom tapped me on the forehead, pushing my hand from my mouth again. "It makes a lot of sense, actually. Maybe he's just got commitment issues."

I shook my head. "I don't think so. He full-on married Erika and didn't seem to have problems with that."

"Maybe that's the point: he went into a serious relationship too fast without thinking and then he lost her."

I turned my head to look at her, wondering where she got that kind of sensitive information. "He talks to you?"

She smiled. "He misses his mom and loves me because I'm yours. And for the record, I absolutely adore him. Permission granted."

I turned my head back around so she didn't see my smile.

"The real question is what you think of him," she went on, fishing for a confession as she let the finished braid fall against my back. "Because I already know what he thinks of you."

I folded my arms across my chest, the subject of my favorite person in the world still not quite enough to thaw out my cynicism. "It's too dangerous to love people."

She laughed—not the reaction I was hoping for. "Baby, you sure love a lot of people for someone who thinks that way."

I sighed, the acid butterflies in my stomach flaring up. "Yeah, I know."

It wasn't long after that the lady came back in and told me to say my last goodbyes. Mom hugged me forever, trying to hide her tears, but I could feel her body trembling and hear her muffled sniffles. Then she pulled away to look me in the eyes.

"Is there anything you want me to tell them?" she asked, her voice breaking.

That question sent my brain into a frenzy. Because there were only a million things I wanted to tell them—tell Jacklynn yet again that Hadley's death wasn't her fault and she'll find a friend again, tell Peter I'd somehow learned to love him despite our rocky first start, tell Brennan and Lucy that they'd be the best parents the world would ever see, tell Alaina I was so sorry I let our friendship die once it got hard, tell Ellen I didn't know how to thank her for accepting me and loving me in a way I never thought I could be. And Sark? I could fill books with how much I wanted to tell him, ask him, thank him.

Yes, there were only a million things I wanted her to tell them. But when she asked, my eyes filled with tears and I couldn't get past, "Tell them...tell them that I...that..."

Mom wiped the water from her eyes and gave me another hug. "I will, baby. I will." She took a shaky breath. "I love you so much. I always have."

"I know. I love you too." Then because this might be the last time for me to say cheesy things,

I added, "You really are the best mom. You just got the worst luck in kids."

She laughed once. "Arie, I wouldn't trade you for anything."

The lady came back with another official woman who took Mom away. My hands and feet tingled as I followed the lady—and the six guards followed me—down a short white hallway and into an operating room, making sure to keep my head down so I didn't see anything that would make me throw up. Still, the familiar feeling was almost too much to bear. I stood next to the table, flashes of horrible memories searing my mind.

No, you can't do this, I'd begged. *Please, you don't know what you're doing.*

Gritting my teeth, I forced myself to lie down on the table. The ceiling stared back at me, a blank canvas for the images I'd spend the rest of my short life trying to forget.

Please, don't do this, please! You don't understand. You can't take her out, please.

Then a familiar face popped into my line of vision. Kayla. They must've taken my recommendation to have her on the team. Her green eyes were teary behind her glasses as she looked at me.

I made sure my voice was clear to keep from adding to her conscience. "Do it for them, okay?"

She nodded then shook my hand—probably as close to physical contact as I'd ever seen her have with anyone. "It's been an honor to know you, Arie."

Then a mask was put over my face and I fought the urge to run.

Help! I'd screamed at the top of my lungs. *Somebody, please stop him! Help! Please, don't, please.*

Only this time I wasn't strapped down. This time the process would be a good thing, regardless of what happened to me.

She will bring me perfection, he'd told me, not realizing how much ignorance he was drowning in. *She will bring peace.*

She'll bring death. She's not going to listen to you. She will hurt everyone, just like she hurt me.

My vision started to get hazy on the edges the more I breathed. Each breath I thought of an infected. A person I knew who would get their life back. They wouldn't have to be infected anymore.

Unfortunately, you will not survive the process, he'd said, *but it will be an honorable death. One to be proud of. That's much more than most people can say.*

I struggled to be still on the table, to keep my tears inside.

No.

No, please.

Please don't.

Please make it stop.

A thought occurred to me then, sending a flash of raging panic through my veins. I wasn't going to be infected anymore. I wasn't going to be the key. Not that I had ever enjoyed being the key, but it was such a part of my identity now. Arie Nolan, the key to the formula. For years, that had been my name, who I was. That's all I knew how to be. What if I *did* wake up somehow? Who would I be? How would I know how to live?

I didn't have time to work through an answer for that. I took one last look at the white ceiling, the last image of life, before the darkness swallowed me, pulling me deep under.

10

I couldn't remember anything.

That made me panic. I tried to open my eyes. They wouldn't. Just darkness. So much darkness.

I listened. I heard beeping. Loud beeping. Constant. A stark contrast from my labored and panicked gasping. Those were the only sounds.

I stretched my body, feeling my hands against something underneath me. Something soft. Squishy but hard. What was it?

A bed, I remembered. *It's called a bed.* I felt my hands around more, around the bed.

Where am I?

A new sound penetrated the quiet. Then again. I knew that sound.

The door. Someone came inside.

Footsteps sounded, quick and purposeful, tapping against a hard surface below me.

"Arie?" a voice asked me. "Are you awake?" A hand grabbed my arm, the hold firm but gentle. "It's okay. It's Dr. Bran. Do you remember?"

Oh. Now I did. My name was Arie Nolan. I was a patient of Dr. Bran's. Dr. Bran was nice. I could trust him.

I slumped in tired resignation and nodded, then the hold on my arm disappeared. My hand felt along the mattress until I found the railing on the side of my hospital bed. I tapped my fingers against it six times.

"It's been twenty-one days," Dr. Bran answered, adhering to the tapping code we made up so I could communicate with him. "It's your three-week anniversary. Too bad we haven't mastered solid foods yet or I'd get you a cake."

Three-week anniversary. Three weeks ago I woke up from the near two-month coma reversal had put me in—that was probably one of the scariest experiences of my life. I couldn't see, hear, speak, or move, and I couldn't remember anything, not even my own name or how I'd gotten there.

Finally, the doctors put me out again because I was completely freaking out and they had no way of communicating with me. When they brought me out of it the next day, I had regained spotty hearing and sensations. Slowly, it got better as I remembered more and more: about me or about the world in general. I remembered things like I used to be infected or the sky was blue or that I had two hands. Dr. Bran worked with me and now I had full movement of my upper body—though the movement was weak—could mostly hear again, and had an iffy memory, but I continued to remain blind and speechless.

"Let's go through the routine, okay?"

I wrinkled my nose, jostling my oxygen tube. I hated the routine. But Dr. Bran was a wonderfully nice man and I always found myself doing what he asked. We had an understanding with each other, even though I'd never actually seen him, that gave us an unspoken connection. I liked him. I relied on him. And he never let me down even though he asked me to do ridiculous and painful things in the name of my health.

I kept my jaw clenched in case I winced, then raised my arm in the direction of what I thought would be the…the hard surface. The…what was it called?

Dr. Bran clicked his tongue once in approval and I did the other arm, my brain working overdrive on getting around the wall it had built in front of itself.

What the heck is that stupid thing called?

I turned my head side to side, then open and closed my mouth.

"Good job," Dr. Bran said, his usual positive and encouraging voice a comfort to me. "Let's sit up now."

I dragged myself to a sitting position, feeling the ghost of his hand on my back, ready to offer help if I needed it. I felt dizzy and almost fell backwards but didn't.

It's a ceiling. I relaxed as the burst of insight came to me, knocking down the barrier in my mind. *It's called a ceiling.*

A circle of cold metal pressed itself against my chest, moving the stiff fabric of my hospital gown slightly. I stayed still while he listened.

"Heart's going a little fast," Dr. Bran told me after a moment. "Can we work on bringing it down?"

I nodded but I didn't have much hope. My heart was always pumping way too fast, as if in overdrive, making my breathing short and gasping. It made me even more tired, but I couldn't take in more air. If I tried to take a deep breath, my chest would constrict inside of me like my lungs just couldn't hold that much oxygen.

Focusing, I attempted to slow down my breathing, but it just had the opposite effect—my lungs were sucked dry and I found myself choking, my body screaming for oxygen. My hand found Dr. Bran's holding the stethoscope and I clamped down on it in response to the fiery pain.

My bed shifted underneath me, then Dr. Bran pressed my oxygen mask against my face. Out of energy, I slumped forward, and he quickly sat next to me on my bed so he could put his arm around my body for support, keeping me from falling and hitting my head. That had happened a few times.

"It's okay," he told me. "You're okay. You're just fine. Just wait a minute and it'll come back."

It did. I sucked in the processed air over and over again, focusing on his voice and my heart that was almost pounding through my chest. Slowly the fire was put to rest, and I gained a handle on a more natural breathing pattern. It still wasn't normal, but it was better. I unclamped my hand on his and held the oxygen mask on my own.

"Great job, Arie," Dr. Bran complimented. "That was really fast. You're getting better. Great job."

He waited until I sat up on my own again before standing up, and I heard his stylus tapping against the tablet he always bragged to me about. Apparently, it was one of the best inventions ever and he couldn't wait for me to see it. Dr. Bran was always very positive without being unrealistic—a talent I admired—and was sure I'd get my sight back eventually. It was a good thing, I guess, positivity came so naturally to him because he had to supply it for the both of us.

I tapped my fingers against the rail three times. A step sounded, then Dr. Bran slid his hand in mine, face up so I could trace letters on his palm with my pointer finger. Letting the oxygen mask fall for a moment, I wrote *B-U-R-N*.

There was always a half second reaction time as he pieced together what I'd said. Then his hand was gone. "Show me where."

I pressed my fingers softly against my left temple, right in the corner of my eye. He moved my hand and replaced it with his own practiced fingers, gently probing different parts of my head where the burning feeling was coming from.

"Give me a number."

I was planning on lowballing the pain scale, but then a new burst of the burning came. I held up six fingers.

"Six? How long have you been feeling this burning?"

Thinking for a moment, I reached out my pointer finger until he put his hand in my other one. I wrote *W-O-K-E-U-P*.

"Since you woke up, huh?" His fingers left my face. "And it's a new feeling?"

I nodded and it made the burning worse. I held up seven fingers.

"Hmm. There aren't any visual signs. I could have Raoul come take a look at it."

I made a face. Dr. Bran was one of seven people I'd had contact with since waking up, all of them nice doctors or government people who didn't like me. They quickly found Dr. Bran was the only doctor I'd respond to. I tried to pretend like I was just too tired for them or didn't care, but really I was absolutely terrified of everyone except him. I mean, I couldn't even *see* them, let alone walk away from them. I was completely at their mercy. And I wasn't okay with that.

My behavior made it difficult, I knew, but Dr. Bran never complained. He understood, at least on some level. He made it a point to be in the room during my interviews and interrogations, and always met with the other scientists in a different room and would tell me all about it when he came back. Since none of them had ever had a patient like me, nobody knew how to explain the weird ways my body responded or the best ways to treat me. They just had to make it up as they went. I tried not to think about that too hard.

Dr. Bran laughed, a throaty sound. "You mean you don't want visitors? What a surprise." I felt him lean closer. "From my preliminary findings, I would guess you have a case of the classic zombie infection. I'm sorry but there's just nothing I can do."

I had to reach out and find his shoulder, then I pushed it, the tiniest of grins on my face. That was why we got along so well. Unlike some of his coworkers who had degrees in seriousness and killing the joy, Dr. Bran was a dorky geek. When I first decided to be his friend, he insisted on playing a get-to-know-you game where we asked each other anything. The first question he'd asked was if I'd ever been exposed to large amounts of gamma radiation or had any rage problems. That's when I decided that maybe this could work.

"Well, what are you going to do about it?" a hard male voice asked, coming from my right.

I jumped at the sound, instantly shying away from it. The door was to my left. I knew that. Somebody was on the other side of my bed and I didn't notice.

I strained my eyes, but only saw nothing. A slight whimper escaped from behind my teeth as I tried to scramble away from the unknown without getting too tangled in my thousands of cords.

How could he not tell me?

"Whoa, Arie, it's okay," Dr. Bran said, trying to mask his disapproval, stepping closer so my hand could find his arm and grip it tight. "I'm sorry, I should've told you there are others in here.

But it's okay. You're not in any danger." He cleared his throat. "I just need you to listen for a moment, all right?"

Listen? Listen to what?

The male voice spoke again, much softer this time, as if afraid it would break me. "Arie? Do you know who I am?"

I stopped, tilting my head toward the sound now. I knew it. At least, I thought I did. Maybe I was playing tricks with myself.

My eyebrows furrowed as I concentrated, making the burning by my eyes get worse, and I let go of Dr. Bran's arm. No, I definitely recognized that voice. I found myself nodding as the name echoed in the back of my head.

I reached out my pointer finger. A few seconds passed before a hand slid into my other one, palm facing up, and I stiffened. It wasn't Dr. Bran's smooth hands that were always covered by a film of hand sanitizer. It was about the same size as his, but the skin was rougher but softer somehow, a sense of unpredictability that differed from the practiced hands of the doctor. The break in consistency made me pause. Though it took a painful amount of time, I'd had to learn to trust Dr. Bran—and *only* Dr. Bran—really because I had no other choice. I spelled my speaking to him and no one else. Ever.

"Go ahead," Dr. Bran told me, his voice highlighted with encouragement. "It's all right."

Slowly, I dragged my pointer finger along the unknown palm, spelling the name in my head that held a familiarity I couldn't place. *S-A-*

Bam. The imaginary wall slammed down, blocking my path, and I couldn't get around it. What came next?

A frustrated breath escaped me. I could see it, taste it, I just couldn't translate it. I knew that I knew it. It was the alphabet, for crying out loud. S-A-what? It had to be easy. S-A…

"Are you missing a letter?" Dr. Bran asked, as patient as always.

I didn't have the patience he did. Nodding, I poked my head with my finger over and over as though that would help free the letter from wherever it got stuck inside my mess of a brain.

"Let's go through the alphabet again, okay?" Per usual, he tapped my shoulder softly with each slow letter. "A, B, C, D, E, F, G, H, I, J, K, L—"

A short gasp went through my teeth as the light bulb came on and the wall broke down. I went back to the strange palm still held in my other hand.

S-A-R-K. Sark.

Once I remembered the name, the floodgate opened up and I was suddenly drowning in flashes of imaged memory, the force of it knocking me back against the bed. A Ferris wheel. A glass box. A library. The starry sky. City lights blurring past the windshield. Painful blows and warm hugs and worried nights and carefree laughs and protective stances and knowing glances and soft words and shouted anger and slow kisses and fast kisses and blue eyes.

The hand I'd been tracing on closed around mine, as if reflexively, and I recognized it then. Sark. Of course.

I smiled and a burst of excited breathes escaped through my panting at the mental exertion, not even caring about the pounding headache that was forming.

"You remember Sark?" Dr. Bran asked, a slight hint of worry tinting the positivity.

I nodded, ecstatic at the remembered revelation. To know something. To recognize something amidst the confusing nothingness and scary unknown that was my world now.

I know him. He's here.

"Good," Dr. Bran said in approval. "Wow, that's very good, Arie."

I reached my other hand out, wanting more proof in case the universe was messing with me. It took a few seconds but eventually he found me, pressing my hand softly against his face, and I nearly laughed in disbelief at the recognition. Wanting so badly to talk to him, I opened my mouth, but nothing came out and I remembered that I couldn't.

A soft pressure appeared on my blanketed ankle, and I knew her voice seconds after she spoke, as though the path of remembering had been opened by Sark. "Hey, baby."

I wrote on my leg: *M-O-M.*

"Yeah." Her voice broke and I knew she was crying. "I'm right here, baby. I'm right here."

"Excellent, Arie." Dr. Bran was surprised. "That's great. Just don't push it too much, okay? Let's work on retaining what you've got."

"Push what?" Mom asked. "Can she hurt herself by trying to remember?"

"Not necessarily. I just worry about her mentality. Her body is already under an incredible amount of pressure, I don't want to cause further damage by excessive mental strain. Especially considering the unpredictability of her body's reactions and her..." He hesitated. "Unpleasant history."

They continued to talk about my misadventures, but I stopped paying attention when I sensed Sark's face get closer to mine and he held his hand against my cheek.

"I'm here now," he whispered to me, his breath on my face. It smelled like spearmint gum. "I'm here now, Arie, and they can't keep me away anymore."

I nodded rapidly, my smile hurting my face, and I wished so badly I could see him. He stroked my hair and sighed.

"I missed you so much. I'm so glad you're...well..." He kissed my forehead ever so softly. "Alive."

I'm alive. Right. It didn't always feel that way.

For no reason I could tell, the burning by my eye suddenly exploded, spreading fire through my face as though my eyeballs themselves were now orbs of flame. I choked on a scream as my head snapped back, breaking my hand out of Sark's to smack the bedrail frantically until Dr. Bran's hand stopped me.

There was a hint of worry among his calm. "Arie, point to what's wrong."

Sark was gone now. I slapped both hands over my eyes as though that could extinguish the flames, painful sounds escaping my mouth.

Can't you see the fire? Put it out!

I felt his hands on my face, prying mine away so he could look for himself. It only lasted a moment. My body slumped forward, and I covered my head with my arms, ready to combust. Then I saw it. I stopped moving. Stopped making sounds. I probably stopped breathing.

White. That was a color. Bright. White. Then a half second of black. More white. Texturized white. It looked soft.

It's a blanket. It's your blanket.

My eyebrows furrowed and the shape of the white changed slightly. *I have a blanket?*

Ever so slowly, I lifted my head, squinting at the light. I was in a room. It was white. A long white counter with a silver sink and cabinets lined the wall to my left, next to a wide door with a skinny rectangular window. A thirty-something man in a lab coat stood on the left side of my bed, his white uniform a stark contrast from his thick dark beard, extending a restraining hand across my bed, as if to hold in place a younger man in a brown leather jacket who was standing on the right side of my bed, his stance tense and ready. A woman peeked around, sitting on a chair behind the man in the leather jacket, her worried eyes on me.

Who are these people? My new eyes glanced between all of them as I clutched my hospital gown. *Where am I?*

The bearded man lowered his arm slowly, watching me with dark eyes, as though the movement was a peace offering. "You can see me now, can't you?"

I knew that voice. It sounded familiar. Hesitating for a moment, I nodded.

He nodded with me, his surer than mine. "Good, Arie, that's great. Do you recognize my voice?"

My nod came faster this time. I glanced back over to the other two in the room, and the familiarity grew stronger. The guy in the leather jacket sat back down in his chair, his deep blue eyes meeting mine, and I could see he was trying to cover up something.

"You don't recognize me?" he asked, his voice nearly shaking.

I sucked in a sharp breath at his pain. I realized I wanted to make it stop. I'd do anything to recognize him if it meant his heartbreaking expression would heal.

Why do I care so much?

It all came back like the snap of a rubber band. I dropped my eyes sheepishly, pulling my fingers through my long hair, and I nodded apologetically.

The tension in the room dissipated. The bearded man—who I guess was Dr. Bran—regained my attention by pulling out a thin pocket flashlight.

"I told you it would come back, now didn't I?" he asked with a grin on his hairy face. He held a finger up. "Let's take a look. Eyes on my finger please."

I did my best to follow his finger with my gaze and not flinch at the light he shone in my eyes, shaking my head when he asked if the burning was still there.

"The good news is I think your sight here to stay," he told me as I finished the checkup. "The bad news is I don't see any signs of laser vision, which is just too bad." He put his flashlight away, then held out his hand. "Now we can officially meet. Hi. I'm Dr. Bran."

I cracked a smile and shook his hand, then traced my name on the back of it.

"Wonderful to meet you, Arie. I think we're going to be great friends."

"So, what, that's it?" Sark asked, the hardened impatient tone back. He gestured to me though his distrustful eyes were on Dr. Bran. "What just happened to her?"

Dr. Bran wasn't put off by the hostility, though I thought his shoulders tensed slightly. "I don't know. Like I told you earlier, we have enough knowledge and research to be able to perform reversal, but we're in the dark as to what happens after or why. Your guess is as good as mine."

"So what are you good for?" Sark muttered. I shot him a disapproving look, but he ignored it.

Don't scare away my only friend, Sark.

"I understand your frustrations," Dr. Bran said, his voice tighter. "They're mine too, as well as Arie's. I wish I could do more, but unfortunately that's just the way it is." Then he looked at me. "It's exciting, but let's take it slow, okay? I'm going to dim the lights and say no to reading or the TV, at least until tomorrow. No extra strain."

I nodded, then tapped twice on the bedrail.

Dr. Bran gave a small grin. "You're welcome. I'm going to do an update. Have someone holler if you need me." Giving a nod to Sark and Mom, he turned and dimmed the lights before stepping out.

I pressed the button on the bed control panel until I was sitting up, then I began exploring. I started with my hands, noting how long my fingernails were, running my fingers over the scars on my wrist. Now that I could see again, I'd need to get some long sleeves. There were two IVs—one in each arm—which were just two of the many cords that hooked me up to one of three monitors that hung on the wall behind me. Sitting down my hair fell almost to my waist, the strands appearing darker against the blue and green printed white hospital gown I was in. The lower half of my body was covered with white blankets.

Once my inspection was complete, I reached for Sark's hand. Mom scooted her chair closer to the bed as I traced on Sark's palm. *Y-O-U-?*

Sark concentrated for a moment, then he got it, looking up to meet my eyes. "I'm fine. Just been waiting around for you."

Creasing my forehead in concern, I leaned forward to gently touch my fingers against a jagged scar on the side of his head, feeling the ghost of stitches underneath.

Sark just took my hand in his and shook his head. "It's no big deal now. I'm okay. Besides, it doesn't even compare to you."

I didn't really like that statement, but it would be hard to refute with only palm-traced communication. Instead, I glanced at Mom who just gave a sad smile and nodded.

"I'm okay too," she told me. "Now that I can see you, that is. You wouldn't believe how rude

251

some of these people here are about you. What happened to innocent until proven guilty?"

I nodded. I believed it. Turning Sark's hand over, I traced his palm again. *O-T-H-E-R-S-?*

Again, it took Sark a few seconds to know what I meant. "They've reversed everyone, and all of them survived and are in recovery. Both Peter and Brennan were in the last wave. We've been to see them."

I waited for him to continue. He didn't. I tapped his hand.

He sighed. "They're both fine except Brennan's blind too and they say Peter's developed some kind of muscle problem, but…I guess you know how unpredictable this all is. If it weren't for your test run, though, they all could've had it much worse."

The information made me more worried, but at the same time, it was better than hearing they were dead. Once the government team assigned to our 'case' found out I had survived reversal—even though I was still pretty much brain dead in a coma—they decided that was enough. Every infected was mandated to go through reversal. No exceptions. That was the only information Dr. Bran gave me though.

"Lucy's doing good too," Mom told me, knowing I would ask. "They have her on bed rest and won't do reversal until after the baby comes, which will probably be soon." Her mouth turned down. "They aren't sure…how well it's going to go."

I sighed. Of course. Couldn't there be just one thing that worked out for us? Just one. I wasn't feeling picky.

Don't you think we deserve a break? I asked the universe. I guess I shouldn't have been surprised when no one answered me.

~~~

Nothing noteworthy happened until a few days later. At least, I was pretty sure it was a few days. It was hard for me to keep track.

I'd been sleeping, which wasn't anything new or fascinating by any means since I spent a good eighty percent of my time that way. Dr. Bran said sleeping was good for me—my poor body needed all the energy it could get—but soon he was going to start keeping me awake for a bit longer. I didn't know what I was going to do when I was forced into even more consciousness.

My arms woke me up. From time to time I'd get a quick sharp pang of fire right where the symbols on my wrist used to be. I was almost a hundred percent sure the feeling was completely psychological, but that didn't keep me from snapping awake, jerking the long sleeves of my new hospital gown up, and checking my arms for blue, just to be sure. Like every other time, there were only scars.

Taking the giant oxygen mask off my face, I glanced around the room, which still felt like a new thing to me. It was empty. That was strange— usually there was always someone with me now—
~~~

but not too unusual. They probably all had to go to the bathroom or something.

I relaxed again and closed my eyes, knowing I should put my oxygen mask back on if I was planning on sleeping again. Typically I'd stop breathing at least six to ten times while I was asleep. Though the giant mask was bulky and annoying, it saved my life all the time.

Oh, the joy.

Groaning—because heaven forbid I had to move—I prepared to lift my arm and grab the mask. Then the door opened. Then it shut. I stayed still, debating on the risk of opening my eyes, because if it was the physical therapist then I definitely was going to be asleep.

It was silent for a moment, then there were a few footsteps that stayed on the left side of the bed. Probably by the counter. The sound of a long zipper coming undone, then slight shuffling. My curiosity got the best of me and I cracked my eyes open.

It wasn't the physical therapist or Dr. Bran, though he wore a lab coat. He stood at the counter, his back to me, arms moving as he assembled something. I only saw the back of his head: it was buzzed to reveal a gross bony skull and a thick scar that wrapped its way almost from ear to ear.

Wonder what his story is.

The stranger turned around and did a slight double take, as though startled I was awake. Then I realized I recognized him. But from where?

From the hospital, duh. He works here. I probably just forgot his face, like I forgot everything.

"I apologize," he murmured, keeping his voice low. "I thought you were asleep. I didn't mean to wake you."

I shook my head to tell him it was no big deal. Then my eyebrows furrowed in confusion when I saw the syringe in his hand. I never let anyone put anything in me unless it was Dr. Bran. And Dr. Bran knew that.

The stranger gestured to the syringe. "Dr. Bran sent me in here to give this to you. Change of protocol since the new revelations."

I shook my head again, this time without understanding, and twisted the edge of my hospital gown in my fingers. I didn't feel good about this.

He arched a thin eyebrow. "They haven't told you yet? It is new, I suppose. They found traces of drugs in your bloodstream. From before reversal. And that changes your case dramatically."

What? Drugs in me? A pit formed in my stomach. That would not be good. I was halfway to life in prison as it was.

My heart started pounding faster, my gasping picking up. I needed to talk to Dr. Bran. Now. Not this stranger who was making me more and more uncomfortable.

He took a step toward me, and I decided I really wasn't okay with that. I glanced to the door, outside the thin window. Someone couldn't have been far.

The stranger spoke again, regaining my attention. "You still can't speak yet, can you?"

My hands closed into fists, my long fingernails digging into my palm. Something was wrong. His lab coat was too crisp, too new, not worn and soft like Dr. Bran's, who practically slept in the thing.

That's when my brain wall came down and I remembered: yes, I knew this man. Yes, he was a doctor, but not at this place. At the Compound. For Cyrus.

Dr. Bragenhurst.

He smiled at my panicked silence, raising the syringe. "Good."

The volume of my scream surprised both of us. Someone must've been close to the door because it swung open almost instantly, quick footsteps following.

I didn't wait to see who it was. I surged forward, ripping cords off of me, feeling skin tear but not really feeling it. I heard Dr. Bran order, "Grab her," and someone seized both my arms, then forced me back, sitting next to me to pin me against my bed. My terrified gaze found Sark's. I tried to tell him what was going on but only a blubbered mess came out of my mouth.

"What happened?" Dr. Bran asked, stepping closer to my bed.

"I apologize for the alarm, Doctor," Bragenhurst said, gesturing hopelessly to me. "It's an ordered cleanse. In response to the drug predicament."

No it's not! I wanted to scream. *He's lying!*

But I still couldn't find a way to form the words. I pushed against Sark's hold, but the feeble attempt was almost laughable.

"I didn't know anything had been mandated yet," Dr. Bran said, scrolling through his tablet. "Was that recent?"

"This morning. They asked me to come down and give it to her immediately to avoid further complication."

Liar, liar, liar, liar, liar. What was I going to do?

"I tried to explain it to her," the creep went on, "but she just started screaming. I've been told her mental state is rather fragile and she doesn't handle things well, however I didn't prepare for that reaction. I apologize I caused an issue." He took another step, closing the rest of the distance between him and me. "I'll just inject it quickly and be on my way."

I shrieked and tried to thrash under Sark, shaking my head violently as the silent 'no' I was trying to scream. Tears fell down my face as I met Sark's broken eyes.

Please don't let him. Please hear me. Please.

He watched me with a stone face, but I could see it in his eyes—watching me like this killed him. Right when I thought he was going to cry with me, he spoke up.

"Just give her a minute to calm down," he said, glancing at Dr. Bran.

Bragenhurst jumped in. "Certainly, I'll just give this to her and leave in peace." He brought the syringe closer to my arm and somehow my scream got louder, nearly ripping through my esophagus.

Dr. Bran stopped him, then nodded, and Sark let go of my arms. I lurched forward and threw my arms around him, legs like jelly noodles underneath me as I tried to climb up him and out of there. Sark held me tight so I couldn't get off the bed, my tears soaking the shoulder of his shirt, and

I finally just yanked his hand away to write on his palm.

C-Y-R-U-S.

Sark's arms instantly clamped around me, his body angling in protection, and he jerked his head to the intruder. "Who are you?"

I saw Dr. Bran's hand slide into his pocket, and the door burst open a few seconds later, two security guards barging in. They secured the threat as Dr. Bran rushed to me.

"Arie, calm down before your breathing—"

But it was too late—it had already set in. My body slumped forward and my chest seemed to cave in on itself, my lungs constricting, as though a giant snake had wrapped itself around me and was squeezing the air out of me. I felt Sark flinch when my fingernails dug into his neck, and broken airless moans escaped me.

The oxygen mask was slapped over my face with too much force, but I didn't care. Choking on the air, I was nearly seeing double when I looked over to the enraged Dr. Bragenhurst who was now in handcuffs.

"I want all passwords updated," Dr. Bran told the guards, as much anger in his voice as I'd ever heard. "Fingerprint scanners need to be installed and image ID cards made for everyone. Nobody gets in or out of this facility unless they're supposed to be here."

The guards nodded and pulled their prisoner toward the door, who just fought against their hold, his vengeful eyes on me.

"You may have killed her," he spat at me, "but you'll never be able to escape her." Then with one last jerk of the guards, he was gone.

I was shaking so hard I could hear my teeth snapping together through the oxygen mask, clinging to Sark with everything I had.

"It's okay," he whispered softly in my ear while still trying to keep a hold on me. "It's okay. You're okay. It's okay."

Dr. Bran bent down so he was eye level with me, his concerned face blurred by my tears. "He threatened you?"

I just nodded as I cried and wheezed.

He stood and retrieved the small whiteboard and marker he brought in a few days ago for me to practice remembering the alphabet on, then kneeled down on the ground in front of me. Gingerly, he uncapped the marker and offered it to me.

"I know you can't defend yourself anymore like you're used to," he told me, his words slow so I could keep up. "You're vulnerable and that scares you. Rightly so. You need to feel safe here, so you make a list of all the people you know you can trust and they will be the only souls allowed in this room. Anyone else will need to go through someone on the list. No exceptions, no matter what. Is that okay with you?"

I considered that for a moment, my half sobbing subsiding enough that I could get a handle on breathing, then nodded. Unclenching one arm from around Sark, I hesitantly took the marker in my fist like a two-year-old—the only way I knew how to hold it—and Dr. Bran held the whiteboard while I produced shaky letters. They weren't pretty but they were mostly legible.

S-A-R-K

B-R-A-N

M-O-M

Then I stopped. Infecteds weren't allowed back here and I wasn't sure I wanted anyone to see me like this anyway.

Dr. Bran gave me a few moments to think before speaking. "Three people?" I couldn't tell if he thought that was too much or not enough. "I spoke to a woman earlier who wanted to see you. She said her name was Lindsey Carter."

I nodded and went back to the board.

L-I-N-D-

Then I stopped, the wall in my brain up again.

"S," Sark said softly before I could get frustrated. "It's an S."

L-I-N-D-S-E-Y

I gave the marker back to Dr. Bran and he inspected my list. "Four people. That's a great start." He met my eyes again. "Thank you for considering me one of them. That's a high honor I don't take lightly."

He patted my knee then stood to position the whiteboard on the counter so I could see it. I latched back onto Sark, my breathing spiking dangerously fast again.

"Hey, it's okay," Sark told me, rubbing my back gently. "It's okay. It's over now."

I buried my face in his shoulder and shook my head furiously. Because it wouldn't matter if I improved or even made a miraculous full recovery. It wouldn't matter if they finally nailed Cyrus and locked him away forever with his cronies and nobody had a reason to shut me up anymore. It wouldn't matter if I changed my name and moved to France and lived in a cabin without internet and only went outside during the nighttime.

He held his hand out to me, palm up. "Tell me why."

Hesitating at first, I used a shaky hand to trace the words that were seared onto my skin.

N-E-V-E-R-E-S-C-A-P-E

11

Dr. Bran bought me a week and a half. That's how long I had until I had to face a council assigned to our investigations about my alleged drug problem.

A few things happened in that week and a half. For one, I spoke my first word since waking up. Apparently, I started mumbling strings of words in my sleep without knowing it, then forgot when I woke up. Dr. Bran worked with me, though, and I got to the point where I could say a sentence at a time if I really concentrated. At first, I was excited, but quickly decided to stick to palm writing or the whiteboard. I sounded like an idiot trying to find the right words and remember how to use my voice to say them and put them in an order that made sense.

Both Dr. Bran and Sark were as patient as ever with my broken communication. I told Mom to divide her time between me and Jacklynn—the poor girl needed so much help. Reversal went pretty well for her, and she was already up and walking, leaving no side effects except an allergy. To everything. They'd yet to find a food she didn't have a reaction to, but to be fair, she hadn't allowed them to try very hard. She just stopped eating. She'd do her physical therapy and worked with the child psychologist, but most of the time she just spent crying or sleeping or catatonically watching the TV.

Eventually Dr. Bran got clearance to bring Jacklynn to my room. In a question that took ten years for me to say, I asked her if she'd help me learn to talk again. She was thrilled that I would ask her for such a task and readily agreed. The next week she spent mostly in my room, writing letters on the whiteboard or drawing simple things and having me guess what they were, pretending that she was the teacher and I her student. I had homework and report cards and a lunch hour and even recess. The game was a wonderful distraction for her.

After a while, Dr. Bran came up with the idea of using music. We'd play songs that I knew really well and I would try to keep up with it, the pre-learned lyrics coming much more naturally to me than an actual conversation. Jacklynn and I spoke-sang songs together, which helped my vocabulary and sentence structure grow.

It still wasn't enough though. I nearly threw up when Dr. Bran came in one morning and said he couldn't buy any more time—the council had to question me today.

Once I'd calmed down from the scary experience a week and a half ago, Dr. Bran looked me in the eyes and asked me if I'd ever abused any kind of drugs. I answered honestly: no. He believed me and said he'd wait until I was ready to explain the presence of drugs in my system. I wasn't yet. But apparently, I would have to be today.

After transferring to a wheelchair and making sure my cords weren't tangled, I put a blanket over my lap to keep me warm, hide my shaking hands, and be my friend. It reminded me of the blanket I used to have at the Compound.

With Dr. Bran pushing me and Sark pushing the pole that held my IV bags and oxygen, I made my way out of the world that was my room and into a much larger world that was the hospital facility.

The white walls matched the ones in my room, though they were accented with a deep red. The hallway outside didn't go far—there was a thick glass door about ten feet in front of me, a security guard posted next to what looked like some form of number pad. I looked through the glass to catch a glimpse of the different people in lab coats and scrubs going from one room to the next, each taking care of another reversed infected. My view was obstructed when Dr. Bran pushed me into the elevator right off my room door.

I adjusted the oxygen tube on my face, re-securing it behind my ears even though it didn't need to be, then tucked my hands back under the blanket. This would be my first interrogation where I could speak, rather than having to write everything out. What if I forgot every word I know? What if they didn't believe that I actually struggled with speech and thought I was faking it as a way out? What if they decided they found me guilty right there?

Stay calm, I ordered myself. *Just stay calm.*

I couldn't remember ever getting out of the elevator. All of a sudden I was pushed into a conference room, getting a blast of air conditioning, which I was grateful for. I was already sweating both from nerves and the energy expended just to get here.

The medium-sized room was filled up with a long conference table, a woman and two men sitting on the far end. Dr. Bran parked me on the other end, closest to the door, and I caught a whiff of peppers, the stench making me nauseous. The door shut and I was trapped inside.

Dr. Bran and Sark took a seat on either side of the table next to me. We'd rigged it so they could stay: Dr. Bran said he needed to stay in case anything I said was important to my medical standing. Sark was allowed to stay as my 'security' after the breach a week and a half ago. I couldn't decide if it would be worse to have them there or to be alone.

One of the men—he said to call him Jensen—got the ball rolling. He was nice enough, I guess. We went through several formalities like my name and age and birth date. He asked me how I was doing physically and even had Dr. Bran give a quick update on my health.

Then Jensen took a deep breath. "I assume you know why you're here, Miss Nolan?"

I nodded.

"About two weeks ago now, readings from your previous blood samples came back with an unknown substance we believe to be a form of drug. I don't think I have to explain to you why that's a huge setback for the case you're trying to make." He sat back in his chair and gestured to me. "Can you explain this?"

I had to wait for a few seconds to make sure I had the right words. "I'm guessing. In the Compound it was punishment. If you broke rules or tried to leave. They put you in a…" I forgot the word, tracing a square in the air over and over until it came back to me. "A box. It's dark. They lock it. They shoot you with a hallo—hallu…" I struggled with the term, feeling my veins get hot with embarrassment.

"Hallucinogen?" Jensen supplied.

I nodded, thankful and humiliated. "I don't know exactly what it is. Something they made. It makes you see and…and feel things. Things that aren't real. But you don't know that un…un…until after."

"Did you feel pain when under the influence of this hallucinogen?"

I didn't stop the wince in time. I nodded. "Whatever you see, you feel. Bleed. Choke. Arm ripped off."

Jensen's mouth hung half open. "And when you woke up…?"

I shrugged. "Checked to see if it was still there. It was. Only real damage is self-inflicted while brain is gone."

I had to clear my dry throat, which sounded like an engine turning over, and Dr. Bran handed me a water bottle. The guy was always prepared. I took it with a grateful nod, not meeting his eyes, and screwed off the lid.

"Wow," Jensen remarked as I drank. "That sounds intense. Describe for me the last hallucination you had while under the influence. Just so we can get an idea."

I nearly choked on the water when I realized what the answer to that would be.

Cyrus, you stupid smart idiot.

Now I truly understood the logic behind magically bringing the drug problem to light. This could bury me and any shred of belief that I was innocent.

Where are your guys planted, Cyrus?

The silence was prolonged as I kept drinking. If I stopped, they'd expect an answer. Did I dare try to lie? Or would that just make it worse?

Jensen cleared his throat. "Miss Nolan?"

The water bottle made a smacking sound when I pulled it from my lips. Concentrating intently on my work, I screwed the lid back on, placing the bottle with great care on the table.

"Miss Nolan?" Jensen asked again, impatience shining through. "What did you see?"

I sighed as I watched condensation bead down the water bottle. "Monsters," I finally answered in defeat. "Blue monsters. Mutts."

There were a few beats of silence. Everyone probably stopped breathing. Then a chair creaked and Jensen asked, "Like the ones that attacked the public?"

I gritted my teeth. "Not *un*like them. Cyrus had them. Like pets. I trained with them."

Harsh disbelief colored his tone. "You're telling me you hallucinated the very monsters you'd allegedly unleash later in time?"

Laughing once, a miserable sound, I rubbed my face over and over. "Yeah. Not exact same. People I knew were turned to mutts. Then they'd torture me until I died."

"Did you ever abuse this drug, Miss Nolan? Take it when you weren't forced? Maybe act rashly when under the influence of these hallucinations?"

Dropping my hands to my lap, I watched my fidgeting fingers. "No. I didn't."

It's your word against mine, Hammond had warned me. *I think you of all people know our organization isn't something you can go up against.*

No kidding.

"Well…" A chair creaked again. "I'd call that very…telling. What would you call that, Miss Nolan?"

My eyes snapped up to meet his. "Convenient. For them." I had to admit that Cyrus won the award for most backup plans. "Make me look crazy and wrong until they can get out."

"By 'they' you mean Cyrus, Hammond, those arrested?"

I nodded.

"And what would happen if 'they' got out?"

I shrugged. "I die. Those who know die. He starts all over. Waits years until next key. This happens again."

Jensen raised an eyebrow. "He'd kill you? That would debunk the theory you were on the same side."

I glared. "I was never on his side."

"And yet you claim he's the actual leader—an old, crippled scientist who's borderline insane. That he's the one that actually concocted all of this, he's the blackmailer, rather than you—the younger, stronger, much more capable one. The one we have actual evidence condemning."

"I know what it sounds like," I said, not sure what else I could say. "That's why it's hard. He told me never go against him. He'll always win."

Never escape.

Jensen cleared his throat and straightened up, his silent stoic associates doing the same. They were probably celebrating on the inside—they'd pretty much gotten the evidence they needed. Just another thing to add to my ledger: Arie Nolan, half key, ex-infected, mentally fragile and, now, druggie plus mass murderer. What a great person I was turning out to be.

"Miss Nolan, thank you for your honesty and cooperation in our discussion. I just have one more question for you."

I nodded as my shoulders slumped slightly, my exhaustion catching up with me.

"Besides this case we discussed with the hallucinogen, have you ever taken any other drug at any other time for any other reason rather than medical?"

Making sure my gaze didn't waver from his, I answered, "No."

Part of me felt guilty for lying to him after he kindly thanked me for honesty. What did it matter anyway? It was too long ago to prove it now and it had nothing to do with this situation.

"Really?" Jensen asked, a new edge to his tone. "That's the answer you're sticking with?"

"The answer is no."

"I don't know if I believe you."

He knows. Not everything. But something.

My hands clenched into fists. "I don't think it's you. But some…someone who tells you things…they're on the wrong side." I glared at him. "Make sure you know…who you work for."

With that, I decided our discussion was over. Grabbing onto the wheels of my wheelchair, I started rolling myself toward the door, dragging my IV pole behind me. I stuck my arms out and tried to push the door open, but I didn't have time to wheel myself all the way through before it shut on me. I was trapped halfway.

Humiliation burned again. What a statement I was making.

A hand came from behind me and held open the door. I pushed myself through, screeching to a halt when Jensen jumped in front of me, blocking my path.

Dr. Bran had to push back Sark, who looked like he was going to kill Jensen. "This discussion is over," Dr. Bran told Jensen. "You can go."

"This is a matter of national security," Jensen countered before looking at me. "What was it that you took?"

"I don't know what you're talk…talking about." I pushed forward but he stopped me. "Let me go."

"It was over a year ago. I know that. Was it while you were allegedly incarcerated or not?"

My jaw clenched. "Not your business."

"Drugs circulate in prisons. The inmates love a good stash. What did you take?"

I'm an inmate now? "I didn't take anything!" I half shouted. "He gave it to me. No choice."

I slumped in resignation, holding my head in my hands, the weight of the memory dragging me down to places I'd sworn I would never go again.

Jensen's voice was quieter when he spoke again. "According to the timeline you gave us, 'he' would be referring to Richard Dalton?"

I winced at the name, staring at my blanket. Then I nodded.

"A means to keep you there," Jensen realized, thinking out loud. "If you were addicted then you couldn't get yourself to leave." He cleared his throat. "Are you still on it?"

I shook my head without looking up.

"Did you take it for the entirety of your imprisonment?"

I shook my head again.

"He cut you off."

I nodded.

"And the withdrawals?"

I shuddered and wrapped my arms around myself. "Awful."

The edge was gone from his voice now. He was gentler than I thought possible. "Did he ever try to put you back on it?"

I raised my head to look at him. "He was an idiot. He had no plan. When others at his work came for building inspection he…panicked. Thought we would try something. He was so far in. Didn't want to get caught. So he tried to put us back on them."

"So, you did then?"

Tears stung my eyes as I shook my head. "I didn't want to. I refused. But they would make me—we knew that. So my friend took mine for me. Tricked them. I didn't ask him to. He just did it."

Sunshine and roses, Arie. That's where you're headed.

"And they found out?" Jensen guessed.

I nodded. "By then it didn't matter."

His eyebrows furrowed, then raised with understanding, a hint of sympathy in his eyes. "It didn't matter."

I strained my eyeballs to keep my tears inside them, making my tone hard. "He didn't need an addiction to keep me there."

That's what happens when you give up, Jensen. Have you ever been pushed to that point?

Jensen nodded slowly, taking it in. "So your friend—the murderer—helped you?"

I shook my head. "Not murderer. Not then. Just my friend."

That made Jensen scoff. "The blood doesn't lie. He was a murderer."

My throat closed up with fury and I tried to melt Jensen with my eyes. No one could talk bad about that person except me.

You have no right.

Grabbing my wheels again, I rammed into Jensen's legs over and over until he moved out of my way, desperate to leave before I completely lost it. Jensen grabbed my wheelchair as I passed him, bringing me to a halt. I had to clench my teeth to keep from screaming in frustration. How dare he use my injuries against me.

Finally, I decided to bag this crap and just walk. My legs couldn't be *that* bad.

I was wrong. The second I stood I dropped like ten bags of bricks, smacking my head against the floor. Everything went black. I felt my heart start hammering, chest heaving, lungs constricting, setting my core on fire. I didn't realize my ears had been stuffy until they cleared up. I heard Dr. Bran calling my name, frantic worry instead of his usual composure. Then the mask against my face.

There was no distinction of time, no difference between past and present, real and fake. The plastic mask was secured to my face, and suddenly I was screaming, begging, fighting my restraints in a desperate attempt to keep Cyrus from damning me to my fate.

It was happening. It was happening again.

Please don't. Please make it stop.

I opened my eyes and started clawing at my face, ripping the plastic away. The back of my hand hit a bearded face as I struggled to get away.

I managed to bolt upright, my vision stabilizing just long enough for me to see my empty wheelchair, get confused and really dizzy, then throw up clear liquid all over the floor. My body crumpled in on itself, and arms caught me on the way down. All I cared about was the plastic mask that was making its way toward my face yet again.

"No!" I shrieked, thrashing around my dying body, falling into hysterics. "No, please! Please, please, please stop! Stop! You can't take her out! You can't! Please!"

Thankfully, the mask disappeared, a dark fuzzy beard taking up my vision.

"Arie," a calm voice said. "It's Dr. Bran. Do you remember where you are? It's okay. You're in the research facility. You're okay."

I shook my head, not understanding. "Please don't. Please. I'll do anything. Anything. You can't."

"Nobody is going to do anything you don't want to do."

Then I was crying. Hot tears stung my cheeks as they streamed down, and I started to realize where I really was. "I didn't want them to. I screamed. I screamed so loud. And nobody came. Nobody stopped it. And it hurt so bad." Finally, I got ahold of myself enough to actually focus on Dr. Bran's face, one that I recognized. My voice cleared, fragile, as I considered his kind eyes. "Are you going to hurt me?"

The kindness in his eyes just deepened, matching his sincere tone. "No, Arie. I'm not going to hurt you. Do you believe me?"

I watched him for a moment. I believed him. Nodding, I carefully curled myself into a ball and turned my head into his shoulder, gripping the edge of his lab coat in my fists. My body trembled as I whimpered softly, slowly remembering how I got there on the floor.

He let me cry for a minute before speaking softly. "You're carrying a lot, Arie, and I know you've been carrying it for a long time. I've been waiting for the day when you finally swallow the act and admit to me that you're having a hard time. That you need help. Is today that day?"

Even if I wanted to tell the truth, I was afraid I'd choke on it. Despite his mild probing, I'd never really told him a whole lot about what happened to me—there were some things that I'd never said out loud, period, even to the government agents who questioned me. He only knew what he was told by other people, and I knew that bothered him, more for my sake than anything. He knew a ticking time bomb when he saw one.

"He was talking about my friend," I blurted without lifting my head.

I felt Dr. Bran nod slowly as he hesitated, his voice filled with concern. "Your friend who was your prison mate? The, uh…assassin?"

"Nobody knows." Rogue tears fell into my mouth as I trembled. "Nobody knows what they did to him. Awful things. Way worse than to me. For years. The things they did to him to…to make him that way. He told me one day. People hate him but they…they have no idea." My voice broke. "He was just a *kid*."

I closed my eyes, like that could somehow keep the nightmares away. "He had a…a…" I tried to think of the expression. "Mental disorder. And kind of brainwash. So many problems. Not all was his fault. He could be good." I stopped to catch my breath. "But he killed people. When he was with me. He hurt others and me. But I still loved him. He got shot. He never gets shot. But she got him because…because he thought it was me. And now he's dead. I watched him die. He told me it was better he died. I don't know if that's right. I miss him." A dry sob escaped me. "What am I supposed to do with that?"

Dr. Bran let out a long breath. "I don't know. But we're going to work through it. You're going to be okay."

If I hadn't been crying then I would've laughed. The 'okay' ship had sailed long ago and it was never coming back.

My breathing was ragged; it hurt my chest. I tried to adjust myself, but then I caught a whiff of my vomit and gagged.

"Can I take you back to your room now?" Dr. Bran asked me.

I thought for a moment before nodding, sniffing a few times and slowing my tears. "I want…I want to go. Everything hurts."

"You hang in there with me. Let's get you back and comfortable, okay?"

Going slowly just in case, I lifted my head and opened my eyes. They filled with tears again when I saw who was bending next to Dr. Bran, watching me with an unreadable expression on their face.

My voice broke again. "Sark?"

He tried to give me an encouraging smile, but it just made him look miserable. I reached for him and Dr. Bran shifted me into his arms instead. A weird sound—a mix between a sob and sigh and groan—escaped me as I rested my heavy head on Sark's shoulder, clutching his jacket and shaking. He was here with me.

"You're okay," he told me quietly, his voice rough, as he wrapped my blanket around my shoulders. "You're okay. You're safe. We'll take you back upstairs and it'll be okay."

I relaxed a bit, because somewhere inside me I knew I could trust him.

"You're not going to hurt me," I stated through my teeth. "I know that. You won't...I'm...I'm okay with you."

"Yes. I'm not going to hurt you." He rubbed my arm softly. "I won't hurt you. Tell me when you're ready to go."

A couple more deep breaths. I buried my face farther into his jacket, trying to block out the throw up and cleaner smell with leather and Sark.

"Sark?" I asked, my cracked voice barely above a whisper. "Can...can you...I'm sorry."

"Yes, I can. Anything. What can I do?"

"Can you carry me?" I thought of the wheelchair and shivered. "I don't want...get back in. You're nicer. And safer. And I can trust you."

"Of course I will." He promptly adjusted me so he could pick me up, placing my hand on my IV pole. I held onto it as he carried me to the elevator.

"Sark?" I asked, the taste of bile in my mouth.

His voice was slightly strained. "Yeah?"

"Do you...do you think I'm a...a druggie?"

I almost expected him to laugh but he didn't. It made him angry. I felt the muscles in his neck tense. "No, Arie. Of course not."

"Oh." I had to take some breaths before I could talk again. "Thank you."

He didn't answer but his arms tightened on me. I suddenly felt desperate that he really understood that.

"No…no, Sark." I tried to lift my head up. It barely even budged. "Sark, you…you have to know. Do you know?"

The hardness to his tone ebbed slightly. "Know what?"

"You…you're the best person I've ever…I've ever met. Best thing that ever happened to me. You are always there for me. Always." I closed my eyes. "Too many thank you's. I can't say them all. But I know…I know it's been real…real hard. All the time. I make life so hard."

I really needed him to know that, how much he'd done for me. Because the people who don't give up on you—even after the world gives up on you and even after you give up on yourself—are the people worth anything and everything.

"Do you know that?" I asked him, insistent while I still could be. "Do you?"

The smile in his voice warmed my insides as he whispered to me, "You're worth all of it, Arie. That's why I do it."

"Really?"

He kissed the top of my head. "Someday I hope you can see yourself the way I see you." He shifted me in his arms so he could press the elevator button. "Don't listen to them, Arie.

They're doing their job, but they're looking to take you down any way they can. You know what happened. You stick to what you know, okay?"

I nodded, even though I didn't really get everything he said. "Okay."

"You're doing just fine," he said as he slid us into the elevator. "Don't give up yet."

I drifted in and out of consciousness, barely aware of the blast of air conditioning that blew my hair everywhere. Then I fell asleep. When I woke up, I found myself curled in a bed, every part of my body whining and aching and wheezing away. My eyebrows furrowed as I registered the man and woman standing next to me, but my attention was snatched by a bearded man in a lab coat coming toward my arm with a full syringe.

I screamed and swatted and hit my head against the railing and screamed, not stopping until the other guy reached over the bed to hold me still.

"Please," I choked, hoping the guy with the sad blue eyes would take pity on me. "Please don't. Please don't let them."

"Arie." The man in the lab coat placed a hand on my shoulder. I instantly relaxed at the familiarity of the gesture. "These are painkillers. You asked me for them just a minute ago when we got you back in your room." Worry edged around the words. "Do you not remember that?"

That sounded like it might be right, but I shook my head, confused and overwhelmed, and in so much pain—in my body and my heart—I didn't know what to do. Where did it all come from?

I pulled my arms away from the guy holding me down. He hesitated as he watched me but let me go. I held my head in my hands and squeezed my eyes shut and took deep breaths even though it hurt.

"I don't know you," I said, my body trembling, tears flowing. "I don't know any of you. I don't know! Don't hurt me! Please! Please, stop, please."

I felt pressure on my feet and froze. Someone was rubbing them. Something fluttered in my head, a feather in the wind trying to get picked up and fly.

The room was silent. I'd stopped breathing. The pressure on my feet felt nice, and my body loosened up. I knew that feeling, from eons ago. Rather, I knew that feeling was always paired with one person.

My eyebrows scrunched together, but I kept my eyes closed. "Mom?" I whimpered.

The pressure stopped, disappeared, then picked up again, the pattern of movement different than before. Then there was a frail hand underneath mine, on my face, gently brushing my cheek over and over again, as though my skin were as fragile as it was the day I was born.

"Hey, baby," she said in her slow, deep, calming tone. "It's okay. You're okay."

I nodded. "I'm scared, Mom."

"I know, sweetie, but you don't need to be. It's okay." She started humming. I turned my head slightly to hear her better. I knew the tune from somewhere.

The humming turned to quiet words as she crooned a song. I must've heard it before, because the missing notes filled in my head even though there was no music. Just Mom's voice. And with the combination of the song and the foot rubbing—Mom's signature 'Calm Arie Down' tactic—I knew that even if I didn't remember anything, I must be home. And with that knowledge helping me, I finally fell asleep.

12

I've heard people say that miracles don't exist. I'm somewhat partial to them, though I'm not sure why. Maybe just because my grandpa used to talk about them all the time.

"Miracles are all around us," he would tell me, "you just have to be smart enough to see them." And I would nod and think he was the smartest man in the whole world because he lived as though life itself were a miracle.

I never got that positive about life, especially after infection, but whether I actually believed in miracles or not, I got one. It came in the form of a man named Gustave Ferdinand.

Dr. Bran was the first to realize something was going on—he came in and told me about all of these government big wigs that had shown up at the hospital. Sure enough, I was called down to a special hearing and told to come alone. That made both Dr. Bran and me nervous, especially considering how well my last conversation with Jensen had gone. I didn't really have a choice though.

Again, I was loaded into a wheelchair—a nicer one with my IV pole attached—and was taken downstairs. There we ran into Lindsey who told me she was going too and could take me. I was so grateful to be able to have a friend with me, but when Dr. Bran handed me off, I felt like I was nine years old, being passed from one parent to another.

Dr. Bran, Sark and Mom waited in the common room; Lindsey pushed me down the hallway and into a lecture room, parking me on the end of the first row, then sitting next to me. I glanced around the buzzing full room at all the men and women in fancy suits, recognizing several from my many interviews and questionings. Jensen and his pals were on the top row. Agent Grant, the woman who had questioned me before the first hearing, sat on the second row. The section to my left was taken up with all those who had sat around the circle table at the first hearing, including Senator Whyme.

Keaton and Brody were some of the last people who came in. Each shook my hand, then sat on the other side of Lindsey. I hid my hands under my blanket, tapping my fingers against my leg nervously, anticipating what was coming. What if I had to talk in front of all these people? What if I had to *defend* myself? What if they incriminated me right here?

I can't do this. I need to leave.

Right when I was about to make a wheelchair dash for the door, the lights dimmed. A man stepped up in the front and began a presentation. A presentation that started with Gustave Ferdinand.

Gustave Ferdinand was not a good guy. He was in deep with gangs and drugs and money laundering, all under the table of course. Local authorities could never nail him on anything. But Gustave Ferdinand made a mistake—he had a prolonged affair with his gold-digging mistress, then dumped her when she wanted him to leave his wife. She was angry, to say the least. A hit was put on her to keep her from ratting Gustave and his pals out, but she stole his money and accounts and skipped town before they could kill her. Unfortunately, the mistress wasn't the cunning type and got caught by the authorities three days later.

I was really confused as to what Gustave Ferdinand and his problems had to do with me, until they got to the part where the authorities investigated where the money came from, tracking it back to accounts that technically didn't exist. It took some digging, but someone finally connected the illegal money to an account that belonged to a doctor by the name of Ben Hammond.

After that, the whole thing cracked open. Hammond and dozens of his employees were implicated and pegged to over twenty different unsolved scandals. The web only widened, connecting manufacturers and lawyers and government agents all over the world, every single person latching on to a family tree that eventually all led to one person: Cyrus.

Once they knew who and what to look for, evidence got dug up from the thousands of places Cyrus tried to bury it. As of today, two hundred and thirty-seven people had been officially arrested—including Cyrus, Hammond, a few agents who had been assigned to this case, and even three of the scientists at this hospital—and the investigation was still ongoing. The presentation man promised they would get them all.

Then the slideshow turned personal. Countless files had been uncovered detailing Cyrus' different experiments on hundreds of kids over the years, experiments that I knew as infection. Hundreds of cases, hundreds of people, victimized by Cyrus, often kidnapped and kept in a place called the Compound and forced to work or fight or do whatever he wanted. There were files on my comrade—the assassin—and how his mental conditioning worked to utilize his killing capabilities. There were files on the kids kept in the Dome. There were files on Stephen White and his partner and their crusade for reversal. There were files on all seven keys Cyrus had ever come in contact with, including me.

Everything they found had been cross-referenced with the stories my family and I had given during questioning—everything checked out.

There was the order Cyrus sent out to grab my family and bring them to the Compound. There were ledgers of all of the assassination orders, including Laurent Bridges and Alexis. There were pictures of me during the transfer process, and I winced at the perfect new me lying unconscious next to the battered, blue-ridden me. Very clearly in his notes, Cyrus spoke of there being two of us, of the frustrations he faced that I didn't give him enough and Vanessa gave him too much. He made consistent remarks about how I resisted what he wanted and detailed all the tactics he used to try to break me down. Later he wrote about Vanessa, about how uncontrollable and unpredictable she was, and how he was planning on trying a new kind of brainwash on her, after learning what worked with Micah and me.

Turns out, Arie Nolan was right. There was another one who caused the death and destruction. She and the infecteds put their lives on the line to save others'. And within a one-hour presentation, I went from blacklisted criminal to celebrated hero.

A round of applause went to Lindsey Carter and her team, who took their own initiative in the investigation and became a key part in uncovering the truth. They were to receive more funding and the Office of Cultist Intelligence would be reinstated as a verifiable government institution.

It wasn't until everyone started clapping for me that the truth of everything set in. I was innocent. I was free. They believed me. My story was validated.

I'm not crazy after all.

After the presentation closed, I shook so many hands, everyone too eager to meet me and thank me for what I did, even though a week ago they all were ready to burn me at the stake. If I ever needed anything, a gazillion people in fancy suits told me, I could give them a call.

I was flying high, my hands shaking in excited disbelief, as I wheeled myself out of the lecture room. Down the hallway I could see Dr. Bran, Sark and Mom sitting on chairs in the common room, each staring at the ground and fidgeting with nerves. Sark must've heard the door open or something because he glanced up right when I came wheeling down the hallway.

We locked eyes and a new burst of excitement went through me. My eyes filled with tears, a triumphant grin stretching my face as I nodded.

It took a few seconds for him to connect the dots, then he broke into a giant smile, the happiest I'd seen him since waking up in this miserable place. He jumped up and ran down the hallway to me. I threw my arms around him and he actually picked me up out of my wheelchair, crushing me in a huge hug.

"We did it," I whispered to him, the euphoria taking my voice. "We did it."

Mom practically ran into us, somehow wrapping her arms around both of us, and kissed the top of my head. Someone patted my arm and I turned to see an ecstatic Lindsey.

I gave her the best hug I could while still being held up by Sark. "Thank you," I said, unsure of how I could adequately express my gratitude. "Thank you so much."

She just smiled. "You're so welcome."

Then there was Dr. Bran, a grin underneath his beard as he put a hand on my shoulder. "Congratulations, Arie. Do you want to go break the news? I know a few people who'd be really excited to see you."

I nodded. Sark carried me, Mom pushing the wheelchair behind us, as Dr. Bran led our small victory parade back up the elevator, turning right instead of left. For the first time, I went through the guarded glass door outside my room, down an unfamiliar hallway and into a huge common room filled with couches and TVs and books and toys and people. Infecteds. Everyone. I watched them with their backs to me, chatting with each other, some in wheelchairs or on crutches or hooked up to IV stands, as everyone had been through reversal by now.

Dr. Bran cleared his throat loudly, gaining the attention. "Excuse me, everyone, we have an announcement to make."

At that, everyone turned around, eyes widening, mouths grinning when they saw Sark and I in the doorway.

I pumped my fist in the air. "We won!"

The room erupted in joyful chaos. Sark put me back in my wheelchair just as Jacklynn found me. Then Ellen. Brennan and Lucy, Peter and Alaina, Kayla and Daxton. I couldn't keep up with everyone. Carl and Tristan and Sasha and Dustin and Elijah and Zoe and so many others I only recognized.

My reunioning was interrupted by the senator. Apparently, the government felt pretty darn stupid and guilty that they'd been prosecuting us this whole time rather than thanking us (or just treating us like human beings). The senator gave me a card with both his office and cell number, then told me he would do or get anything I wanted. Anything. He said he'd be back tomorrow to talk logistics with me, but was there anything I wanted right then?

I said the first thing that came to my mind. "Pizza." It was a celebration, after all. "A lot of pizza."

My wish was granted. A half hour later, two pizza delivery guys showed up with enough pizza to feed Finland.

Despite the fact we were all disabled in one way or another, it was one of the best nights ever. Pizza was downed by the box, the best meal any of us had had in a long time, then music was turned on, mini dance parties held by those who still had that kind of motion. Laughter was the primary sound, and it echoed off the walls from every spot in the room.

I parked myself next to Sark, eating much more pizza than was probably healthy and saying hi to people as they came and went, recounting the presentation at least three times. We got quieter as the night went on, the excitement tiring us all out. I wasn't sure which of us had instigated it, but eventually I found my hand in Sark's, and I rested my head on his shoulder, content for the first time in a long time.

~~~
~~~

True to his word, the senator came back the next day. He told me about how they'd put out a call for infecteds who were arriving by the truckloads from all over the world to get reversed themselves—a process that had already been improved and made more humane—and the government had started a program to help them get back into life. The committee of that program had also begun tracking down relatives of each infected and letting them know where to find their kids. We should expect family members to start showing up anytime, he told me. He asked me to write down greeting messages and protocols for what to do for survivors that found us.

Once we'd finished that, Senator Whyme told me about the memorial service they were arranging that would take place next week. It was for all the victims of the attacks, as well as anyone—infected or not—who had lost their life to the cause. After reviewing, adding to and approving of a list of the deceased to honor, the senator asked if I'd say a few words at the service, to commemorate those who had fallen. I thought it was stupid to ask me but I couldn't find it in me to say no.

Before he left, he asked again if I'd thought of anything I wanted. I said I just wanted my name kept out of the press, my face censored from every press conference and interview in the past and in ones to come. We battled on that topic yet again— didn't I want to be the face of the infected populace to the public?—but I didn't back down. Eventually he nodded, typing something into his phone, then said to let him know if I thought of anything else. Something popped into my head when he was halfway through the door.

"Destroy it."

The senator paused, turning to look at me. "Excuse me?"

"Destroy it," I repeated. "All Cyrus' notes. Everything on infection. All of it. No exceptions."

His eyes clouded over, but he gave me a fake, courteous smile perfected for the camera. "It's being reviewed for usefulness. If we could change the formula to—"

"Destroy it all," I ordered, my voice hardening as I glared lasers at him. "Destroy it all or I swear you will see why Cyrus almost got away with calling me a monster."

That shook his presentation stance. A sense of fear came into his eyes and he nodded once, as if in a daze, before leaving.

Over the next few days, the hospital got a lot more crowded as relatives poured in from all over: moms, dads, aunts, uncles, grandparents, cousins, neighbors, friends. I don't think so many tears had ever been shed in one place in such a short amount of time. I was in Ellen's room when her aunt and new uncle came in—the aunt that pretty much raised her, who she hadn't seen since Cyrus took her over seven years ago—and I caught myself tearing up as I slipped out, the reunion scene just too sweet.

A wobbly, skin and bone Peter tracked me down just so I could meet his parents. A balding man stood behind a woman in a tan pantsuit, her hair swept up in a regal fashion, mascara smeared all over her face.

Peter grinned. "Arie, these are my parents. Mom, this is Arie."

I reached my hand out. "Nice to meet you Mrs…" I stopped and glanced at Peter, realizing after all this time I didn't even know his last name.

"Wyman," Peter muttered in a fake cough.

"Mrs. Wyman."

She looked like the handshake type of person, so it caught me off guard when she bent down to hug me, squeezing me like a long lost relative.

"Thank you," she whispered in my ear, her soft and shaky voice genuine.

Hesitating, I hugged her back. "I'm so sorry about your daughter."

She sniffed and nodded as she straightened up. "I am too. There are so many things I wanted her…were so many things, I…" She blew out a long breath. "Though it's a miracle I got even one of them back. I can't believe he's been so brave."

Peter snickered at that, and I gave him a small grin. "Actually, he was kind of a wimp, but we pulled him through." He flicked my shoulder in mock annoyance, but the gleam in his eyes matched his carefree laughter.

The Wymans were only two of the dozens of people I met. There were Brennan's parents and older sister, Lucy's parents and younger brother, Ellen's aunt, Elijah's grandparents, Jacklynn's mom and aunt…the list went on and on. Neil, Mark, Mara and Liam were finally allowed back to see Alaina, and I waved as they went by instead of stopping to chat.

Zoe was one of the few who didn't have anyone show up, which was really sad because, unlike others, the government had actually found her parents—her parents just didn't want anything to do with her. I told her she was welcome in my room anytime, really just so she didn't have to hang around everyone else who was getting their families back. She surprised me by taking me up on my offer, and spent quite a bit of time the next few days hanging out in my room with me, Sark, Mom and whoever else happened to come in. It wasn't like we were BFFs, so our interaction was tinted with slight awkwardness, but Mom was good at talking with her and made her feel at home. At least I hoped so.

I spent the time leading up to the service panicking and doing physical therapy. I told Dr. Bran I'd rather die than go the memorial service in a wheelchair, so he gave me simple exercises I could do with the warning I'd probably still have to use the chair.

Despite my hard efforts, I was only able to stand for about thirty seconds. Dr. Bran applauded my progress, but I was just frustrated. It wasn't enough.

The day before the service, Dr. Bran could tell I was really freaking out about the whole thing, so he went against his better judgment and brought out these weird leg contraptions. He said I probably wasn't ready for them, but I could give them a try.

They looked like those fancy metal knee braces except they stretched from my hip to around my foot. They were bulky, ugly, and hurt really bad, but with them I eventually was able to limp from one side of my room to the other.

Knowing I would abuse the braces and probably hurt myself, Dr. Bran made me a deal: he would let me wear them to the service if I still went in a wheelchair and only stood when I absolutely had to. That way I didn't have to give my speech in the chair, which was what I was mainly worried about. I thought the deal was a little one-sided, but I reluctantly agreed.

I didn't sleep at all the night before. At three I finally turned on the TV and watched cartoons until everyone else woke up and it was time to get ready.

Mom had bought me a black dress to wear—a long one, at my request—and she was the one that helped me into it after the adventure that was the shower. It was a good thing she was there because I had no motivation for anything. She dried my hair, pulled it into a ponytail and did my makeup, then Dr. Bran came to put the braces on. I clenched my teeth and fists in response to the pain as they were latched on to my legs, trying to ignore the fact that a man's hands were basically up my skirt. I was way too reserved for this ridiculous medical world, where they expected you to check your dignity at the door.

Then began the long process of loading everyone and their families into cars and getting to the park where the memorial would take place. Though the weather was still on the chilly side, we'd all voted to have the service outside. It seemed more fitting than being stuffed in some fancy building.

I watched the world pass by the car window without really seeing it. The sky was gray and cloudy, a perfect reflection of the day. At least the sky cared about us.

The park was decorated beautifully, hundreds of white folding chairs set up in front of a podium with a microphone, giant standing flower arrangements bringing bursts of color every few feet. A huge slab of concrete stood taller than me behind the podium, hundreds of names etched on it. The names of the dead.

Peter gave me a saluting nod from a few yards away as Mom pushed me toward the chairs—we were the only ones who still needed a wheelchair and it annoyed both of us to no end.

My dress sat weird on my lap, the braces underneath protruding in random places, giving it a funny look. I wrung my skirt in my hands over and over, afraid the crazy amount of different emotions in me would make me explode.

I told Mom to hurry and park me on the third row before someone told me to sit in the front. Sark sat next to me while she went back to the car to retrieve her forgotten purse, and I watched as the crowd began to assemble. The right side of chairs were reserved for the victims of the mutt attacks and their families. The left side was for the infecteds and theirs. I saw Brennan squinting through his new glasses—even after the laser eye surgery they performed, his vision was awful. A no longer pregnant Lucy sat next to him, her face pinched up with worry, as I knew she hadn't stopped thinking about her baby in the NICU since it was born a few days ago. Both of their parents sat on either side of them. Jacklynn sat with her mom and aunt on the other side of Mom, who was now next to Sark. Ellen took a seat in front of me with her aunt and uncle. Alaina and her family sat behind us, the Wymans tacked on the end with Peter. Kayla and three other blondes helped a staggering Daxton to his seat. His reversal took an unexplained nosedive, and he now walked on a prosthetic leg due to an emergency amputation. I hadn't seen him down about it, but Kayla told me he cried when he woke up.

My eyes avoided the right side of chairs, but my peripheral still caught the crowds of people that kept coming in. Kept coming. Kept coming. Would they ever end?

Is this what you wanted, Vanessa? Does this amount of suffering make you happy?

A stab of burning hit my wrists. I jerked my sleeves to check—of course there was nothing there but scars—then hurried and moved them back when Sark glanced at me.

I almost didn't recognize Dr. Bran in a black suit rather than his lab coat. He and his nice wife with a vivacious cloud of orange hair on her head came over, and he gave me an encouraging pat on the shoulder before heading to take his seat in the back with the other scientists.

Then all the government people showed up. I was happy to see Lindsey, but everyone else was a chore, as they all came up to shake my hand and babble on and on about how amazing I was, and how they would do anything for me. Funny how they all cared about me now that I was really worth something to them. I barely got through it. Sweaty creases formed on my skirt from me clenching it in my fists, and finally Sark took my hand and smoothed it out and whispered horrible but hilarious things in my ear about the pretentious people that congratulated me. My smiles to the government people became completely real, but I had to bite my tongue to keep from laughing at Sark's secret observations. Though the joke about Mr. Tameran's many chins may have been a little too below the belt.

I waded through the wave of important people, slumping in relief when they petered out. There had been a rumor that the President of the United States himself was going to show up, but the senator informed me he couldn't make it and sent his thanks and condolences.

Figures.

I shifted uncomfortably in my wheelchair as everyone found their seats and went quiet, the service beginning. Senator Whyme led the memorial, speaking in a powerful voice about the founding of our country, those who fought and died for our safety and rights, and the principles that brought us all together. I thought it was a bit much, but then I remembered that, at least to the victims' families, this had been chalked up to terrorism. They had no real grasp of how twisted the situation that killed their loved ones really was.

They began with the victims, a handful of pre-selected family members coming up to the podium to recount short eulogies to their loved ones and the others lost. I was doing okay until a six-year-old girl with dark hair read a poem she wrote about her dad.

A screen was hung over the cement slab to project a slideshow on. Hundreds of pictures of different people came up—at family barbecues, with their dogs, on a boat—each only getting a second of time, while piano music played in the background. Muffled sobbing echoed through the brisk air from the right side of the seating as hundreds of people paid a last tribute to their loved ones. I had to blink back tears, but I couldn't tear my eyes from the screen.

Then the senator got back up and talked about us—the brave infecteds who pushed against the minority standing and chose to fight a battle it didn't seem they could win, losing so many of their own along the way. He gave a quick account of what happened, how Cyrus had unleashed the monsters that killed so many, how we went in on our own to stop it. Again, I thought it was a little too much, but whatever. It was all about the presentation, I guess.

It's still all just a show.

The projector played another slideshow, this one rolling through pictures of us, containing each infected who had gone to fight. A ridiculous blue sky background was behind each of us as we looked off into the distance. It was stupid. I hated it.

The slideshow went black, then words popped up: *We are survivors. We did not survive in vain.* I guess it was better than the lame hero quote they were going to put before I told them not to.

We aren't heroes, I had said to the team in charge of the service. *We aren't victims. We're survivors.*

A big 'Thank you for your sacrifice' went across the screen, then it was over. I'd been so focused on the production that it wasn't until the senator introduced me and Sark nudged my leg that I realized it was my turn.

My legs shook as I dragged myself up from my wheelchair, Sark's hand on my waist for support until he knew I was standing steady. Then began the longest walk of my entire life.

The tips of my fingers were numb. My whole body was numb. I didn't look up from the ground as I limped up to the podium, touching the cement slab softly before turning to face the ginormous crowd.

Suddenly I forgot how to talk. My hands shook harder as I cleared my throat, my heart speeding up, my veins burning, and I didn't know if it'd be worse to have a breathing attack or not talk at all or just die right there on the spot.

This was a bad idea. Bad idea. Bad idea.

The silence drug out for another painful thirty seconds. I looked over the ocean of people, all the ones I knew and the ones I didn't. I caught sight of Ellen. She gave me a small, sad smile and somehow that helped me find my voice.

"I thought a long time," I said, wincing as my voice exploded out the speakers behind me, "about what to say here today. A very long time. I came up with a lot of things you usually hear at funerals, you know, like 'they were great people' and 'they'll be missed' and 'we'll always remember them but they're in a better place' and stuff like that. And even though it's all true, I realized saying that doesn't matter. Because they're still dead. And there's nothing we can do to bring them back to us.

And there are no words to be said that can justify that or make it better."

I took a shaky breath, focusing on a spot of grass behind all the people, reciting the words in my head first so I wouldn't mess them up. "So then I started thinking about what I learned from them, what they taught me. It seemed like a small way to keep them alive, you know? To help them live on somehow."

I had to clear my throat again. "I learned the true meaning of bravery. And loyalty. From these people who I've lost, I've learned what it truly means to love and to hate. To sacrifice. To give freely. To appreciate every small and big thing you're given or work to attain." My voice was cracking. "Even from the smallest minds, I learned the most. I learned why it was important to have fun and to always believe in yourself. I learned that sometimes we get so caught up in life and sorrows and responsibilities, we forget how much we need to be childlike. To believe in magic and the impossible. I learned that there is strength in caring and there is no weakness in fear. And I feel really lucky that I knew amazing people who showed all this to me."

I thought of those not on the official 'fight' list. I thought of Hadley's parents and Sark's mom and Erika. I thought of Alaina's mom and Ellen's mom and my dad and Mom's dad. I thought of my brother Kieran and Peter's sister Leslie.

"Because we aren't just here to honor them." I pointed to the cement slab behind me. "Not just those lost in this fight. We're here to honor others too: mothers and fathers and sisters and brothers and grandparents and friends. We're also here to honor the parts of us who died with them. To honor kids—" My voice broke and I had to blink back tears. "Kids who were robbed mercilessly of their childhood and the rest of their lives. Not just the children we'd come to adore, but the child inside all of us."

Get back on track. You're derailing this whole thing.

Cleared my throat again. "But one thing I learned a lot about is choices. Our choices. Their choices. One person I'm mourning here today still had his innocence. He was too young. He didn't live long enough to get to make a lot of choices, and now he'll never get to make them. Another one was stuck in cruel circumstances and had the chance to choose taken from him. But of the few choices he did get to make, most of them were the wrong ones. And that makes people look over the fewer—but no less significant—right ones. And yet another person I knew had spent his whole life making the wrong choices and had just started on the path of fixing things and finding forgiveness."

Now I was playing with my ponytail. I couldn't stop fidgeting. "All of them were taken too soon. All needed more time. It seems unfair, the way we lost them, the timing, the fact that they had so much left to experience, not just for themselves but with us."

I stole a glance at my bawling mother, which was a mistake. I stared at the grass again. "I heard once that we always have a choice. Always. I don't believe that anymore. We don't get to choose the bad things that find us. We don't get the choice of whether or not the darkness affects us, whether or not we break. When your feet get swept out from under you, you don't get to choose if you fall. You can only let your eyes adjust, gather the pieces, and drag yourself up."

Then my mind went blank, so I just stole the line from the slideshow. "We are survivors. And those we lost would want to make sure we don't survive in vain."

The crowd gave me a respectful round of applause. I turned to get the heck out of there when I caught sight of the little girl who'd read the poem about her dad. I froze. She sat on a woman's lap, a sad but confused look on her face.

She doesn't understand. She doesn't know he's really gone.

"I'm so sorry," I said, my voice breaking. "I'm so sorry." Then I ducked my head and limped back to my seat, practically collapsing in my wheelchair. Sark took my shaking hand, but I couldn't bring myself to look up from the ground.

That was awful. They deserved better than that.

Senator Whyme went back up to the podium, thanking everyone for a beautiful ceremony. He then announced that the infecteds had prepared a special tribute and for everyone to remain in their seats and let us have our time.

Brennan and Elijah found me first, each holding a guitar. Brennan offered one to me.

"Do you want to take the lead?"

I held up a shaky hand. "I can't play yet. Slow reaction time."

He nodded. "You can just do vocals then, if you want."

"I never learned all the words," I lied. "It's okay, you guys go ahead." Thankfully they were okay with that and went to set up.

My legs were not ready to get back up, but I didn't want to sit for this. Using Sark's hand for support, I stood again, trading his hand for Jacklynn's, who'd come down the row. Ellen took my other hand and we made our way to the pile of firewood assembled a little ways off from the cement slab. Even Peter rose and Alaina helped him walk the distance to the circle we all formed around the firewood.

The crowd was silent as the medium-sized bonfire was lit. Fire was how we'd send off infecteds at the Compound. It was our way of sending off everyone today.

At some unknown cue, Brennan and Elijah started strumming a tune on the guitar, then began singing the song they'd written for the occasion. Their voices worked beautifully together, almost haunting, as they sung of fire and loss, the real flames reaching up to the gray sky.

I didn't let go of Jacklynn or Ellen's hands, so I didn't have fingers to wipe the tear that rolled down my cheek. I just watched the flames crackle.

I'm so sorry. All of you. I'm so sorry.

The end was the most powerful: we all joined in for the last verse, Brennan and Elijah's soft voices now backed with ninety others. Tears flowed freely down my face, and I felt Jacklynn shudder with a quiet sob.

Then it was over. Nobody moved for a few moments, hanging heads silently in respect. It felt like we were all frozen in the scene—all of us, even the audience—the power and imagery of the tribute immobilizing us. After what seemed like an eternity of us all united together, the senator's voice came back over the speakers, thanking everyone again and dismissing them. The spell was lifted. We could move again.

Our circle broke, the crowd standing up, some leaving and others starting up quiet conversations. Jacklynn ran back to her mom. Ellen turned and gave me a giant hug, and, for once, I didn't hesitate. I just hugged her back. We stood like that forever. Over her shoulder I caught a glimpse of Peter wheeling up to check out the memorial, his body stiffening slightly, then his arm reaching forward slowly, touching the bottom middle of the concrete. He turned his head to see me, his tear-filled eyes finding mine.

"Thank you," he mouthed to me.

I gave a small grin. "She deserved it," I mouthed back. I didn't know if he'd understand me, but he grinned and nodded, so I guess he did, pressing his fingers again against what I assumed was his sister's name.

Ellen broke away from me to look at my face. "I love you, Arie. And I know it was awful but I'm so glad we met each other."

That made me choke on my tears. "Me too."

She started walking to her aunt just as Jacklynn ran back to me, Sark and Mom following a ways behind her. With a sad smile through her tears, she held up a thin stack of printer paper. I just nodded.

Jacklynn plopped down on the ground, and I had to bend awkwardly to get myself down there too. She took two pieces, handed one to me, then motioned to Sark. He sat down next to us.

"Paper airplanes?" he asked softly.

Both Jacklynn and I nodded. "It's what Hadley would want, right?" Jacklynn asked.

Sark nodded. "I think it's exactly what he would want."

Jacklynn smiled at that response and started working on hers. She stopped when she saw me staring blankly at my flat page.

"Don't you know how to make one?" she asked, her voice in awe that I wouldn't know that survival skill.

"He, uh…he showed me once, but I…" I rubbed my forehead, frustration bubbling. "I don't remember."

"Here." Sark took my paper, braced it against his black pants, then started folding it into an airplane. A gasp of excitement escaped Jacklynn when she saw his expertise, and she scooted over to sit in his lap while they both crafted their planes.

Sark handed me mine when he was done, then grabbed another paper to make his own. Brennan, Lucy, Mark, and Alaina made one too. On Jacklynn's cue, we all flew them into the fire, the flames licking up the paper and sending the embers to the sky.

"Whoa," Jacklynn muttered, watching the fire in wonder. "Hadley would've thought that was cool. Huh?"

"Yeah," I murmured. "I think he would've." I patted her knee. "You're a great friend."

She beamed, then jumped up and ran to tell her mom about it.

I watched the fire for a few more seconds before staggering to my feet. These braces had to go soon. I was about to go find the wheelchair when I saw Mom standing a few feet from me, tears falling down her face as she stared at the fire.

I limped to her and stood next to her. She grabbed my hand.

"Thank you," she said. "For mentioning him. That was very noble of you."

'Noble' wasn't the word I would use, but I was glad it meant something to her. My mind travelled back in time to the moment that I'd replayed over and over.

"I should've talked to him," I said out of nowhere. I could almost see the scene in the flames: us in the hotel room. Me confessing the truth about Kieran's death. My dad stepping to give me a hug, only to have me walk away. "He tried to hug me. He tried to take me back." My voice got shaky. "And now he's gone."

Mom squeezed my hand. "Arie, he was a great man and we both loved him in our own ways. But he made a lot of wrong, awful choices. You can't martyr him, baby." She took a deep breath, as if composing herself, then turned and smiled softly at me. "I'll be waiting in the car. Whenever you're ready." Then she left.

I watched her go, seeing the group of government agents and reporters gathered and talking with the senator, probably waiting to snag me again—the senator didn't really grasp what I meant when I said I wanted out of the media period. I sighed. I was too tired to talk, especially the inordinate way they expected.

"You want me to be your security?" Sark asked as he walked up next to me, his gaze following mine. "I'm even wearing a suit. I'll pretend I have an earpiece and everything."

I cracked a smile. "You do look more official."

You look great. Handsome and charming and...

Our hands reached for each other's at the same time, and I smiled again when our fingers interlocked. He stood in between me and the group of fancy suits, as if to shield me from interaction, and I concentrated on putting one foot in front of the other. My legs were killing me. I almost asked Sark to go get my wheelchair so I didn't have to walk anymore, but I didn't want to let go of his hand and be left exposed in the open.

"How are your legs?" Sark asked after several staggering steps. "Are you doing okay?"

I need a saw to cut them off.

"They're fine," I answered. "A little tired."

He nudged me with his shoulder. "I'm sure. You did great, by the way. Your speech or whatever you want to call it."

"Thanks."

"I mean it. I don't know why you were so worried. It seemed like it came naturally to you, like it was...well, not *easy*, but you know what I mean."

I just sighed, getting sick of unnecessary praise even though it was really nice. "I guess. You should've done it. Be grateful they didn't ask you."

"Oh, I am," he told me. "If they'd asked me to speak, it would've been about you."

I didn't have a response for that. We finally made it to the wheelchair, and I immediately turned my oxygen on and shoved the little tubes in my nose, taking deep breaths.

The drive back to the hospital went by fast, thank goodness. It wasn't long before I was back in my room. Nearly in tears and not able to wait for Dr. Bran, I asked Sark to help me take the awful braces off—I couldn't decide if the major distraction of having *his* hands up my skirt was worth almost holding in all yelps of pain—claiming over and over that the red patches of skin didn't hurt that bad. Then I told him to go do whatever: I was just going to take a nap.

Once I was alone, I changed into sweats and a t-shirt, my planned boycott of hospital gowns put into action. Then I wrapped my blanket around my shoulders, put the oxygen mask on my face, and curled into a ball, waiting to drown in the tsunami inside of me.

I jumped when the door opened. I'd thought nobody would come in since I put the 'sleeping' sign on my door, so I was unprepared to fake asleep.

Dr. Bran caught me. Back in his trusty lab coat, he came and sat on the foot of my bed. I felt like an idiot at the thought of how stupid I must've looked: smeared makeup, red eyes, tearstained face, shaking body, gasping breath. I actually looked how I felt. And that was something I'd hoped to hide.

"That was a beautiful service," he said, his tone conversational. "Were you happy with it?"

I just shrugged. *Enough, I guess.*

He looked me in the eyes. "Is there anything you want to talk about?"

I shook my head.

"All right, then." He gave me a knowing stare. "If you don't want to talk then I guess I have nothing else to do but check your legs."

I froze. I was sure Dr. Bran would not approve of the nasty red welts. I'd never be allowed to walk again.

With a trembling hand, I took off my oxygen mask. My voice was small and raspy with tears and shame as I uttered the words that were years overdue coming from my mouth. "I need help. I'm having a hard time."

Dr. Bran's eyes softened. "You're grieving. That's natural."

I shook my head. "It's not just grief. I'm…" I held my head in my hands, unable to face my own confessions. "I'm so messed up."

"In what way?"

"In every way. And I can't get a handle on it—on anything. I have no idea in the world how to deal with any of it. And it feels like…it feels like I never will."

"The things you've experienced—"

"Are hard," I interrupted harshly. That's what everyone has been telling me, as though I wasn't aware. "They're hard and hellish and would destroy anyone. I know that. It doesn't make it easier."

"Do you think about what would've happened if you were never infected? What life you might have had?"

"Not anymore. Not really. It feels inevitable, that I would be this way. I don't know, maybe I'm just used to it—being such a big part of my life. Of me. It's just..."I took a shaky breath. "I had to hold up my world for so long. I cracked. I cracked and darkness got inside of me. It changed me." My voice got quieter. "Life didn't break me. She did. And I can't put myself back together." I finally peeked up to look at him. "Am I just stupid? Or weak? Or what?"

Dr. Bran paused thoughtfully for a moment. "My brother's a psychiatrist. He works with people who have seen a lot of things. A lot of hard things. They have a lot to deal with."

My tone went flat. "I'm not going to therapy. That's for…"

He raised an eyebrow. "Weak people?"

"Well…no." That sounded awful. "Other people. It's just not for me."

"It's not for you or it's not for your ego?"

For that, I didn't have an answer.

Weakness is death.

"That's not what I was saying," he went on when I didn't. "He has several phrases he uses to help his patients. One of them is the 'D-Zone' or the "Die and Deal Zone.' I believe that's where you are."

"What's that?"

He stood and picked up a book of fairytales off the counter that Jacklynn and I had been reading. "It's the hardest part of the healing process. It's depression. Anger. Bitterness. It's hopelessness and defeat and turmoil in the face of traumatic experiences. And it's the part that's often left out.

You have to let yourself arrive at an emotion before you can move past it." He sat back down and flipped through the book. "Look at these stories you love, for example. These people go through awful things, then just jump right to their supposed happily ever after. The writers left out what must've happened in between."

My forehead creased. "You mean the D-zone?"

"Yes." The page stopped on a story and he pointed to the title. "Take Cinderella. You think she just got a prince? No, she got a lifetime of self-confidence issues and a case of OCD." More page flipping. "And you can't tell me that Sleeping Beauty didn't become an insomniac because she was scared of not waking up again." More pages. "And Snow White here, will question everything she eats, her paranoia growing until she stops eating all together and starves herself. That's called anorexia."

Dr. Bran shut the book and placed it on the bed. "It feels like you're losing, like you'll never get to the happily ever after, but the D-zone is a part of the healing process. You're angry. You're confused. You're depressed. You're arriving at and feeling hard emotions, and you're doing a wonderful job so far. So, no I don't think you're stupid or weak for being in the D-Zone. Do you know why?"

"Why?"

"Because it's the part nobody is exempt from. Which I find ironic because it's the part nobody talks about." He tapped the book. "It's a part of the story. Just remember it's not the end of it."

I thought about that for a moment, then realized I should say something. "Thank you."

Thanks for not judging me.

He gave me a small smile. "You're welcome. Now, I'm going to give you the benefit of the doubt and check on your legs tomorrow." He hesitated. "I know you don't like them, but just know I can—"

"Yes please," I interrupted, surprising him. "I just want to be done for right now."

Dr. Bran pursed his lips and nodded. "Okay." Then he hooked me up to a new IV and shot sedatives through it, putting me out of my misery.

13

Julianne Lucille Jennings-Welker was born on April thirtieth, weighed five pounds, six ounces, and was arguably the cutest thing I'd ever seen.

Lucy's baby girl was whisked to the NICU right after she was born, as she was premature and the doctors wanted to make sure she was okay. Lucy was put straight through reversal and made one of the fastest recoveries of all of us. Both she and Brennan waited in fear for news of their baby girl.

Julianne was released from the NICU within four days. Much to the doctors' disbelief, the baby was perfectly healthy. They ran a million different tests but couldn't find any anomalies or traces of the formula in the child—there was nothing to do but let her go. The small family was finally reunited.

Between Lucy, Brennan, their moms, and everyone else in the universe who wanted time holding Julianne—including *my* mom—I had a hard time finding a chance to even meet the girl. Once most of the excitement had died down and there wasn't a line anymore, I wheeled down to Lucy's room to get my turn.

I fell in love the second I saw her. Brennan took her from Lucy, just a pink bundle, then walked over to place the girl in my arms.

"Arie, meet Jules."

"Oh my gosh, Brennan," I murmured as I stared into giant brown eyes, the soft baby smell wafting up in my nose. "She's absolutely beautiful."

"She is, huh?" He had the biggest, proudest smile on his face as he looked at his daughter.

I smiled, looking back and forth between him and Lucy. "Great job, guys."

"I'm just so glad she's here," Lucy said, her eyes on Jules. "She's here and safe with us. And now we can actually give her a home." She sighed in contentment. "Everything worked out after all."

I stayed for almost an hour holding baby Jules while Brennan and Lucy told me all about what color they wanted to paint her room and how each of their parents took the news and how Lucy's name was Lucille too, after her grandma. It was so sweet to see them, so happy and proud, after so many months of worry and fear.

Before I left, I made them promise to come say goodbye before they left the hospital, as many infecteds were beginning to be discharged. They both promised, I reluctantly gave Jules back to her dad, then I wheeled to my room.

Ellen came by later with some awful and wonderful news. I knew she was being discharged in three days, but for some reason it never occurred to me that she would actually leave.

"So guess what happened?" she asked, practically shaking my bed as she failed to contain her bouncing excitement.

I couldn't help but grin. "What?"

"Remember right before we went into the building and we were all talking about what we would do if we lived?"

"Yeah."

"Well Peter remembered too. I guess his mom is a lawyer or something and has some really high political contacts. He told her that's what I wanted to do, so she got me an intern position on a campaign! Isn't that awesome?"

"What?" I exclaimed. "Are you serious? That's amazing!"

"I know! They said I can start as soon as I want to. I'm flying out to D.C. next week."

My voice went flat without my permission. "Next week? Wow, that's…" I tried to bring back my excitement. "That's so soon. That's really cool. Congratulations, Elle."

She nodded, beaming. "Thanks. I figured, why wait, you know? I'm so excited, I could die." Her face fell. "I'm going to miss you. So much."

"Yeah. I'm going to miss you too."

"But I'll come visit. It's not like we'll never see each other again, right?"

I shook my head to clear it. "No, yeah. Right. You better come visit. They'll probably give you your own fancy jet or something."

She waved her hand. "No, I'm just an intern." She winked at me. "At least for now."

"I'll be waiting for the day when I hear you're running the country. Remember us little people, okay?"

She laughed, but I sensed a realism to it. That's what she wanted. After years of being trapped at the Compound, she was ready to go start her life.

I was happy for her. I really was. And so proud. I just really really *really* didn't want her to leave. But I felt like telling her that would ruin her excitement.

Over half the infecteds were discharged the same day as Ellen, and more left every day after that, until it was just me, Peter and Jacklynn that were left. The trifecta team, I guess.

If I wasn't wasting my life on the TV or typing on a laptop, then I was in therapy. Peter and I were often in the gym at the same time, and we'd come up with games to play or competitions to make the torture more bearable. We were both frustrated beyond belief—reversal had left him with a kind of disease that made it really difficult to build back muscle. And for the star football player, that was about the worst thing that could possibly happen to him. He was making progress though. It would just take time.

Alaina was around often to act as moral support for Peter even though she'd been one of the first discharged. We spoke from time to time, mostly just small talk stuff. If it ever got prolonged, I just asked the right questions that would get her to talk so I didn't have to. She told me all about how nervous she was to meet Peter's mom, and I had to stifle a laugh at the thought of how proper Mrs. Wyman would've reacted to Alaina's crimson hair alone.

Unfortunately, I also started another kind of therapy—the kind where you're supposed to just spill your guts to a complete stranger. Dr. Bran asked me to just try a few sessions with his psychologist brother. If I truly hated it then I wouldn't have to keep it up.

"Your physical health is tied to your mental," he would tell me over and over. "You're not going to get better if your brain doesn't want to."

Or at all, I would bite back in my head.

Dr. Bran Psychologist was nice enough. I couldn't help a double take when he walked in: a tall, bald black man. The near opposite of my Dr. Bran's short, bearded pastiness.

"I'm Dr. Bran," he told me in a deep voice as he shook my hand. "My brother is your doctor."

I tried so hard to curb my surprise because I knew that was just rude. "Yeah. Yeah, he is. He's great."

"Yeah, he is. I like to think we share a lot of the same qualities as brothers. Sense of humor." He rubbed his shiny head. "I didn't get the hair gene—pretty sure he took mine and put in on his face—but we have the same chin."

That made me laugh and relax slightly. Dr. Bran Psychologist was willing to poke fun at any part of himself just to get me to trust him. And slowly I came to, like his brother. He was a good guy and truly wanted to help me, which was good because I needed him to pry if anything was ever going to come out. The more sessions we had, the easier it got to talk.

I rarely talked about it, as though therapy itself were a felony—Dr. Bran and Mom were the only ones who knew. I wasn't even brave enough to tell Sark.

Something was wrong with him too. I'd been noticing it since the first day I woke up from reversal, but I could never pinpoint exactly what it was. I just assumed he was stressed and tired and probably traumatized too, just like the rest of us. I was too caught up in everything else going on to really think about what was bugging him.

It was just another day. Another trudging day amidst a million boring and useless days. We were sitting in my room, alone, and somehow got on the topic of my dad. It was still a soft spot for me, but I was surprised too at how much it upset Sark. I knew he and Mom were one step away from swapping BFF necklaces, but I didn't think he cared too much about Kurt Nolan.

"I should've hugged him," I muttered. "He wanted to hug me and take the next step, and I wouldn't let him. I should've."

Sark shook his head. "No, Arie, your mom's right: you can't martyr him. You just needed time that you didn't have. The world doesn't expect that much of you."

But it does. It expects so much of me and I keep falling short.

I started biting my thumbnail—the last fingernail I hadn't torn apart—thinking about how stupid the whole cancer thing was. That's when it hit me, so obvious I felt like an awful excuse for a human being for not thinking of it earlier.

I sucked in a sharp breath, feeling my soul crush. "Oh, Sark, I'm so sorry. I didn't even…I didn't even think."

His eyes met mine, then they got misty with tears—which was how I knew I was right—and he clenched his jaw to try and fight them.

"It's not a big deal, Arie," he muttered harshly through his teeth.

But it was. I knew it was. Because the last time he had to stay in the hospital for an extended period of time—not as a patient but as a waiter—the last time he'd been forced to stay at a place that claimed to heal—the last time he'd been somewhat close to a parent taken by cancer—was when he watched the most important person in his life die, his mother, leaving him all alone.

Arie, you idiot! How could you not see what this was doing to him?

"I'm sorry," I whispered. "You shouldn't…you shouldn't have had to watch all this. You should've left when it was too much."

He ducked his head so I couldn't see his face, running his hands through his hair. "And what? Left you to die?" He shook his head. "I couldn't do that again. I couldn't…"

He cleared his throat and stood, jerking his way toward the door. I tried to grab his arm, but he pulled away.

"Sark, please don't go," I said, my voice cracking.

That made him stop halfway between my bed and the door, his back to me. "Why?"

"Because…because you're going to…probably…" I took a deep breath. "You're going to go get wasted. I know that and I really wish you wouldn't."

He didn't refute me. He didn't say anything.

"How have you done it?" I finally asked softly. "So far. Without alcohol. What helps you stay…sane, I guess?"

I didn't think he would answer, but his quiet voice came through after a minute. "You. Your reasoning. Your voice. For years now. You keep me grounded."

That was about that sweetest thing he—or anyone—had ever said to me, and in any other circumstance it would've been a million times better. "Yeah, but right now that's not enough. Please let me help you. You don't have to deal with this alone." I had no clue how I could help him, but I was desperate to try. "Please."

Sark hung his head, running his hand through his hair, then let out a breath that lasted years. I was afraid he was just going to leave anyway—and I wouldn't be able to follow him—but instead he did the opposite. Without meeting my eyes, he sat down on my bed. I reached for his arm and he let me take it, then he scooted back. Confused and surprised, I moved over to make room for him as he lied down next to me, wrapped an arm around my waist to pull me down next to him, then rested his head on my shoulder and buried his face in my neck. He trembled slightly under my arms, as though trying to contain a storm, and I saw a flash of a memory that wasn't mine: a sixteen-year-old kid. Just a kid. Lying in his mom's hospital bed, holding her frail frame tight, after months of watching her waste away, unknowingly giving her the last hug they'd ever have, days or maybe hours before he lost her forever.

A shaky breath went through him, spreading warmth on my neck. "I miss her," he whispered.

I thought I'd already exceeded the amount of crushing sadness I could feel at one time, but this now topped it. Pulling the blankets over both of us, I just held him tight, not sure what I could possibly say.

Next thing I knew, I was being shaken awake. Disoriented, I opened my eyes to darkness, a woman leaning over me. It took me a moment to recognize her as Jacklynn's doctor.

"I'm sorry to bother you, Arie," she whispered, which is when I realized Sark was still asleep next to me. "But Jacklynn's having an emotional breakdown. I can't bring her through it. Is there any way you could try to talk her down?"

I nodded, rubbing the sleep out of my eyes. Gently so I didn't wake him, I slid out from underneath Sark's arm and sat in my wheelchair, the doctor at the helm. She pushed me out of my room and down the hallway to Jacklynn's.

I could hear her crying before I even got inside. If I thought the sounds were bad, they were nothing compared to the scene.

Jacklynn's aunt was sitting in the corner with puffy eyes—apparently, she'd given up. Her mom was sitting on the edge of the bed, her voice broken as she tried to reason through the mess that was Jacklynn. The girl sat on her bed, tears rolling down her face as she sobbed, her eyes narrowed and concentrated but wide at the same time. It made her look manic. Her frail arms worked furiously with white paper while she muttered to herself, the inside of her hands red with paper cuts. Crumpled sheets of paper littered the floor everywhere.

The doctor wheeled me up and I took her mom's place on the bed. She patted my hand before going to join her sister.

"I've got to fix it," Jacklynn was muttering. "I have to fix them."

I put my hand on the airplane she was making. "Jacklynn, please stop."

"They won't fly!" she screamed at me. "They're broken! I can't get them to fly!"

"Okay, we can fix that. Can you just take a break for a second?" I paused before adding, "I don't think Hadley would mind."

The name was like a magic password to shut her down. She froze exactly where she was, her labored breathing going silent. Afraid I'd just triggered something worse, I waited for her to speak, the silence stretching out for almost ten minutes.

Then out of nowhere she spoke, her voice tired and monotone. "If I hadn't gotten stuck then Hadley would be here. I was the one who got stuck. I wish the Dome would've crushed me instead. Life is stupid anyway."

"It is stupid," I agreed. "I wish the Dome wouldn't have crushed either of you."

She met my eyes. "But it did. So what am I supposed to do?" Her voice broke. "Even when I went to school before I was infected, I was shy. He was my best friend, Arie. He was my *only* friend."

A lump formed in my throat. "I miss him too. But you know what? If he could talk to us, he'd be saying how you were the best friend he'd ever had too. He would tell the whole world to go be your friend because he had so much fun with you."

She shook her head violently. "Nobody would choose to be my friend. The other infected kids that came are already all better and I know that they would look at me funny 'cause I'm not." Her breathing picked up, her voice rising. "The doctors keep telling me I'll get better! And I'm not! I'm still sad all the time. I'm stuck here forever."

I put my hand on her leg. "Healing takes time. People forget that sometimes. You'll be better again someday, I know it."

She glared at me. "No you don't. Do you think *you'll* be better someday?"

I blinked in surprise, my mouth falling halfway open. "Well, um…yeah. I do. Just maybe not that soon." The words burned my mouth like the Bible burned hypocrites.

Jacklynn started crying again. "No! We're never getting better! We're never…" She slumped forward and held her face in her hands as she broke into sobs. "Hadley's *gone*."

I was in her room for hours, talking to her, listening to her, restraining her, helping her. She sobbed and screamed and whispered and even laughed a few times. I was trying so hard to keep myself awake when she asked me to sing her a song.

"Remember the one from that night at the club in Denver?" she asked. "When there was the storm and everyone was really scared?"

I did, actually. Singing the song to her, my mind wandered back to that night—the night we'd all thought was doomsday. Lennon had found our hideout. I was going to be turned over to Alexis. The infecteds were going to die. Sark was going to be butchered as punishment. My best friend Alaina was barely talking to me. I was trying to work up the courage to make a run for it. A record-breaking storm ruined our escape. At the time, I thought that night was the worst it could possibly get.

Of course, those giant monsters then turned out to be shadows compared to the real monsters that lurked on the outskirts, in the future. We didn't know that at the time, though. I remembered being absolutely terrified, sure that we had reached our end.

And yet we made it through.

It was awful. It was terrible. Things only got impossibly worse, then nosedived from there, crash landing into four layers of rock bottom. But we made it through. We survived.

"It's just a little rain," I murmured to Jacklynn after the song was over, caught in time between past and present. "We'll be okay."

14

I wheeled myself back to my room the next morning, utterly exhausted. Physically and emotionally drained after my all-nighter with Jacklynn, I practically threw myself onto my bed, preparing to fall asleep on impact. Once I lied down I saw the hand that was holding onto my bed railing. Peeking over the other side of the bed, I found Sark sitting on the floor, staring at the wall with a face of stone.

Slowly, I wrapped my hand over his. "I'm not going to die here," I murmured to him.

His voice was as hard as his expression. "You don't know that."

"Yeah, I do, actually. I can just tell." I sighed, trying not to sound tired. "I'm still going to be around for a long time."

He didn't answer. He just stared.

"Did your mom tell you that? Once she was hospitalized. Did she tell you she wasn't going to die?"

There was silence. "No. She didn't. She knew."

I rubbed his hand softly with my fingers. "It's hell for you here. Just leave. I promise I'll still be here whenever you can come back."

That cracked him. He turned his head to look at me. "You'll promise me that?"

"Yes." We both knew how important promises were to me. "But only if you promise me something too."

"What?"

"No alcohol. At all. If you need someone to listen, call me instead."

Part of me didn't think he'd actually take me up on it. He thought for a few minutes before nodding. As if he were wounded, he dragged himself up and shifted, like he was testing to see if his legs still worked. Then without meeting my eyes, he leaned over and kissed my forehead before walking stiffly out the door.

He really did it. He really left. My eyes stung at the thought of how much pain he had to be in to actually leave, and I wished with my whole broken soul that I could've gone with him.

Mom came back a few hours later. She'd spent some time apartment hunting ever since the first infecteds were discharged. I almost told her she shouldn't—really, was I getting out of here any time soon?—but then I realized she was probably sick of sleeping on the fold out guest couches downstairs. She deserved to find a home.

She plopped down in the chair, shedding her purple jacket as she gushed about the place she considered to be the 'one.'

"It's going to be perfect," she finished, then looked around. "Is Sark down in the cafeteria? I should ask him to bring me caffeine."

I shook my head, playing it cool, not even looking away from the TV I wasn't really watching. "No."

"Oh. Did they call him down for another one of those one-on-one meetings? I know how much he hates those."

"No."

As always, she had to know everything. "Well, where is he?"

I kept my voice even. "He left."

"To the store?" She started rummaging through her purse. "I thought I still had my credit card…"

"No." I met her eyes, my voice hardening so it didn't crack. "He. Left."

Mom dropped her purse to the ground and her eyes filled with concern. "Oh, no, baby, you two didn't have a fight, did you?"

"No." I looked at the TV again. "I told him to."

"Why? I thought you'd want him here."

I do. "He needed to leave. He really did. It was bad. I couldn't help him." My voice broke and tears stung my eyes without my permission.

"Oh, baby." She sat on my bed next to me, wrapping her arms around me. "I'm sorry." At first I resisted—hadn't I promised myself I wouldn't cry about this?—but then I just gave up, threw my arms around her and cried into her shoulder.

The hours turned into days, the days into weeks. After being put on some kind of anti-depressant, Jacklynn made enough progress that she was discharged. Mom and I threw a party with Jacklynn's family, her doctor, Dr. Bran, Peter and his parents, Alaina, Mark and Mara, plus a few of the nurses as guests. We decorated the common room with streamers and balloons, a table spread out with water and these special granola bars—one of the few foods she could eat that she liked. She was ecstatic when we surprised her and later told me it was one of the funnest things she'd done in a long time. Then, after a few tears and many hugs, she left.

And then there were two. Me and Peter.

We played poker a lot. I didn't know why. Since neither of us had money, we'd assign each color chip a different thing, like stolen M&Ms or pillows or pills. Peter remarked it was fun to gamble with something other than our lives or sanity, which made his mom huff quietly in concerned surprise. When Mrs. Wyman wasn't around, Peter cracked open and told me all about his sister Leslie—his best friend in the world— how they came to be infected, and eventually how she died. I pretended not to notice when a single tear fell down his face. We compared survival notes and held contests for who had ever dumpster-dived for the worst thing, and I wondered why it had taken us so long to be such great friends.

I met with the senator a few more times, which I learned to hate. He was nice. I just had no patience for the publicity aspect he cared about so much, and finally I just told him I wouldn't take part in it anymore. The war was over. Time for them to go home and get a new hobby.

The only true excitement for me was when I walked down the hallway by myself for the first time. That inspired Peter to try harder and soon enough we were both staggering down the hallway, having contests to see who could go farthest or fastest, each encouraging the other. Dr. Bran allowed us a delicacy to celebrate our success—ice cream—and when I found myself sitting on the floor of the hallway sharing mint chocolate chip out of the carton, I realized I didn't know what in the world I would've done the past weeks without Peter.

After I could go up and down the hallway, Dr. Bran asked me what I thought about being discharged even though I hadn't technically 'fully recovered.' That's when I realized a whole new problem.

"I don't even know what I would do," I said quietly, twisting my blanket in my hands. "I don't really…I don't really belong anywhere. I don't even want to do anything, but if I did…I don't know."

I don't know how to live.

Dr. Bran thought for a moment. "You've been in survival mode for a long time now. There's nothing wrong with that. It's kept you alive, right?

And because it's kept you alive, you're attached to it. You don't know how to let it go." He patted my knee. "But someday you're going to feel the need again to do more than survive. You're going to want to live again."

I shrugged. "Then what?"

He gave a small grin. "Don't survive in vain." I rolled my eyes, but he went on. "No, I'm not joking. Turn this around. Use what's happened to you to your advantage rather than have it keep dragging you down. Own it."

I raised a mocking eyebrow. "*Own* it? Really?"

He nodded, not put off by the cynicism. "Work as a counselor. Blog about the struggles of health issues. Raise awareness for domestic abuse. Become a social worker. Volunteer your time to help homeless youth."

I dropped my eyes and shook my head, my voice getting small. "I can barely walk. I can't do anything. I'd just be useless to them. Other people should do it."

"No." Dr. Bran tapped my hand until I looked up at him. "You should. You have more to offer than any other person you'd deem 'normal.'"

My forehead creased. "Why?"

"Because when those patients or victims or kids look at you and say, 'it hurts,' you'll be able to look them square in the eye and say, 'I know.'"

That struck a chord with me. I thought of how comforting it would've been any of the nights I'd spent in an alley or a gross motel, any time I'd cried because I was scared of someone or because I was stuck in a hospital or because I knew I was going to lose the ultimate battle of my life—if I had someone look at me and understand.

Dr. Bran nodded at my thoughtful silence. "Experience is the most valuable thing a person can have—that's why it costs so much to get it."

I thought for another moment. "You know, I don't know what I'll do when I don't have my on-demand fortune cookie dispenser on hand."

Dr. Bran just laughed. "I'm going to miss you too."

~~~

I didn't hear from Sark for seventeen days. I didn't know where he was or where he'd gone or if he was okay. I just made myself sick worrying about him. Eventually I started to wonder if he ever would come back.

Maybe he stayed out of duty or obligation. Once he got an out, he took it.

On day eighteen, I woke up to find him there, sitting in his chair as though he'd never left, and he acted as though nothing had happened and wanted to keep it that way. He did seem looser though. More relaxed. I gave him space and didn't ask, but I hoped that the time away had helped at least a little bit.

Unfortunately, he picked a bad day to come back. I woke up in the mother of all nasty moods, the kind where I just considered going back to sleep for the rest of the day because I knew nothing good would come of being awake. Not wanting Sark to fall victim, sensing he wanted to keep things normal anyway, I asked him if he'd go
~~~

down to the cafeteria and get me food. Anything. I didn't even care what it was.

I think he knew I was giving him an out because I didn't have to ask him twice. He nodded and left.

Not knowing what else to do, I turned on the TV. Within five minutes I was so annoyed at nothing that I turned it off. I tapped my fingers against my bed. I doodled on the whiteboard. I stared at the wall. Finally, I stood and went to the counter, finding the little plastic cup of pills for the morning. My head hurt and my body ached and my stomach was upset and I'd need help if I wanted to last the day.

Taking the cup in my hands, I grabbed a water bottle from the mini fridge underneath the cabinet. I fumbled with the new bottle, unable to twist the cap off. My fingers burned as they scraped against the rough plastic lid, only adding to my frustration.

Sark came back in with a cinnamon roll and a bottle of apple juice—had I been happier, I would've smiled that he knew me so well. He set my food on the counter, then reached for the water bottle, but I pulled away, not willing to admit I didn't have the strength or coordination to get it open. He backed off and went to sit in his chair.

"You know, I talked to one of the senator's guys the other day," he started, his tone conversational. "He told me about the compensation they were going to give you."

I stiffened, then went back to my struggle, not wanting to make it a big deal. Nobody was supposed to know about that.

Sark went on when I didn't. "He said you declined the offer and gave it to the victims' families instead."

"And?" I asked harshly, finally hearing the plastic tear.

He hesitated. "Arie, that was a lot of money. You could've had a life."

Maybe I don't want one.

I jerked the bottle open with too much force: water spilled over the side and I lost my grip on my cup, sending pills everywhere. Frustration exploding, I chucked the bottle across the room and it smacked against the wall, the rest of the liquid drenching the floor.

My outburst stunned Sark to silence. I held my face in my hands, embarrassed I'd made such a scene, then tried to bend down.

Sark jumped to his feet, rushing to me. "Don't you—"

But it was too late. I practically fell to the ground, killing my knees, but at least I was down. With shaking hands, I started picking up the soggy pills.

Sark kneeled next to me and nudged my shoulder. "Arie."

I ignored him, continuing my task. He pulled gently on my arm and I yanked away. My vision started to go blurry with tears of sadness and anger and humiliation.

"Arie, just stop for a second," Sark said softly, pulling on my arm again. I caved, dumping the few pills I'd collected back on the ground, and let him pull me into his lap. He wrapped his arms around me and I buried my face in his shoulder.

I'm sorry, I wanted to say. *I'm just being stupid. I'm sorry.*

I turned my head to breathe and speak, but he beat me to it.

"Maybe we can get you a water jug or something, with a straw," he suggested, his chin brushing against my nose as he talked. "Get rid of the hard lids."

"Thank you," I murmured, my voice fragile. I hated it. "That's sweet but I don't think you can fix this problem."

He sighed, hugging me tighter. "You know you can cry if you need to, right?"

"I'm not going to cry," I muttered, glad he couldn't see the rogue tear rolling down my cheek. "I'm not going to cry because I spilled some water. That's stupid."

"I don't think that's the real problem."

Sark was being exceptionally nice when I didn't deserve it, but I was in no mood for therapy sessions. I sat up, trying to push myself away from him and stand, but he wouldn't let me go.

"Don't look at me like that," I snapped.

"Like what?"

"Like you feel sorry for me. I'm so sick of sympathy."

He nodded, his eyes hardening slightly. "Fine. I'll just take my cinnamon roll and go find someone who will truly appreciate it."

That made me feel guilty. My shoulders slumped. "I'm sorry, I didn't mean to—"

"I was kidding, Arie."

"I know you were, but I wasn't." I let out a breath. "Can I get a restart?"

He pretended to think for a moment. "Yeah, I *guess* I can let that slide."

I cracked a smile, my voice turning overly gracious. "Thank you for your impeccable kindness in retrieving the cinnamon roll. The kingdom applauds your…" I forgot the word I was going to say.

"Strength?" Sark supplied. "Charm? Astounding good looks?"

I laughed as I remembered. "I was going to say bravery. Some of those cafeteria ladies scare me. Though all of the above applies."

Sark grinned. "Really? You think I'm astoundingly good looking?"

I reached my hand up to run my fingers through his hair. "Don't let that go to your good-looking head."

As if through muscle memory, my hand automatically traced down his face until I held his cheek in my palm. I didn't realize I'd done it until after we started gravitating toward each other. I felt his hand slide up my back and rest behind my head, pulling me closer until our foreheads touched, then our noses. Right before our lips met, I suddenly realized what I was doing. A burst of nerves went through me and I turned my head.

What the heck was that?

I felt Sark stiffen in surprise and my veins heated with mortification, wishing on every star in the universe that I would melt into the ground.

Thankfully Sark didn't seem that upset. He leaned forward to kiss my cheek instead, then spoke softly in my car.

"You know, I'm still waiting for that serious conversation I was promised. About you and me."

I straightened up to look at his face, my forehead creasing with confusion. "Really?"

Sark was puzzled by my response. "Yeah, of course. Why wouldn't I?"

"But I'm…" I stuttered like an idiot, stunned. "I'm not strong anymore. I can't fight with you. I can't be…normal for you. I'm not even special anymore. I just spill pills and forget my own name half the time."

His eyes widened in bewilderment, a hint of sadness in them. "Arie Nolan, please tell me you don't actually think that I love you less because of where you are now."

I dropped my eyes, wishing I hadn't said anything, scratching the back of my neck while I tried to figure out how to smooth that over. He took my face in his hands and tilted it up until I met his penetrating gaze.

"If you don't know that I care about you unconditionally, then I've done a terrible job of—"

The door opened, making both of us jump, and I pushed myself out of Sark's lap just in time to see Dr. Bran close the door. He stopped when he saw us on the ground next to a giant puddle of water.

"There was an accident," I said. "Sorry."

Dr. Bran composed himself quickly. "No problem. Don't even worry about it." Then he took a deep breath. "I have good news: you're being discharged."

I blinked in surprise. "What? Seriously?"

He nodded. "Yes. Unfortunately, I've concluded that there's not much else I can do for you. There's no point in keeping you here."

There's nothing else they can do for me. My heart sank. *I really am going to be this way for the rest of my life.*

"When?" I asked.

"Tomorrow. I gave you a night to prepare."

I nodded slowly, then a thought occurred to me. "What about Peter? I can't leave him here alone."

"He's going next week." He sighed. "Unfortunately, there's not much we can do for either of you. I imagine you'll both continue to make small progress as the days go on, but that progress won't be helped here."

The next twenty-four hours were some of the longest and shortest of my life. I was excited to leave the hospital room I had memorized. I was terrified to leave the hospital room that was comfortable and safe. Despite hating it, I still loved it. I belonged there.

Home is home.

But the time came anyway. Dr. Bran let me take a pillow and blanket from the hospital, then gave me a bag full of all my medications, my oxygen mask and the small square oxygen tank. Sark took it all down to Mom's car while I said my goodbyes.

Dr. Bran put his hands on my shoulders. "Take care of yourself, okay? You have my cell number, so call me if you need absolutely anything. If you feel something strange or know something isn't right, you don't tough it out. You call me."

I nodded. "Okay."

He gave me a knowing look. "I know you still won't, so Sark and your mom have it too. Remember not to use your oxygen mask unless you really need it, and always have someone sleeping in the same room as you, at least for the next few months."

I nodded again. "Check."

"And remember that therapy hasn't killed you yet. It's okay to be scared of things. It's okay to talk." Then he smiled. "It's a new chapter for you, Arie. That's both exciting and frightening. Only look back to remember how far you've come."

I took a deep breath. "Right." I'd planned on keeping it cool, but I ended up throwing my arms around him. "Thank you…so so much. I don't even have the words."

He hugged me back. "Arie, I've never been happier to do something in my life. Thank you for the opportunity."

Then it was time to go. I gave a last glance to what had been my home for months, then turned and walked away.

Mom's new apartment was about a ten-minute drive from the hospital. Thanks to our new fancy hang card, we were able to park in the handicap stall closest to the front door so I didn't have to walk as far. I watched my feet as the cement underneath them changed to cream tile flooring, half listening to Mom gush all about the amenities of the place and concentrating on not freaking out about the people we had to stand in the elevator with. We were room number four hundred and ten, Mom said. Our feet tapped against the shiny hardwood floor as we made our way down the hallway and to our door. The wood floor smelled new. Actually, the whole place seemed pretty new, from what I could tell watching the ground.

The apartment wasn't big, but it was nicer than I expected. A kitchen, living room, two bedrooms and two bathrooms, with everything already furnished. The furniture looked fairly new too, the place smelling like leather and lavender air freshener.

That became my new home.

Mom and I stayed in the master bedroom—it was kind of the unspoken understanding of all of us that Sark would stay in the other. We never actually talked about the living arrangements, at least not in any conversation I was a part of, but we all knew that's what would happen.

As the first hours turned to days, I started to adjust. Kind of. It was hard. Mom had to get up with me almost every night, quickly putting the oxygen mask on my face and shaking me awake when I started gasping for air in my sleep. She didn't say anything, but I knew it made her exhausted.

While I spent my days sprawled on the couch, Mom was busy keeping herself busy. She went shopping for clothes and dishes and paintings and decorations, slowly bringing the apartment to life. She got a part time job at an animal shelter and loved it. She cooked and cleaned and went to yoga classes, keeping herself from dwelling on things she didn't want to.

Meanwhile, Sark had started a few online classes, working to get a degree—Mom set it up with the contacts she had from when she worked in education. Watching him do homework was entertainment on its own: either he got it in two seconds flat or he ended up ranting about the fall of the educational system. Sometimes I'd throw bits of paper at him or help him study or he'd have me read his textbook to him. He claimed reading was good for me—which it was—and he could concentrate better on boring things when hearing them in my voice. I thought it was just an excuse for him to tune out and still claim to be working.

In all this, I just existed. I kept up with Ellen's adventures in D.C., baby Jules, Jacklynn and Peter. It seemed Peter and I were always texting. Alaina's reversal hadn't been that bad, relatively speaking, and she didn't have much understanding—or patience, often—for Peter's constant fatigue, something that I was too familiar with because I lived with it too. He'd message me paragraphs of venting, and I was glad he could get it out. They were living together for the time being and heaven knows that bowl of gunpowder didn't need any extra sparks.

But that was it. Life went on. I got more comfortable in the apartment. Mom noticed when I started singing to myself again. I was grabbing some apple juice from the kitchen while she was doing dishes, and suddenly she stopped. Closing her eyes, she sighed in contentment and murmured, "Now it sounds like home."

The next day, Sark left the apartment to go pick up a book he needed and, probably, to breathe fresh air. Once he was gone, Mom cornered me like a poacher in the African wild.

"You're avoiding him," she accused.

"No I'm not," I muttered defensively even before realizing it was true. Sark and I spent almost every waking moment together. I made no effort to change that. I didn't want to change it.

She rolled her eyes. "Come on, Arie. I don't mean literally. You know what I mean."

I just stared at her and pretended I had no clue what she was talking about.

"You avoid contact," she explained. "You'll hold his hand when he knows you're not paying close attention but that's it. It's like you're making a point not to touch him. It's weird." She narrowed her eyes, as if analyzing me. "Have you even kissed him yet?"

I felt like I should've been blushing. "Yes. Duh. Of course I have. A lot. It's great. Just…"

Just not since I woke up.

Mom raised her eyebrows and nodded knowingly, like she just read my mind. "Do you even notice him? Physically, I mean."

My words got all jumbled in my mouth as I gently pulled on the ends of my hair, unsure how I wanted to answer that question. Because *of course* I did. I noticed the way he ran a hand through his hair, somehow making it better rather than just messing it up. I noticed when he was concentrating really hard and his top lip would curl and he would chew softly on his thumbnail and his eyes were wide but narrow at the same time. I noticed how much space he filled when he stretched his arms, how the muscles in his back and shoulders constricted and flexed underneath his shirt, how his chest would puff then deflate again as he settled back into whatever he was doing.

And—even more noticeably—I noticed how conscious I was of him, how each movement, each breath of his made my insides flutter and squelch and knot and fly all at the same time. Because I wanted nothing more than to be the one running a hand through his hair, making his lips move, be the one held by his arms with my head against his chest, feeling it rise and fall over and over again while I listened to his heartbeat. And that yearning made me always dangerously close to either acting on it or moving to China so I could put half the world in between us.

I tried to find a happy medium between those two options. I watched him a lot. I watched him and waited for nothing and held my irrational desires at bay. And sometimes I'd glance up or over to watch him only to find he was already watching me, his blue eyes not quite sad but almost. Contemplative, maybe. Then he'd smile and say something funny or ask for my help and I would try not to be too eager or laugh too hard. And that moment of eye contact was forgotten. At least by him. I didn't forget. Sometimes I wondered if he didn't either.

Mom was waiting for an answer, so I just shook my head and shrugged. "Yeah, I guess I do."

"You're still attracted to him, aren't you? He didn't morph back into best friend brother status, did he?"

"No," I said, surprised she'd come to that conclusion. I'd been hiding it better than I thought.

"I just…" I was too tired to be honest, so I stuck with my lame excuse. "I just need time."

She nodded in understanding and left me alone.

The time card. It always worked to get people off my back. Trouble was, I really didn't know how time could help me in this case. It wasn't like I was going to suddenly wake up one day and be ready for anything. But part of me really wanted to.

Why is this so confusing?

Time flew by, as I was so preoccupied with 'noticing' Sark and trying not to be weird and deciding what to do and figuring out how to live. It was almost three weeks into our new living arrangements when Mom made a big announcement.

"Aunt Karen's coming tomorrow!" she exclaimed. "She's bringing Austin and his friend—well, you remember Conrad, don't you?"

I could barely bring myself to nod. Of course I remembered. Austin and I used to play all the time when we were kids, and Conrad had been his best friend since elementary school. I hadn't seen any of them since I'd run away from home. Not that I had anything against them, but the thought of seeing them again—or them seeing me—made me want to barf. I didn't even know what Mom had told them about our mysterious adventures in the past years or why we'd essentially disappeared off the face of the planet or why I had even run away in the first place. But Mom was so excited about seeing her sister again, I couldn't bring myself to say anything.

Despite my wishing on stars that something would fall through, the visitors showed up. Mom and Aunt Karen squealed like little girls when they saw each other. They hugged, and I saw Austin and Conrad and had to do a double take. There was no way the two pimple-ridden punk fifteen-year-olds I remembered could be the two grown twenty-year-olds standing in my doorway.

"Wow," Conrad said in his usually teasing voice—though it was much deeper now—as he looked me up and down. "Someone grew up."

"You guys too," I said, having to look *up* at them now. "Last time I saw you, you were pushing what? Four eleven?"

Austin snickered. "Yeah, we had to get Conrad heeled sneakers just so he could ride the roller coaster."

Aunt Karen found me, wrapping me up in a hug, the familiar smell of fresh cotton flowing off of her. "Oh, Arie, it's so great to see you." She broke away and looked to Sark. "I'm sorry, I haven't met you."

"This is my…" I didn't know what to call him. "My friend, Sark."

Sark shook all their hands nicely and answered their few introductory questions, then went in his room with the excuse he had work to do, making random trips to the fridge from time to time. Mom whisked Aunt Karen away for a tour of the place, leaving me on the couch with the two boys.

This. This is a new kind of torture. I would rather take a mutt on my own than face anyone with social expectations.

I tried my best to be calm. I asked all about their lives and schooling and hobbies, keeping the focus on them. They told me about life on college campus, the tricks they learned on their skateboards, and the girl Conrad had made out with behind the biology building—giving too much detail, in my opinion. They laughed at inside jokes, and I found quickly that I had absolutely nothing in common with them.

"What about you, Arie?" Conrad asked. "How's your love life?"

Austin nodded. "Yeah, are you still with that one kid…uh, what was his name? Gunther? No…oh, uh, Connor?"

Mom piped up from the kitchen like a tiger who'd been waiting all day to pounce. "Oh, no, Arie's been done with that jerk for a long time now. You wouldn't believe the way he trea—"

"Mom," I cut in, before answering myself. "Nah, not anymore. Not my type."

"Yeah, I get you." Austin cleared his throat, trying but failing to keep his tone conversational. "So…what you been up to?"

"What have *I* been up to?" I thought for a minute, desperately trying to stall, twisting my hair around my finger. "Well…let's see…"

What am I supposed to say? There was no way I was giving the full-length story. And there was no way to shorten it without making zero sense.

I took a deep breath to keep from panicking. "I guess…I've just been around. You know, travelled and stuff. Trying to find a place I like."

He knows you ran away from home, idiot.

My answer was pathetic. Austin tried to help me out, though he did nothing to hide his discomfort. "My mom said you spent some time in the hospital. Are you doing better?"

"Yeah, what happened with that?" Conrad asked. "'Cause we got, like, no deets."

Oh man. "Um, yeah. Yeah, I'm doing a lot better now, actually. In fact, I just remembered it's time to take a pill. I'll be right back."

I didn't wait to see if they believed me—I just made a dash for my room, heading into the bathroom to splash cold water on my face. When I turned around, I saw Sark walk into the bedroom and lean against the bathroom doorway.

"How's social hour?" he asked, trying to keep a straight face.

I sighed hopelessly. "Awful. I don't even know how to talk to them."

"I've been listening. You're not doing as bad as you think."

"No, it's bad." I turned back to the mirror, grabbing a brush as I worked on redoing my limp ponytail.

"They're an interesting pair," Sark remarked casually, though I sensed something under his tone. "That Conrad sure likes looking at you."

That made me laugh. "Conrad has been hitting on me—and every other female in the country—since the second grade. 'Desperation' is his middle name." I pulled my hair through the elastic. "Plus, I hope I look different from the last time he saw me. Junior high was not kind to me; they called me Braceface."

Sark walked up to stand behind me, his expression almost annoyed, and I couldn't help the alarmed thought in my head that I was bugging him. I focused on my ponytail. Once my hair was secure, I turned around to find him standing a lot closer to me than I'd thought.

"Still," he said. "I don't care if you've grown up. He looks at you like…"

I grinned as I realized what was going on. "Sark, are you telling me you're *jealous* of Conrad Johnston?"

He set his jaw. "No, of course I'm not. Why would I be? He's immature and disrespectful and sounds like he has no sense of responsibility or a future in anything."

"Oh my gosh." I laughed. "You are totally jealous."

He rolled his eyes. "Not even close. He should know there's already a line, though, which might have gone over his head when I was first introduced." His expression turned more serious, but the corner of his mouth was still turned up. "I guess I just want to know where I stand."

Where does he stand? I couldn't help but give a small grin as I looked him over, this guy who always made me laugh and feel safe and cared about. This guy who I was worlds more comfortable with in any situation than the two in the living room who I was actually related to and a childhood friend. Mom had been right—I should be giving him more. For both of us.

Deciding to take the chance before I chickened out, I leaned my hands on his shoulders for balance and reached up to kiss his cheek. "You're the only one standing."

He raised an eyebrow as he hesitantly wrapped an arm around my waist. "Really?"

I nodded and nuzzled my nose on the side of his face, not able to help noticing how perfectly I fit against him. "Yep. Conrad's got nothing on you."

He took a moment to mull that over. "Well…in that case, how do you feel about maybe going to dinner with me tomorrow?"

I blinked and took a step back to look him. "Dinner?" I asked, the common word tasting absolutely foreign in my mouth. "You mean…you mean like a…"

"Like a date." His lips pursed as he struggled to keep his grin from growing. "I hear that's what normal people do these days."

"Oh." I scratched the back of my neck, then folded my arms tight across my chest. After a deep breath, I nodded slowly, lost in thought. "Okay, yeah. A date. I'd…I'd like that."

"You sure?"

I raised an eyebrow at him. "Well don't lose your confidence now. You've almost got the girl."

He laughed. "Thanks for the advice. I'm really nervous, you know. I really like her."

My gaze dropped to the floor, my smile hurting my cheeks. I tried to rein it in but failed. "She's lucky then."

"She's something." Then he nudged me with his shoulder. "Pick you up at six?"

I rolled my eyes. "From my mom's room? Yeah, sure. Sounds like it'll be a great date."

That didn't deter him at all though. He just smiled again and winked at me. "I plan on it."

Buzzing now with new plans, I headed back toward the living room, knowing Mom would be suspicious if I took too long taking my fake medicine. I turned out the light and started walking slowly out of the bathroom, Sark following behind me.

"You want me to start a fire or something so you don't have to talk to them?" he asked quietly.

I laughed. "I might take you up on that."

"I would."

"I know you would. That's why I love you."

My feet stopped in their tracks the second I realized what I said—well, not so much what I *said*, but what I knew I *meant*. Sark nearly walked into me, and I wondered what the odds were that he hadn't heard me. When I glanced sideways at him, the expression on his face told me those odds were nonexistent. It had a different effect on him, though, than on me.

"I just told you I loved you," I said stupidly, almost in a daze.

Sark just nodded like he won MVP of the national championship of something important and was trying to keep his cool. "I heard."

I frowned and shook my head. "That doesn't scare you?"

"Kind of." He shrugged, but he didn't look that indifferent. "But there are other stronger emotions involved I tend to focus on more when things like this arise. I guess all I really care about is if you meant it."

I bit my lip and watched him for a second, a sincerity that I'd never felt before coming over me, then I took a breath. "Yeah. I meant it."

Sark's eyes glinted with something that made my heart leap, but instead of pushing the point, he leaned down to stage whisper in my ear, glancing to the door. "Can I tell Conrad you said that?"

I cracked a smile and pushed him playfully before making my exit. "No, you may not."

Somehow I made it through the rest of the visit. Aunt Karen had brought a box of old home videos from back when Austin and I were about five, and watching them together was actually really fun. I felt a bit of bittersweet fondness, though, watching the adorable younger me, wishing I could change what was coming for her. Of course I couldn't, and when she told the camera she wanted to be a real princess someday, I found myself feeling like I owed her.

Sark took a break from 'studying' to watch them with us, and he sat on the couch next to me, getting a kick out of my princess bow I did for the camera in my pink dress and curlers. And when he slyly took my hand, I decided to keep it there.

After dinner and much family gossip, the visitors finally left with promises to return. Upon my request, Aunt Karen left the home videos with us, and I spent the next few days watching them over and over, obsessed with the little girl in the pink dress.

15

I tapped my fingers against my arm slowly, one at a time, counting each tap. Since it was dark in the room, I had my sleeve rolled up, allowing the skin on my arms to feel other skin for once rather than the brush of cotton fabric. Every third tap I'd touch a line of scarring, and a weird tingle would go through me, and I'd wrap my blanket tighter around myself.

One, two, three, four, five. One, two, three, four, five.

It was roughly four thirty or so in the morning—I didn't want to interrupt my tapping rhythm to check my phone again. Sometimes Mom had crazy early shifts at the animal shelter, and whenever she'd leave, I'd grab my pillow and blanket and breathing machine, tiptoe into Sark's room, and sleep on his floor. Both he and Mom knew I did it and both disapproved since laying on the floor too long tended to make me sore, but nobody really stopped me. I liked to do it. Sometimes the world just makes more sense on the floor, and Mom couldn't argue that I may need help sometime in the night, and while she didn't have any objections to me crawling into Sark's bed, she decided one day it wasn't very motherly to encourage it and changed direction on me. Sark never really commented on the issue besides the standard 'that could hurt you' and the occasional rebuttal after I argued that I didn't want to wake him up (which was completely true but also I think we both just felt weird about it. Or, at least I did). But one time he woke up and rolled over to find me on his floor, and I pretended I was asleep and peeked through my eyelashes, and in the dark I saw him smile softly and watch me for a while in a way that made me all fuzzy inside.

He was asleep now, though. His arm was half hanging over the side of the bed, and I had to stop myself from scooting closer and reaching out to take his hand. He'd been restless, tossing and turning incessantly since I'd come in almost an hour ago, which wasn't like him. For the billionth time that morning, I wondered if he was dreaming or not, even though he told me once he didn't dream a lot. I was always embarrassed at how much he popped up in my head while I was asleep, and I secretly hoped that I invaded his unconsciousness sometimes too.

That's silly, I thought as I continued to tap. *One, two, three, four, five.*

Eventually I thought I heard him stirring and mumble my name. I froze, trying to decide if I was going to be 'asleep' or not, but when he said it again, the word mushing in on itself, it didn't sound like he was awake. Instead, he started tossing again, breathing heavy, and once I heard the next name tumble out of his mouth, I knew what was happening: Hadley.

I pushed myself up on my hands too fast, making me dizzy, and Sark gave a mangled gasp before bolting upright. I couldn't tell if he registered my shadow in the darkness, but he didn't trip over me as he jerked himself out of bed, threw the door open, and lurched out into the hall. Clumsy and shaky, I pulled myself to my feet and stumbled after him.

Sark was kneeling on the bathroom floor, one hand braced against the bathtub and the other on the side of the counter, coughing into the toilet like he was going to throw up. His hair stuck out everywhere, part of it plastered to the cold sweat on the back of his neck. Going softly, I put a hand on his back and stepped around him, then settled on the ground between him and the bathtub. He trembled underneath my touch. My insides ached, knowing all the horrible things Sark had seen in his time, wondering what was so bad, so awful, that seeing it would leave him like this.

Finally, he stopped coughing and leaned his forehead against the counter, his breaths still shuddering. He didn't even turn to look at me when he spoke.

"Get off the floor," he snapped, his frosty tone biting at me. "Can't you at least *try* to take care of yourself?"

I blinked in surprise, willing myself not to feel the sting of the remark.

He doesn't mean it, I chanted to myself. *He doesn't mean it, and you know it.*

"Sark," I whispered softly, forcing my hand to stay put. "It's okay. It's just me."

Sark shook his head, forcing a frustrated breath through his teeth. I clenched my free hand into a fist and repeated my silent chant. "Get off..." he tried again, but tapered off, then punched the cupboard as hard as he could. I flinched, then stilled myself, hoping against hope he hadn't seen it. That would only make this worse.

Acting on my suspicion, I gently pushed him away from the counter and wedged myself in front of him, taking his face in my hands and forcing him to look at me. His neck and jaw were tight, but his eyes were a tsunami—a dangerous, welled up storm that just had to burst before he drowned.

"It's okay," I said again. "You've seen me lose it before. A lot."

He closed his eyes and shook his head, making his eyelashes wet. "It's different," he managed to get out.

It's different when you're the one that's falling apart.

"I know," I said, my voice trembling now too. "I know. I know you want to hit someone, or drink something, or do something you shouldn't, but you can't. You have to let this one bleed."

Sark gritted his teeth and shook his head again, but I could sense him breaking. All at once he took my hands off his face, buried himself in my shoulder, and let his shaky control go.

He didn't cry for very long. I just held him in my arms, stroking his hair, the corner of the cabinet painfully digging into my back as my legs fell asleep. I didn't move though. I'd never seen him so exposed, and I wanted him to know he was safe with me. Heaven knows how many times the roles had been reversed.

Eventually, the tears trailed off and he just sat there, breathing into me, the air prickly cold against my wet skin.

"Please," he murmured, his voice cracking. "You really need to get off the floor."

I hesitated, deciding what to do. "Will you come with me?"

He took another three deep breaths before nodding slowly. His knees shook slightly as he dragged himself up, pulling me with him. I had to lean against the counter for a second as blood rushed back into my limbs. Then Sark took my hand and I flipped the light off on our way out.

I half expected him to go crash back in his bed again, but he purposefully avoided his room and led me to the living room instead. After setting me gently on the couch, he sat down and focused on anything else. Once he'd readjusted the pillows for the third time, I took his hands in mine.

"What can I do for you?" I asked. "Anything at all?"

Sark pursed his lips, still avoiding eye contact. His face was ghastly pale, even in the shadows, and his eyes were rimmed red. We were both still for a minute until he slowly raised my hand to cradle his cheek in my palm.

I broke into a sad, small smile before lying down on the couch and pulling him with me. He hesitated only a second before caving—that's how I knew I was doing the right thing. Fidgeting for a moment until I was comfortable, I had Sark lie next to me in my arms, resting his head on my chest. My hand was still against his cheek; he tapped it until I figured out what he wanted. I traced lines on his face over and over, feeling him take another shuddering breath before relaxing slightly.

After a minute of peaceful stillness, his thick voice broke the silence.

"Arie?"

"Yeah?"

"Will you...will you sing?"

My eyebrows furrowed and my finger stopped on his face for a second. "What?"

"Will you sing?" he asked again. "Your voice...your voice helps me stay calm."

I bit my lip, nerves spiking. "Um...I'm not...well, okay. What do you want me to sing?"

"The one from Denver. You sang to the kids. That one."

I nodded. I could've guessed. "Okay. I just...I might not be, like...I might ruin it. I don't know if I'm still good at it, you know, with everything."

He wasn't concerned. "You will be."

"Okay."

I cleared my throat excessively, then realized I had no other way to stall. Heart stuttering inside me, I softly sang the song I'd come up with all those months ago. I messed up several times—forgetting words, of course—but Sark just relaxed further and further, and by the third time through it I'd remembered all of the words and he was sound asleep.

Sark slept for a while, at least, based on the sun that had started peeking through the kitchen windows. I faded in and out myself but stayed pretty alert for the most part. And that was very bad.

I counted for a while. I counted the specks on the ceiling (I got to 251), the leaves on Mom's plants (78.5—one was just about to poke out of the stem), the hairs on Sark's head (I gave up after I hit 300), the number of times my index finger brushed his nose (I did this in increments of ten, four times). I tried to count the number of times I'd seen him cry (inconclusive, but I knew they were limited to one hand), then the number of times he'd seen *me* cry (innumerable at this point, really), then the number of times we'd cried together (once). One time we'd broken together, in a hospital, buckled under the words of a soft nurse wearing the bright sun and carrying the darkest cloud in the sky.

Then the ceiling and the couch and the apartment seemed to melt away. I felt the gas dripping from my clothes, the blood from my face, the terror in my bones.

Arie, don't let me fall!

It's okay, I promise. I promise, but you have to trust me. You have to let go.

Arie, please! Don't leave me.

It'll be okay, I promise. You have to be brave.

I want to stay with you.

Sark will catch you, I swear.

Please, I'm too scared.

I promise.

Arie!

I promise.

It'll be okay.

I promise.

I promise.

I promise.

Then my hands were sweaty and my heart was pounding and my eyes were stinging and my lip was bleeding because I bit it so hard and I was stuck. Stuck in the darkness, too far from the numbers. I focused on the numbers because they were safe, safe and far away from the edge because once my mind went over the edge, I fell into the abyss and there was never a way to come back out. I spun in the darkness, again and again, stuck in places and things and people and so much darkness, the thick, oozing kind that stuck to your skin and held you down, captive, and even if you managed to yank yourself free, you'd still be discolored from the black tar of it.

Then I saw *her*, my eyes glaring back at me, and a choked gasp escaped my mouth, and I knew I was doomed to suffocate in blackness.

Sark lifted his head to look at me, and I could see by his face that he'd been awake for a minute, patiently waiting to see if I'd come out of it myself. I clenched my hands into fists, stabbing my nails into my palms and digging them deeper. It helped me focus a little, but not completely, and the helplessness started to overwhelm me because I couldn't escape the ghosts in my mind.

"Arie?" Sark asked softly. "Arie, it's okay. You're okay. You're here."

I tried to take deep breaths like Dr. Bran had taught me, but it didn't always work and breathing was stupid anyway. The only adequate distractions I could think of that Sark wouldn't deem 'unhealthy' and disapprove of entirely was either food or him. And since it was six in the morning and my stomach would react explosively if given anything, I opted for my other option.

"Sark?" I asked, hesitating, because while he'd proven himself a master at distracting me through conversation, I'd never really asked him this before. "Will you kiss me?"

His forehead creased in confused surprise. "What?"

"Will you kiss me?" I dug my fingernails further into my palms. "Please?"

He watched me for an eternal second, his eyes scouring my face before he slowly brought his mouth to mine and brushed my lips so softly I hardly even felt it.

"No," I said before he'd even fully pulled away, meeting his eyes almost desperately. "I need you to kiss me like you want me to forget every name except yours."

Sark raised an eyebrow, but a flicker of light in his eyes told me a different story as he pushed himself closer to me. I didn't have to ask him again, and this time he got what I meant.

I forgot everything I was trying to forget—at least I thought so—because Sark was everywhere and I could only focus on him and his mouth and his hands and his breath and his urgency and wanting...of me. And when he pretty much broke my lungs and I was wheezing away like an idiot, he was just as happy kissing my face and hair and neck—and that's when I forgot my own name and where I was and everything besides the need for him.

The need sent electric currents through me, but it still couldn't fizzle out the darkness clawing at the edges of my hazy brain, and even though every nerve in my body and heart begged me to keep going, the thought of where we were headed forced me to stop.

Suddenly the electricity running in my veins was replaced with the panic I'd become so familiar with, and for a half second I was frozen with the fear of being stuck.

Just tell him, some little voice in the back of my head piped up. *He's different.* So I did.

"Sark," I whispered hoarsely, partly out of fear and partly out of lack of breath. "Stop. Please."

His mouth left my skin instantly, his eyes finding mine, his face twisted with fearful remorse.

I stared at him with a mix of awe and confusion. "You stopped."

He glanced over me, breathless too. "Of course I did. You told me to."

At that, something clicked together in my head, an important puzzle piece that was filed away in my brain for future use—a new layer of trust.

"Thank you," I told him, voice still airy with disbelief.

"No." He shook his head. "Don't say thank you. You should expect that from me. Always. That's really...that one's really important to me."

I stared at him for another moment, and he seemed to think I was still scared.

"Sorry," he said, quickly trying to untangle himself from me to sit up. "That was...that was probably too much."

I hugged his arm to prevent him from moving, already comfortable with him again. "You did exactly what I asked." I felt my face get warm—warmer than it already was, anyway. "And you did it very well."

Sark grinned, a playful light dancing in his eyes that made my heart stutter and veins thrum. "I think I would trade just about anything to have this—you and me alone on the couch like that—forever."

That was so hard for me to wrap my head around, that he could see me that way.

"I think I could get used to that," I decided. "You'd have to teach me your masterful ways though. We'd have to practice."

"I think practicing is a great idea."

Suddenly I heard the jangle of keys and Mom's bubbling voice coming from the other side of the front door, talking on the phone. Instantly Sark and I bolted up; he smoothly switched himself so he was lying against the other side of the couch, while

I frantically tried to fix my messy hair and rumpled shirt.

"You look better like that," Sark said with a mischievous smile, winking at me.

I rolled my eyes but couldn't help the tingle that went down my spine. "You're the one that messed me all up."

Two clicks had sounded—Mom still had the third lock to go—and I snatched the blanket off the other couch and spread it out over me, trying to seem casual.

"We have to work on your guilty face," Sark told me, teasing. "You're going to give us away."

"Please," I muttered. "She thinks you walk on water. I think everyone assumes you're too much of a saint to lay a finger on me."

"Next time she's gone, I will enthusiastically debunk that theory entirely."

Part of me actually considered coming up with some stupid excuse to get Mom out of the house so Sark could make good on his promise *now*, but all elation got sucked out of me when the front door finally swung open and I saw that Mom wasn't on the phone but with someone.

"Like I said, Candace," Senator Whyme was saying as they walked in. "I'm just here to drop by and then get out of your hair."

Sark tensed next to me, and I automatically straightened up, annoyed that the senator had come so early in a pristine suit, catching me in my eight-day-old pajamas. He held the door open for Mom as she carried in paper bags full of groceries—more of her new organic stuff, probably—and I noticed a pile of assorted papers in his other hand.

"Oh good, you're awake," Mom said when she saw us, walking into the kitchen to put the bags down and put the groceries away. "I didn't want the Senator to miss you."

I bit my lip to keep from rolling my eyes. *Wouldn't that be a shame?*

"Arie," the senator nodded at me pleasantly, then gave the slightest glance to Sark. "Sark."

Sark nodded back, not quite reaching the level of fake pleasantries the senator had, but doing his best given the morning we had. "Senator. I'd say it's nice to see you, but that usually means something's wrong."

Underneath the blanket, I kicked Sark's leg as hard as I dared.

The senator gave a laugh, thankfully, and waved his hand. "No, not today." Then his eyes fell onto me. "Besides, traditionally it seems you guys are the magnets for trouble."

There was a beat of tense silence before Mom piped up. "The senator was nice enough to bring our mail up for us."

At that, Whyme tossed the contents of his hand onto the coffee table. Out of habit, I guess, I glanced down at the pile of mail, then did a double take. My stomach twisted painfully, and I felt the color drain out of my face as I stared at the sturdy envelope on top, bearing my name in immaculate flowing cursive. I'd know the handwriting anywhere.

How did that get here?

Mom had been blabbing on about the kale she found but trailed off once she realized the senator was focused on me. I stuffed my hands underneath the blanket to hide their shaking, then took a breath and forced myself to look at Senator Whyme. His face was impassive, neutral, and camera-ready, but I could see the calculating curiosity in his eyes.

"You can't keep doing this to me," I said, my voice hoarse and hollow and not nearly as strong as I wanted it to be. "You can't keep checking up on me. I'm innocent."

"I didn't say you weren't," the senator insisted, still pleasant. "You've been through quite the ordeal, as we all know, and it wouldn't be right if I didn't check up on you now and again."

"Thanks," I said coldly, and Mom huffed as a warning to be polite. I was sick of the pretenses though, so freaking annoyed that they followed me everywhere. "I'm doing okay. I'll see you next time."

The smile on Whyme's face turned plastic, his tone hardening slightly as he gestured to the envelope. "Yes, well, I'd really like you to open that before I go."

"So you're going through my mail now? Isn't that against the law or something?"

"Depends on the kind of mail, I suppose." He took a breath, as if filling himself up with his ego. "Really, though, Miss Nolan, I need to see you open that."

I forced the words through my teeth. "Not a chance."

"Arie," Mom chastised under her breath from the kitchen. Sark took the opposite stance, stiffening and sitting up straighter, focused, as though the senator were a derailing train headed

368

straight for me and Sark was ready to yank me out of the way.

"Down, boy," Whyme muttered to Sark, and I pushed myself off the couch before Sark acted on the murder glinting in his eyes.

"Thank you for your visit, Senator," I said, folding my arms across my chest. "I'll be sure to let you know if I need anything else."

Whyme folded his arms across his chest too, wrinkling the folds of his navy suit. "Arie, please be reasonable. Acting this way casts you in a very bad light."

"I'm asking for privacy, a basic humane—no, I mean, human right as a person of the country that *you* serve. You're the one that needs to be reasonable."

He narrowed his eyes. I finally hit a nerve. "I'm serving this country, Miss Nolan, by protecting them from potential threats."

"That doesn't—no, that doesn't include me anymore."

"How am I to know that? Especially with this kind of behavior?"

"You *proved* it." I took a deep breath, trying to keep myself in check, keep my words slow and calculated. The more upset I got, the more I tended to forget things and mess up. "We've been through this before. I'm not in...cro...correspondence with anyone I shouldn't be. Now please *please* just leave me alone."

"I hope you realize your own hypocrisy," the senator said, the most disgust in his voice I'd ever heard. "Someone who claims to be unfairly judged casts the same on others. Why won't you trust me?

Is it because I work for the government? Are you so blinded by your prejudiced hatred that you can't trust the person who can help you the most?"

"No!" I exploded, my mind getting achy and airy and fuzzy. "I don't...that's not my...my..." I pressed my fingers against my temples. "It's not like that."

"You don't trust me, Miss Nolan," he said, like I was committing a federal offense. "That's clear to see. I guess I was hoping you'd grow out of your immature bias eventually."

I glowered at him, clenching my hands into fists. "Lindsey Carter saved my leg—I mean my life. It's not about the job. I don't trust you because you are a living, breathing human being. I don't trust *anyone*, Senator, not just you. I'm sorry you thought you were so special."

"You can't use that as an excuse to further endanger the public. You need to get over this irrational fear of authority *now*."

Too far. That was too far. Way too far, and everyone knew it too. You could hear a pin drop, break the tight glass atmosphere with a flick of a finger, sense the way Mom was too afraid or shocked to speak and Sark was too infuriated to move without socking Whyme in the face. You could hear my breathing as it sped up and back down, as I filed through the chaos in my head and fury in my fingers, nearly seeing red around the edges of the disaster scene.

I took a deep breath. Then a second. Counted to twelve. My livid glare didn't break from the senator's as I collected my thoughts enough to speak coherently.

"You want to know..." I started, my voice quieter than I thought it'd be. "You want to know the last time I talked to a government officer? At the Compound. Ken...Klend...Keene..." I shook my head, frustrated. "I can't remember his name now. But he was one of the inside guys. To the government. Had a direct line to the military."

The senator actually widened his eyes. "Kendler Blake."

"You knew him?"

A second of pause. "Yes."

"So you know he's dead."

A sigh. "Yes, I do."

"And before that he was under arres—no, investigation. For shady activity."

Whyme eyed me warily. "How do you know anything about that?"

"He was one of Cyrus' guys. Betrayed him too, stupidly. One day they brought him into my training session—a torture day. They tied him to a chair and ordered me to make him scream. And I did." My throat felt dry and cracked, but somehow it felt good to say it, to put the truthful words into the universe. "I made a grown up, stoic, solid wall of a military man scream and cry and beg the devil to take me away."

Senator Whyme pursed his lips, his face going slightly pale. I got a weird sense of satisfaction from that, like he was finally getting the gravity, the magnitude, of these horrible things.

"I admit I had less hard...revers...reservations than usual. Usually I'd cry or throw up before and after something like that. But Cyrus had brought

371

this man in on purpose. That man basically pressed the button that blew my innocent brother to bits."

Whyme raised his eyebrows, realization dawning. I heard Mom choke on silent tears; I didn't have it in me to break my gaze from Whyme to glance at Sark.

"After hours of torture, Cyrus ordered me to murder him. I'd never killed a person before. That was the point. He thought I was hyped up enough on revenge to see it through." I took a deep breath, trying to keep myself in the room. "But I didn't. I stopped. I knew if I crossed that line then I'd never ever come back. So I said no. And you know what they did?"

I had the senator captivated now. His eyes were horror struck as he waited for me to finish.

"They strapped me to a chair next to him and turned on me."

That broke him. Whyme closed his eyes and rubbed his forehead, taking a second before he could look at me again.

My voice was thicker now, edgier. "He spat blood at me. Said I deserved it. They forgot about him. Kendler Blake eventually died in the chair."

"Because his injuries were so severe?" the senator asked, accusing, as though he finally found something he could successfully pin on me.

I tried to glare harder, if that was possible. "No. Because he was left alone *so long*."

Whyme's face went whiter. He cleared his throat and readjusted his tie. "Ah. I see."

Suddenly exhausted, I ran my hands over my face and through my hair, the anger draining out of me slowly. "I don't know--I've *never* known—

what kind of hellish game Cyrus is playing, but I promise you again I've only ever wanted out. I know we all have nightmares, Senator, and you and I both lose sleep over protecting those around us. But I guarantee your nightmares are not the same as mine. Please don't assume you have me all figured out."

Whyme cleared his throat again, surprising me by spreading his hands out in apology. "I'm sorry for the unannounced visit. I hope we can both be more forward with each other in the future."

I nodded, impressed by the direction he'd taken. "I would appreciate that."

He nodded back at me. "All right then." He glanced at Mom and Sark. "Candace. Sark. Have a good day." He started to turn for the door, but then stopped himself, not facing me anymore. "In the name of that honesty, Arie, I'll tell you that Cyrus' people are pressing for a fast trial. He's going to go for the insanity plea. And with the people he's somehow got on his team, there's a chance he could get it."

The information sat in the air, hanging, a dead weight. Thick and black and something nobody would ever be able to carry.

Whyme sighed, the most tired sound I'd ever heard him make. "You know better than I do what he's capable of. If he lands himself in a mental ward, how soon do you think it'll be before someone gets him out?"

I wasn't sure if I couldn't breathe or if I was holding my breath. Either way, I felt lightheaded.

"I would like you on my team, Arie," the senator finished. "We need you if any of us have a chance, and I need us to trust each other. Please let me know how I can facilitate that, and I will do better to trust you in the days ahead."

And with that, he turned and walked out the front door, clicking it securely behind him as though making sure my monsters didn't follow him out.

The second the door shut, I lost my presentable posture and started shaking so hard I could hear my teeth hitting together. I clawed my fingers through my tangled ponytail and squeezed my eyes shut, panicking at the feeling of control slipping out of my grasp.

"I'm going to take a shower," I announced to the silent room. "I'll be back later."

"Arie," Mom piped up, quiet and infuriatingly patronizing. "Dr. Bran says you're not supposed to be left alone after triggering situations."

The only words I could think to say were ones I learned from Peter while he was doing physical therapy—not the best words for the situation. "I'll be fine," I told her, though my strained voice said otherwise.

The same fight we always had ensued—the *only* fight we ever really had. Mom had the annoying habit of switching mothering versions on me, not sure how much authority she had over me now since I was so old and had lived so long without her. We were different kinds of stubborn, and they did not mesh well when presented at the same time.

She'd always win though, when her eyes would well up and her voice would crack and she would say, "Arie, I'm just doing the best I can."

And I'd choke on nothing and say, "I know. Me too."

I didn't have as much energy for this fight, though, so it didn't last as long. Sark was quiet and still on the couch while Mom and I went back and forth, then she consented that I could take a bath so long as she was in the bathroom with me. I caved, knowing that was as close as I was going to get, even though I didn't even want a shower anymore anyway. She went ahead to get bath salts or something, and I waited until her back was turned to snatch the envelope off the table to take with me, knowing Sark saw but deciding I didn't care.

Mom took charge of setting the bath up for me in her (our? I still wasn't sure) bathroom, which was probably good because I barely had the control of mind to walk in a semi-straight line. The only thing I did was pull the water temperature handle to max heat; Mom noticed and pursed her lips but didn't say anything. Within five minutes of the senator's departure, I was soaking in steamy soapy water that smelled like citrus.

I made my mind go blank. I numbed myself to everything but the scalding on my skin from the water. Mom brought in a chair, perched her glasses on her nose, and continued reading one of her new self-help books.

There isn't a book that can help us, I almost snapped at her. *We are what we are.* But I held my tongue because that was a mean thing to say and Mom didn't deserve me being mean to her. Really, it was a miracle she still claimed me as a daughter, with all the baggage I came with.

At the word miracle, I heard my grandpa's voice in my head. *See, little miss, don't roll your eyes at me no more. Miracles are all around us— every breath, every star, every splash of color is a miracle. It's our job to see 'em.*

Miracle, huh? I swirled my finger in the bubbles. *The only miraculous thing about this is how much it sucks.* I stole a glance to where Cyrus' letter was hidden under my pile of dirty clothes. *And any second it could get even worse. Now wouldn't* that *be a miracle.*

For a second, I wondered what Grandpa would say to that, if he were still here, besides noting my impressive sarcasm. Being the only religious person I'd ever been close to, Dad never liked me to listen to what he had to say, but I remembered Grandpa talking once about angels and devils. The devils hadn't come from Hell originally, he'd once told me. Everyone who'd ever fallen had started out on a high plain in heaven. How else could they have fallen so far?

That's when it hit me: anyone could be a Cyrus. Anyone could be so morphed and disfigured by the pain in their lives—disfigured into something awful. A real monster.

Everyone will have pain that destroys them. Anyone has the chance to turn it into something evil. Even me.

I swore to myself right then that I'd never again wish my pain on anyone else, even if the loneliness swallowed me and the need for understanding suffocated my last breath.

My eyes automatically found the scars on my wrist. *You may kill me, but you will never turn me into you.*

I sunk deeper into the water, trying to tune out my own thoughts. Eventually, Mom flipped her book shut. She'd finished it. That's when she realized how long I'd been in there—my skin had puckered and the suds had fallen flat and the water was verging on icy.

"You should probably get out now, sweetie," she said, trying to be casual and careful at the same time. "It's been hours. I'm afraid you're going to get sore from sitting in a hard tub for so long."

Too late. I watched the murky suds float from one side of the tub to the other. *Too late for everything.*

Five minutes later, she tried again. "Arie, you have to get out. Come on."

I barely even heard her. Three minutes later she pulled the plug on the drain. I watched the water level sink and sink and sink and sink until there was nothing left. Instantly goosebumps rose on my skin from the chilly air.

"Come on," Mom said with her hand on her hip. "Let's go."

I didn't move. I didn't even look at her. I watched my wrinkled fingers drum against the side of the tub, the only movement I could handle.

I stayed like that for a long time. Mom tried everything she could think of, but I wouldn't budge, and eventually she managed to get me into one of her robes: the big white fluffy one with little pink roses on it. I didn't know how she did it since my limbs were like noodles and she wasn't strong enough to pull up all my dead weight, but somehow she tucked my arms in and rolled me around until the robe was tied tight around me. Then she left. It was then I realized the loud clicking sound I'd been hearing forever was my teeth chattering violently. I actually looked at myself for once. I was nearly bent in half and trembling out of control, the deep cold settling into my bones, and my bare legs were splotchy pink and purple. The big toenail on my right foot was turning dark; I must've slammed it against the side of the tub more than I thought.

You're scaring her, I realized. *You're scaring her really bad. You have to get up. At least go get in bed and pretend you're sleeping.* Taking a raking breath, I braced myself for effort. *If not for yourself, then for her.*

Sark walked in then, surprising me. Eyes on the ground, he took slow steps across the bathroom to the bathtub, then turned to put his back against the wall and slid down, sitting on the floor next to me. He watched his hands on his knees. I watched the blueish spot on my left kneecap.

"She sent in the cavalry, huh?" I thought I meant it as a joke, but my voice sounded absolutely dead, the words slaughtered with my teeth chattering.

Out of the corner of my eye, I saw him shrug. "Somehow she thinks you'll listen to me."

I felt the need to apologize, but somehow knew that wasn't what he wanted, and for the millionth time in my existence I wished I were better for him.

He wants me to get up. No, that wasn't it, I realized with an ache. *He wants me to be okay.*

"You know how I knew you were still you?" he asked out of nowhere. "I don't know why, but I was thinking about it this morning."

I took the bait. "When?" I croaked.

"When I got to the Compound. Everybody told me you were a monster. We weren't really talking. And honestly...I was afraid you were. So afraid we were too late, not that we could've really done anything. Even when you saved us in the construction disaster, I wondered, just a little. But you know how I knew for sure?"

"No."

"That night, when I walked you to your place and you made me promise you something." He laughed once softly. "I don't even remember what it was, honestly. But you operate on that so much—on promises. It was such an Arie thing, to rightfully hate the world so much and still consider promises to be a good foundation of honesty." I felt him glance at me. "It's always been one of my favorite things that you do. And that's how I knew you still had to be you, no matter what they'd forced you to do."

My mouth tried to smile, a ghost of an action that I would've done in response to something like that, but it didn't come. Instead, my voice remained monotone and vibrating. "I hurt a lot of people."

"Yeah," Sark said. "You did." That was a better response than what I was expecting. He sighed, readjusting himself on the floor. He couldn't be comfortable. "I threw up my first time too."

"First time what?"

"The first time I ever tortured someone." His voice had a soft, haunting reverence to it. "It was initiation, kind of, for Alexis. He was watching. I didn't want to disappoint him. But when it was over, I snuck out, locked myself in a bathroom, and threw up. Twice."

"Oh." With my teeth chattering, it sounded like "Ro-oh."

We sat there for another few minutes before he spoke again.

"Will you get up?" he asked. "Please?"

I thought about it for a second without really thinking at all. "Yes."

"Okay." He stood up and stretched himself out, and while his back was to me I snatched up the envelope from underneath my crumpled pile of dirty pajamas on the floor and stuffed it in my robe. Then I braced my arms and tried to get up.

Clenching my jaw shut, I was able to catch the cry of pain before it left my mouth. I was so stiff and sore, and the bitter cold had settled inside of me, making my bones ache horribly and my limbs tremble so hard that I couldn't use them very well.

I felt something then—helplessness. A hint of frustration. Enough to overwhelm me after my hours of nothing. Tears pricked my eyes, and for the billionth and thirty-first time in the last months I begged the stars to give myself back to me. This vulnerable, fragile, needy mess wasn't supposed to be me.

I closed my eyes to keep from crying or seeing any more of myself. "Sark?" I asked, nearly inaudible, the word cracked. "I need..." I took a breath, willing myself to say the 'h' word Dr. Bran had made me promise to practice. "I need help. Please."

My eyes stayed closed as I felt Sark scoop me up in his arms and pick me up. My body automatically curled into him, desperate for his body heat since I was seconds away from becoming a human popsicle. At first he flinched away from my touch, but then he leaned into me, letting me burrow my frozen nose into his neck and suck up some of his warmth. I let him bundle me up like a burrito in one of Mom's huge fuzzy blankets, only because he said if my core temperature dropped too low then I'd probably have to go to the hospital.

"Do you want something to eat, Arie?" I heard Mom ask me quietly while Sark wrapped me up. I shrugged indifferently, but she must've not seen underneath the layers of fabric. "How about some soup? That will warm you right up."

I nodded, my teeth still chattering. "Thank you."

"Of course, baby." She touched my head before she left. "I'll heat it right up."

While she was gone, I lied down on my pillow with my eyes still closed and Sark played with a loose strand of my hair. When she came back, I sat up and cracked my eyes open and forced myself to eat, not really tasting anything but I couldn't help the slight sigh that came when the hot broth coursed through me.

Mom turned on the TV. I made a point of staring at it, so hopefully she thought I was watching, but I couldn't really get myself to concentrate on anything. Eventually Sark deflated, curling up next to me and intertwining his fingers in mine. Instead of going with pretenses himself, he let it down—I sensed his sadness and we sat in our mess together. Once Mom got the idea to put in our home videos, I found myself perking up a little and paying attention. She held my other hand while she ate chicken salad and commented on her horrendous video commentary.

I watched the little me in her princess dress twirl for the camera. "Again!" she squealed, eyes lighting up as she watched her skirt whirl around her.

Then a pudgy blond boy wearing an oversized soccer jersey sauntered in front of the camera. "You're hogging it!" Kieran accused the princess, trying to do some soccer drills for the camera in our hopelessly cramped living room. He ended up tripping over the pink skirt, sending little me down with him, and the two kids erupted in a burst of giggles on the floor.

I didn't want this, I imagined her saying to me. *You're too sad. I know it's not all your fault, but I didn't want to be this sad. I wanted to be happy. Can't you make us happy?*

My hands pulsed with the warmth from the two people next to me, the only tethers holding me here. *It's possible to be happy and sad at the same time,* I imagined telling her, a new idea I was just starting to realize. *I know it's not what you wanted, but it might be something, you know?*

She would make a face at me, like the one I used to make at Kieran. *If you say so.*

For some reason that got me thinking about all the days since I was discharged from the hospital. There had been a lot of ones like this: sad, empty, mundane days where any kind of functioning was a laughable hopeless fantasy. There had been explosive ones, days where I had to keep myself in a gridlock and talk myself down every five seconds, where even the slightest thing, like burnt toast, sent me into a dangerous spiral.

But there had also been decent days. Good days. Days when I actually had enough energy to do things I wanted to do; days when I sat at the kitchen table in the mornings and watched the sun come up, flooding the room with such peaceful and beautiful rays of gold; days when Sark and I went to the movie theater, and I was engulfed in the smell of buttery popcorn and enchanted by the dancing pictures on the screen; days when Mom and I laughed about nothing, when our connection was so tight I couldn't imagine it had ever been broken at all; nights when I sat in my bed with the lamp on and read a book, feeling so safe and comfortable and just so *grateful* I was where I was. There were times when I felt my insides would burst with gratitude for simple things, like running water or decent pasta or my choice of socks or getting myself my toothbrush or walking in the grass on a sunny day or a stranger's genuine smile—times when I had a different kind of gratitude, a gratitude *for* gratitude. Because I knew I'd only reached that level of thankfulness because at one time I'd had those things taken away from me.

Today had been awful. It was a day to survive, to grit your teeth, curl yourself up, and get through, not one to really live. But a little voice inside me whispered that at least I was beginning to learn the difference.

16

My lungs burned. The darkness was disorienting as I suffocated, my fingers clawing at oxygen that my lungs couldn't find. Consciousness came. I felt the plastic mask on my face. The processed air mercifully made its way into my body, and I struggled to sit up, remembering that it helped. I felt a hand on my back. My shoulders slumped as the pain began to drain out of me, the gasping sending vibrations through my body, and my mind started to focus.

It's okay. You're okay. It's fine.

Slowly, I cracked my eyes open to see my darkened room. It was still the middle of the night. Prepared to apologize yet again to her, I glanced to my right, surprised to find Sark sitting on the other side of the bed, holding the mask to my face, rather than Mom.

Suddenly I was wide awake. I reached up to move his hand and take the mask off, but he reaffirmed his hold on it.

"Just a minute," he said softly. "You always take it off too fast. Be patient." He rubbed my back, making me tense and relax at the same time, and I obeyed, sucking in the air, giving time for my heart to slow down and my breaths to regulate.

After a moment, Sark took off the mask and set it down on the bed next to my leg. He was wearing sweats and a t-shirt, and I noticed his blue pillow next to my white one rather than Mom's pink one.

I opened my mouth to ask but he answered me first, keeping his voice quiet. "She needed a night off."

"Oh." The guilt made me feel heavy. "Thank you. Really. I know this is exhausting."

He shrugged. "Nah, it's not so bad. Can't be worse than it is for you. Almost dying every night has got to take it out of you."

I gave a small smile, confused as to how he could make me be at ease so quickly. "You know, it's not really a new thing for me."

He laughed once. "No kidding."

Folding over, I rested my forehead on my knee and focused on breathing again. I held my fist to my chest as though the pressure would better contain the repercussive stabs of pain my breathing attacks brought. It was silent, except for me. The back of my neck prickled because I was pretty much doubled over trying to breathe and all I could think about was how close Sark was to me.

After a minute, I blindly reached out for the water bottle I hoped was still on my nightstand. Judging by the air that raked through my hands, I must've not even been close, because I felt the bed shift as Sark said, "I got it."

I tilted my head up just in time to see his arm reach across me, grab my water bottle, and sit back to hand it to me. I glanced at him before taking it.

"Thanks," I muttered, then poured the stagnant liquid down my dried throat. It was lukewarm, but it still felt nice, and it helped my heart slow down a bit from its frantic racing. When I dropped my arm, the water bottle disappeared from my hand. This time, I was more prepared when he reached across me to put it back.

"You okay?" he asked me. "Do you think you could go back to sleep?"

The question made me feel so warm and fuzzy inside that I smiled, though I didn't know why. "Yeah, I'm okay. I think…I think I was dreaming, but I'm not sure." My forehead creased as I tried to remember the images that kept escaping the more I chased them. "Something about a horse in a storm, or…it got scared, and ran from the zombie monst—"

A sharp burning pain stabbed my wrist. I yanked my sleeves up, but, like always, I only saw the scars on my skin. No blue. A shaky breath escaped me as a shiver ran down my body.

It's nothing, like always. Calm down.

"It's never coming back," Sark told me quietly, making me look up at him. "You know that."

"No, I know." I shrugged, trying to sound like I was over it. "Just double checking, you know?"

With my skin prickling in slight embarrassment, I pulled my one sleeve down and went to pull the other, but Sark stopped me. Taking my arm in his hand, he raised it higher and used his other hand to brush the scars softly with his fingers. I had to hold back a gasp of disbelief.

It took a few moments for me to talk; I was mesmerized by what I was seeing. "How can you do that?" I breathed.

His fingers retracted and he glanced up at me, his eyebrows pulling down. "Why, it doesn't hurt, does it?"

I had to process that train of thought. "Oh, no. It doesn't."

The worry left his face and he stroked my scar again, making my skin tingle, his eyes contemplative.

"They're gross," I tried again, wanting to understand. "They're just…"

Sark shook his head without looking up, rustling the sheets as he stretched out his legs. "They're not as bad as you think they are."

"Of course that's what you'd say. You're way too nice to tell me the truth."

"The truth?" He thought for a moment, still touching my arm. "I don't like them. Of course I don't think they're pretty and I wish you didn't have them. Most of the time, I'm glad you keep them covered, because they're hard to see—not because they disfigure you, like you think, but because I know where they came from. And I don't always like being reminded of your pain." He glanced up to meet my gaze. "But sometimes I like to see them. It helps me remember in whose presence I'm standing."

I just stared at him with my mouth hanging half open, my soul touched to the core. When had anyone ever said something like that to me?

Who is this guy? And how did I wind up being lucky enough to be next to him right now?

Sark squeezed my hand, then set it back down in closing, as if expecting me to settle back in and go to sleep. I kept staring at him, until the whispered words slipped out of my mouth knowing I really did want them out in the world.

"I meant it. What I said a few weeks ago. I love you. So much."

That made him smile, but it was only a half smile that didn't quite light up his eyes like usual. Like he was purposefully holding it back. Like he maybe thought that I didn't mean it.

I didn't think through much else. I just leaned over and kissed him. One soft, quick one that easily morphed into another one. The second my lips touched his, Sark froze. It wasn't like he didn't kiss me back, because he did, kind of, his mouth moving against mine, but it was uncertain and the rest of him remained rigid and still.

He tilted his head just enough for our mouths to separate, and a huff of annoyance slipped out of me. "Are you actually awake?" he asked me, putting his hands on my shoulders as if he were going to push me away. "I don't think you're completely here."

"I'm awake," I insisted, nodding. "I'm here." Then I acted again without really thinking—I pushed through his hands on my shoulders, crawled into his lap and planted my mouth on his again, this time with a little more force, as if I could get him to wake up too.

A deep sound came from the back of his throat, so low I almost didn't hear it, but besides that he stayed frozen, his lips hesitating at the contact. For a crushing few seconds I decided that I'd read everything completely wrong about us and should get off him *now*, before I made this horrifying situation catastrophically worse.

Sark broke from me before I could, holding his hand against my shoulder though I couldn't tell if he was restraining him or me. His expression was torn as he studied me. "Arie, I…"

"I'm sorry," I blurted. "If you don't—"

"I always want to kiss you. I just don't…" He sighed, a sad and anxious breath. "I don't want to hurt you."

I shook my head. "You won't."

"You'll tell me?" he asked sincerely, though he was already pulling me closer to him, his eyes fixed on my mouth. "Promise."

"Yes."

Sark pulled me back into him and crushed his lips again mine. I ran my fingers through his hair, hands over his chest, loving the way he held me. I sunk into it, determined to focus on the blissful electricity his touch brought rather than my oxygen-starved body.

I didn't know how long I lasted, but any time would have been way too short. My lungs were going to explode. I pushed against them as hard as I could, wanting just another second with him, but eventually I couldn't take it. Practically wheezing over nothing, I broke away from him just as I thought I was going to collapse in on myself.

"Sorry," I gasped, resting my head against his cheek while I burned with hatred at myself for ruining perfection. "Sorry. I can't…I can't…"

If I was the murderer of all romance, Sark was its rescuer and protector. Instead of admitting the dying animal sounds coming from my throat had slaughtered the moment, he turned his head to whisper in my ear. "I'm flexible." Then he kissed my ear, cheek, jaw, neck, head, nose, back to my neck…everywhere. I sucked in oxygen until the burning was mostly gone, weighing the chances that it would be manageable for the foreseeable future.

"Breathe," Sark told me quietly, like an afterthought, as though it took everything he had to break and spare the reminder.

"I am," I mumbled, fingers in his hair again. "You're distracting me." I felt him smile and then we were kissing again, and I didn't care about anything else because it was just us, here, and I felt kind of okay. Maybe more than okay.

I heard a bump from the living room, and it reminded me where we were: in a room, alone, with my mom next door, and I was suddenly mortified at the idea of her walking in here now for whatever reason. Then I realized that was the most normal thought I'd had in forever.

For some reason, that made me start laughing. Sark stopped and leaned back to look at me, eyes shining in the dim light like the late sun dancing on the ocean waves.

"What's funny?" he asked me, playing with a strand of my hair.

I had to take a few deep breaths to help my angry lungs out. "Nothing. I was just thinking how…interesting it would be if my mom walked in right now. And how that's such a normal person thing to think, you know? I guess I thought it was funny."

Sark propped up the pillows behind him so he could lean back, then he pulled me down against him. "You know, she'd probably apologize for interrupting, tell us to keep going, then go call Karen." I laughed again because it was true. He continued to play with my hair as I nestled myself into his chest and relaxed. After a few minutes of quiet, he asked, "What are you thinking about?"

"That you're a great kisser."

He snorted. "Obviously. Besides that."

"I was thinking about…us"

"Yeah? You're still okay with it?"

I nodded. "More than okay."

He held my chin and tilted my head up to look at him. "But?"

I studied him for a second. "You're really worried about this, aren't you?"

"No, not this." He stroked my face with his finger. "This, I'm more than okay with. I just want to make sure you are."

I nodded again.

"But?"

"But I…" I stopped and thought, really thought, about the ideas that were right underneath the surface of what I admitted to myself. It wasn't the easiest thing ever, but I'd thought a lot about it since Aunt Karen had brought over the home videos.

Dr. Bran Psychologist had made me promise that I'd be more honest with the people I wanted to have a good relationship with, so I bit my lip and started talking before I could stop myself.

"I think…I think I'm afraid to be happy," I admitted. "All I do is think about everything wrong or bad or sad, and sometimes I just can't help it but other times it's kind of on purpose. And when something good happens, even if it's small, like this, I'm afraid to like it. Because I think it will get ruined or disappear, and I'm…I'm not sure how to handle happiness yet. But I think for the first time…I kind of want to. I mean, I don't have to be bursting with joy for the rest of my life, but maybe I could find a balance, you know, so there is some goodness in there somewhere."

Sark nodded, thoughtful, and I loved him even more for taking me seriously. "That's a great goal, actually. I think you should go for it."

"It'll be hard, I think," I said, "because it's something I have to do on my own. It'll take a lot of work. But hopefully I can get better at it. Feeling happy. Like now." I smiled. "I'm doing pretty good now."

He grinned. "I could stay like this forever."

"Me too."

I want to be with you forever.

Just then, something in Sark's expression changed, as if he read my mind. An uneasiness came over him and his eyes shifted away from me. The change was subtle, but I still noticed it.

"What's wrong?" I asked, lifting my head to look at him even better.

He shook his head and chuckled softly, a nervous sound. "You know, I like to think I'm harder to read than that."

All good feelings vanished and paranoia shot into overdrive. I pushed myself up on my hands, prepared to move away. "What did I do?" I asked, hating the thought I'd just ruined something.

He grabbed my arms and pulled me back to him, his forehead creased. "Why do you always think you're the problem?"

"I…" That brought me up short. "I don't know. I guess…well, am I?"

"No, you're not the problem. You're ridiculous, but you're not the problem."

"Then what?"

"Well, I…" He met my eyes evenly, then stopped, as though my gaze paralyzed him.

"Sark?" I asked after a moment. "You're kind of scaring me. Please tell me what's wrong."

He shook his head slowly. "No, nothing's wrong. Sorry, I'm giving you the wrong idea." He took a deep breath and that stabilized him. "I just need your opinion on something. Complete and total one hundred percent honesty. No matter what."

I nodded. "Okay."

"You swear?"

"Of course. What's this about?"

What if it's about me?

Instead of answering, he took my hand and kissed my palm, as if for reassurances, then gently rolled me off of him, stood up, and slipped out the door. My hands played with the end of the sheet nervously and I glanced at the clock. It was past two in the morning.

What is he doing?

Sark came back a minute later. Watching the ground, he used one hand to shut the door quietly behind him, his other hand in the pocket of his sweats. Then he came and sat across from me.

I waited in anticipation. He stared at his hand. I considered the probability of him being a CIA agent who'd been compromised and was about to flee to witness protection. The more probable idea came that somehow I'd scared him with commitment, even though I didn't really say anything too telling out loud. Neither options were ideal and Sark looked miserably uncomfortable.

"Are you okay?" I scooted a little closer and took his hand.

"Yeah." He took a deep breath. "Yep, I'm okay. I just…" He laughed once. "I don't think I've ever been this nervous in my life."

"You can tell me anything," I said. "It doesn't matter what it is."

"I know I can." He finally looked over at me, gazing over me, the kind of look that made me want to drop my eyes and blush and smile sheepishly, but also made me want to jump up and down and shout at the top of my lungs that the greatest person ever thought the world of me.

I squeezed his hand and nodded, then felt his aura relax slightly and the hand in his pocket move. I glanced down and gasped, slapping my hands over my mouth. He was holding a ring.

"It doesn't have to happen now," Sark told me, as if reassuring. "But maybe…maybe we could think about it. I don't know. What do you think?"

My hands dropped to my lap, my eyes still bugged open and on the silver band. My brain flipped through a thousand different thoughts and emotions and scenarios and reactions, but I didn't really see any of them—I was at a blank. Finally, I was able to breathe out, barely audibly, "You want to marry me?"

The anxiety came through his voice even though I knew he was trying to bury it. "I've seen two marriages up close in my life, and both of them were complete disasters. And that makes me…scared to even think about it." He stopped to take a breath. "But I love you. I want to be with you. I want to be tied to you. I want to be able to tell everyone that I'm the lucky guy that gets to have you. And then I thought maybe we just aren't ready, that we should wait. But wait for what? Wait for us to get to know each other better?" He shook his head. "I feel like you know me better than anyone ever will. And I love that because somehow it doesn't make me feel vulnerable or exposed. It feels…right."

Sark stopped talking, picking up my hand and placing the ring in my palm so I could look at it. It was beautiful. The diamond was small but no less gorgeous, and I loved how it wasn't flashy but still stunning. Beautiful in the background.

"Now this is the part where you tell me what you think," Sark said, "because if you don't say something soon, I think the nerves will kill me."

My hand had started shaking, so I put the ring back in his hand, unsure how to filter through the thousands of chaotic thoughts running through my head.

"You're serious?" I asked, feeling like I had to triple thousand check this because it was just too good to be true.

He laughed once. "Well, I just offered you my mom's ring, so I'd say probably yes. I mean it."

That made my fingers tingle, the thought that I'd just touched one of the most sacred things on this planet to him.

He's completely serious.

"You would marry me?" I asked. "Like full on, complete commitment, together for the rest of our lives?"

"That's what marriage is. Or what it's supposed to be, anyway." He sighed again. "It's just that we have a chance to rebuild our lives and start over. And I want to rebuild mine with you." The nerves came back into his voice, the words picking up speed. "But like I said, it doesn't have be now, or ever, really. If that's not what you want then we can—"

"Yes," I whispered.

That brought him to a screeching halt that seemed to make him trip over himself. "What?"

"Yes." I nodded. "Four thousand times yes."

Sark broke into a beaming smile, nerves melting away and triumphant confidence rising up to fill their place. "Then I guess I should tell you my three conditions."

I raised an eyebrow but burst out laughing. "Conditions?"

"Yep. I want to do this right. No cutting corners."

I want to do this right too. "Okay. Lay it on me. What are they?"

He nodded, as if going over the checklist in his head. "We have to have a real wedding. At a church. A courthouse. Wherever you want. It's just going to be a real wedding and we will invite real people and—the first condition—you will wear a real wedding dress."

I grinned and nodded. "I *guess* I can work with that."

"Good." He counted on his fingers. "Then we have to dance at our wedding."

"Whoa, hold on." I shook my head. "Dancing? I used to be dicey, but now it would be a catastrophe."

"Well, we're doing it. It's condition number two."

"Do you even know how?"

He grinned and shrugged. "Can't be that hard. It doesn't have to even be in front of anyone. Just any time after we're officially married on our wedding day with you still in your dress, we have to dance. Deal?"

I couldn't say no—it was just too adorable. "Fine. Deal."

"Excellent." His enthusiasm seemed to falter for a moment, and he hesitated. "The third…it's not really a condition. It's more of…need to know information. But I still want you to be okay with it.”

I shifted my position on the bed, so I was sitting cross-legged. “Okay. What?”

“When I talked to the senator, he said he would give me whatever I wanted—whatever I needed help with. So, officially now…” He took a deep breath. “Mr. Sark died. Everything he did, everything he was wanted for, all died with him. I can’t be incriminated for anything he did or was.”

I took a few seconds to really process that. “Wow. That’s…wow.”

Sark nodded. “I know. They’re legally treating us as different people, so I’m going back to my old, real name: Aiden McCoy. So your name would be—” He stopped himself hastily. “Only if you want it to. There’s no pressure to—”

“Arie McCoy,” I said, a smile spreading across my face. “I love it.”

He smiled too. “I do too.” Then the smile faded, his eyes dropping to the ring in his hand. “The only thing is…Sark had a life in prison, but he could’ve easily provided for you. Aiden, on the other hand, is clean besides a few spots here and there, but…he’s got nothing. I can’t offer you—”

I took his hand. “I love *you*. I don’t care what your name is or how much money you have.”

His eyes flicked up to mine, and I saw the dwindling anxiety. “Really? We’re going to be dirt poor, Arie.”

The corners of my mouth pulled up. *He said ‘we.’*

"I don't care about that," I told him. Then I remembered something and I hung my head, reality setting in. "But my hospital bills are—"

"I know. We'll figure it out."

But now the magic of the moment was gone as the thousands of possibilities wheeled around and around in my mind.

"But what if it gets to be too much?" I asked, unable to hide the fear in my voice. "We both know I'm going to be in and out of that hospital probably for the rest of my life. What if…what if you get sick of it? Will you tell me?"

He chuckled. "No offense, Arie, but if you were too much to handle, don't you think I would've walked out on you a long time ago?"

I didn't laugh with him because this was different than everything else. This was completely trusting myself to another person and hoping that they would stay. This was terrifying.

His eyes softened at my expression. "I love *you*. I don't care what scars you have or what medicine you take." He squeezed my hand. "And everything else that comes, we'll do it together."

I smiled. I liked the sound of that. "Together, then."

Sark cleared his throat ostentatiously, got off the bed, then kneeled down on the floor in front of me. "Arie Nolan, I love you, and I promise to keep loving you unconditionally for the rest of my life." He held up the ring pinched in his fingers. "Will you marry me?"

My surging happiness took my words, so I just nodded. Sark took my left hand and slid the ring on my finger, then I practically fell off the bed onto him, threw my arms around him and kissed him. Unable to wipe the smile off my face, I glanced down to admire the ring on my hand.

"It's beautiful," I murmured.

Sark kissed my cheek. "Like you."

A crash sounded from outside the room, like a cup had fallen onto the kitchen floor. I knew that sound a little too well.

Sark nudged me with his nose. "Want to go break the news?"

"I think she'll be more excited than both of us combined," I said as we stood up. Sark took my hand, then we left the room and went down the hallway, into the kitchen. A single light was on, illuminating Mom in a pink robe with frazzled hair and baggy eyes.

"Oh, I'm so sorry," she said when she saw us. She'd retrieved her cup from the floor and was now working on the coffee machine. "I just couldn't sleep. I didn't mean to be so loud."

I'd planned on saying something funny or witty or at least cool, but when I opened my mouth, nothing came out, my eyes filling with tears instead.

She did a double take when she saw my face. "Baby, what's wrong?"

I couldn't speak—the words were just too great. Instead, I lifted up my left hand and broke into a smile.

Mom threw her hands over her mouth and screamed, the cup she was holding clattering to the floor again. "It's about time!" She grabbed my hand to inspect the ring, then hugged me, hugged Sark, grabbed my hand again, then hugged us both.

I found myself crying with her. I literally could not remember the last time I cried because I was happy.

"I've been waiting for so long!" she squealed. "It was so hard to keep it a secret!"

I opened my mouth, but Sark beat me to it. "You really think I wouldn't ask permission first?" He grinned at Mom. "Good thing too, because I probably wouldn't have mustered the courage to ask you without her."

"Nonsense," Mom scoffed. "You would've. You love her. You just needed a little help." She took my hand again. "Oh, baby, it's beautiful. I'm so happy for you."

I couldn't believe this. "You're telling me you knew this whole time?"

She waved her hand at me. "Sweetie, half the world knows. On their breaks the nurses would look at wedding dresses for you."

My eyebrows shot up. "What? The people at the *hospital* knew?"

Mom looked at Sark, so I did too. He gave an almost embarrassed smile.

"The government refused to let us see you for weeks," he explained, "but eventually Lindsey helped us get through the barrier. When the day came, though, the rule was only immediate family would be let through."

I scoffed. "You *are* my immediate family."

"I know, but to them everything had to be official. They were going to shut me out, so I told them I was your fiancé."

My mouth dropped open in wondrous surprise.

Mom grinned and nodded. "Yeah, he really did."

Sark laughed. "It just came out. They didn't believe me, though. Candace didn't even blink. She just backed me up. They believed her, at least, so that's all that matters."

I glanced at Mom with a smile. "You backed him up?"

"Of course I did." She shrugged like lying in that scenario was the most natural thing ever. "Besides, if you weren't going to marry him, then I was planning on adopting him. I have to claim him somehow."

My smile just grew, my heart along with it, and I decided it was nearly impossible for anyone to love two people more than I loved these two.

Nobody went back to sleep. We spent the next hours going over possible wedding dates, researching caterers, and electing bridesmaids and groomsmen. You would've thought Mom found her new calling in life, and it made me so happy to see her so happy. It was true. I'd missed my mom. Never had I thought it would be so great to have her back.

Once the sun came up, Mom was calling different reception centers to request availability. In between her quests, she'd call Aunt Karen or her other long-lost friends, and Sark and I stifled laughs when her conversations went from the business-like 'my daughter's wedding must be perfect' to her screaming in excitement like a twelve-year-old girl.

As a thank you to him for waking up with me so I didn't die in my sleep, I told Sark I'd make him breakfast. It was a lame gesture, I thought, that didn't at all make up for it, but he was okay with it. We left Mom to her phone calling in the living room to go make pancakes.

I was practically bent over in concentration as I measured the flour. Sark bumped my arm right as I went to level it, sending a spray of white powder right in my face. He claimed it was an accident and tried to plead the fifth. I wasn't very merciful.

It wasn't long before we were both caked, the threats and laughing only stopping because Sark had pinned me against the counter, and I used my mouth against his to win my freedom. It worked; he melted and tangled his fingers in my hair, both of us forgetting all about the flour fight.

I jumped in surprise when Mom's voice called from the living room. "I don't hear much talking going on in there."

I ducked my head in embarrassment, but Sark stole one more kiss before we cleaned up our mess. All three of us ate pancakes together, debating on the guest list in between bites of syrup-soaked goodness, then threw our dishes in the sink to be dealt with later. Wedding came first, Mom said.

My phone rang as we retired to the living room, and I hung back in the kitchen to answer it. Mr. Freeman's voice came on the other end—he was my case officer, my tie to the government, keeping me updated on what was going on as well as keeping tabs on me.

"Good morning, Miss Nolan. How are you doing today?"

"I'm doing well, thank you," I answered.

"That's great to hear. Just calling to see if you can join us for a meeting next Tuesday?"

I paced slowly along the length of the kitchen, withholding a huff of annoyance. Government meetings weren't really my favorite things ever.

I glanced at the living room absentmindedly. "Yeah, sure. When is it?"

He answered, but I only heard his voice instead of words. The scene in the living room momentarily stole my attention, Mom hunched over her laptop and Sark sprawled easily on the couch as they discussed the pros and cons of different flower arrangements. I'd been smiling so much today that my cheeks were starting to hurt.

"Miss Nolan?" Freeman asked. "Are you okay?"

"Yeah, I think so," I responded, a little late. "Eventually, I'm going to be just fine."

One Year Later

I glanced over my reflection for the millionth time, afraid I'd forgotten something. Black dress. Check. Hair up. Check. Makeup on. Check. Earrings secured. Check.

Am I missing something?

Tapping my fingers against the bathroom counter, I bit my glossed lip. Today was not the day I wanted to be forgetting something. Today had to be good.

I turned off the bathroom light and walked back into the motel room, finding Aiden sitting on the bed, staring at the ground with expressionless eyes. He'd managed to change into his worn black suit, though. That was a good sign.

Grabbing my black flats from the suitcase—I still wasn't even close to having the walking skills for heels—I sat on the bed next to him and slipped them on. We sat for a moment in silence.

Finally, I put a hand on his shoulder. "You ready?"

His head moved, but he wasn't agreeing or disagreeing. He didn't say anything.

"Look," I said softly, "if you don't want to do this today—"

He put his hand on my knee, leaning on me so his head was on my shoulder, then let out a long breath. "No, it's all right. Let's go." He stood up and pulled me with him.

He's moving. Another good sign.

Aiden grabbed the motel key from the desk, then took my hand as we walked outside into the sun, getting into our rental car. The vehicle was hot and stuffy, the air thick. I wasn't used to the heat. Once Aiden turned the car on, I instantly flipped the air conditioning, pleased when I didn't even have to wait for the air to cool down, like in our car.

It's a good feeling when your rental is better than what you own.

Our financial situation didn't bother me too much, but it was a constant struggle for Aiden. I didn't see the big deal: we could afford what we needed. We had an apartment. We had food. We had clothes. What else was there?

He didn't care about owning anything for himself—buying presents for the guy was the trickiest quest in the book—but he wanted to buy me everything. I would look so great in that dress,

I need a nicer car, I only have two pairs of shoes…the list went on forever. He was so concerned about what I might need, he never considered that maybe I already had it. I wasn't used to having nice stuff, or even stuff at all, making me so easily pleased it was almost laughable. Actually, he did laugh at me. Often. He just had to buy me a pen and I thought I was the luckiest girl in the world.

Aiden didn't talk much throughout the drive. I almost asked him if he needed the GPS, but when I watched him closer, I could see he didn't need it. He'd glance around in confusion for a moment, then his eyes would clear and I could tell he knew where he was going. I tried to keep my hands from fidgeting, not wanting him to know how nervous I was. I wanted to keep him calm. If he knew I wasn't, then he really might bag the whole thing, and I didn't want that to happen.

My phone buzzed, the screen popping to life with Ellen's name and a picture of us at my wedding. It'd been awhile since I'd talked to her—she was doing so well, it was crazy for her—and I realized she probably didn't know about our trip since Aiden and I had planned it so spontaneously, finally cashing in our wedding present from the senator.

I let the call go to voicemail. I'd talk to her later.

Out of nowhere, Aiden reached over and grabbed my hand, holding it slightly too tight. I glanced at him to see a square jaw. He was thinking of backing out. He needed help.

Aiden and I had gotten a lot better at helping each other. As two very non-communicative people, we'd learned to recognize when the other needed help but couldn't say it. Our connection was relaxing and reliable for both of us, which just made me love our decision to get married even more. Of course, Cyrus' trial had almost slaughtered our marriage—and us—before it really even began. Somehow that hell ended eventually. Cyrus met the electric chair three weeks after our wedding. One of the officials poorly joked that it was a wedding present; he didn't know that that night I went home and threw up so much that I had to be hospitalized for a day.

We got through it, though. We made it. On to the next thing.

The next thing was Aiden. Aiden didn't sleep. I knew he had problems with that since the beginning of time, so many stressful situations over the years forcing him to stay awake until his body decided he didn't need sleep. He could function without it. The past few weeks though, it'd gotten way worse. It started affecting his energy and attitude during the day, like he was tied to an invisible weight that kept dragging him down.

Several times in the past weeks I'd woken up in the middle of the night to find him staring at the ceiling or playing with something small, like the slinky I'd given him as a joke present once. It took a ton of prodding but eventually over the evenings I was able to coax the problem out of him. As usual, once I could break through his initial wall, he'd talk to me for hours and I wouldn't have to do anything but listen.

Of course, sleepy, vulnerable Aiden was much different than guarded, wide awake Aiden. Even though I'd somehow managed to get him on a plane out here—which was a miracle in itself—his resolve wasn't nearly as strong now as it'd been the night he finally confessed what was bothering him.

We made minimal small talk in the car, mostly about how the air conditioning actually worked or how nice the California weather was this afternoon. My phone buzzed again, a message this time: a picture of Mom with Cinnamon. After Aiden and I moved out of her apartment, Mom was so lonely she couldn't stand it. So one day she brought home one of the dogs from the animal shelter she worked at. He was small and brown— hence the name 'Cinnamon'—and it took a while for me to admit that I actually liked a dog. The two were practically inseparable. I was afraid one of these days the dog would oust me out of favorite child standing.

I showed Aiden the picture when stopped at a red light, and he actually laughed at Mom's ridiculous expression. Laughter. That was a good sign.

Calm down. I was nervous. For him. For me. The whole thing just made me want to crawl under the covers and never come out, so I didn't have to watch it unfold.

I asked Aiden to make a stop at a grocery store—I ran inside to pick up a bouquet of flowers, hoping they would calm me down. Aiden nodded in approval when I came back with the white daisies, so I guess I did the right thing for him too.

His hold on my hand got harder and harder the closer we came, and he was practically cutting off blood flow when I caught sight of the iron gates. The car stopped at the entrance. I just waited patiently, admiring the scenery outside my window, giving him time. Eventually the car moved again. We followed the winding road for a moment and then stopped. Aiden turned off the car.

I guess we're here.

I glanced at Aiden, but his focus was everywhere else—in front of us, behind us, to his left, down the street—as if waiting for something to pop out and catch him by surprise.

"You made it this far," I said softly. "That's great. We can try again tomorrow if you want."

He didn't answer me and part of me wondered if he was afraid to speak. Afraid to wake something up in the place he abandoned.

I wasn't going to force him into anything, but I had stuff to do here too. I'd spent so much time the past few days building it up in my head, I just needed to get it over with before I went crazy. I was this close. Better now than never, even if I did it alone.

Grabbing my phone and the flowers, I got out of the car, the beating sun sending prickles over my skin after the blasting air conditioning. I didn't have the first clue of where my destination was, but I figured out the general direction: the only way Aiden *wasn't* looking. Slightly to my right.

Taking a deep breath to steel myself, I started walking.

The smell of freshly cut grass filled the air. Several people were scattered over the large grassy area, some sitting in camp chairs or just on the ground, children running around and laughing as their parents called after them to settle down. Even with them, though, there was a peaceful stillness here that I knew I couldn't find anywhere else.

I had to watch my feet so I didn't trip over any flowers or pinwheels or decorations dotting the grass, my eyes scanning the slabs of stones I passed. It took several minutes of searching—I really hoped nobody was watching me—but I finally found the headstone I was looking for.

I sucked in a sharp breath upon my discovery, automatically standing up straighter, smoothing my skirt, tucking invisible hair behind my ear. My nerves shot into overdrive, my palms sweaty.

Knowing I was walking on sacred ground, I took a step closer to the small, square headstone, getting a better look at the dusty words that had been etched on years ago and almost seemed forgotten.

Kristen Allison McCoy
April 14, 1970—August 2, 2006.
Loving Mother and Wonderful Friend.
"Be still, my soul: the hour is hast'ning on
when disappointment, grief, and fear are gone,
sorrow forgot, love's purest joys restored. Be still,
my soul: when change and tears are past, all safe
and blessed we shall meet at last."

The words gave me chills. I shifted uneasily on my feet, feeling as though she was really here, watching me, waiting for me. I was terrified. I felt like I was really meeting my mother-in-law for the first time.

Finally, I cleared my throat. "Um, hi. I…I don't know how much you've been watching from wherever you are, but, um, I'm Arie. I married Aiden, your son. I know you probably know that, and this…this is stupid, probably, but I just wanted to meet you. Introduce myself."

I felt way too hot, like I was melting, and I couldn't tell if it was from the heat outside or from my muddled embarrassment. Then I remembered I was holding flowers.

"I brought you these," I said, leaning down to set the bouquet next to her headstone. I stood there for a few moments in silence, all of my pre-planned words fleeing my head. It frustrated me. I wanted this to be good.

I gestured to the space behind me, in the general direction of our parked car. "Don't feel bad if he doesn't come over here," I told her. "I'm really surprised he made it as far as he did. It's difficult for him to be here. But I guess…I guess you'd know that." I sighed. "He's having a hard time reconciling…himself, I guess. He pretended to be someone else for so long. Using his own name again and stuff…it's caught up with him, you know? He's trying to figure out who he is and who he wants to be and what to do about it all. And he…he thinks about you all the time. He feels like he let you down."

I rubbed my arm and shook my head. "I keep telling him it's not true. He just can't bring himself to believe me. The guilt's been eating at him too long. Just…just know he loves you so much. You mean the world to him. And he misses you every day."

Rocking on my heels, I looked up at the clear blue sky. It was pretty. It was soothing. I let it calm me before looking back at my company.

"But I didn't come here to tell you that," I said, my tone timid. "I came to apologize. And to say thank you."

I paused, digging my toe into the grass, watching my feet now. "I'm sorry he's mine now, that you don't get to be as close to him as I know you'd want to be. It's not fair that you got to spend so little time with him and now I get to claim him for the rest of my life. I don't know, you're probably a better person than me, but if…if our places were reversed, I don't think I could help being a little jealous. And if I could find a way to give you more time with him, I'd do it in a heartbeat. I don't want you to think I'm…like, competing with you, or anything. I wish you were here for him too."

The thought of him filled my mind, and I couldn't help but smile. "He treats me with so much respect and love, and he…he's just a wonderful human being. You'd be proud; I know you would be. Thank you for raising such an exceptional person and sharing him with me, because I really don't know where I'd be without him. And thank you for letting him take care of you. I know it had to have been just awful, but now…now he's wonderful at taking care of me. And I know I owe that to you."

I had to shift on my feet again—standing was still a difficulty. "I just want you to know that I love him. I'll treat him the amazing way he treats me, I'll stand by him and support him all the time, for everything. No matter what. I know that I'm…I'm probably not the kind of girl you imagined for him. But I've recommitted myself and really have been trying to pull myself and my life together. And I'll keep trying every day." I took a breath. "I will spend the rest of my life working to deserve him. And I hope that maybe someday I can earn your approval."

That was it. I'd said what I'd come to say. I felt a slight weight fall off my shoulders, but I couldn't erase the blaring self-consciousness, the thought that Kristen still didn't like me. I wanted her to. Really bad. But, like I told her, I was willing to do anything.

About to say goodbye, my words were interrupted by slow footsteps through the grass behind me. I was surprised to see Aiden trudging toward me, steps heavy and head bowed, stopping right next to me. The silence was thick. I thought he might want a moment alone, so I turned to go, but he snatched my hand, saying without speaking.

Please stay.

I did, waiting with anxious anticipation for his reaction. Finally, he shifted his eyes up from his feet to the headstone. He flinched. A shaky breath escaped him as his hold on my hand tightened and he slowly lowered himself to his knees, half leaning against my legs. I felt his body tremble next to me before I heard the quiet words leave his mouth.

"I'm sorry," he whispered, his voice husky while he choked back tears. "I'm so sorry."

I looked up at the sky again, blinking back my own tears as a mother and son reconnected after so many years apart.

I didn't know how long we stayed like that: me standing over him kneeling over her, a tear rolling down my cheek as he murmured broken confessions and apologies. Time seemed to stretch and bend around us, giving us an eternity to make up for past years lost.

Eventually Aiden's words tapered off. His breaths got progressively less ragged and more even, the trembling subsiding. It was silent again. I stared at a spot on the grass, sensing a new kind of distress coming from him. I knew what it was: a crossroads.

He can do this, I knew. *He just needs a little help.*

My sore joints cracked as I bent down. Aiden offered his support when he realized what I was doing, letting me use his arm so I didn't hurt myself. I sat on the ground next to him, bending my legs and fixing my skirt, then leaned myself into Aiden, facing Kristen.

I nudged him with my shoulder gently, a small smile on my face. "Tell her about that guy at your work."

Aiden stiffened slightly. I glanced up at him to see his red eyes wide with surprise.

I decided to take the lead for him. "So Aiden got this job," I told Kristen, as though we were all sitting out for a nice picnic. "It's at this company that sells like…medical equipment or something. Anyway, there's this guy that works in his department that's the biggest…"

"Idiot?" Aiden supplied, finally recovering. He laughed once and shook his head. "Oh, Mom, it's bad. I know you'd tell me to give him a chance, but—believe me—there is such thing as too many chances."

He took it then, retelling the funny and memorable stories he'd told me about the misadventures of the people at his work, getting more and more relaxed the longer we sat there. We told Kristen all about our wedding, our apartment, our car, Mom's dog, my part-time desk job, the one neighbors with a billion kids and the other neighbors that were always hosting a party. Then we branched off to others: like how Jacklynn came over once a week for our club meetings, how Ellen was dominating the campaign in D.C., how Peter now coached football at the high school and Alaina volunteered at a troubled girls' home, how baby Jules was the cutest thing ever created and Lucy always kept us heavily stocked on adorable photos. Kayla was accepted to Harvard and had been making a name for herself there. Daxton spent most of his time volunteering with injured veterans. Carl now worked as a web developer. They were doing good, we told her. Everyone was working on putting their lives together again.

I'd learned to trust Kristen pretty fast, because when Aiden brought up harder topics, I didn't shy away as much as I'd thought I would. Like how Cyrus' trial almost killed both of us, and not in the mortal danger way we were used to; how we both went to see Dr. Bran Psychologist for separate therapy and had made peace with it; how we worried constantly about Mom being on her own and made sure to visit at least once a week; how it was scary for me to go anywhere, especially without Aiden, because my breathing attacks would still pop up randomly all the time; how several government people hadn't left us alone so we'd started 'missing' their calls from time to time. We were really trying. We were trying together to make a relationship work, but we were also trying separately as individuals. Healing took time and we were learning to have patience with ourselves.

The sun was on the other side of the sky when the conversation tapered off. Aiden had taken off his jacket and tie and had rolled up the sleeves on his white shirt; I had shed my shoes and long-sleeved sweater that I'd worn over my sleeveless dress, baring my arms with only an ounce of self-consciousness rather than the usual truckloads. We'd traded laying our heads in each other's lap as the hours went by, just hanging out casually as we would in our living room. It was nice.

Aiden let out a long breath, and I knew he was good. He could go. We both staggered to our feet, stretched out our legs, and I gathered up our array of discarded clothing. Slipping my shoes back on, I turned to go, noticing Aiden hanging back.

I looked at Kristen's headstone again and smiled. "It was wonderful to meet you. We'll come back to visit again soon."

Out of the corner of my eye, I saw Aiden smile. "Yes, we will."

I patted Aiden's arm before walking away, meandering around the cemetery to give him some time alone. The air had cooled down a smidge from earlier. It was easier to enjoy now. I admired the different flower arrangements as I walked through the rows of stones, reading name after name. Some were fairly new. Others had been here for years.

I was watching a giant blue pinwheel try to catch some dry air when Aiden made his way over to me. The sight of him made me happy—it looked as though the past few hours had transformed him. His steps were lighter, eyes brighter and looking outward, shoulders straight and relaxed.

He nudged me with his shoulder. "You ready to go? I'm starving."

"Yeah." I nodded. "Let's go."

We walked slowly back to the car, taking our time. He opened the passenger door for me, but his quiet voice stopped me from getting in.

"You have it," he told me, almost like an afterthought.

"Have what? The keys?" I glanced at the pile of things in my hands but there wasn't any sign of the key ring.

He shook his head. "No." He motioned back toward the cemetery. "Her approval. Since day one."

"Oh." A small smile spread across my face as I realized how much of a compliment that was. "Thanks."

Ducking in the car, I found this ride to be much better than the last. The rest of the day was fun as we drove around in our own version of sightseeing and ended up having a picnic in a park for dinner. By the time we got back to the motel that night, I was exhausted but so content. It was a perfect day.

I was heading into the bathroom to get ready for bed, but Aiden grabbed my wrist and pulled me back, wrapping his arms around me and kissing me softly.

"Thank you," he murmured, resting his forehead on mine. "That was…I don't even know."

"I didn't really do anything," I said. "It wasn't a big deal."

"No, it was everything. I mean it. Thank you. You're amazing."

I grinned and kissed him on the cheek. "And you're biased. But you're welcome." I hugged him before continuing my quest for comfortable clothes. "I love you."

He smiled. "Love you too."

It took him less than half the time it took me to get ready for bed. By the time I made my way out of the bathroom, the lights were off and the TV was on with the volume low, Aiden watching it casually from the bed. I grabbed my laptop from my bag before climbing in next to him and opening it up.

The screen glowed to life, displaying my screensaver of my favorite wedding picture: the one of Aiden and I dancing. I paused to admire it for a second before pulling up the internet browser and clicking on the bookmark that led me straight to my private blog. I'd started it way back when I was still at the hospital. After showing Dr. Bran parts of the history I'd written about my life before reversal, he suggested I keep it up, taking time each day to type things that I didn't want to forget. Then when my brain wasn't cooperating with me, I'd have a place to go that held any major memory I might be missing.

I still struggled with memory, but I mostly used the blog now as a cathartic outlet, writing down all my frustrations and hardships as well as triumphs and good moments I wanted to remember. Like the day Aiden landed his job and we 'splurged' by ordering pizza. Or the time we stayed up all night together helping him study for one of his tests and ended up talking until six in the morning. Or after our first real fight when I was so ticked off at him, so he turned on a song Elijah and Brennan had sung at our wedding and started dancing in the middle of the kitchen with me until I thawed out.

The blog was my life. Literally. I rarely missed a day without writing at least something down, commemorating at least a small part of my existence. I got so detailed that I never shared it with anyone—I'd let Aiden and Dr. Bran Psychologist read different parts at times, but always with me mandating how far they could go. It was one place I could truly be myself, as I still hadn't figured out a good answer for when people asked me why I carried a fancy inhaler or took so many medications or couldn't walk for very long or got sick all the time.

I didn't go back to read the first ones very often, the ones about early infection days or shortly after reversal. It was hard to relive it all again. I tended to stay away from them, but sometimes I found myself needing them, pouring over my old words as though they were a source of life. Because sometimes I got too caught up in the normalcy that was my life now. Sometimes I'd look down and see my scarred wrist and my mind would get fuzzy. Because when I was sitting at my desk at work, filing reports and taking customer calls and covering while Rachele went on her coffee break, it was easy to forget that I lived in a world where things like infection and running away and the Compound happened. Things like having an assassin as a best friend or escaping corrupted government agents or watching unexplainable experiments go awry seemed a lot less real. That's when I went back and read about them, not to dwell but to remind myself. It really happened. I wasn't crazy. I survived it. And I was moving on.

My fingers flew across the keyboard as I detailed the adventures of the day, how everything had gone from nerves and tension to release and serenity. I'd finally talked to my mother-in-law—*the* Kristen McCoy, no less—and I thought it went mostly well. Certainly better than it could've. I summarized what we talked about, described how Aiden seemed better afterward, especially compared to the last few weeks, then wrote about the fun evening we had.

I stole a glance at Aiden, who was now sound asleep, and I felt my heart swell inside me.

I really do love him, I typed. *And that's amazing to me. That I'm capable of loving someone so completely, and even more that he's capable of loving me. Me. The girl who just a year ago truly believed she wasn't worth the dirt on her shoe. The girl who thought she was a waste of space, an accident, a soul broken and tainted beyond repair.*

It's amazing to me how far we've come in just the last year, or even just how far I've come. I know I don't seem like much. In the grand scheme of things, I guess it would look like I haven't come far at all. But just over a year ago, I didn't even want to live. A year ago, I was scared to live. And now, twelve months later, I'm trying to build a life for myself. I'm trying to get better. Dr. Bran was right after all: I feel the need to live again. I never would've believed that a year ago, but the urge is here now. For the first time ever, I want to get better. Of course, that prospect is terrifying in and of itself, so I focus on daily life, small and simple things to take my life day by day. You have to start somewhere.

The darkness will always be a part of me, but I've finally started to accept it—not in a hopeless way, like I have so many times before, but a way that gives me hope. Just like Dr. Bran told me, I have to allow myself to arrive at an emotion before I can move past it.

They say you aren't what happens to you. I don't completely buy that. I am what happened to me. I know I am. But now I've finally come to realize that it's not the only thing I am. I'm a lot of other things too, a lot of things that—dare I say it—might be useful. Right. Good. I'm finally learning to embrace all aspects of my life, all aspects and parts of me, and put them together. My experiences have made me who I am. And I'm teaching myself to like her.

It's been hard. Really hard. I've had to completely readjust my thought processes. I've had to relearn how to talk to myself, to treat myself, to take care of myself: how to use soft words and have patience and give myself time. Whenever I have a self-destructive thought pop into my head, I imagine saying it to the little girl in the pink dress and curlers. I owe that little girl a future and I'm building the best one I can.

That isn't to say I'm perfect now. I'm not, unfortunately. I still see a therapist to work on depression and PTSD and all my other thousands of issues. I still have the days where I can't get out of bed and it's not my body's fault. I still have anxiety attacks in the grocery store, and I have to abandon my cart and make a break for my car to calm down. I still have nightmares that haunt me and moments that last lifetimes as I talk myself down from my mental cliffs. On more than one occasion, Aiden has found me in a corner somewhere, sobbing and clutching a paper airplane to my chest. The same goes for him too. There have been way too many nights I've waited up in worry until my phone rang with a slightly drunken Aiden on the other end, apologizing profusely that he'd let the memories take over again. I'm working on not getting mad or frustrated with myself when bad days come around. I try not to see them as setbacks anymore. I try to allow myself to have bad days. I don't hold myself to this impossible standard I know I'll never be able to achieve.

I guess that's it: I don't try to be perfect anymore. I'm not the Arie Nolan who felt so much pressure to be good, to be right, to be useful, that she wouldn't allow her weakness to be shown. I see the destruction in that thought process now, how it was my pride more than anything that truly caused damage. Now I allow myself to be weak. I'm more honest with a few trusted others and myself. This is who I am. And maybe I'm not quite who I want to be yet, but maybe someday I can be.

Of course, recovery road is much steeper and meaner and rockier and harder to walk than anything I could've imagined. It's cruel, in a way. You think it would be an amazing and poetic and inspiring journey of 'rediscovery' or whatever, but it's not. It's finally climbing up to your dusty old attic and turning on the light and taking inventory of all the skeletons and rats and worn books of memories you'd rather forget. It's finally taking the bandage off the wound and looking at it in all its blood and damaged glory and trying not to be sick as you decide how to treat it. It's an effort to give up the demons that have tortured you for years, which is harder than it sounds—when you spend so much time in the dark, often your demons are the only things you've got. It's confusing to work through, to try and understand who you actually are when your head has been telling you so many wrong things for so long. It's scary. You have to change your whole world and somehow trust that it'll stay stable when it hasn't before.

No, recovery road hasn't been kind, but on my good days I'm glad I've at least found the road. After so many years of being sure I'd never be okay again, I'm mostly willing to work with the small hope I have. I'll be okay someday. I'll be whole again. And I look forward to the moment when I look back and realize everything was worth it. Because I think back to that day we stormed Vanessa's fortress all the time. I think of the moment I told Carl to the blow the place with the decision I wasn't leaving. I was ten thousand miles past done. I was so exhausted—my soul was exhausted—and I just wanted it to be over. I just wanted a break, and it seemed I would never get one. I just wanted it all to stop.

I realize now that out of all of the crazy or otherwise admirable things I've managed to do or get through in the past years, the bravest thing I ever did wasn't walking into the building. It was walking out. And I still have to choose to walk out every day. It's such a difficult choice, but I'm always glad I made it in the end, even if it takes days or weeks or months to realize it.

After all, I didn't survive everything I did for nothing. I know it became a joke at the hospital, but I really want to make sure I didn't survive in vain. Against all odds, the sun came up. It's time to try another day. And every day after that. Sometimes I get tired at the thought of how many days I have left to live. I try to focus on the moment and live in it, no matter how good or bad it is, until the next moment comes. And the next. Keep going. Keep breathing. Don't give up.

Darkness is a part of my life now. A part of me. I know I can't change that, and I know I've got a lot of work ahead of me. Somehow, though, on my good days I know that it's okay. I know to trust the little girl in the pink dress, the new person I see in the mirror who's battle-scarred but stronger and wiser and more compassionate because of it. I know I have to keep going on with life. I have to survive.

After all, it's still worth doing.
It's still worth living.
It's still worth telling.
It's still worth writing.

It's still my story.

—A

To little Em, in your beautiful curlers and pink princess dress—I really hope this makes you proud

ACKNOWLEDGEMENTS

To my Executive Producer, Padre: thank you for believing that I could do this when I didn't, for pushing me to do my best, and for dedicating so much time to my projects. I owe so much of who I am to you and Mom.

To Nan, my best friend: thank you for being my best friend, calming me during my panic, and helping me shape my words into something beautiful that I could be proud of. I hope you know you mean the world to me, and I'm so incredibly proud of everything you are.

To Mom: thank you for always being on my team even when I can't play the game very well. I wouldn't be here without your endless supply of unconditional love and midnight venting sessions. I can't even say how much I love you, which is super embarrassing since I'm a writer and all.

To Court, my little cheerleader: I adore you. Thank you for keeping the magic in my life and reminding me time and time again what's really important. Never lose the things that make you so perfectly you. Also, coming from a professional secretary, you make a great secretary.

To everyone who helped me with this book in some way: I'll never be able to properly thank you for your help, which, again, is embarrassing since I write books. And a shoutout to Robbin, for putting so much time and passion into my writing, not only teaching me about words and stories but about life too.

To NaNoWriMo: thank you for your incredible program. I wouldn't be writing the acknowledgements to a novel without you.

To my favorite authors, directors, and all other creators
of fiction: thank you for creating art that inspires me.
Fiction saved my life—and continues to save it—and I
owe a lot of that to you.

To the countless people that inspired or influenced my
life or this story in some way, that took the time to know
me or spared a simple reminder that I'm not alone: some
of you are integral parts of my life, while others will
remain nameless strangers in my memory, but I thank
you for your kindness, compassion, and love. I truly
believe that empathetic people with good hearts can save
this world, and you are all examples of that. Thank you
for saving me.

To the lady at the book club that told me thank you for
writing my books: that's one of the highest compliments
I've ever received. Thank you for reading them.

To you, the reader, who just finished this book: I can't
tell you how much it means that you'd dedicate some of
your time to my words. I hope you got something out of
them.

And finally, to Arie: I have tears in my eyes as I write this,
but I hope you know how much I love you and how
grateful I am to you. You were my sister in so much
suffering—my sad story brought yours to life, and in turn
your story saved me in ways I'll never be able to explain. I
couldn't have done the past five years without you, and
while it hurts so badly to say goodbye, I can only hope
that I did your story justice.

Until next time, everyone.

—E

ABOUT THE AUTHOR

Emilee King is the author of the Arie's Story survival series and the Elarian Chronicles. She loves fairy tales, superheroes, fantasy, and murder mysteries, and is constantly on the hunt for good stories. When she's not writing, you can find her reorganizing her bookshelves, eating pasta, beating the high score on Galaga, or spending time with her family. Visit her website at emileeking.com